# *Portraits of the Wind*

**Written by: Janix Pacle**

Edited By:

Marcel Villanueva

Charmaine Cordero

Published by:

Jan Xavier Pacle, 2020

Copyright © 2020 Jan Xavier Pacle

This novel is entirely a work of fiction. The names, characters and incidents portrayed in it are the work of the author's imagination. Any resemblance to actual persons, living or dead, events or localities is entirely coincidental.

Designations used by companies to distinguish their products are often claimed as trademarks. All brand names and product names used in this book and on its cover are trade names, service marks, trademarks and registered trademarks of their respective owners.

The publishers and the book are not associated with any product or vendor mentioned in this book. None of the companies referenced within the book have endorsed the book.

All rights reserved. No part of this book may be reproduced, or stored in a retrieval system, or transmitted in any form or by any means, electronic, mechanical, photocopying, recording, or otherwise, without express written permission of the publisher.

Cover design by the author.

ISBN: 9798656013550

First published by Jan Xavier Pacle 2020
www.janixpacle.com

## DEDICATION

*This book is dedicated to those who dreamt and fell short, and to those who loved and lost. May we all find obscure joys in a world abounding with hurt and pain.*

*To my wife and daughter, Papi loves you. Tika!!!*

## PORTRAITS OF THE WIND

"And to me, it's no longer working." Nicola scowled and walked away.

"Wait! What?" Xavi began chasing her through a sea of unwitting faces. "Nicola, wait! What do you mean not working?" He gasped for breath as his flabs got in the way.

Nicola was Xavi's first girlfriend, and it seemed to him that there would be no other. He never did when, fair or not, a storm hit them, and their relationship was buried by a landslide.

Since then, Xavi lived a life of powerful nostalgia in which everything seemed to point back to the days of Nicola—the days when the wind sang the song of Nicola's name, the days whose night skies were filled with glistening stars resembling her sparkling eyes.

Now, nostalgia isn't the only thing consuming Xavi's days. Something more sinister is lurking beneath his sullen heart. And if not careful, nostalgia's big brother will devour him inside out, leaving only bitter tears in its wake.

# Chapter 1: Brain Farts

Thud! Thud! Thud! Thud!

That was the sound of jackhammer excavators outside our office. It didn't bother me anymore as much as it used to two years ago. When you hear something for so long, it just becomes white noise, allowing your mind to fly wherever it pleases, hopping from memory to memory, from imagination to imagination.

DING!

The computer beeped, hauling me back from my nostalgic side trip. I glanced at my computer screen; the thousand photos that I was copying from an external memory card finished after thirty minutes. Thirty minutes. That's how long that took. These were the photos I took to document the progress of a new skyscraper we're building.

Progress photos used to be outsourced from a production company. But my company, Al-Zubara Contracting, had employed me to do just that, saving them tens of thousands per year from hiring freelancers. Smart move.

I took another memory card from my camera bag and started copying the photos from it.

*Copying: 50 minutes left...*

"Wait, what? Fifty minutes?" I said.

I looked at the number of photos. They were almost double the previous transfer. I didn't know if I should be pleased that I had a lot of spare time or should be pissed that I won't be able to do anything else. So, with almost an hour to kill, I decided to clean my DSLR. Yeah, my DSLR, my own gear, my personal equipment. They should be paying me extra for using my stuff. But... well... that's a moot point.

# PORTRAITS OF THE WIND

"It's only for documentation. Cellphones are enough. There's no need for award-winning photos," the management would always say.

I know it's not an insult, but I can't help to be insulted a little bit. As a photographer, I always want to take the best photos. That's why I'm using my gear for free. I remember one time when I took a group photo at our church, it took me about two minutes before I pressed the shutter.

"Why did it take you so long?" my dad asked me in private afterward.

"I was making sure my framing and exposure were correct," I answered.

"Then you have to do it more quickly. Our smiles were straining."

"But... you told me to make sure everything is correct because films are expensive."

"I know! But don't you want to be a photojournalist? You need to be quick, boy. You must train your eyes to see as the camera sees. Instinct! That's what you need!"

Thud! Thud! Thud! Thud! The hydraulic jackhammer resumed its hammering outside.

I arrived in Doha in 1994. Twenty-five years later, 2019, they still haven't even begun to slow down on Qatar's makeover.

Wait, twenty-five years? That means I've been living in Doha for like ninety percent of my life! Wow!

Back in the early '90s, everywhere you looked, Doha was a barren desert. There were only three skyscrapers at that time. Well, to be honest, they're barely skyscrapers. They're simply tall, in the sense that they were the only buildings to have more than fifteen floors.

The year we arrived was a defining moment for the country. That year marked an era of economic and educational revolution. The government ensured every riyal spent was spent on expanding human knowledge. So, they built Education City, a thousand-hectare piece of land where foreign universities had set up shop.

Unfortunately, that wasn't where I studied. My school was roughly fifteen kilometers away from Education City, and they had a creative name for it: The Philippine School. Obviously, it was established to serve the growing number of Filipino children in the country.

DING!

The second card finished copying. I accessed our cloud servers and started the archiving process. Upon pressing the "Start Upload" button, I had the least pleasing realization: the whole side trip to 1994 took fifty minutes. Fifty minutes! See, that's how my life is; I regularly jump back in time remembering the good times of the years gone by. But fifty minutes? Wow. Lately, my nostalgia adventures are getting longer, and that is not good.

"Wait. Hold on. How did my thoughts drift back to 1994?" I asked myself.

You know, being a nostalgiac, I can tell you for sure that people don't purposely dive into reverie. Something would always tickle the brain's uvula causing it to regurgitate the memories deep within its belly. Was it the sound of the doorbell? A barking dog? An acoustic guitar? The two-stroke engine of a motorcycle? Or maybe it was a random brain fart?

My brows furrowed and my eyes narrowed as I scanned the office for clues on how I descended into throwback mode, just as if I were looking for the person who ate my chicken nuggets last week. (Dammit!) I studied every person in the room and listened to all the sounds they made: the keyboards clacking, the phones ringing, and the pencils tapping on the desks. Nothing was awry.

I switched my attention to my desk. First, I checked my camera, then the items on my desk. Nothing. What about my computer desktop? Nothing. Maybe that tiny blue LED light on my monitor? Nope. What about the creaking sound of my swivel chair? I swiveled, adjusted the height, rocked back and forth... Nope. Nothing. I slouched on my chair then, dissatisfied.

Maybe it's a brain fart. Maybe. If there's no trigger, then fine, it's a brain fart! I give up.

Thud! Thud! Thud! Thud!

My spine snapped straight. Oh wow! Oh wow! Dammit, Mia! The jackhammers! It's the jackhammers! Isn't it incredible how such a mundane sound can command a horde of memories running back to you?

"Xavi, do you have five minutes?" Saeed, my Qatari boss, called aloud from his glass office.

"Sure," I answered as I walked towards him with the knowledge that the five minutes would probably stretch to fifteen minutes.

When I entered Saeed's office, his brows raised in surprise, then dipped in confusion.

"Wow! You're getting wooly," he said. "Are you trying to look like an imam?"

Saeed was referring to the growing bush in my face, which made me look manlier, I think.

I used to keep my face clean-shaven, as wished by my then beloved. But lately, I seem to be ignoring her will. Definitely not intentional, though. It's more like growing neglect over time. For example, I used to keep an expensive fancy razor with extreme features such as five blades, ergonomic handles, and other marketing scams. This razor now rests under the sink collecting dead hair and gunk. It fell there, and I didn't bother recovering it.

"Yeah, I'm— I have no money to buy a new razor," I blurted. It was met with a half-hearted chuckle. Yeah, I'm not really good with quips.

"What are you doing right now?" Saeed asked.

"Archiving photos from this month's shoot."

"Until now? It's past eleven."

"Yeah, well, they're about a hundred gigabytes."

"A hundred?!" Saeed gasped.

"Yeah, they're raw photos and our internet—you know our internet."

"I told you to just use your cellphone. That's all we need."

Here we go again. "I know," I said. "Trust me. For archiving, you'll thank me for these hi-res photos in the future." That's what came out of my mouth. What I really wanted to say was: *Hey, if I'm taking photos, I'd make sure it's something worth bearing my name.*

Saeed fixed his ghutra and said, "Fine. Anyway, how would you respond if the CEO personally requested you to take his portrait? I sent him your Flickr account. I guess he liked what he saw."

I smiled ear to ear inside. But I don't do portraits anymore, so, the smile dwindled. "Um, I don't do portraits," I responded.

"But you're a photographer," he said matter-of-factly.

"I'm into photojournalism, capturing real life."

"But you're a photographer. Portraits are the basics, aren't they?"

I sighed softly. "Okay… I'll check my schedule first."

"I hold your schedule," he said matter-of-factly, again.

Dammit, Mia! "Alright, fine. I'll do it."

"Will you be using your camera?" he asked.

"Not unless you want to use cellphones."

Saeed chuckled. "No, no. With your camera. We want it professionally done. We'll pay for it."

## PORTRAITS OF THE WIND

I smiled again, this time also on the outside. Finally, real work! I was thrilled!

As I walked back to my desk, some questions arose: How am I going to do it? I've never done portraits for a long time. How can I deliver good work if it's something I'm not confident about? Maybe I could do it in the same way I did *her* portrait.

Her portrait? Her… Oh wow. That was a long time ago. I can still vividly remember the day that our principal introduced her to our class.

*\*\*\**

Let's see… I remember a classmate adjusting the thermostat of the lone window air conditioner, and it still struggled to cool down the classroom.

It was a warm and sunny July 2003 afternoon. The sweat brigade did not withhold in attacking each one of us. Some of them camped in our napes, while some rappelled down our sideburns. Worse were the secret agents who penetrated the pits of the underground bunkers. They were so active what with the mercury reaching 48 degrees Celsius. They called it "mission complete" when the room began stinking of vinegar.

Unfazed by the heat, the teacher, who spoke with a voice of a horse race commentator who forgot to eat breakfast, droned on about the ancient system of trade called barter. Now combine that with the heat, the blinding sun blazing through the windows, and the constant whirr of the air conditioner, some of us couldn't help but succumb to siesta.

Myself, I tried many tricks to stay awake. I played with my pen; perched at the very edge of my chair to sit up straight; I even attempted to slap myself, to no effect. I was helpless. When the AC swiveled towards me and blew its dry, cold air, I slowly, slowly bowed my head, closed my eyes, and dozed off...

"Ow!" I screamed discreetly when someone pinched my flabs. "Dammit, Mia, why?"

Mia, my seatmate, always pinched me. Sometimes for no reason. She was annoying and irritating that way.

A loud knock at the door echoed across the room, waking everyone up. Mr. Dosado, the school principal, entered without prompt.

Everybody stood up and said, "Goood mooornig misteeer Dooosadooo." We still sounded like grade-schoolers.

"Good morning, seniors," he replied as he walked towards the front of the class. An unfamiliar face followed him. A new girl. "Please welcome your new classmate."

Murmurs arose from everyone: "New classmate? New classmate? What? New classmate? Oh, new classmate?" For a moment, we sounded like chickens.

"Please introduce yourself," Mr. Dosado told the new girl.

I observed this new girl. She had short bob hair; her skin was fair (neither light nor dark); she had a petite build; and she wore glasses with a thick black frame. Unlike some other new students, she didn't have any mannerisms that showed shyness. The others probably would just look down, or have a deadpan face, or grab the side of their clothes and grip it hard, or maybe fail to speak at all. But not her; she stood there with solid confidence.

"My name is Nicola Cueto, and I'm sixteen years old," she said, bowing slightly like a Japanese anime.

Then she smiled.

When she smiled, cute little wrinkles formed at the bridge of her nose, and her eyes narrowed to the point of closing. The crescent on her lips was— aw, dammit! I couldn't even describe her smile without nuclear bombs lighting up all the darkness in my world.

I didn't let that smile fool me though. By how she carries herself, I can tell she was a handful. She boasted the air of confidence with every step, outstaring everyone gawking at her. And she projected her voice without a hint of anxiety. But as she sat down at the other end of the room, I can't help imagining, what if she sat next to me and replaced this she-devil Mia?

"How do you prefer to be called, Nicola? Do you have any nickname?" our teacher asked when the principal left.

"Just Nicola," she answered politely.

"Could you tell us more about yourself?"

"I live in—"

"Stand up," the teacher said.

She pushed her chair back and stood up.

At that moment, I surveyed the other boys, checking if anyone was leering at her. Turned out, none. All the stares were about curiosity only.

The new girl spoke without fear. "We live in Las Piñas. We're originally from Angeles, Pampanga. Um… We live in Al Nasser here in Doha."

"Do you have any siblings here too?"

"No, I'm an only child."

I find it amazing what the fear of being apart from a loved one can do. Cola (Yes, that's Nicola. I prefer to call her Cola) was pulled out from her school in Las Piñas so she could fly to Doha with the family. It all seemed impractical, knowing that there were only eight months left in the school year. After that, she would fly back home to the Philippines for college (given that college fees in Doha are impractical if you're a mid-income family). I guess being the only child was the only reason her parents needed to take her with them. Spend all minutes together as much as possible, right?

# Chapter 2:
# A Sunflower in the Desert

Cola found her new circle of friends right away, faster than I anticipated.

I theorized that there are four stages to successful integration into a new class. In stage one, the new student would first get an impression of the schoolroom. He or she would brood in a corner, and when someone approaches, he or she would politely agree to whatever pedestrian thing that someone would say.

Stage two would be selecting the right group to hang out with. Movies would usually show us some stereotypes such as the goths and emos, the mean girls, the nerds, the jocks. But our class didn't work that way. We mingled with everyone, and we're comfortable with everyone. Groups do form, not out of common interests, but when each member of that group are drawn together by the gravity of their personalities.

Stage three would see the new student cracking simple jokes and laughing meekly.

Stage four would be full integration with the chosen group and gradually in the class, as if she had been a long-time classmate. Usually, it takes around three to four weeks to reach stage four. The fastest I've seen was one week. Cola reached stage four in a record-breaking three days.

I remember the time when I tried to start a small talk with my aunt whom I've known for years. She stood by the sink, washing dishes, and I pretended to get something from the fridge.

"How's Jason?" I asked.

"He's great; he's already graduating," my aunt said with a mighty grin. "It took him a little longer because he shifted courses. But he's almost there. Now, he's about to graduate with a business administration degree. I'm going to have a businessman! Isn't that great?"

I tried to cook up a follow-up question or anything to keep the conversation going, but only the howling wind made a sound at the follow-up department. I DO NOT CONVERSE IF I DO NOT HAVE TO! I don't want to waste other people's time with my meaningless twaddle.

But to Cola, it was so easy. Words freely rolled out her mouth. She moved with grace and without effort from one desk to another to meet and greet. Finally, on her third day, she loitered onto the chair behind Mia and looked at me. I prepared myself for some small talk, but... she talked to Mia first.

"Hi, sorry, what's your name again?" Cola asked.

"Hello! I'm Mia!"

"And you?" she turned to me.

"Xavi," I answered.

"Nice name! What does it mean?"

"Short for Xavier."

"Oh! So, is Xavi spelled with an H or an X?"

"X."

"That's nice!"

She waited for me to say something, maybe to return the compliment, but I stayed silent. Waiting for my response, she locked her eyes onto mine. Whoosh! Smoke billowed from my ears as her stare caused a firestorm inside my head. Dammit! Say something, Xavi!

"So, how do you like Doha so far?" Mia asked, breaking the disjointed silence. (Dammit, Mia! Thank you!)

## PORTRAITS OF THE WIND

"So basic!" Cola said. "It's like watching paint dry! I think this is how birds feel like when they're locked in a cage. You're stuck in one place, looking at the same things forever and ever again."

"Not entirely true. I mean, you can always go to the mall," Mia said.

"Ermergahd! The mall again! I've been there twice, and I already know where each store is!" Cola roared. "Back in the Philippines, after school, we could just take a stroll and hang out eating *taho*. Here, after school, it's either the mall or you go home. God, I miss taho!"

"You could hang out at a shawarma place," Mia said.

"I heard about these shawarmas. Are they good?"

"You haven't tried shawarma? They're better than BJs!" Mia abruptly laughed.

I groaned and spun away. Behind me, they began whispering. I can still hear everything, though. Their whispers were loud.

Cola spoke while giggling. "You slut! Who? Who did you BJ? Come on, spill!"

Mia keenly whispered back, "Not me! I heard Bernadette did it to Nard and said she'd rather suck shawarma over and over again than his dick."

I flinched at the thought.

"Eww! Maybe it's not so boring here, after all!" Cola said.

"So, you wanna hang out at a shawarma place sometime?" Mia asked.

"Only if it's the real shawarma, not Nard's shawarma."

They burst out laughing so loud that the whole class whirled to them. I recoiled when Mia laughed, out of instinct. Thank goodness she didn't pinch me.

And that was that. Stage four completed. Since then, Cola would exchange seats with the student behind Mia so they could talk whenever they can, disturbing what used to be a quiet corner of the room.

I was right. Cola was a handful. She was also right though. Life in Doha is dull, according to all those who grew up in any other place but here. For a sunflower like her, this desert city might as well be a city without a sun.

***

Let's fast forward to two months later, to a September day. I was staring at the scene of the classroom, observing the different groups of four, all huddled around in their own spaces, creating a poster about the motto of our graduation ("Cherish Today, and Live for Tomorrow"). Undiscernible chatter echoed across the room, nevertheless, when you focus on one person, you can catch each word that they say. These are moments that you know you'll never experience again after graduating.

The scene playing in front of me had generously intoxicated me with comfort to the point that my wooden classroom chair now felt like a leather recliner. It imparted me a feeling synonymous with the feeling I get when watching the sunset: a gloomy happiness.

"Where would you like to finish this?" Cola asked our activity group, which was chosen randomly by our teacher. Random as it may be, Mia and Cola were in my group.

"Let's do it at Joie's place so we can go play billiards afterward!" Mia said.

My scalp slid backward.

I hate spending time outside school. It's tiresome. I like my routine as it was: home–school–home. That's it. Sure, go out if I really, really, only really need to. But we still had thirty minutes left in class; we could have easily finished the poster. I was done doing the drawing, all they had to do was to color it.

I wanted to say no to Mia's suggestion, but what I said was: "You have a pool table, Joie?"

"Nope, but we're close to Rendezvous," Joie answered.

"Rendezvous?" I asked.

"It's the new billiards place, Wey," Mia said, stretching the last word. Joie cackled.

"Wey?" asked Cola.

"That's how he answers the phone! Like in Meteor Garden! Wey? Wey?" Mia said.

I gritted my teeth at Mia.

"So, Wey, Joie's place it is," Cola said. And the girls giggled once more.

"Fine. I'll let my mom know."

I excused myself from class for a phone call. Eight minutes later, I was sauntering back to the three ladies of my group.

"And?" Cola asked as I flopped back down.

"My mom said no," I said without making eye contact with anyone.

"No. You're lying. I can see it!" Mia pointed the butt of her pencil to my face.

I frowned, feigning innocence.

At that time, I wished Mom had actually said no. Going out, and billiards at that? That scared the bejesus out of me. First, I don't like the smell of smoke. I imagined the place would be like in the movies: hazy, cloudy, and cigarette-ish. I don't like that. Second, the game of billiards, as portrayed in films, is prone to violence. I don't like that either. Third, I inherently hate crowded places. I like empty spaces where my eyes can wander around without locking with another human being.

I told Mom we'll be doing a project at Joie's house and we'll be playing billiards afterward.

"I'll be home by ten," I said.

Mother was the typical strict mom. She required us to be home by seven whenever we had to go out. Eight, if we're doing something really fundamentally important. Nine, sure, if we were accompanied by adults. Ten? Absolutely not! Or so I thought. I guess she also wanted me to "enjoy" the remaining few months of high school. Dammit.

"Don't be a killjoy, Xavi," Joie said.

"Fine!" I said. "Fine! I'm coming!"

Cola playfully pushed my shoulder. "You're gonna have fun! I promise!"

"Hey, Xavi!" exclaimed a man with a thick Qatari accent.

\*\*\*

I snapped back to 2019 and spun towards the voice. It was Saeed beaming down his mean grey eyes on me. But don't let those aged eyes fool you, he is as friendly as a hungry cat and as talkative as a toddler who discovered his own voice for the first time.

With a bachelor's degree in computer science, he started his twenty-year journey in Al-Zubara Contracting as an IT officer. Later, he upgraded his knowledge and finished graduate school carrying a Ph.D. in Computer Science and Engineering. With such a degree, you'd assume he'd be able to fix my internet speed. But he said, due to things that I do not understand, our workstations are capped to specific rates. And that includes mine because, according to him, all that they require are freakin' cellphone photos.

## PORTRAITS OF THE WIND

"Xavi!" his commanding voice echoed once more.

"Mr. Saeed, hi," I said as I collected myself.

"What's wrong with the wall?" he asked.

The wall? Oh, was I staring at the wall? Think of a believable response, Xavi. Think!

I grinned and said, "What's up?"

Pfft!

Saeed walked away. "It would help if you'd look at your screen from time to time," he said from afar.

I glanced at my screen: *Upload failed. Please check your internet connection.*

Damn you, internet! I stood up from my cubicle and looked around the office. Alright, who's downloading movies?

"Hey guys, does anyone have new movies to share?" I murmured so the bosses wouldn't hear.

Everyone furtively glanced at one another, as if they were also curious to know. But nobody answered. They only shook their heads.

"Okay, but is there anyone downloading anything?" I asked loudly now. "I need the speed for archiving."

Once more, everyone shook their heads.

Maybe I am the one downloading something, I thought.

I sat and opened my torrent software. There was nothing on the download list; however, it was seeding Miyazaki animes from my childhood. Maybe that could be the reason. So, I stopped the seeding.

I restarted the archiving process.

*Uploading: 97GB left. Approximately five hours.*

There goes my day! With nothing else to do, I decided to take my lunch.

I took a small plastic grocery bag under my desk and headed to the breakroom. Inside, Saeed and a co-worker were conversing by the coffee machine. No, no, no, no, no. I looped around and walked out. I knew if I ate inside the breakroom and Saeed started talking to me, he'll begin machine-gunning words and I won't be able to put anything in my mouth.

Approaching my desk, I glimpsed at the notice posted at the entrance of every cubicle: NO FOOD ALLOWED INSIDE

Great. Just great. With a heavy heart, I dragged myself back into the break room. I tiptoed towards the farthest corner to be away from Saeed's proximity sensors. It was good that Saeed was chatting with another person; otherwise, he would hurtle to me like a magnet.

I opened my lunch. I smiled. Big. Chicken nuggets and rice, the champion food of my childhood and all Middle Eastern childhood. I took a small sachet of ketchup I saved from a previous take-away and emptied the red sauce over my yummy nuggets. When I reached for my spoon and fork, I caught a glimpse of Saeed. He was already alone, pressing buttons on the coffee maker. Oh no!

I discreetly took my first bite so I wouldn't attract his attention. But he had a sonar built for hunter submarines. The crunch of the crumbly nugget sent him hurtling towards me with an expectant demeanor. No!!!

Saeed implanted himself to the opposite chair, fixed his ghutra, leaned back, relaxed, and took a deep breath. That was a sure sign that a long conversation was about to dawn.

"So…" he began.

I tried to listen as I took another bite of my nugget. But as I chewed, his voice started to trail away from my ears.

## PORTRAITS OF THE WIND

It's incredible how people can pretend to listen while their minds hitch a ride with dandelions floating in the wind. And with a piece of the nugget (my childhood favorite), my mind leaped beyond my cranium and drifted away. With one bite, the flavor took me to the night where, let's say, a new chapter in my life began, on a September evening in 2003.

# Chapter 3:
# We Can Be Insignificant Together

Even with the ubiquity of single-lens reflex cameras with autofocus and auto-exposure in 2003, I was still using my father's Nikon FM2, a robust manual camera. Why? One reason: it allowed me to further train my eyes to see what the camera sees.

The camera was already ten years old when I first held it. Aside from its musky odor, I love what time had done to its viewfinder. Dust, moisture, and other stuff had camped in and around the viewfinder, creating a preview that is brown, grainy, and vignetting around the edges. It's the encapsulation of what I see whenever I remember the past.

For example, when I peered through the viewfinder and framed the silhouette of three girls playing billiards, I knew that that scene would sink, second by second, into obscurity. Soon, only our imagination would catch a glimpse of that fleeting image. The problem is, even those stored in our memories will quickly fade into nothingness. Hence there is the need for pictures. We need something that our mortal minds can latch onto forever.

I checked my settings: F/5.6, 1/60 seconds.

CLICK!

The moment I pressed the shutter, the reflex mirror swung up, and the shutter curtain opened a slit that moved from top to bottom, allowing light to touch the photographic film in one-sixtieth of a second. Once molecules of light have hit the film, the magic of photography happens.

## PORTRAITS OF THE WIND

Most consumer photo films use the silver halide chemical compound based on silver bromide. Once photons pass through the shutter, they enter the silver halide crystals and excite bromide electrons. The latent image forms when the electrons attract the silver ions and combine to form a dark metallic image on the film, which will later be accentuated by the chemical solution "developer agent." Longer exposure time and a wider aperture will allow more light, which means more photons on the film, causing more electrons to get excited, resulting in what we call overexposure. I'm proud I know this process. Not a lot can enumerate it now in the digital age.

I peered through the viewfinder once more and re-assessed the play of light and shadows that the low-hanging pool table light created. The light produced neither hard nor soft shadows over the faces of the three girls that stood under it, but it still gave a sparkle in their beaming eyes. I changed the aperture to F/2.8 to isolate them even more and throw the smokey background into a glittering, colorful bokeh.

CLICK!

That's it, I thought. That's the perfect setting.

CLICK!

I pressed the shutter again when Cola and Joie laughed hard after Mia overshot the cue ball. After a few more minutes of watching them, I decided that I had enough of the noisy crowd, the loud music, and the smoke that filled Rendezvous. So, out I went.

\*\*\*

I sat on the curb next to a lamp post facing the huge parking lot. My bottom flinched upon feeling the heat of the cement that radiated onto my butt cheeks. Although, I would still choose that over the racket inside Rendezvous. Besides, the yellowish light that shone from the sodium-vapor streetlamps gave the atmosphere another one of those gloomy happinesses. Happinesses? Combine that with the distant sound of whooshing cars— My body relaxed and leaned against the lamp post there.

"Hey stranger…" A soft voice said somewhere from my right.

I spun towards the voice. There, a figure emerged, gracefully floating into the rays of the yellow light. If it wasn't Cola, I would have had thought it was a ghost.

"I thought you left," she continued.

"Nope."

She gave me an amused side stare. "Are you just worried about us? Who's gonna take us home? You boy scout."

"What are you doing out here?" I asked.

"Taking a break. It's getting loud and crowded inside. My ears are getting tired," she said as she settled herself only inches away from me. "So, Wey…"

I rolled my eyes.

"Which character do you like?" She paused and studied my quiet demeanor. "I watch it too, don't worry. I think boys who watch it are cool."

I like Meteor Garden, and it felt good to know that I was cool for watching it. I became curious about the show upon hearing the song "Broken Vow" from a classmate who got cheated on. It was such an emotional song that it pulled me into binging the whole season. I even had to beg a classmate who was on vacation in the Philippines to get me a bootlegged VCD copy of it. The song, the way it was written and sang, was in all sense nostalgic. I had no idea about nostalgia back then. All I knew was I liked anything that induced longing for something that time had buried in the past.

# PORTRAITS OF THE WIND

"Qing He," I replied to Cola's question.

"What? That loser? Really?"

"Why not?"

"What do you mean 'why not?' In the first place, why?"

The gears in my head churned to construct my thoughts. "Well, everybody likes the F4, Shan Cai. Qing He is the underdog. It's tragic that he can't fully be honest about his feelings with Shan Cai. I mean, I know it's never gonna happen, but I do hope somehow they end up together."

"Millions are gonna freak out if that happens."

"Yeah, well, who are they to choose for someone else's happiness," I said.

She chuckled and playfully punched my shoulders before facing the parking lot.

Nobody talked for a while, which heightened the sound of the whooshing cars. And through the corner of my eye, I caught her fidgeting. It figures. For an extrovert like her, the quiet should be unbearable. So, I started a new conversation using an established method of small talk openers.

"How's the weather?" I asked.

"Yeah, it's freezing hot," she said, her voice trailing off. She did not take her attention away from the parking lot. "It's so beautiful," she added.

"Hmm?"

She gestured with both arms towards the car park. "The calmness... It's relaxing. It's so different from what I'm used to."

"It's therapeutic," I said.

"I could get used to this. Maybe it's not so bad being a wallflower, like you, after all."

Observing her, I felt something inside me. Something weird.

"Can I show you something?" I asked. Then I pulled her up and dragged her to the side of the building.

When we arrived at Rendezvous about an hour ago, I spotted a ladder mounted on the side of the building that led to the roof.

I have always enjoyed rooftops; it's a mountaintop in the city. It's serene, peaceful, and undisturbed. All the noises of the busy life down below are replaced with tranquility.

"Here. Climb up." I pointed to the ladder.

"What's up there?"

"I'll show you."

She shook the ladder and a couple of loose bolts rattled. "Why don't you go up first."

"Ladies first, right?"

"I'm wearing a skirt," she said matter-of-factly.

Yes, we were all still in our school uniforms: blouse and skirt for her, polo and khaki pants for me.

Trying to be a gentleman, I took a deep breath of courage, grabbed the first step, and started climbing up. While we were ascending the precarious ladder, the lively wind blew thoughts into my head. It wasn't about the risk we were taking by climbing up, it was about Cola looking straight up my ass and picking up some funky odor from my bottom. With that thought in mind, the muscles on my arms began burning as they pulled me up faster, me and my flabs.

As I helped Cola over the ledge, several water tanks greeted us. Silhouetted by the moonlight, the tanks sang a chorus of clicks and whirs as their pumps turned on and off. Apart from that, the rooftop was empty.

Up there, the wind kept whipping and messing Cola's hair. At first, she was allowing her hair to riot freely, but when she got annoyed, she gracefully moved her hands to sweep the strands neatly behind her ear. I shuddered internally then. Somehow, my entire body would always warm up pleasantly whenever I see her doing that.

Cola didn't say anything after we crossed the ledge, but her body language screamed amusement. Her lips fluttered, hinting that she wanted to smile. Letting the wind ruffle her hair once more, she visited the four corners of the rooftop, bouncing on her toes, to admire the serene sights and sounds of the city. On her way back to me, her face shone the salient glow of the streetlamps below, and her lips gave way to that suppressed smile.

"Can I show you something else?" I asked.

"What? Another rooftop?"

I started unbuttoning my shirt.

"What are you doing?" she asked incredulously, the color draining from her face.

"It's not what it looks like, trust me." I took off my polo shirt and laid it down on the floor. (I still had an undershirt, don't worry.) "Come, lie down," I continued.

"I'm not what you think I am," she said.

I removed my shoes. "I'm not what you think I am either. Just trust me. Remove your shoes and lie down."

She reluctantly did as I asked, and lay down beside me on the small surface that my polo shirt covered.

A palpable edginess crept in her voice. "What are we doing?"

"Relaxing," I said meekly as I put my feet up on the ledge. "Go on. Put your feet up."

She did; but not before giving me a stern look.

"Now, take a deep breath," I continued.

She inhaled deeply.

"And look up."

We both looked up simultaneously. The night sky said hello.

"How does it feel?" I asked. "Better than the parking lot, right?"

Cola's lungs released a deep, rich, and relaxing exhale, then her body dissolved into the floor there. She didn't say anything. Her mouth was just open as she looked up at the infinite blackness of the heavens at night. I understood her; above us was a cloudless ceiling littered with glistening white stars.

We stayed quiet for a long while, only feeling the wind dancing between our toes. Mesmerized, I took my camera and pointed it at our feet. I set it to bulb, held my breath, pressed the shutter and held it for three seconds.

CLICK! The reflex mirror swung up, and the shutter curtain dropped, exposing the film to the celestial beauty of the night.

When I take a photograph, I don't do it to capture the scenery. I take a photo to preserve what I'm feeling at that moment. And that moment with Cola felt like nothing I have felt before. There was a strong sensation that wanted me to create more moments with her. That's the emotion I wanted to capture through the image of our feet under the backdrop of a starry sky.

"Do you always carry a camera?" she asked.

I answered without looking at her. "You'll never know when a magical moment will happen."

When I turned to her I… I froze. In her almond eyes that glinted under the starlight, I saw my own reflection. And with a blink, I saw the whole universe staring back at me. My heart started to race. I couldn't help it. Her stare injected a hundred energy drinks into my heart, which was now thumping audibly. I think she might have heard my heart because she panned back to the sky and focused on the stars. We fell silent then.

## PORTRAITS OF THE WIND

Lying down and staring at the vast night sky can make you feel insignificant. It's a dazzling emotion. But if you have someone lying beside you, someone whose heart beats the same rhythm as yours, that feeling is washed away. It's as if somehow, your petty feelings are overpowered by your pounding heart, saying, "It's alright, you can be insignificant together."

Cola was right. I did have fun.

# Chapter 4:
# Tinikling, a Philippine Folk Dance

"I'm going to grade you with the following criteria: execution, sixty percent; costume, thirty percent; and facial expression, ten percent," the teacher had announced as he walked about the stage. "Your third quarter grades depend on this." He then proceeded to give us tips for combatting stage fright.

I can tell from everyone's bouncing knees that the teacher's words were doing everything but to encourage us. Nervousness had cloaked us so heavily that it prompted the guy beside me to discreetly release tension through his backdoor. Thankfully for him, his fishy aroma went unnoticed owing to everyone's neurosis from performing on stage. Myself, I had cold sweats on places that shouldn't even be sweating.

Let me give you an idea about why we were so terrified. Two months ago, folk dances were assigned to either groups or individuals, and we will be performing at the stage of Court A.

Court A, which is about a third of the size of a basketball court, was situated between the campus' main gate and the school building. On one end of the yard was the stage for performances. It would not have been a big deal to perform there if it didn't coincide with the break time of other classes. Now, that afternoon, students, teachers, staff, the whole school for all I care, were waiting for us to begin. Worst of all, I will be performing solo! Thank goodness the teacher did not choose the larger Court B.

We were called to perform in no particular order. The teacher asked for volunteers at first, and as expected, nobody got the guts to volunteer. So, our fate depended on the tip of the teacher's pencil landing randomly on a name in his grading sheet.

All eyes were fixed on the teacher as he lifted the pencil. When he released it, everyone held their breath as the pencil fell in slow motion. The pencil dropped with a loud (inaudible) thump. Everyone's heart stopped.

"Mia and Khalil!" the teacher said.

Everyone took a sigh of relief. Everyone, except those two.

Mia and Khalil performed the Cariñosa, a dance depicting the courtship of two lovers. I tried to watch them as everyone did; however, I could not concentrate due to my stomach turning over fifty times. Clutching it seemed to have made it worse. In hindsight, I should've volunteered so I wouldn't have to wait and leave my fate to a pencil.

The Philippines had many folk dances that I always found funny. Unfortunately, I would be performing one of them. It's called Maglalatik, a dance where I have to hit various halves of coconut shells strapped onto my body. I practiced the dance at home, and my sister said I looked like a fat dog trying to swat fleas in its fur.

Someone began drumming the coconut shell on my left shoulder. I turned and saw… Cola! I gasped. She was sitting from over there and then she transferred here next to me.

"Are you nervous?" she asked.

"Aren't you?"

She shrugged. "I try not to think about it. We're all gonna look stupid up there anyway."

A little later, the Cariñosa music stopped. Mia and Khalil froze in a tableau, and we all applauded to be polite. Then everybody was once again covered with anxiety as we waited for whom the pencil will name. The cycle repeated after every performance: anxiety, relief, applause, anxiety. At least, with Cola next to me, I was a little bit more relaxed.

"Nicola, Nard, Gio, and Sherry," the teacher announced.

"Break a leg!" I said.

Right there, watching Cola march up onto the stage had washed away all my anxieties. She glanced at me before they began. I gave her a thumbs-up, and she gave me a sweet half-smile. The music played, and the bamboo poles started to *clack* together.

Cola's group performed the Tinikling, which is a form of bamboo dance. To perform it, a pair would open and shut two bamboo poles on the floor, while the other couple danced in and out of the shuttering poles. If someone committed a mistake and a performer's foot was caught in between the bamboo poles… well… someone won't be walking properly for a while.

Gio and Sherry were the first dancing pair, whereas Cola and Nard clacked the bamboo poles on the floor. They all visibly counted the beats so none of them would commit a mistake.

I watched with furtive intensity when it was Cola and Nard's turn to be the dancing pair. I tried to observe Nard at first, and when my gaze had shifted to Cola, I couldn't take it away from her anymore. She was gorgeous. The way her Filipiñana costume imparted more grace on her, the way she wore a subtle delight on her face as she enjoyed the dance, made her look like a painting from heaven.

For the whole time that they performed, Cola and Nard kept their eyes on each other. They must be in sync, I thought. If they looked down at the pair of bamboo poles shuttering under their feet, points would be deducted from their score. I hated that. I hated that they had to look at each other. I didn't know why I hated it back then; it simply didn't sit well with me. Then as the music started to fall to a crescendo, she broke the eye contact with Nard, glanced at me, and... she laughed!

The next thing we all heard was a high-pitched scream after the shuttering poles crushed her feet.

*\*\**

The school clinic was a meager room with beds and dividers, attended by one school nurse. The typical case the clinic received was a headache, which is the go-to excuse for slackers wanting to get out of class. A nosebleed was the next usual case. Common causes include the summer heat, a punch in the nose, and the English subject (ha-ha, how original, Xavi). Sprains and fractures ranked last on the clinic's "common list." Next to it, at only one case per never, was a Tinikling catastrophe.

I entered the clinic and searched for the school nurse. She wasn't there. Only some voices were there. Familiar voices. I tiptoed towards the end of the room and peeked through the narrow opening between the cloth dividers. Oh heavens, Cola was resting on a bed, still on her Filipiñana attire that made her quaintly attractive. Standing beside her, Mia and Joie gossiped about the rest of the performances.

"Sir Ariel told me you got a 90," Joie said.

"Was that a pity score?" Cola replied.

"Nah, you were doing great until you laughed. Why did you laugh?" Joie asked.

Cola paused and bit her lip. "I've been wondering the same thing! I don't remember. Shouldn't you guys be having lunch already?"

"Yeah I know, we just wanted to check up on you," Mia said, "Get well soon!"

Pivoting to leave, Mia recoiled. She caught my nose sticking out between the dividers. She hurtled towards me, her shoes slapping the floor. "What are you doing there, fat robot?" She raised an eyebrow until it reached the back of her head.

I kept a straight face. "Checking on Nicola."

"What's that?" Joie pointed to my hand.

I glanced at my right hand that was carrying a plastic bag and tried to cook up a quick retort, but my stove didn't have a fire. I kept staring at the bag, waiting for an idea, a flame, or…

"Whatever," Joie said, giving me a dismissive wave of her hand. Together with Mia, they left without further questioning.

As I came into her view, Cola sat up and pulled the blanket to cover her legs. "Hey, stranger…"

"Why'd you laugh?" were my first words.

"You looked stupid with your mouth open. You were gawking like a moron!"

I knew it. It was my fault! I suppose my face drooped because Cola quickly recanted.

"No, no, no, no! It's not your fault. Alright? I lost focus," she said.

I ignored her. Even if she denies it, she can't hide the fact that my face made her laugh.

"How're your feet?" I asked, trying to change the topic.

"Mrs. Boots says it's only bruising. But it really, really hurts when I put pressure on it. I can't walk!"

"I hope it gets better soon. I'm so sorry." I wanted to sit down but there were no chairs beside the bed. Obviously. The school didn't expect patients to have visitors; they were required to rest until they got home or be transferred to a real hospital. So, I took the nurse's swivel chair and pushed it next to Cola's bed.

"And you? How was your coconut dance?" she asked while I settled down.

"Mia said I looked like a malfunctioning chubby robot who was looking for the reset button all over his body."

Cola snorted. "Yeah? Don't listen to her. She just loves to annoy you. She thinks you're her plaything."

"I got a 78."

"At least you passed!" she said with a big smile.

"Sure. Anyway, I brought you food." I took out a container from the plastic bag.

"Why?"

"Because I don't know if you've eaten or not."

"Why?"

"Aren't you hungry?"

"I am, but why?"

I hunched my shoulders. "I don't know! Stop asking why!" Removing the lid of the container, the mouth-watering aroma of the food overpowered the alcohol scent of the clinic.

Cola leaned backward. "Wait, Is that your food? I can't eat that. What will you eat?"

I gave her my nuggets and rice. NUGGETS! I supposed it was the safest food to give her. A patient wouldn't want fried fish like what the school canteen was offering. They want feel-good foods such as pizzas, or burgers, or nuggets. Nuggets are safe. Everyone loves nuggets.

At first, Cola didn't want to accept it, so I kept saying "please" until she took a bite. At the crunch of the crispy goodness, her face lit up.

NUGGETS!

Now that she was eating, I decided to leave her alone because eating is for eating (to enjoy food), not for talking. I hated it whenever someone would talk to me while I'm eating, so I assumed she did too. When I stood up, she shifted on her bed, almost reaching out to grab my arm.

"Please don't leave," she said, begging. Then she changed her tone. "Sit, stay. C'mon, boy. Sit! Sit!" She pointed to the chair. "Don't let me eat your food alone. You have to share it with me. Sit!"

I didn't know how to respond to that, but I sensed a peculiar sensation in my body. That sensation compelled me to sit. As I resettled, she extended the fork towards me with a piece of nugget on its end. I ogled it. Am I supposed to bite it? She wiggled the nugget, gesturing me to indeed take a bite.

It was only in the movies that I see two people feeding each other. Now, I know what it felt like. It was weirdly delightful. But I'm leaning towards the weird side.

After the nugget, she fed me a spoonful of rice. "Now, who's the patient here? Is it me or you?" she asked, taking a bite from the nugget I bit.

The food was almost consumed when the nurse returned. It was obviously time for me to leave. I was disappointed, of course, and Cola's unexpected sulky face showed it too.

"Hi Mrs. Boots," I said, rolling the chair back to her.

She returned the greeting with an agog lift of one eyebrow as she sized up Cola and me back and forth. I was about to walk out of the door when, out of the blue, an idea came to my head.

"Mrs. Boots, my head hurts," I said.

She dryly asked, "Why?"

"I think it's a severe headache."

Mrs. Boots analyzed me. I have never visited the clinic before with any ailment. This was the first time. Even more suspiciously, I developed the headache precisely a minute after she had walked in on us laughing and joking around.

"Lie down over there," she said.

Wow, it worked! I pretended to massage my head as I dramatically dragged myself towards the bed next to Cola.

"No," Mrs. Boots said. "Over there where I can observe you." She pointed to the other end of the room

Gah, she knows!

She continued watching me as I lie down on the bed. "Should I prescribe something for your heart?"

"We're just friends," I answered. I checked to see how Cola was reacting, and there, beyond my view, were all those dividers in between.

\*\*\*

Cola came to class a little later the following morning. Noticing that she was limping and dragging her right foot, a classmate dashed to help her. Another peer saw the other classmate helping Cola and rushed to help too. The willingness to help Cola cascaded from one person to another until everyone was flocking around her and showering her with kind words.

I, on the other hand, stayed on my seat and observed from the distance the gaggle of compassionate geese flock Cola. My help won't be of use anyway what with all those people already there. Besides, I had something better: a peace offering.

That afternoon, I made a break from my seat to Cola's the moment our teacher dismissed us for lunch. The ten meters between us stretched to a ten-kilometer obstacle course of chairs, desks, and students who moved slower than sloths. I squeezed through butts, ducked swinging arms, and jumped over bags. I only had one goal: get to Cola before Mia and Joie could hover around us like flies when I give my peace offering.

From my left, Mia overtook me. From my right, Joie buzzed by. What the… How were they doing it?! They weren't even running!

By the time I got to Cola's desk, the flies had already picked her up. I ran after them towards the hallway.

"Nicola!"

The three of them spun around. I jogged towards them. In my mind, I emulated a hunk, trotting in slow motion. But in reality, my flabs were flapping their wings to the beat of every step.

"Wazzap hunky-chunky?" Mia said, reaching over to pinch my side. I ignored her.

"May I speak with you," I asked Cola.

She nodded. Mia and Joie, as I predicted, hovered like flies. WHAPAK! That would be the sound if I hit them with a fly swatter. Unfortunately, I didn't carry one around.

"Can you just come with me for a minute?" I continued.

"Sure," Cola answered.

We started walking back to the room.

Joie yelled, "Nicola's limping; do you really want to let her walk back?"

Cola and I stopped short and moved to the side of the hallway.

"Alright, fine." I bit my lips. "I brought…"

"Quickly, Xavi! The line is gonna get long in the canteen!" Mia yelled.

That. Was. It. With a voice that reverberated across the halls of the school and a voice that had absolute power, I boldly exclaimed, "Shut up Mia! Can't you see I'm talking here?"

## PORTRAITS OF THE WIND

Everybody who was walking stopped and stared, amazed by the power of my voice. A second later, they resumed walking as if nothing happened. Three people remained, though, that was Mia, Joie, and Cola who were paralyzed in shock. I felt ridiculous! Ridiculously powerful!

"Whatever." Mia smirked to feign composure and then buzzed away.

Cola's eyes grew wide. "What was that?"

I felt fearless. "Listen, I didn't know if you'd come today, that's why I didn't leave this under your desk." I handed her a sandwich in a zip-lock bag.

She looked confused.

"It's my peace offering," I said.

"You don't have to—"

"Yes, I do. I was the reason you got hurt."

"No—"

My remarkable, fearless voice continued. "No arguments. Just take my peace offering."

She made a small lopsided smile.

Then, the fearless voice was replaced by the usual quirky me. "Just don't tell those two about this, alright?"

"Fine. I'll tell them it's mine."

That day, I gave her a Nutella sandwich with a note that says: "I'm sorry :(" I know it wasn't much of a peace offering, but I didn't want to buy her a necklace, or an earring, or a bracelet, or a cane. First, I do not have the money. Second, if I'd ask money from my parents, my mom will start interrogating me. Not ideal. I'd try to cook, then again, it will raise some questions. A sandwich was the perfect offering for three reasons: One, all the ingredients were available at home. Two, I made an effort to prepare it. Three, it wouldn't raise any suspicions.

"Why are you making another sandwich?" my mom asked when she saw me that morning.

"I'm hungry," I answered. Boom! As simple as that, I have a peace offering.

I didn't give Cola a sandwich for just one day, though. My culinary prowess for sandwich-making continued for a fortnight and a week. The following day, I left her a Nutella sandwich at the storage under her desk, together with a note that says: "I'm really sorry :("

She already asked me to stop the second day; I didn't, naturally. I wanted her to know that I am really sorry. On the third day, I prepared another Nutella sandwich, but then I thought I should spice things up a bit. So, on the third day, I left her a peanut butter sandwich. The fourth day was peanut butter with jelly. The fifth was jelly only. The sixth was a different flavor of jam. The seventh, still another flavor. The eighth, I made an egg sandwich. Then, egg and cheese. Then, egg and cheese and turkey ham. Then, cheese and ham. Then, just cheese. Then, just ham. Then, chicken ham and cheese. And so on…

During those three weeks, preparing her a sandwich every morning gave me something to look forward to at the start of the day. It added vigor to my usual home–school–home routine. It energized me, activating something in my heart.

After the nth time I gave Cola a sandwich, she leaned in and whispered, "I forgive you."

Only then did I agree to cease my sandwich production. What we both didn't expect was how we would feel about the sudden halt. Do you know the feeling of jogging on a treadmill and then stopping abruptly, then your legs still felt like it was running? That was us. We were the legs. Our cheesy mornings came into an abrupt, jarring halt, and we secretly wanted more.

On the first day of stopping, still carrying that earnest look, she plopped onto her chair and dived under her desk to look for a sandwich. When there was none, the sunshine that followed her also disappeared. Every day since then, she would only give me a joyless smile when she arrives. I did the same. I hated not being able to give her a reason to set-off her dynamite smile.

Something had to be done.

After a week, I replaced the sandwich with something simple: notes. Hand-written notes. The letters simply said: "Good morning! Have a beautiful day!" To enliven it, I drew some of my masterpieces such as a stickman, a boat, the sun, a nugget, or a bitten nugget.

Since then, the spirited walk-ins and the morning smiles returned. My routine now became home–school–make note–watch Cola read my note–home–call Cola–sleep. Yes, I was also now phoning her.

***

I obtained Cola's number from Mia. I thought I would have to pry it out from her, and as it turned out, I just had to tell her some lie about collecting phone numbers for our upcoming yearbook production (which I took no part in). Of course, to keep up with the charade, it wasn't only Cola's phone number I took, I also had to ask for everyone else's.

When I got home, I punched in the numbers, and a steely man's voice answered the phone. "Hello?"

I gulped. I glanced at the wall clock, 8:30 p.m. That's still a reasonable hour for a boy to call a girl, right? "Hi, it's Xavi, Nicola's classmate. May I speak with her?"

The line fell eerily quiet, save for the man's heavy breathing vibrating through the earpiece.

"Stay cool. Just stay cool," my brain said to my drumming heart.

A minute later, a sweet voice said, "Hello?"

BOOM!

Chills blossomed from my ears down to every part of my body, rendering me weak. I dropped down, sprawled over the couch. Hearing her voice over the phone sounded even sweeter than in real life. "Hi, Nicola. It's… uh… Xavi. I just wanted to say goodnight."

I heard her chuckle. "Is that all?"

"Yes, that's all."

She chuckled again. "Goodnight, Xavi."

I then ran to bed, jumped face down, and rolled the blanket over me like a Swiss roll. My heart freely rejoiced by pumping blood all over my face… and that part down there.

\*\*\*

In only about two weeks of the good mornings and the goodnights, something unpredictable happened.

As the clock struck 1:00 p.m., as usual, everybody rushed out to go to the canteen for lunch. And as usual, I stayed behind so I could eat my lunch alone. When the room was clear, I took my lunch box, opened it, and marveled at the glory of— The door burst open. I whirled towards the ungodly people who dared to disturb me at such a sacred hour. But what I saw ironed out the wrinkles on my eyebrows. From the door, Cola floated towards me, gracefully as always, carrying a take-out container from the canteen. Then, the two flies shadowing her appeared and laid their malicious eyes on me. My brows wrinkled anew. I knew I should have brought a fly swatter!

"Just go, please!" Cola told the flies.

The flies buzzed away, and Cola continued her graceful advance towards me. She poised herself onto Mia's chair beside mine, opened the take-out container, and started eating. I gaped at her for a long time before I fully understood that she was right there beside me, eating. I didn't ask her why, she didn't tell me why either, but for some reason, I'm in love with it. Normally, I would be appalled, but with Cola, I didn't feel any kind of repulsion at all.

I never ate lunch alone after that.

# Chapter 5:
# Serendipity Underground

Driving home from work, I recalled the events of the day as a reprieve from the tangle of cars clogging the road ahead. First, I was uploading photos to our cloud servers; then, I had lunch while Saeed loquaciously babbled on about something; now, here I sat listening to the horns of cars, trucks, and buses. Gah! That took my mind off the traffic for only three minutes! I tried to come up with ideas for the CEO's portrait instead.

One hour and some minutes later, I opened the door to my apartment, walked in, closed the door, and I was still conceptualizing for the portrait. Growing desperate, I turned my attention to my tiny studio apartment, hoping to find some inspiration there. Scrutinizing the small dining table, the two-seater couch, the poster of a rhino with glowing eyes, the flatscreen TV, and the PlayStation 2, did nothing to open the tap of creative juices.

I sought help from Mr. Google. Within an hour, I viewed a wide selection of instructional videos and tutorials about portrait lighting. Brilliant as they seem, none had the touch I was looking for. Nothing seemed right. There was a disconnect between the screen, the photo, and the emotions. Unlike back in the late '90s when I read books about photography or held actual prints that I— Whenever I held prints! That's the answer!

Tangible photos echo sentiments. As I see it, this is the result of prints having larger grains of noise, which screams nostalgia, especially photos taken with film cameras. Perhaps knowing that I'm touching paper that was printed who knows how long ago stirs a stronger subconscious that yearns for the past. There's something inherent with print that transcends time and touch. Computer screens, on the other hand, only projects emotionless electronic pixels. And where would there be a huge collection of printed books and photographs? The library.

Taking the keys to my car, I caught a glimpse of the view outside my window. There, under the waning sun, the glimmering sight of the newly opened metro, just a hundred meters away from my apartment, captured my interest.

Hmm... Should I take that instead?

I weighed the pros and cons. On the pro side: I get to save on gasoline, and I would get to the library faster. On the con side: it's crowded. But! Ideas always pop up in the most random places. Who knows? Maybe I could get inspiration inside the train. That's reason enough for me.

I slipped into my jacket, strolled a hundred meters along whizzing cars and babbling construction workers, and there I was.

***

With its arching roofs, the subway entrance reminded me of a mini Sydney Opera House, only beige. At night, strips of LED lights lined the arches, making it glow brightly against an urban landscape of rectangular buildings. I stepped onto the escalator that led down to the driverless trains, revealing a vast platform littered with people milling about, whose chatter overpowered the automated public address system.

One person seemed lost in the middle of it. That was me. I had no idea what to do. This was literally the first time I will be riding any subway. Logically, though, a ticket is the first thing I need. So, I purchased a prepaid metro card, then I queued at the turnstile. That's when I felt inept.

To get to the other side of the barrier, you must tap your card somewhere over it. But knowing where to tap your card is key, otherwise, you'll spend all day tapping your card with nothing happening. The commuters ahead of me tapped their card onto some sensor on top of the gate. BEEP! The turnstile opened, and it closed as each person walked through.

Easy enough, I thought. Now, it's my turn.

I glanced at the sensor. There was a circle that emitted green light. Below it was an illustration of a Wi-Fi symbol inside a rectangle. I tapped my card over that emblem.

Nothing happened.

I tried it again, lingering a little longer.

Nothing happened.

I glanced over my shoulder. My stomach heaved. Everyone in the queue was looking at me. Beads of sweat started forming on my forehead as my scalp heated up in panic. Driven by embarrassment, I slid the card around, hoping that the sensor would probably catch it.

Nope.

Dammit, Mia! Work! I tapped the card once more with the force of dropping an Ace in a card game. Nothing happened. I tried to— Someone yanked out the card from my hands and tapped it on the circle with the green light.

BEEP!

The turnstile opened. I dashed to cross over without thinking. Thank goodness! My pits were also starting to sweat. I spun around and a lady with wavy red hair—correction: wavy crimson hair—extended her arm and held up my prepaid card to my face.

"Thank you," I said in hushed sincerity.

## PORTRAITS OF THE WIND

At that moment, an Indian family started arguing over at the next turnstile. The father was tapping the card on the wrong place, while the mother kept pointing to the circle with the green light. Alright! Welcome to the club!

When I boarded the driverless train, the phobia of being sardined together evaporated. I seized a seat and reclined. There were enough seats for everyone. None had to stand.

The train rocked as it began to move. I peeked out the window and watched with suppressed excitement the train entering the tunnel. When there was only darkness outside, I switched my attention to the passengers, surveying them and— I snapped to attention, for there, sitting in front of me, was the crimson woman. She was bristling with distress for some reason, which made me stare at her a tad bit longer.

The cellphone of the dude sitting beside me rang. Out of reflex, the crimson lady turned to our direction, glanced at the dude with the phone, then to me. Dammit, Mia! She caught me gaping at her. Embarrassed, I closed my mouth and nodded. She nodded too and looked away.

***

In ten minutes, we reached our stop. The train doors opened, I stepped out, scanned my metro card (successfully), walked to the surface, and moved towards the library. Wouldn't you know it, by some random act, the crimson woman was already ahead of me, oddly limping on her right leg.

BOOM!

My ears rang from the explosive crack that came from the station. I spun around to check what was going on. BOOM! Faint laughter. Kids. Teenagers. Turned out, they were only students who were deliberately backfiring their luxury SUVs. Whew!

When I faced the front again… Boom! The crimson-head was now staring at me. Boom! We shared eye contact for an awkward second before she glowered and walked away. (Understandable.)

I probably looked like some kind of perv who's following her. If not, maybe just some "curious" person "curious" of the opposite sex. Man, you don't know how many "curious" persons are there in this country. Like Mia and Joie, they're flies. They are harmless and annoying, but they sometimes follow you to stare "curiously." So, to give the woman the benefit of the doubt, I stayed behind for five minutes and enjoyed the cool breeze. Once I was certain that she had left, I headed for the library.

The library's design is a marvel of architecture. It has an expansive foyer in the middle of the building for lounging and reading. There are beanbags, desks, and believe it or not, it even has some games for little children to scream and play around on. Also, there's a cafeteria in the middle of the open space. So much for a quiet library! Lastly, the ubiquitous bookshelves are placed on ascending steps that lead towards the wavy glass walls. So, when you're at the top level where the photography books are, you are treated with either the view of the entire city or the whole interior of the library.

I ascended the hundred steps towards the photography section. BOOM! The crimson woman stepped out from a row of shelves. The explosion was only in my head, though.

The woman cocked her head towards me, one eyebrow raised. I stopped; I didn't know what to do, so I happily showed my teeth once more. I didn't know what kind of smile I contorted because she returned a crooked brow before frantically looking around as if trying to seek for help. I raised my left hand to signal *"wait,"* and I placed my right hand on my chest to tell her that I'm a friend. She stayed in her position, frozen and glaring. To appease the situation, I headed for the digital library, feeling the weight of her eyes on the back of my neck.

Inside, I was the lone living being within rows and rows of black computers with 24-inch monitors. Tiny blue status LED lights pulsated from the CPUs and monitors like stars. Nice. While waiting for the lady to disappear, I decided to do some internet research about our CEO. I mean, I know who he was, but I didn't know who he is. A little background info would always help in crafting a good portrait. Just like I did for Cola's portrait.

Reading various interviews and articles about the CEO, an apparition appeared in the middle of the screen. I jolted, banging my knees under the desk. Ow! It was the crimson head!

I rolled the chair backward and scanned the room. Nope, not a sight of her. Weird. Her image sitting across me inside the train popped up for no reason. Peekaboo! Just like that. My imagination must be going haywire.

SNORT!

I jolted again. The snort sounded familiar. Sinister. I hunched over, closed my eyes, and listened for another snort. I knew what it was, but I hoped it wasn't *that*. When my ears only heard my own breathing and there were no more snorts, I went back to reading about the CEO.

An hour had passed, and my stomach grumbled. I haven't even gotten to see what I came to see. Time to move towards the photography section. But first, I took a peek outside the digital library. A few patrons were browsing the shelves; no sight of the crimson lady. Perfect! Onwards to the books!

Along the way, I passed many other sections, including sports where a book, lying on its side, caught my attention. On its cover was a striking picture of a former Tour de France champion who fought his way out of cancer to win the race seven years in a row. Later, he was stripped of the titles for doping.

I scrutinized this man's portrait. I have already seen it on the internet before, but looking at it printed on a book exuded more depth. The lighting, the shadow plays, the expression of the eyes, showed a man who was tired of lying. It was a picture that encouraged me to open the book and read more. Interesting, I thought.

I closed the book, and I noticed a wet spot on the back cover. Running my finger over the wrinkled and damp blemish, it felt like a teardrop. Or it could be saliva. Eww! I threw the book back to the shelf.

"Please don't," a woman said.

The hair on my arms stood up. Please don't be the crimson-head, please don't be the crimson-head.

I spun around and saw a female librarian. I sighed in relief.

"Pardon?" I asked.

"Don't reshelve books. Just put it on its side. We will take care of it."

"Sorry..." I said, nodding to her.

As the librarian left and attended to other books, my stomach growled anew. That brought thoughts of nuggets. Nuggets from 2003.

# Chapter 6:
# Where Cats Come and Die

"You wanna eat now?" Cola asked me.

Slouched at the couch, scissoring some images for Cola's visual aids on Philippine History, I can already smell the mouth-watering aroma coming from the kitchen. "No thanks, I'll eat at home," I answered.

"What? Come on, don't be a dick! My mom cooked for you! It's nuggets! Yummy-yummy!"

Cola's parents already met most of her friends, including Mia and Joie. They have this policy of knowing who their only daughter hangs out with. I have been friends with Cola for six months now, and I got by without meeting them. It was only a matter of time when my turn would come.

"H... Hello? Hello? Nicola, are you still on the phone?" It was her dad. He picked up the phone extension while Cola and I were talking for about... probably more than two hours already.

"Yes, Dad. We'll hang up in a few minutes."

"Alright, fine." Click!

We talked for a few more seconds. Clack! The sound of the other line being picked up resounded once more on our earpiece.

"Wait, is that Xavi you're talking to?" her dad asked.

"Yes, Dad."

"Great. Tell him we want to meet him. We'll have dinner. Evelyn will cook. Something good. Maybe his favorite, so he'll come. No excuses," he said. He had the voice of a bull, if a bull could speak.

"Okay..." she said.

Me, "..."

Cola then told me that her dad was a former first lieutenant in the Philippine Army and a Korean War veteran. Hearing that, the hair on my head stood up like I was touching a Van Der Graaf generator.

"Xavi? Xavi? Are you still there?"

Me, "…"

Two days later, there I sat at their house helping Cola with her project and then later having nuggets with her parents.

"Are you the one Nicola had been talking to for hours on the phone?" Her dad asked me in his bull-ish voice during dinner.

I took a bite of nugget before answering. He didn't appreciate that, and the raging veins under his white sidewall haircut confirmed it. I stopped chewing, keeping the food at the side of my mouth. "Yes po," I answered, furtively glimpsing at Cola.

Cola's dad pointed a fork at me. "You love my daughter?"

I. Literally. Froze. The nugget I bit lodged in my throat.

"Rodrigo!" his wife, Evelyn, snapped.

"Dad!" Cola simultaneously protested.

"What? She's my daughter, I have the right to know," he said.

"Stop it! He's turning red!" Evelyn said.

I was. Blood was rushing to my face like a geyser.

Rodrigo turned to Cola. "You like this boy?" he asked as he pointed his fork at me, again.

I coughed, trying to dislodge the stuck nugget.

"Dad! Stop it! You're embarrassing me!" Cola said.

"Xavi, sweetie, ignore him," Evelyn said, glaring at Rodrigo.

Rodrigo laughed aloud. "I'm just messing with you. I always dreamed of scaring Nicola's boyfriend and see his frightened face. See, look at you now. I got you good, didn't I?"

"He's not my boyfriend, Dad!" Cola said.

Rodrigo feigned surprise. "He's not?" Then he looked at me. "Don't you know you're the first boy she brought home? She talked about many boys. You're the first one we've met."

"We're doing a project!" Cola snapped.

"Cola! Don't shout!" Evelyn's voice killed all the sound in the room, save for the dripping kitchen tap.

Drip. Drip. Drip.

Evelyn dropped her shoulders and turned to me with a close-lipped smile. "So, where do your parents work?" she asked.

Finally, I was able to swallow that damn piece of nugget. "My father works in an advertising agency as an art director; my mom works as a secretary at the same agency." While I answered, I can see Rodrigo studying every tiny aspect of me.

"I see, so what are your plans for college? Are they going back to the Philippines with you?" Evelyn asked.

I shook my head. "No, it's just me flying back home. Baguio is a small place. It's an easy city to live in. The university I am going to is only a fifteen-minute downhill walk from our house."

Evelyn leaned in, her eyes turning bright. "Oh, you're from Baguio? I would love to have a place over there. Such cold weather. And the view! The view of the mountains peering over the fog is what enchants me."

Ah, Baguio, my hometown—the city sitting above the sky, where your eyes would feast on green pines and silver clouds covering a sweeping vista of towering hills and mountains. It's a city whose winds carry the icy breath of the stars that makes every tick of the clock a memory splashed in gold.

"How long is the travel time again from Las Piñas?" Evelyn asked.

"About eight hours by bus."

"So, what don't you like about my daughter?" Rodrigo asked in his hardened voice, giving me an inkling on how POWs probably felt like inside an interrogation room.

"Dad!!!" Cola banged the table.

"Are you gay?" Rodrigo followed up.

"Rodrigo!" Evelyn yelled, "Enough!" Her voice didn't kill any sound anymore, but it killed Rodrigo's parade of questioning.

"Fine," Rodrigo said. "Sorry, Xavi. You two spend too much time together, you might as well be a couple. Come to think of it, you're spending more time together as friends than Evelyn and I did as a couple. Isn't that right, Eve?" he asked his wife, who wagged her eyebrows.

"You're really embarrassing, Dad," Cola said.

"He's right though," Evelyn said, tilting her head. "When your dad was courting me, we would spend three, four hours together. Maybe five tops. You guys see each other every day, from morning till night. And then that's not enough; you'll phone each other. You can easily be mistaken as a couple!"

Cola and I glanced at each other. Our eyes opened their mouths as they began to talk.

*"I told you this is a bad idea,"* my eyes said.

*"Yeah, I know. Sorry,"* her eyes replied.

After dinner, I offered to wash the dishes. Naturally, as I anticipated, they refused. So, instead, I helped take out the trash.

"Xavi!" Rodrigo's footsteps echoed across the hall as he chased me towards the garbage chute. "Please pardon me for earlier."

"It's alright," I said, stuffing the trash into the chute.

"Stop being polite. It's not alright. I embarrassed you."

I insisted that it was okay.

"Well, I apologize," he said. "Sincerely, I do. Listen, the army took pride in my ability to judge a man's character, and…" He rubbed his chin, looking to the ceiling. "You know, Eve and I have been talking, and… You know, when I first met Eve, I knew that… um… Never mind, I'm just rambling here. Never mind. See you back inside." He skedaddled back into the apartment, scratching his head. Weird.

Sitting on the floor, knees bent sideways, Cola and I continued to work on her visual aid for another hour, using the center table as our desk. The stereo softly played acoustic songs, and the ceiling fan provided a mellow draft of cold air, stirring Cola's lilac-lavender cologne. Her parents kept to their own while reading a book and doing yesterday's crossword puzzle. It was a simple tableau, and it felt as romantic as it sounded.

\*\*\*

Remember Gio and Sherry? Cola and Nard's groupmates during the fateful Tinikling dance? On the first day of December 2003, they announced that they were now a couple. Well, they did not announce it to the class per se. It was revealed by the form of gossip. Gio told his basketball bros and they gave each other a high five. Sherry confided to her circle of friends and they shrieked in joy. Then through the grapevine, it became common knowledge. In the past, I wouldn't know of such things until it became old news. Not that I cared anyway. This time, I learned about it through Cola.

Gio and Sherry's relationship was a mystery to me. They weren't even that close with each other to begin with. But somehow, sometime between October and December, starting from that Tinikling dance, something formed between them.

I've always wanted to ask someone about what I felt whenever I see, talk, or hear anything that is Cola. The feeling was like drowning in a sugary syrup collected from the essence of her soul. As time wore on, that feeling intensified until I can no longer ignore it. There will be days during my quiet moments that Cola's face would pop up randomly, then my whole body will sink in that syrupy lake to search for her presence within its depths. I could never forget that feeling. I knew it was something extraordinary. I knew it was deep, but I wasn't sure what it was. If it was only friendship, then it was too extreme. And I knew it wasn't a simple crush either, for it wasn't the same shallow feeling I experienced with others.

I had nobody to ask. My sister? Nope, she'll laugh at me. My mom? Nope, she'll say I'm too young for relationships. My dad? Nope, he'll tell my mom. Mia? Nope, she'll be lampooning me and then tell Joie. The movies? Nope. They "show," not tell. So, who are the next people on my list? Gio and Sherry.

"It's not something you study, you just know," Gio said.

"Yeah, I think of it, like, a sort of hunger. You know? You know you're hungry, but you don't know what to eat. But when you finally find the right food, then you know it's the food you want to eat. Does that make sense?" said Sherry.

"It's really difficult to explain. It's not something that you can describe," added Gio.

"It's more like, when the first time you meet each other, you are drawn to each other. Like magnets, you know. They even say opposites attract. So, yes, exactly like magnets," explained Sherry.

"I don't know man, there are no words, it's just a wonderful feeling," Gio exclaimed.

These were their exact words when I asked them about deciphering the code of feelings. Satisfactory? Nope. I wanted something more meaningful and substantial, something that sounded mature. But what could I have expected? I asked a bunch of high school students.

The only concrete lesson I picked up from observing others in my school was: when you confess your feeling to someone, it could either lead to a meaningful relationship, or it can ruin your friendship.

\*\*\*

Icy winds churned the clouds over The Philippine School a week before the winter solstice of 2003. Trees swayed and dried leaves drifted in the air. Grade-schoolers, swathed with thick jackets, ran around Court A, throwing paper planes while waiting for their parents to pick them up. Beside me, doing her homework, Cola zipped up her jacket against the wind. Me, sweat dampened my pits and nerves shook my knees, which in turn shook the bleacher we were poised on.

"Stop it!" Cola said, "I can't write properly!"

I pressed my hands down onto my knees. A sheepish grin tugged at my lips. I said nothing. When she turned back to do her homework, a carefree wind messed her hair, and the usual sweeping motion of her hand followed. I picked up my camera and, CLICK! I just captured once more one of the moments that always shuddered me inside. She ignored me.

"If not now, then when, Xavi?" my heart said to my brain. I glanced at my wristwatch; only fifteen minutes left before Cola's dad picks her up.

I held my breath as I traced the afternoon sun over the contours of her figure. With her lips bit and her legs crossed, she stood out against a backdrop of normalcy. I watched her twirl her pen around her long fingers, creating dancing shadows on my thighs. She murmured to herself as she solved a problem. When it was time to write down the answer, she inked her cursive handwriting that resembled a string of pearls. By watching her, time got suspended, and I realized how much more alluringly magnetic she became. She was indeed God's portrait of heaven.

When I first met her back in July, I thought she was pretty. The simple kind, not the type of pretty that jocks chase around, you know, the high-maintenance kind, supermodels, cheerleaders, and whatnot. She was the kind of pretty that you only discover when you get to know her more. Nothing changed in her appearance, she simply became the darling of my soul. Is this what falling in love is? I don't know. How would I know? I have nothing to compare it with.

"Cola..." I said as I formulated my words.

Cola chortled.

"What? What's funny?" I asked.

"I will never get used to being called Cola," she said.

"So, you don't like me calling you Cola?"

"No, I like it. It's you and me." She winked.

You and me, she said. The words wiggled my ears like Dumbo. You, and, me. Cola and—

"Xavi!" she said, snapping her fingers.

I reeled back. "Oh, sorry. I forgot what I was about to say!" No, I didn't. After months of building courage, I just lost it again.

She pulled a face and then continued doing her homework.

"Why don't you have a boyfriend?" I asked. The words went tumbling out my mouth. I couldn't stop myself.

"What?" she asked, "What are you talking about?"

"I mean, you're pretty. And. Uh, smart. And. Um, beautiful. Funny. Energetic. Graceful. Uh..." I ran out of adjectives. I was straining to look for more, but I didn't see words, I only saw her. And there she was, rapidly blinking, waiting. "You're a thesaurus of perfection. You know what I mean?"

"No, I don't! Do you want me to have a boyfriend?"

"No. I mean yes. It depends," I said. It depends if it's me!

"Depends on what?" she asked.

"Depends on who it is," I said.

"So, who should it be?"

"No one! No, not no one—no, wha— You're like my mom! You're twisting my words around."

She laughed derisively. "What? I'm just repeating your words!"

This was not how I envisioned my confession would be.

*"Cola, I think I'm falling in love with you."*

*"I'm falling in love with you too."*

Then we'd hold hands as we walked down the seaside at sunset. That's how I imagined this moment would be. Short, sweet, and nostalgic. Something to look fondly back on down the road. But there we were. It's too late now to turn around and retreat.

"So, did you ever have a boyfriend?" I asked again. Dammit, why do I keep asking that?

She raised her chin. "Never. Since birth."

"Not even a fling?"

"Why would I waste my emotions for a fling? What are you up to? Why are you asking these questions?"

*Because I want to be your boyfriend! I have never looked at anyone with extreme longing. I yearn to be with you so badly; I am running out of words to describe how I feel. You're the person I think of in the morning, and the face I see when I close my eyes. Cliché, but true. I do not want another moment in my sorry life on earth without you by my side. You bring sunshine in places where cobwebs grow!*

*You make the time tick faster when we're together, and crawl light-years long when we're apart! I want to be with you!* Say it! Say it, you coward!

"Just curious," were the words that came out of my mouth.

"Just curious?" she scooted closer to me. Our legs touched. Oh. My. God.

She found my eyes and I saw my own pupils dilate.

"Look, if there's something you want to tell me, tell me now. We only have a few months left. You might never get the chance again," she said.

I rallied my strength. "You see, I..." I began. My lips started quivering, and my heart started doing CPR on its own. I gripped the sides of my sweater, still trying to look composed.

She continued waiting, making the discomfort stretch to forever.

"Would there ever be a chance for. For..." Come on! Say it! My nostrils whistled as I drew in air. "Would you get mad if... if..." Dammit, why? Why does it look so easy in the movies?

"Just say what you want to say, Xavi," she said with a voice that I found very comforting like a fluffy blanket. But I wasn't comforted. Every part of me teetered on the edge of collapse. Fearing a total breakdown, I walked out. I walked out on her, leaving her hanging. I didn't want to do it. I hadn't thought about it. But my feet mindlessly moved up on their own and walked away.

I didn't run when I fled. I kept a constant pace, slowing down at times. A part of me waited for Cola to call my name.

She never did.

In return, I never looked back. I never saw the look on her face. What she did next? I'll never know. That day would continue to live in regret.

Coward.

## PORTRAITS OF THE WIND

I didn't know where to go when I walked out. I just kept walking, skirting classmates, rounding corners, and seeing places around the campus that I didn't know even existed. And when I was far enough not to feel Cola's presence, my body gave way to despair, forcing me to lean against a pile of scrap wood. That's when I realized I was already in a secluded place where all wood and metal scraps were dumped into obscurity. It was a place that stunk of death because in between those scraps of junk, it was a place where cats come and die. And like those cats, I thought our friendship was also crawling between those gaps to slowly die.

Dammit, Mia!

\*\*\*

The winter solstice of 2003 came. Before the start of classes, everyone went standing outside the yard, both young and old, who looked fatter with their thick jackets and sweaters. They craned their heads upward as they exhaled with their mouths. And when a visible puff of moisture rose in the winter air, they would start giggling and wowing. Some would even pretend to be smoking, using their pens as the make-believe cigarette. I would have joined them, but all I desired that day was being close to Cola and be swaddled by her warmth.

I entered the classroom. There were the usual early birds plus Nard.

Like clockwork, Cola arrived ten minutes later. She took her seat and bent down to look through the desk storage.

Hoping we could just forget about the bleachers, I kept the good morning letters going. But when she read my letters, she just folded it back without a trace of twinkle in her eyes. It's as if she can read my conflicting emotions within each pen stroke. It was awful. Obviously, the good nights also ended.

After putting away my letter, Cola took out her notebook from the desk storage. Simultaneously, another letter fell out. She recoiled with raised brows. The letter was not like my little notes. It was, in fact, a letter. And it was a letter written on a white legal pad folded in squares, unlike my intricate origami folded notes.

With knitted eyebrows, Cola opened it and read it. Then in slow motion, her brows slowly lifted as her eyes widened millimeter by millimeter. She took a glimpse of me, a swift one, like a whip, a dart of the eyes, before shifting her gaze to Nard.

Nard? What the hell? Then I remembered something.

"Are you and Nicola still together?" Nard asked me out of the blue while I was having lunch alone in the classroom. That was a day before.

Nard lurked at the doorway a minute after everyone went to the canteen. He kept glancing and checking the room like he was looking for something. When he saw me see him, he gestured an awkward wave and paced towards me.

I sensed that my nuggets were gonna get cold.

Though Nard and I grew up together in the same school, we never really talked to each other (to be fair, I never really talked to anyone). When we were younger, we never saw each other eye to eye. We just sort of co-existed. He was an upcoming basketball athlete; I was an audience under the bleachers. When we entered high school, he became a varsity player, and I remained under the bleachers. Younger kids started looking up to him, and he treated them very nicely. He is a good guy, down-to-earth, not a bully. We just never really talked. So, when he marched towards me, I knew something was up.

"Why do you ask?" I replied, keeping a straight face.

"You just stopped being together. Normally, you'd be together now, having lunch. Now you're... alone."

I chuckled, pretending not to care. "We were never together. We're just friends."

"Really? We thought…" He hesitated for a moment, looked away, pondered, and whirled back with an incredulous look on his face. "Not even MU?"

"What's MU?"

He abruptly laughed. "What? Never heard of MU? Mutual understanding?"

"What's that?"

"Seriously? You don't know? Okay, mutual understanding is, like, you know you like each other, but you don't tell each other. But, you're together. But not exactly. There's just an understanding, a mutual understanding, between the two of you that you know you like each other without telling each other that you like each other. Do you get that?"

Ah… I thought it had something to do with law.

Were Cola and I on an MU relationship? No idea. Even if we were, mutual understanding still meant we were a couple, though not officially in a relationship.

"Yeah, no. We're friends," I said.

Nard gave me a grin of a conman, the type of grin with something devious lurking underneath. "Good to know," he said before departing without even saying goodbye.

# Chapter 7:
# The Portrait That Matters

"Bad nostalgia moment," I said to myself in front of the bathroom mirror while I got ready for work. Remembering the past is like walking on a tightrope; one false move (or a wrong memory) will kill you rather than get you to the other end.

I splashed cold water on my face, hoping it would wash away not only the dead skin cells but also the bad memories that were still clinging in my head. I tried stretching my lips to form a happy face, but the frowning muscles were stronger. I pensively sighed instead, still crestfallen over what happened ages ago.

Coming back to Qatar seemed to be a good idea nine years ago. I was coming back to the place where it all began to start anew.

Initially, I was hoping that I will land a job as a photojournalist, but I didn't know that the 2008 financial crisis would still have some impact on Qatar's economy two years later. When I started looking for work, no one would hire me. Then I stumbled upon this little start-up company. I submitted my credentials, got a call with an offer, and I took it.

"It's only temporary, it's still photography, isn't it?" I told myself, trying to justify my decision to become an in-house documentation photographer. A decade later, I'm still stuck in the same rut. It didn't matter though. I didn't care. The job wasn't as important as the reason I came back.

I came back to fill the gaping hole left by Cola. I assumed it was going to be a healing experience to see the streets that I grew up in, my old school, which is now torn down, and that Rendezvous building which is now a bank. But coming back only raised a question: what if. What if I was actually able to say what I wanted to say on the bleachers? Where would I be now? Where would *we* be now? And what if I picked up on Nard's intention the day he asked me those questions? Would I have answered differently?

What if... They're the parting words of people who went the other way. You can never find any comfort with what-ifs. They only trigger the agony of longing as you picture what could have been.

I rode the metro to work again. I had been taking it since the day I rode it to the library. Aside from saving petrol, riding the subway gave me an inherent sense of calmness and peace. It's similar to the serenity you get when you're alone inside your house, lit by a candle, while a howling tempest rages outside in the night. It's hard to explain. It's a kind of peace known only to those who have experienced it.

Thank goodness the train is not overcrowded yet. God knows if it did become packed, I'd be back behind my steering wheel.

\*\*\*

As soon as I arrived at my office, I flopped onto my squeaky swivel chair and drew in a sharp breath. The train ride today wasn't peaceful at all.

The displeasure didn't come from the train ride itself; it came from the back of my mind. For the whole fifteen-minute train ride, flashes of Nard and Cola together kept manifesting in my thoughts, and I can't seem to keep myself distracted from it. Even if I had thought of other things, their image still popped up on top like unwanted pop-up ads while you're browsing the internet. I was getting ready to jump overboard. It seemed to be the only escape. Fortunately (or unfortunately), we arrived at my stop.

"Xavi, do you have a minute?" The voice came from the glass office. Here we go again. A minute that would turn into ten minutes.

Saeed spoke as soon as I crossed the doorway into his office. I remained standing and he stayed seated behind his desk. "Xavi, I wanted to let you know that the board wished to have the photoshoot sooner. They're planning to publish a self-pleasing article about the company's twentieth anniversary, and they wanted to use the photos you'll be taking. Are you alright with that?"

"Okay," I said while his words tumbled a couple of times in my head. "Uh, did you say the board?"

Saeed's brows crashed into each other. "Yeah, the board."

Me, "…"

Saeed, "…"

"I'm doing the portrait of the CEO, right? That's what you told me."

"Yes, you are. Including the board. I told you that."

"You did? When? Really?" I looked to the side, trying to search for the lost memory.

"At the breakroom. Last week. You were smiling while you ate your nuggets. You don't remember?"

"At the breakroom? Last— Oh, yeah. I remember. Yeah," I said while looking around the room. Nope. I still didn't remember.

Saeed zeroed in on my retinas as if he knew I was lying and was waiting for me to recall. But I didn't. Dammit, Mia! I should pay more attention to conversations. I should pay more attention to everything. Stupid Nard.

"So, can you do it tomorrow?" Saeed continued.

"Tomorrow?!"

"As soon as possible, yes. Tomorrow."

"Okay. Sure," I mumbled before pivoting to the exit.

## PORTRAITS OF THE WIND

"Xavi, hold on." Saeed stood from his chair and marched towards me. He placed his hand on my shoulder and gently directed me to the couch by the doorway. "Have a seat," he said.

I crumpled onto the couch, bewildered. I don't recall him touching me that way. The touch didn't feel natural; it felt clinical.

"How are you feeling?" he asked, plopping down onto the chair opposite mine.

I stared at him questioningly, forcing him to explain his question.

"You see, Xavi, these glass walls over here are not glass for no reason," he explained, "I specifically requested glass walls so I could watch over my employees. Not in the creepy way you're imagining. For example, you see Mohammed there, you know he's not having a good day when his hair is not gelled. Or take for example Satti, right now I can tell by the way she laughs— See that, that's a guffaw, that means something good had happened to her recently. This see-through room is this department's weather station, and it lets me forecast each one's current climate, so I know what kind of face to wear. Like you, right now I am taking my time to ease into my main point because you seem a little... for the past week, and especially today... distracted."

"Distracted?"

"How long have you been working for me? About ten years already, am I right? So, exactly, I know when you're experiencing something. You know what I mean?"

The leather couch creaked and echoed uncomfortably as I tried to look okay.

"It's you know... ups and downs. People have them," I said.

"Are you sure? I mean, today especially, you look more wishy-washy than usual."

I nodded. "Yep! I'm sure," I said, although Nard was still hovering over my head.

"Alright. I'm saying, sometimes people need to rest for health reasons. Just tell me if you need a break to rest and collect yourself. I'm fine with that. In fact, the company encourages you to take breaks. To be honest, I've never seen you take any leave. We do appreciate it if you work tirelessly, but we don't appreciate it if you get all sick because of it."

I chuckled timidly. "I'm fine, I'm alright."

Saeed didn't move in his spot, he kept looking at me, studying me, looking for the truth in my eyes. The eyes speak the words the mouth cannot express. I wanted to blink, but blinking would show weakness. So, I stared right back, uncomfortably so.

After the prolonged awkwardness, Saeed nodded and paced back to his desk while straightening his ghutra. "Alright! Then I'll let the board know you're good to go for tomorrow's shoot," he said.

I stood up and faced the exit.

Saeed added, "Oh, and remember, nothing fancy about the photos. Just ensure they look good. That's all they care about."

As I exited the glass office, a hundred thoughts swirled inside my head: What was that about? Now I have to do the board's portrait too? Rest? I don't need rest!

Stop it Nard! Stop showing your face! Dammit! Portraits... portraits... how did I do Cola's portrait?

\*\*\*

A week after the 14$^{th}$ of February 2004, I sat pensively at our porch, gaping at the shadows of moving clouds. I couldn't help but imagine what Cola did together with Nard during the past

Christmas, New Year, and of course, Valentine's Day. Were there a lot of wild laughter? Did he also meet the parents? Was he afforded the same warmth that I received? Did they kiss? Were they making golden memories together? I tried to bury all these thoughts, but they always forced their way up to the surface akin to a ball pressed down into the water and then released.

"Xavi, are you feeling alright?" someone asked.

I jolted. It was Mom.

"Yeah, why not?" I answered.

"You've been sulking since the new year. Is there something wrong?"

I got on my feet and patted my shorts. Little specks of dust formed a tiny cloud. "No. I'm not sulking. I'm wonderful," I answered, keeping my eyes on the dust particles.

"Is it a girl?" she asked, analyzing me.

"What?!" I marched to the house, trying to avoid her. But there's no avoiding her.

"You know you're too young to have a girlfriend. You're still in high school!" she said, following me into the house.

"No, it's not a girl! What—no! Stop!"

"You're too young to understand these things! You may think you found someone, and then you'll end up getting hurt! I've seen my brothers get hurt; it's not a nice sight!"

"I'm graduating in a month, Ma! I can understand these things already!"

"So, you do have a girlfriend!"

"No, Ma! Stop! Stop!"

"Then why do you look so broken-hearted?"

"I'm not! I'm just wondering about life after we graduate!" Yeah right.

"As long as you're living in my roof, you're not going to have a girlfriend. Not yet! Not when you're still too young!"

Pfft. Mothers. Even if you're already taller than them, they still see you sucking a pacifier. No matter how wrong they are, they will always be right. There's no winning an argument with them. Even the supreme court doesn't stand a chance with them.

Entering the living room, I noticed the phone's handset sitting outside the cradle.

"Phone call for you. Some girl's father," Mom said condescendingly, paying attention to my reaction as I picked up the phone.

"Hello po," I said.

Mom planted herself next to me with her arms crossed, reading me. I turned my back.

"Yes. Yes. Sure po. No problem po," I said while cupping the phone's microphone. "Bye." Click. I replaced the handset with the corners of my lips rising slowly.

"Who's Nicola?" Mom's voice punched me. As soon as the sound of Cola's name traveled through my ears and into my thoughts, my body gnarled in glee. It always does whenever I hear Cola's name. Nicola Cueto. Nicola, Cueto. It still does until now.

"Just a classmate," I replied, absconding to my room, hiding my rainbow-esque emotions.

Mom tailed me. "Why is her father calling you on the weekend? More importantly, why is her father calling you at all? Is she your girlfriend?"

I tittered. "No, Ma. She's not." Oh, how I wish she were. "Her dad wants me to take some graduation portraits for them."

Mom's prying tone made an abrupt about-face. "Are you getting paid?" she asked vibrantly.

## PORTRAITS OF THE WIND

"No, Ma. It's just a favor." At last, I reached my room, locked the door, and an exuberant, soundless scream escaped my mouth.

\*\*\*

Most apartments in Doha were only four floors high, so elevators weren't standard back then. Unfortunately, Cola's apartment was on the fourth floor, so I must haul my photography gear all the way up. I was panting and sweating when I reached their door and rang the bell.

The door swung open and Rodrigo's face emerged from the entrance. "Xavi. Come." His bull voice echoed down the stairwell as he stepped aside to let me pass. "Eve and I have been talking about you. How come you and Nicola are not spending much time anymore?" he asked.

I didn't look at him. "Aren't we? We're probably just busy."

"Or is there another guy?" Rodrigo paused to stare shrewdly.

Nard's face slammed onto my face. I grimaced.

"Nah! I'm messing with you again!" Rodrigo said laughing, giving me a big pat on the back. "I know there's no one. Trust me, I'd know if another boy is hanging around my princess Nicola." He pointed me to a cleared-out space in the living room. "You can set up there. Call us when you're ready. Nicola is almost done with her makeup."

I started setting up my guerilla equipment. Being a student then, I had no access to professional gear. My tripod, with its thin legs, only rose to my chest before I must crank the head's height to a maximum of twenty centimeters. Still, it was perfect for Cola's 5'4" height. For my lens, I decided to go with my 35mm f/2.8 prime. I could have used my zoom, but it would let me lose two stops of light.

My choice of lighting was amateurish too. I used one Speedlight on slave mode and a couple of fluorescent bulbs for backlight and fill light. For light stands, I used broken microphone stands that I foraged from the school scrap yard (that reeked of dead cats).

After setting up all my equipment, I took a step back and appraised the makeshift studio. And you know what? It reminded me of the setup for taking passport pictures. I was abhorred. If I took Cola's portrait there, it wouldn't be different from any other studio portrait. Besides, the school was already providing our studio portraits.

I murmured to myself, "Where could I take her photo that would let her relieve this day, or rather her high-school life?" With that objective in mind, I started prowling around the living room, eyeing and framing different locations, using my fingers as a viewfinder.

"Are you ready?" Rodrigo asked all the way from Cola's room.

"Give me ten more minutes!"

"Alright. Take your time."

I got worried. If I didn't find the right spot, then I would be forced to do a cliché studio portrait. I kept looking around until I encountered the couch behind me. I also noticed a low center table behind it.

"Ah-hah!" I proudly exclaimed.

I hastened to move my lights aside to rearrange the furniture. Then, I scurried around their house inconspicuously to look for some props. Lastly, I rearranged my lighting and then I was jubilant.

I knocked on Cola's room. "I'm ready," I said without opening the door.

"We'll be out in a minute," Evelyn answered.

I waited at the makeshift studio. Thereafter (not a minute but maybe longer) several clacks of footsteps sounded on the marble-tiled floor.

## PORTRAITS OF THE WIND

I about-faced and— My god. A piece of me died upon laying eyes on the peerless splendor beyond me. Cola wore a short light blue satin dress; spaghetti straps on her shoulders; straight cut from bust to the waistline; and skirt pleated on the waist, dropping to a wavy flounce above her knees. Wearing low heels, she floated like silk towards the set with her trademark grace while her medium curled hair sprang up and down. There was little to no makeup at all. Her mesmerizing beauty was all-natural. Imagine a bright minimalistic apartment from an Ikea catalog; she would fit right in with her semblance of guileless elegance.

"Hey, champ! Your mouth is leaking," said Rodrigo as he lightly lifted my chin to close my mouth.

My lips folded inwards, then I began removing imaginary lint from my shirt.

Rodrigo laid a hand on my shoulder. "It's okay. I know. She's beautiful," he said, flashing his brows.

Cola didn't say anything. She just waved tepidly, bit her lips, and avoided eye contact.

"Did you move things around?" Rodrigo asked, perusing the living room.

"Yes. Cola," I coughed awkwardly, "I mean Nicola will be standing here," I darted to where Cola would stand, "and facing this way towards the camera."

Rodrigo's nose wrinkled. "Why?"

I began to explain my rationale for a photo symbolizing Cola's stay in Qatar. It could have been anywhere, really, but I didn't expound on why I chose this spot.

That morning, Rodrigo spent maybe half an hour or so clearing up space in the living room to allow me to set up my gear. Now, everything was back to the way it was; to the way when Cola and I worked on her visual aids. I even placed manila paper (which I scavenged from their storage room) on the table. It was one of the treasured moments in our togetherness. I knew we were both feeling elated that evening. We weren't saying anything, but our eyes were speaking it. Eyes speak the words what the mouth cannot. So, to me, no question, the living room provided the perfect set for Cola's portrait.

To vividly remind her of our time together, I also populated the set with more props such as the shoebox (which I took from their shoe rack) filled with folded papers to signify the letters I sent. I also placed some sandwiches (which I took from their kitchen) on the center table.

Cola never looked at me while I spoke. The equipment, her parents, and her feet were the only things she paid attention to. Mirroring her, I also did not look at her while I explained; although, my peripherals kept catching the flying kisses of her captivating figure.

"Well, that's interesting. I love it," Evelyn said after I finished my explanation.

"Alright. You're the photographer. You know what you're doing," agreed Rodrigo.

I pranced to my camera and called Cola. "Cola..." I coughed awkwardly again.

Rodrigo and Evelyn briefly exchanged curious glances.

"Nicola, could you stand there." I pointed to the floor in front of the camera.

She took her position and then she looked at me. Well, not me per se, but the camera. So, technically, not me. She still didn't look at me.

"Could you turn towards me?" I asked her.

She turned, but too much.

"Turn back a little," I said.

## PORTRAITS OF THE WIND

Again, too much. I approached Cola and gently grabbed her by the shoulders and turned her to how I wanted it. Electricity, with a voltage high enough to execute death-row inmates, ran through my body when my fingers touched her warm skin. It just didn't feel right, though. She flinched.

I brought the key light a little more frontal to lessen the shadow on her left side. Then I studied the light falling over her face, starting from her shiny black hair, to her forehead, to her nose, to her lips, and back to her— I froze. Her eyes were trained on me, causing my heart to slam against the walls of my chest. But when our pupils met, she paled and looked away. My pounding heart stopped short. Well, I guess our friendship was ruined after all. Sigh.

"Ready?" I asked.

She nodded.

"Oh, wait. Hold on," Evelyn said as she puts on the dark blue graduation gown on Cola. "Should I put on the cap?"

"No," I said matter-of-factly, "just let her hold it on her side so we could see her whole face." It was obvious: who would want anything to obscure a sight of beauty?

I peered through the viewfinder and slowly tuned the focus until her face became sharp enough to prick my heart. I set my shutter and aperture, then, CLICK!

That click was the most satisfying shutter I have heard since the three months we weren't speaking with each other.

I took a couple more photos of Cola, varying her position and location. All the while, we never had eye contact.

Finally, I took some family portraits.

"Does your camera have a self-timer?" Rodrigo inquired after the final family shot.

"Yes, po," I nodded.

"Good, set it on the tripod and join us," he genially said.

Evelyn looked excited. Cola turned red. I was conflicted. I knew Cola didn't want me to do that, but her parents were obliging me to join. And what would Nard say about this?

"Are you sure?" I politely asked.

"Yes! You're family now! Get in here!" Rodrigo said, gesturing me to come over.

"Just come on," Cola said in a tone akin to just getting it over with.

But she looked me in the eye. She looked me in the eye! Her light brown eyes lassoed mine. I got confused. I didn't know how she exactly felt. Her words were different from what was coming out from the windows of her soul.

I replied with a courteous nod, placed the camera on the tripod, and set the timer. I stood beside Evelyn at the edge of the group. But before I could smile, Evelyn grabbed me and shoved me between her and Cola. Awkward. Awkward yet… ayeeee!!!

We all held our smiling lips and watched the timer tick down.

"How long is that timer?" Rodrigo asked jokingly.

It was only ten seconds, but to them, it seemed to go on longer. To me, it felt shorter. I was standing shoulder-to-shoulder with Cola, and when you're together with someone your body and soul yearned for, one hour becomes ten minutes, and ten seconds becomes a blink of an eye. I wonder how she felt about the ten seconds I was beside her. Was it a mere breath, or did it go on forever?

# Chapter 8: Mutiny of Memories

Fifteen years after taking Cola's graduation portrait, I now had the CEO of Al-Zubara Contracting surrounded by my professional lighting equipment. Setting up all my gear in his office rescued the magic of photography, digging it up under ten decades of debris borne by dreary progress photos. However, the viewfinder magnified the tiny movements of his face that yelled skepticism. His gaze hopped from one gear to another, and when it landed on me, it shoved my saliva down my throat.

"Isn't it a little too dark?" he asked.

Based on my research, the CEO, Jaber Al-Zubara, is an avid collector of paintings, especially the works of Rembrandt, Caravaggio, and Raphael. What do these artists have in common? Chiaroscuro. Their artworks are bathed with the contrast of shadows and light, like the replica of Rudolph Ernest's *Smoking The Hookah* hanging on the wall beside the chief's desk.

Mimicking those artists, I decided to light Jaber with a lot of shadows. He also got the perfect features for it; the web of wrinkles in his face and the thick bags under his eyes are perfect for catching shadows and showing a life that has gone through a lot of challenges.

"Aren't you going to use more lights? Reflectors, umbrellas, and what do they call them? Softboxes?" he continued.

I hunted for reasons among my gear to validate my lighting. There were two strobes and a flash erected on the three corners of the room. Two strobes and a flash. That was all that clung to me. Two strobes and a flash.

Saeed noticed my thumb that kept flicking my camera's switch on and off. "He knows what he's doing. Don't worry. Let the pro do the work," he said.

Thanks, I thought.

I let Jaber stand far from his desk so my 35mm lens could capture the whole office. This way, the viewer can appreciate the different details embodying this man, the CEO. One of these details was the thick pile of documents on his desk to symbolize that he was still a hands-on executive. There was also the vintage Herman Miller desk clock that his father handed down to him, which represented the years of hard work. On the corner shelf, I placed a scale model of a yacht that he owns to signify his hobby. It was exactly the same concept I did previously for Cola's portrait.

"How about the board members? How are their photos going to be?" asked the CEO.

"We're going to do them in the conference room," I answered, then pressed my lips together. Stop asking too many questions!

CLICK!

I took the first shot, reviewed it, then deleted it before Jaber could ask to see it. It was okay, but not perfect. I adjusted the "sunlight" to quarter power.

CLICK!

I took another shot. This time, I was jubilant when I reviewed it. Hah! Nice!

"Can I see it?" Jaber asked.

"Of course!" I proudly handed him the camera.

"It's too dark, isn't it?" Jaber frowned, peering down the preview screen.

Saeed came over to have a peek. "Maybe a little. What do you think?" He looked at me.

"I think it's perfect. I think the lighting is good."

"Are you sure? You can't even see half my face," said Jaber.

Two strobes and a flash. Shadows. Sunlight. Chiaroscuro. A picture that shows his history. Again, I was trying to come up with a convincing reason, and again, my reasoning machine malfunctioned. Oh, well. Fine. I adjusted the ambient strobe's power to eighth from sixteenth. This would brighten the overall image, but not bright enough to flatten the contrast; the shadows I wanted would still be there.

CLICK!

I showed it to Jaber.

Please be okay with it… please be okay with it…

"I'm not a hundred percent convinced, Xavi. It's still too dark for me."

Dammit, Mia! "Is it okay if it looked a little traditional portrait-ish?" I asked.

"No. I like where you're heading, it's just too dark. That's all."

I reviewed my setup once more. Two strobes and a flash. I didn't know what to do anymore.

"You can edit the brightness, can't you?" Saeed said to my rescue.

"Yes. I can do that in post."

"Alright. If you think so," Jaber said, looking at his watch. "Let's just get on with it, I have a meeting to attend to."

I took a few more shots of Jaber, then a few close-ups.

Now it was the board's turn inside the conference room.

"Isn't it too dark?" one of the board members commented.

Not again!

"This is how we did the CEO's portrait," I said nonchalantly.

An approving nod cascaded from left to right, identical to a Mexican wave on a football stadium. Then I was back to doing my thing.

Overall, despite the complaints of darkness, I was pleased with how the picture came out. If I had a tail, it would be wagging vehemently right now.

*\*\*\**

I took the metro's red line home more elated than usual. Three hours after the photo-shoot, my tail was still wagging. Not only that, but my ears were also wiggling. Driven by my acute satisfaction, I watched—nope—I studied the people around me. I studied the lighting falling around them. If I was going to do more portraits, I need to refresh my portrait lighting skills.

As my attention hopped from one person to the next, I noticed everyone was glued on their phones. Not one soul was not looking at their phone, except me, of course.

If I had a smartphone, I would probably be one of the "normal" people who are glued on their devices. I'd perhaps be browsing social media or something. I do have social media, though, just not a smartphone.

The phone I use is still the same Nokia 7650 I bought during my first year of college. It was officially the world's first camera phone, but technically, it wasn't. The Samsung SCH-V200 predated it by two years. They just didn't have the same hold in the market back then as Nokia did. I've always wanted to change phones, but I couldn't seem to fathom letting go of my trusty 7650.

Fifteen minutes later, the train stopped at the Grand Central Station. When the doors slid open, people flooded in, forgetting or probably ignoring the rule to let people out first before stepping in.

I observed some of the incoming passengers. Some of them were already familiar to me after two weeks of riding. One of them, a guy with a ponytail, stood by the bellows between two train cars. Another one, a woman who three out of five days wore a pink hijab, took a seat in the corner designated for ladies. Then there was this—

Serendipity stepped in and sat down. It was the lady with the wavy crimson hair. That same woman who helped me when I got stuck at the turnstile, and who I inadvertently followed into the library. She planted herself about a good ten to twelve meters away from me, and unlike everyone else, she kept her phone inside her pocket.

I watched her intently as she rocked back and forth innocently with the train's motion. I observed how the overhead LED lights fell on the right side of her chiseled face and softly wrapped around her tall nose and towards her left cheek. To dawdle with the time, she puckered and bit her pale red lips. Staring out the window, her serene hazel eyes glimmered from the whooshing tunnel lights. A pale blue scarf was wrapped around her neck, trapping the bottom of her red hair. A thick jacket covered her short torso, and skinny jeans hugged her hourglass-shaped legs. She was different, a breath of fresh air. In a country where makeup is the measurement of beauty, there she sat without any makeup on, yet she still had the power to hold my attention.

But you know what, I don't think it was her physicality that called my attention. There was something else underneath her, a creature of the deep, slithering beneath her skin.

"Al Mamriya Station," the public address system announced.

That's my stop. Already? Where did the last three stops go?

Passengers got onto their feet, readying to step out. She did too and stood by the next door. When the train doors opened, we both exited at almost the same time. Fearing the same reaction she had back at the library, I stopped for a minute to let other people swarm the space between us. Thankfully, as we got out of the station, she turned left to a different street, whereas I turned right and started walking the hundred meters to my apartment.

Then terror struck.

SNORT!

\*\*\*

Under the gloaming, my strides grew wider and wider until I found myself careering towards my apartment. Behind me, an invisible presence pursued, seething to bury its ivory horns into my chest. Its stampeding paws shook the earth. My own hands and feet lost warmth. It snorted, grunted, trumpeting the sound of dread. I was fleeing not someone nor something, but I was escaping my own thoughts and the emotions it was pouring. It was the thought of the lady with wavy red hair.

When I observed her on the train, my brain spilled a cup of dopamine, making me feel alive after more than a decade of sadness. The more she lingered in my thoughts, the more energized I became. That's not good. I knew these were the early signs of attraction, and I suddenly pictured Cola drifting towards the fringes of my memory. It may sound trivial or stupid, nevertheless, it petrified me.

I got into my apartment dripping cold sweat. I changed clothes as fast as I could, washed my face, then slumped down the sofa.

Silence.

For a full minute.

On the screen of the turned-off TV in front of me, a reflection appeared. A familiar one. It looked like me. It sharpened its gaze on me, telling me something. Something… I didn't know what. Then, bearing the hallmarks of an apparition, the reflection smirked. It whispered, "It feels good to be attracted to someone new, no?"

"No!"

I scrambled to search for the TV remote on the couch, on its creases, under it. When I couldn't find it, I launched towards the TV to turn it on from there. While it powered up, I loaded a racing game onto my PlayStation 2.

I bought the PlayStation back in college as a means of relaxation after a hard day's work at school. Relaxation was also how I saw myself using it by the time I got employed. But by some twist of fate, I was now using it to distract me from unrest, and from the mutiny of my memories.

After three laps on the racetrack, or about thirty minutes of game time, I had taken the lead. My body tensed up as I focused my full attention on keeping the pole position. One oversteer, a slip of the tire, or poorly timed braking could mean losing my edge and losing the race. I couldn't let that happen. I have never finished a race in second place, and I took pride in that.

Peekaboo!

"Dammit, Mia!" I yelled as I lost control over my racecar. I was confidently tackling an s-bend when the crimson lady burst into my imagination's front door, smiling at me.

I tried to regain control of the car. The woman's face appeared again. The racecar spun uncontrollably.

"Dammit!"

Scared to lose the memory of Cola's face, I dropped the gamepad, dashed to my closet, and rummaged through my shoebox of hard drives stored within. These drives contained all the photos I took since I started photography.

I took out a hard drive labeled "Memory Bank 001." It had all the digitized photos from 2000 when I started studying photography, till 2009, when Cola and I became employed.

I plugged it into my laptop and opened a folder named *September 2003*. I opened a subfolder named *Rendezvous with Nicola, Joie, and Mia*. The first photo was the three girls playing billiards.

I pressed the right arrow on my keyboard. The next picture appeared: A close-up of the same scene but with Cola laughing.

Next: It's the shot of the parking lot in front of Rendezvous. I can still hear the whooshing cars in the distance and feel the warm breeze.

Next: A blurry picture of two feet with socks underneath a starry sky. I shrunk back onto my chair, pulse racing, as I recalled that moment of bliss.

I randomly opened a folder named *November 2003*. Folder, *Halloween*. I clicked on one photo. It's Cola humorously grinning at the camera, dressed as a zombie. It was the night when she pulled my arms around her shoulder to keep her warm while we waited for our parents to pick us up. Though she was covered with dense makeup to simulate blood and decomposition, Cola still appeared heavenly. Not the best costume at that party, but she was the most painterly.

*December 2003*. Folder, *Random Photos*. The first photo was Mia about to put a spoonful of rice in her mouth. Hah! Damn you, Mia! I got you!

Next: Children playing in the yard.

Next: Cola sitting on the bleacher tucking her hair behind her ears. A sour taste filled my mouth as I remember that day.

*September 2004*. Folder, *Cola and me*. The first photo: Cola sitting on their porch in Las Piñas with the wind blowing her hair.

Next: Cola looking at some clothes inside a department store.

Next: Cola watching the sunset serenely.

## PORTRAITS OF THE WIND

Next: Cola looking back at me as she pulled my hand along a yellow-lit street.

My insides went tumbling now, rubbing against each other, consistent with clothes in a dryer. These photos remained so vivid in my memory; I can still feel and hear each moment.

I hovered the cursor to the *2009* folder. Undecided to open it, my finger stayed twitching over the left mouse button.

"Click me! Open me! See the pictures!" said the folder.

I moved the cursor to the eject drive icon and then unplugged the hard drive. "Enough," I said to myself, "Before you tear yourself apart."

\*\*\*

The following morning, I came to the office with a heavy feeling of malaise. My head hung low, limbs drooped, feet shuffling, everything sagging. I can't tell if it was despair or loneliness. All I knew was I was still hungover over Cola's photos. Negative and positive emotions had mixed inside of me and consumed my entirety. But for the love and hate of it, I neither wanted nor objected to more of that sweet melancholy and that warm nostalgia.

I collapsed onto my chair and loaded the memory card from the CEO photoshoot.

*Copying, 16 minutes left,* the computer dialogue read.

Watching the progress bar move forward, the profound feeling of longing crept back and wrapped its sinewy fingers around me. "More of Cola," it whispered. Its breath was reminiscent of lilacs and lavenders, evoking that syrupy lake of Cola's essence.

I jumped out of my seat and started rambling around my cubicle. "Don't do it, Xavi... Don't do it. Xavi, don't! Aargh!" I flung myself back onto my chair.

I am weak. Anything Cola can topple the concrete walls I had built around my heart. In defeat, I opened Facebook. Surprisingly, Mr. Saeed didn't block any social media websites. He only capped our internet speed. I guess he used it too sometimes.

I placed the cursor on the search bar and typed: *Nicola Cueto*. I hit enter. No results. We weren't friends, and she wasn't on any social media either. Despite knowing that for a long time already, I still hoped that I would see her account one day and add her as a friend.

I searched for Mia's name instead. Immediately, she appeared in my friends list. I clicked her profile and browsed through the hundreds of photo albums. One album stood out: *High School Pics*. I clicked on it. The first photo was Sherry and Gio sitting beside each other. Sherry was covering her face while Gio was exultant like a victor.

Next picture: Joie playing basketball. God, she loved basketball.

Next: Nard.

Next: Mia and Joie taking a bathroom selfie with a digicam.

Next: close-up of Cola, in her graduation toga, holding her diploma, looking at the camera, laughing.

I clicked the like button. On second thought, it probably wasn't the best idea. I didn't want to look like a stalker, especially on Mia's albums. I pressed the like button again to undo it.

Nothing happened.

Oh, no! I hit the refresh button. A blank page appeared. Nothing. Did the internet stop working? I slapped the monitor.

"Is anyone downloading anything?" I asked aloud as I rose from my seat. No one answered. The workday was only about to begin, and people were still coming in. Dammit! Why does it feel like closing time already?

The router probably restarted, or Saeed's firewalls cycled on and off. Is that the term? I don't know. Either way, the internet was exceedingly terrible. I hit refresh again. It reloaded with the page appearing slowly in parts. First, the header, then some icons, then the picture, then the thumbs-up icon—meaning the like I gave hadn't been removed yet. Mia, dammit! The loading stopped. I reloaded again. This time it refreshed faster. When the page was complete, a chatbox appeared. It's Mia!

*Mia: Xavi!!!! Xavi!!!! Xavi!!!!*

Uh-oh.

*Mia: How are you?*

I didn't want to answer it, but I noticed my cursor was already in the reply box. That meant Mia would already get the prompt that I had seen the message. Dammit, Mia!

I started typing. Then a pause. I deleted the line. I typed again. Pause. I removed the words. Finally, I sent my reply.

*Xavi: I'm good. And you?*

*Mia: I'm okay. I'm between work at the moment. Thinking of coming back to Qatar...*

*Xavi: What kind of work?*

*Mia: Nursing.*

*Xavi: Have you tried*

I was still typing when she sent another message.

*Mia: Are you still thinking about her?*

The cursor blinked for a few times.

*Xavi: Of course. Always.*

I typed that with guilt-ridden fingers, knowing that a crimson-head recently tried to invade my memory. It's not cheating when you're not in a relationship, is it? Although, it felt like cheating on her memory.

*Mia: After ten years, you still think of her?*

*Xavi: It's not easy to forget, you know.*

*Mia: Haven't you found anyone else?*
*Xavi: There's no one else!*
The keyboard's clackity-clack rang around the office.
*Mia: Okay, okay. If you say so.*
I stared at the blinking cursor for a good minute until she sent a message.
*Mia: Alright. Anyway, nice talking to you. It's been a long time!*
I closed the chatbox without sending a reply. In a breath, the chatbox popped up again.

Great.

*Mia: How long has it been since we last saw each other?*
*Xavi: Graduation? I think…*
*Mia: Really? That's 15 years! Wow! You should come to our next reunion!*

I groaned.

*Xavi: When?*
*Mia: Dunno. We'll plan it. But you should come, alright? You should see us! We've all been wondering what you've been up to lately.*

I reclined exasperatedly.

*Xavi: I'll think about it.*
*Mia: Xavi! You should! If you want, we can pay you to be our official photographer!*
*Xavi: I'll see.*
*Mia: We can do it in Doha if you like! In our old campus!*
*Xavi: You can't. It's demolished. It's now an apartment.*
*Mia: Then we'll do it at the new campus!*
*Xavi: It's all new people. Nobody knows us there anymore.*
*Mia: Whatever! You always have something to say to avoid people! You should just come and see us! Alright! Honestly, we do think about you.*

DING! The computer beeped. The photos finished copying. Thank goodness.

*Xavi: Alright. I have to work now.*

*Mia: Xavi! Wait!*

I stared at the ellipsis animation in the chatbox, that ubiquitous animated GIF to let you know the other person is typing a reply. The animation stopped. Two seconds later, it started again. Again, it stopped, then restarted. After thirty seconds, her message appeared.

*Mia: I know you've been told this a hundred times, maybe a thousand. And I know you might be irritated by it already, or just plain pissed. But I just wanna tell you again. For old time's sake. It's time for you to move on. I know it's hard, but you have to. You can't wallow forever in the past. She wants you to move on, you know.*

I felt a phantom pinch on my side. "*Dammit, Mia!*" I typed. I wanted to send it, but instead, I closed the whole browser without sending a reply.

Wait, did I remove the like from the picture? Or should I?

# Chapter 9:
# A Moment from the Movies

After subjecting myself to the deafening impact of the jackhammers, and after hurdling obstacles made of pipes and scaffoldings, I have now completed the hundred-meter walk from the metro station. There I stood in front of my apartment compound, contemplating its uninspiring architecture.

In front of me stood four 5-story boxy structures that are separated by a one-way street. I mean boxy in an almost literal sense; if not for the poured concrete, it would not have been different from a lot of homeless men's cardboard box shelters stacked on top of another. Despite its homeless appeal, I still lodged in it. Not for the price, it is actually more expensive than it should be. The view? Nope. Look out the window and you'd see ugly rooftops. The location? Yup, exactly. Not because of the metro. It was merely a stroke of luck that they built the metro a few blocks away. It was, in fact, the location where the four buildings stood that willed me to choose it.

Twenty years ago, hundreds of school children scampered here and there in this now apartment compound. Shouldering their backpacks, they would cross the street to get into the cars of their parents and guardians.

Getting the picture already?

I started moseying through the parking lot underneath the buildings and walked past the first one, Building 1, which stood over at what used to be Court A. Yeah, I'm living in a place where The Philippine School once stood.

When I first learned the news of the demolition of the old campus and the completion of the apartment compound five years ago, I knew I had to be here. It would be my Mecca, the center of my pilgrimage. If it meant leaving the bigger accommodation that my company was paying for, I didn't care. If I had to shell out my money for this overpriced hole, so what? I had to come back. I had to. Peace and healing would be found here.

Continuing past Buildings 2 and 3 that stood side by side, I was now loitering in memory through classrooms and hallways that were once aromatic of sun-drenched grade-schoolers. I threaded through memories of sawing plywood at the carpentry lab, baking cakes during home economics, and being amazed by litmus paper changing color over at the chemistry lab. Despite reeking of gasoline and tires, the parking lot still fanned the scent of teenage girls brandishing their perfume at boys whose hair was so oily with gel America could invade it at any time. I carried on gallivanting in the past until I reached Building 4, my apartment.

I chose Building 4 over the other three for one main reason: it stands where Court B used to be. And Court B was where a million smiles were born.

***

Before the open-air Court B was built, graduations were held at hotel ballrooms. We were lucky enough to be the first class, the class of 2004, to graduate in it, under the stars, caressed by a wintry breeze. Being outdoor, the noise of the neighborhood outside (vrooms, horns, children heckling) threatened to disrupt the ceremony, but our zealous cheers and applause overpowered everything on the outside.

"Cueto, Nicola," the master of ceremonies announced.

From the right side of the stage, donned in a blue graduation gown, glowing like the stars, Cola took her first steps to ascend to the platform. I clapped with furtive enthusiasm as she took to the center, illuminated by a striking spotlight.

This is it. This is the last day I will see you, I thought, while the hand of separation tried to squeeze my tear ducts.

Cola held up her diploma and posed for the camera. Going down, she waved enthusiastically to her parents. I had hoped that she would glance at me, but alas, she didn't. She looked at Nard, though. Stupid Nard.

Having a surname that starts with $P$ puts me among the last students to be called. When my turn came, the enthusiastic applause from everyone had already waned. Only my parents remained zealous. I glanced at Cola to check if she was clapping too. She was. Clap, clap, clap. Done. Joyless. Sigh. I took to the stage, grabbed my diploma, posed for the picture, waved at my parents, and for the sake of it, glanced again at Cola.

Oh. My. God.

Cola gave me her heavenly smile. And she was the only one looking at me. The wave of faces surrounding her was either talking with their seatmates or had fallen asleep. The longer I beheld her smile, the brighter she shone, making every light in Court B dim in comparison with the ethereal brilliance of her glow. What is happening? I checked left and right, looking if there was anyone else she might be smiling at. No one. It's just me.

The whole time I marched to my seat, I kept glancing at her. Just a subtle glance. A jerk of the head. Every meter. She did it too, I think. I took my seat which was two rows behind, keeping my focus on her. I imagined that this would be like a scene from the movies: the girl looking back surreptitiously and would be bound into a romantic gaze with the boy. Staying true to the script, I aimed my scope to the back of Cola's head. Doing so, the noise of Court B dampened to a low rumble.

Look. At. Me. Look. At. Me.

And you know what? She did look! At Nard. Stupid Nard.

***

We all stayed at Court B to bid our farewells after the emcee had closed the ceremony. On one end of the court, I saw Joie and Mia bawling and hugging each other firmly. On the other end, I saw Gio and Sherry holding hands as they inhaled each other's exhales. I saw Nard. For most of us, that day was the last time we would see one another. Some would already be flying back to the Philippines for college the very next day. I, on the other hand, would be flying the following—

"Can we talk?" a soft and tender voice said.

Adrenaline filled my veins. Warmth rose to the roots of my hair. My heart and my brain asked each other, "Could it be?" I spun around...

No one was there.

"Over here, dumbo!"

I spun around again and... yes! Yes! It was Cola!

My mouth opened, ready to talk, but my tongue got twisted in shock. Without saying anything else, she grabbed my hand and pulled me, and I, like a suitcase being hauled into the airport, allowed myself to be dragged freely. Weeee!

She pulled me into the backstage. It was dark. The stage lights had been switched off. Only the perimeter lights of the campus illuminated our faces. Cola stood before me wearing the trappings of desire. She swayed on her feet, pursing and biting her lower lip until it was glossy as a silver sphere.

"What is it?" I asked softly, wistfully out of breath.

She did not answer. She only looked at me with those liquid eyes that flitted left and right between my own. Our breathing synced into shallow and rapid huffs. I was uncertain of what was happening, yet I took pleasure from her hand that landed on my waist.

No words were said. There was only the sound of our singing hearts that pulsated with the stars.

Within a breath, an intimate breath, her cold quavering hands slid tenderly from my waist to the back of my neck. She gripped it firmly, slowly leaned in, trembling gracefully, and pressed her lips against mine.

I placed my left hand at the small of Cola's back, and my right behind her neck. I kissed back. It was my first time, so I didn't know if what I was doing was right. But it did not matter. For a moment, our world blended into a whirlpool of pleasure and delight. All my senses were heightened; I became aware of everything, on par with a lion hunting in the dark. I can hear the laughter, the farewells, the birds rustling their feathers above. I can smell her makeup, her sweat, her face. And I can taste her lipstick, including the lips that it coated.

This time, the seconds stretched to forever, towards a moment outside of time. It was the moment to be alive. And I was alive, swimming in the syrupy lake of Cola's soul.

She gently pulled back, delicately pulling my lips with hers. When I opened my eyes, there stood a person sculpted from dreams. Our breaths became laborious and deep, echoing those who had run a thousand miles, reducing our voices to a loud whisper.

"What?" That was all I could say at that moment.

"I missed you," she whispered, seizing my hand.

"But you and Nard?"

"Nard is no one. We were never together. He tried his best, but," her tone changed to an effervescent manner of speaking, almost whispery and coy, "but he's not you. And when you took my portrait, I… I just missed you. I missed you so badly, I couldn't even look at you. I was scared your smile would make me cry."

"That's stupid," I said.

She giggled, rubbing her thumb on my knuckles.

Empowered by the taste of her lips, I said, "I didn't dare to tell you before, but I…" Oh, how I wish I could have continued. Courage abandoned me again. So, I pulled my hand away and chewed on my thumb's fingernail while praying inwardly for indestructible nerves.

She peered at me questioningly. In a few heart-stopping seconds, she gave me another peck on the lips. "Don't worry, I know. Your eyes says it all. I can see your beating heart through it."

"Are your eyes saying the same? I can't tell. It's too dark," I said.

"Yes! You dumbass!" she said, tittering.

We cozied onto the backstage stairs. I wrapped my arm around Cola's shoulder, and she rested her head on mine. "What now?" I asked. This time our voice had settled back to normal. "What's next?"

"I'm not sure. I'm flying tonight," she said.

I jerked back. "What?" I shook my head repeatedly and asked again. "What? What time? When?"

"Technically, it's tomorrow, but we leave home tonight at 11:30; our flight is 3:45 a.m. I'm sorry, Xavi. I should have told you sooner how I felt," she said.

My voice cracked with emotion. "Why? I mean, why? Why? Why tell me all these now? Why kiss me now when you're leaving? That's so unfair!"

"I didn't want to leave without telling you the truth. I waited for you for three months to speak to me, but you just kept staring at me, like, well, like a perv!"

"Dammit, Mia!" I said.

"What?"

"Sorry. That's an expression I use when things don't seem to work out right."

"Why Mia?"

"Because she always pinches— never mind. I have my reasons, and it just feels good to say it."

"Well, dammit, Mia!" she said, arching her lips.

"Do you want to, whatever this is, to continue?" I asked.

"Of course I do, dumbass! Of course!"

"So, how do we keep in touch?"

"Serendipity." She paused sheepishly for a moment to let the word sink in. "We do it the romantic way. Just like in the movies. If we're meant to be, the universe will find a way to cross our paths again."

Corny. But I indulged her anyway; it was Cola.

"Nicola! Let's go!" Rodrigo's voice echoed from the court.

That was when we both realized that the chatter in the court had died down, allowing us to hear planes from a thousand miles above. Cola and I read each other's faces; we were both aware of our fleeting time together.

I held her hand. "I'll see you at the airport tonight," I said.

"Don't be stupid. That's past midnight." She giggled.

"Don't worry, I will. I will see you one last time again today."

"It's okay, you don't have to. I completely understand if you can't."

Rodrigo's voice boomed again, "Nicola! We still have to finish packing your luggage!"

Cola shot towards me and fervently kissed me once more, perhaps for the last time if I don't see her again. "Never let me go," she whispered, wrapping her arms around me.

I pressed my face onto her shoulder and mumbled, "There will never be a moment I'm not with you. I promise."

We came out of the backstage together, keeping our faces deadpan and maintaining a space between us. But no matter how hard I tried, my lips kept forcing a thin curve of a smile. When we reached our parents, who were waiting next to each other, Rodrigo, Evelyn, and my dad exhibited discerning looks, while my mom shot me a dirty one.

"Bye po," I said to Cola's parents.

Rodrigo extended his hand, and I shook it. "Well, I'm sure we'll see each other again," he said with that perceptive smug.

Evelyn gave me a hug. Cola shook the hands of my parents, and her parents bid us goodbye. It was kind of dreamy seeing my parents talk with the Cuetos.

As the Cueto family walked towards the exit, Cola twisted on her heels, gave me a smile, and twisted back.

Ah, the movie moment!

Someone knocked on my head. I jolted and saw Mom with a feigned look of disapproval, then in a beat, it descended to teasing.

P.S. If you're assuming that I snuck out in the middle of the night to see Cola to the airport, I didn't. I fell asleep from exhaustion, and I was beating myself over it the following morning.

# Chapter 10:
# LDR

Serendipity my ass. That is the tool of lazy screenwriters. I learned that from film class. But no, I did not major in film. It was a part of the curriculum for a Mass Communications degree. Given that Mass Communications was the closest to my dream of being a photojournalist, I took that course.

The college I went to, atop the mountains of Baguio City, doesn't have one major. When you graduate with a bachelor's degree in communication, it meant you majored in journalism, advertising, film, TV, and radio broadcasting. That way, they reasoned out, we would have a wide gamut of opportunities.

So yeah, serendipity my ass. The character should not wait on chance to happen; he must work towards his goal. That's Screenplay 101.

Cola and I kept in touch via Friendster, back in the good old days of testimonials. We also used instant messaging services such as Yahoo Messenger to call or chat. But no matter how connected we were, a gaping distance still disconnected us. We were separated by roughly 250 kilometers. Driving that would take approximately eight hours through the congested and underdeveloped highway system of the Philippines.

Three months into college, I couldn't hold it any longer. I secretly acquired Cola's address in Las Piñas by placing an overseas call to Rodrigo. He gave me step-by-step instructions on how to get there, from Baguio to Las Piñas. The following weekend, I boarded a bus and traveled south.

***

## PORTRAITS OF THE WIND

Roosters still crowed and taho vendors still peddled the streets when I arrived at Cola's house on the morning of September 2004. Standing in front of her door, I could already smell her fragrance of lilacs and lavenders, overpowering the gasoline stink of two-stroke motorcycle engines vrooming in the streets. With the growing anticipation, my throat dried up, and no amount of swallowing could lubricate it. I glanced at my watch. Instead of the time, the date screamed to me, "One year."

I was standing on her doorstep, holding a bouquet of tulips, precisely one year after our moment at Rendezvous. I did not plan the date of my arrival. That was truly a coincidence. You could say the hands of serendipity had something to do with it (dammit!).

I took out my brand new 7650 and texted her what had now become a tradition: *"Good morning! Have a beautiful day! :)"* She replied with a simple smiley, just like the way she did back in our classroom in Doha (with a simple smile). Right after I had received her reply, I rang the doorbell and held up the bouquet of her favorite flower. Within a minute, the door swung open. Cola stood there emotionless, stolid, and upon recognizing me, colors of emotions exploded from her face.

"Xavi!!!" Her scream reached the heavens. She slammed her body onto me and held me tight. "What are you doing here?"

I gave her the bouquet. "I missed you," I said.

"Did I ever told you where I lived?"

"Nope. But your dad did."

She hugged me again, gracing me with a whiff of her honest fragrance. It wasn't lilacs and lavenders; it was jars of honey on a summer day. I quivered in delight. She was gorgeous. Simply gorgeous. She just woke up, still groggy, hair untidy, pajamas and all, but she was gorgeous. Gorgeous. Need I say it again? Gorgeous.

With only a day to lose, we spent every passing minute of the day together (except for toilet breaks). We went strolling around the eighth largest mall in the world in North EDSA, watched a horror movie in the cinema during midday, walked some more, had lunch, watched the sunset from the mall's balcony, then walked some more, and finally, we watched a comedy.

Yeah, we stayed at the mall. We figured if we roamed across town; we would spend the day trapped in traffic. We wouldn't be able to create a lot of memories stuck inside a vehicle, would we?

\*\*\*

But all days, good or bad, always have to come to an end.

It was close to midnight when the taxi took a right turn to the street towards their house. I patted the driver's shoulder. "Please stop there," I said. The driver pulled over in front of a 24-hour corner restaurant. One last stop before the day ends.

"How long is the travel to Baguio?" Cola asked as we entered the restaurant.

"About seven to eight hours, depending on traffic," I answered.

She checked the clock on her phone. "It's almost midnight. What time is your first class?"

"Eight-thirty."

Her shoulders dropped. "You have to go," she said, devoid of the vigor we had that morning.

Until now, I couldn't understand the mechanics of time. When you want it to slow down, it will speed up; when you want it to speed up, it slows down. Time itself is an oxymoron. No matter how many hours it was, time still swept away all the minutes I spent with Cola that day.

"I'll be late anyways. Besides, I'm hungry. Aren't you?" I said, ignoring Cola's statement.

"Hey, I don't want to be a bad influence on you! Your mom would kill me if she knew you're skipping class because of me!"

"She won't know. And I'm not skipping class; I'm missing it," I said, widening my eyes with a toothy grin before turning my back and marching towards the order counter.

"Xavi," she called with a flat voice, "let's go!"

"Just a quick bite! I'm starving. Please?" I begged and gave her a guilty dog look. It worked.

"Dammit, Mia! Fine!" she exclaimed.

I giggled. Cola was now using my expression too.

While we ate, I related to Cola why I purchased my new phone. I told her that I would be able to take pictures anytime without toting a bulky camera. I frequently took a bite of my burger and kept the food at the side of my mouth whilst speaking. Noticing that Cola was watching me with a gentle curve on her lips, I stopped.

"What?" I asked, wiping the burger juices from my mouth.

"Nothing." She looked away and bit a stick of french fries.

"What?" I asked again.

She gave me an astute side glance.

"What is it??"

"Nothing! You're just talking too much." She giggled. "You used to say eating is for eating and—"

"You want me to stop talking?"

"No. I'm just saying—"

I silently took another bite and mockingly pivoted toward the window while I chewed, giving her an occasional glance.

"Oh my god!" she screamed in horror.

I was still looking out the window when she had lurched forward to try and pinch me. In her random act, she toppled her drink, spilling it all over the table and her pants.

"What have you done?!" she continued.

"Me? Why me?" Embarrassed, I looked around. The crew was looking at us; we were the only customers at the restaurant, and we were being loud. I dissolved into my seat then.

"I'm soaking! It's so cold!"

"Shh! Keep your voice down!" I said before grabbing a tissue and leaning in to help her wipe.

She slapped my hand. "That's my boobs!"

I froze midway, absent-minded.

"They're not wet! You perv!" she yelled.

"Oh my god, I'm sorry!" I cried, jerking backward. "I'm so sorry!"

Cola creased up in rowdy laughter. She almost spilled her drink again. "Oh shucks! Mwahaha!"

I discreetly peeked at the crew behind the counter; they were shaking their heads. "I think we look like a bunch of *pokpoks*," I whispered.

"Yeah, well, we're a couple who's acting loudly at midnight. And you're touching my boobs. Yeah, we probably look like hookers or whatever," she said.

I stared at her, evaluating her, my mouth agape from the incredulous emotion I felt.

"It's a joke! I'm not mad, okay?" she said, "I know you didn't mean to touch my boobs."

I shook my head repeatedly, still trying to wrap it around that one word she said.

"We're a couple?" I asked, swallowing my saliva.

We both paused.

"Aren't we?" she asked.

"I'm not sure. Are we?"

"Well..." She started counting with her fingers. "We kissed; we chat every day; we call if the chat wasn't enough; you came here and surprised me; you touched my boob and I'm not mad." She leaned in to whisper loudly, "And it somehow felt good. Hahaha!" She now held up five fingers. "So, I guess we're just best friends?"

"I'm serious, Cola. I'm not good at this."

She held up a sixth finger. "And you're the only one I allow to call me Cola. Not even my parents call me by that name." She lingered and studied me. Then her shoulders dropped before asking, "Do you want us to be a couple?"

The restaurant fell silent then. Machines stopped whirring. The stereo playing '90s music also went mute. I had a feeling even the crew was leaning in to eavesdrop on us.

"You'll be my first girlfriend," I said.

"And you'll be my last," she said.

"Wait, how many did you have?"

"I never told you?"

I shook my head.

"Just one," she said through her grinning teeth.

"What? When?" My voice rose involuntarily.

"He's this quiet guy I met about a year ago. He's reticent, but he's deep like an ocean, full of surprises. He's also adorable. Every day he gives me letters. They're nothing but simple good mornings. Never missed a day. Even the days that we're not talking with each other. He also makes sure I never go hungry. He used to bring me all these sandwiches. My parents actually like him, but I like him more. Although, for some reason, I think he likes nuggets more."

My mouth hung open. "So, are we... a couple?"

"Dammit, Mia! How dense can you be?" She took two pieces of fries and squished them together as she spoke. "Yes, if you want to put a label on it, we're a couple. You're my boyfriend, and I'm your girlfriend! I'm yours, and you're mine!"

My appetite had gone then. I couldn't swallow even my own saliva. Electric energy had consumed my body from the inside out that I involuntarily stood up with my arms raised like a victor. I started pacing around the restaurant. The crew wasn't impressed. They probably had seen a lot of this already. But I didn't care. It was our moment. I was high.

"Sit down! You're embarrassing!" Cola said, her face taking the color of a ripe tomato. When I didn't sit down, she hurriedly took our things, grabbed my arm, and pulled me out of the restaurant.

She kept on pulling until we were both running towards their house. Our galloping footsteps and our prancing glee caused sleeping dogs to bark and howl for miles.

"Hold on! Hold on!" I shouted.

I wanted to take a picture with my 7650, but she kept on running and pulling. So, with my free hand, I pulled out the phone and clumsily adjusted the settings.

"Cola!" I called her name, rich and deep, sonorous, and aloud.

She whirled with the perfect blend of beauty.

CLICK!

We reached their gate. She banged it open like a drunk person would (I guess we're both drunk with happiness). I pulled her close to me, saw the moon glistening in her almond eyes, and this time I was the one who gave her a wistful kiss worth six months.

Again, our voices were reduced to whispers. "I... I... I..." I said.

She waited patiently.

My voice started trailing off. "I've been feeling this way since the bleachers, you know. So, I'm not sure. But I'm pretty sure I am," I said.

"Sure of what?"

"I'm in love. I love you." I held the gate for support, to keep me from fainting.

She tilted her head sideways. "Haven't we been in-love since the first time we met? And wasn't that what you wanted to tell me at the backstage after graduation?"

I pressed my hands on my twisting stomach. "Yeah. But this time, I'm very pretty sure, unquestionably sure, I am."

She leaned in and whispered tenderly in my ears, "I love you too."

As soon as I heard those words, I got dizzy and I almost blacked out. I wanted to cry. I wanted to smile. I wanted to laugh. I lost balance, yet I wanted to leap into the stars. My heart and my brain were finally in sync with their thoughts and emotions. I was terrified and high. Love is indeed the most potent drug.

"Are you okay?" Cola held my shoulders, snickering at me.

"I don't want to go. Can I stay? I can, can't I? It's okay. Right? Let me stay? Please? I want to stay," I babbled on and on.

Cola hugged me to sedate my racing emotions. "I want you to stay as well."

My face lit up.

"But," she said, "you have classes tomorrow. You must go, alright? We'll talk over the phone if you can't sleep on the bus. We'll chat every day like we always do, even more. You just have to go now. You can't miss class, alright?"

I started shouting to the heavens. "Damn you, Mia! Damn you!" I screamed, cursed Mia, just because. My god, emotions were soaring that night.

Cola joined. "You suck, Mia!"

"Damn yoouuuu!"

Dogs once more barked from the recesses of the night, and our exultant howls led their choir.

"Alright, alright! You must go! Seriously!" Cola said as she shoved me out the gate.

I kissed her goodbye and started walking—correction—started sailing in a river of dreams, shimmering under the amber wash of streetlamps, towards the main road.

"Hey, stranger!" she called aloud.

Even when I was already well over two hundred meters away, even with the rage of the howling dogs in between, I still heard her whisper: "Never let me go…"

\*\*\*

I have heard of many stories of jealousies and third-parties severing long-distance relationships. Sometimes, it's as straightforward as falling out of love. Long-distance is only for the brave. I guess we can be counted as one since ours worked when everyone else's failed. Gio and Sherry? Only two hours separated them, yet their love crumbled after two months of separation. Long-distance is a team effort to keep the boat afloat.

I started doing freelance photography so I had extra money for the weekly bus fare to Las Piñas. I took all sorts of photography jobs: birthdays, modeling, prenups, anything. I earned enough money to never miss a weekend with Cola for four years, except when I deliberately must, such as during school projects or work. Sometimes, to avoid monotony, she'd be the one visiting me to the city above the clouds, and I'd pay for her trip.

Cola did her fair share of effort too. Sometimes she would place an order to deliver food to me whenever she knows I'm studying or working late. I had to pay for it, of course; online payments weren't a thing yet in the country back in the day. And when we met over the weekend, she'd pay me back.

At other times, I would be receiving unexpected snail mails or random greeting cards that she simply thought were cute, and she would lace it with her perfume so I could smell her. I would sometimes return the effort by sending her an airtight container with my flatulence enclosed. She'd then text me with an angry emoticon.

Sure, there were some petty fights about trivial stuff like forgotten birthdays and anniversaries. Occasionally, we'd fight during our weekend visits, like should we go out? Should we stay at home? Should we do this, should we do that?

One of the usual fights was about where or what to eat.

"Anywhere, you decide," she'd say.

"No, you choose. I'm paying," I'd answer.

"I don't know. Anywhere. You choose"

"Jollibee?"

"No. We ate there last time."

"Then where?"

"Wherever you want."

"Do you want a burger?"

"No."

"Pizza?"

"Nope."

"Pasta?"

"Nah."

"Arabic?"

"Ugh."

"Mexican?"

"Anything, Xavi! You decide!"

You experience this too, right?

Our next most common fight was about petty jealousies. That is the bane of long-distance relationships.

"Why do you have to go and have dinner with her?" she shouted over the phone. She called right after I sent her a message that I was having dinner with a female client.

Sometimes, I would be the one jealous. "Who's that guy you're always with in your pictures?" I asked, after browsing her new album in Friendster. Later, I found out his name was Josefine. It used to be Joseph, but he preferred to be called Josefine. So, all's well on that front.

All our fights, whatever they were, never lasted more than a day. If we had a row in the morning, we never retired for the night until it was resolved. No matter who's fault it was, one of us must give way. I believe this was a significant factor as to why our relationship was so strong. We acknowledged that we're not perfect, and we worked hard to make it better for both of us.

Reasonable humility and forgiveness, those are the secrets to our longevity, I think.

# Chapter 11:
# It's a Tightrope

My nostalgia bubble burst again when the new progress photos I was archiving stopped due to the damn slow internet.

While restarting the upload, I noticed Saeed kept glancing at me from the confines of his glass office. He lowered his gaze when our eyes connected. After a beat, he pushed his chair backward, stood up, and marched towards me with the hallmarks of another long conversation coming up.

"Xavi, do you have a minute?" Saeed asked, his face smothered with uncertainty.

"Sure," I said, "What's up?"

Saeed hesitated momentarily, rubbing the back of his neck. "Let's go to my office."

I nodded and followed him. As he carefully perched on the edge of his expensive swivel chair, I asked, "Are you okay?"

"What?" He shot me a confused glance before understanding my question, "Oh, yeah. No, I'm fine. Have a seat." He maintained a cautionary tone while straightening the ghutra over his head. "How are you feeling?"

I cautiously answered, "I'm okay."

"Okay, well, there's no other way to say this, so I'm going to lay it out plainly."

He sounded serious. I crossed my feet to stop my heels from bouncing nervously.

"The CEO wasn't pleased with his portrait. Nor was the board. They rejected it."

My heart plummeted down to my stomach. "Why not?"

"They said it's too, uhm, sad. That's the word they used. Sad."
"Sad?"
"It was too dark."
"It's low-key lighting. It's supposed to be dark."
Saeed pulled out a copy of the photo from an A4 envelope and showed it to me. "See, it doesn't show energy. It's too dark and… sad." He pointed to Jaber's face.

I lit Jaber's face half and half. Half bright, half dark. Side lighting. The contrast was about three and a half stops to one. It's not that dark.

"See, you can clearly see the wrinkles on his face," continued Saeed.

"Yeah, that's the idea!" I said.

Saeed's glance switched to me, "Really?"

I nodded.

Trying to figure out my intention with the lighting, Saeed once more perused the whole photograph with his hand hovering over it. He dropped the photo and twisted both his hands palm side up questioningly and asked, "Why?"

"It's symbolic of the years of hard work to achieve where he is now," I said.

Saeed raised the photo to his face and squinted at it. "I see where you're going. But to them, and to me, it comes off as sad and old. This is a picture of someone about to retire and walk out of his office."

Sure.

Saeed glanced at the photo again. "Look, I admit this is a wonderful photo. You've done a great job with the lighting and everything. But it's not what they're looking for. It doesn't show a CEO who is at the top of his game. They want something bright, cheerful, and energetic. Something showing vigor, not darkness and sorrow."

## PORTRAITS OF THE WIND

I just nodded and took it all in, frailly at that. Creative people mostly don't handle criticism well. Hours were spent, or days, sometimes years, contemplating, crafting, and sweating over their work. Their fingers worked to the bone, and a substantial amount of energy were drained from their souls. And then with one look, people are going to criticize their *obra maestra* with disparaging words. In my case, I spent a week doing research and looking for inspiration, then these eggheads with no knowledge of photography and its symbolism took liberty in belittling my work.

"And the board's, it's the same," Saeed continued, "They are photos of age, not photos of a brighter future. Do you get what I mean? What they wanted to show? Light. Happiness. Life. Bam, bam, bam! Simple and bright. I told you this before."

I shifted on my chair to hide the crackling in my voice. "Let's do a reshoot then."

Saeed slowly slid the photos back into the envelope while he raised his eyebrows slyly. "Well, that's another thing." He closed the envelope and fixed his ghutra. "They assumed you wouldn't be able to pull it off. They wish to hire another photographer."

"..."

My heart hiccupped. What he said was worse than an insult. That's rejection and denunciation altogether. Saeed proceeded with encouragements, uttering words to lighten the moment, but it only invited malevolence, the beast. Somewhere in the office, there was a low growling, a snorting, an invisible presence. I uncrossed my feet to allow my knees to bounce and pump away the terror seeping in my veins.

"Are you okay?" Saeed asked. "Look, don't take this too hard, alright. It's just a comment. I'm sure you got a lot of similar comments when you started off, right? Don't take it personally. Use it to grow your skills. Take it as a challenge to yourself."

I nodded silently while the muscles in my face contorted and contracted as I tried to look unaffected.

"One last thing, can you recommend someone? Another photographer?" he asked.

Yeah. Shoot me in the face, now shoot me in the heart. I'm double-dead. What's worse was, my mood had already been subjected to the firing squad after reminiscing my golden days with Cola. Yeah, you'd think her memories would make me smile. It does, sometimes. It's Russian roulette; sometimes you live, sometimes you die. Now, I was staring down at a loaded barrel. And this simple yet stern rejection was the silver bullet with the eyes of the beast etched on its tip.

*** 

Going home that afternoon was similar to clomping through gravel and mud while dragging a piece of oversized luggage. All happiness and energy drained away from me. It was replaced with anxiety, despair, gloom, and hopelessness all coalesced together into a massive block of lead strapped to my chest—nostalgia on steroids. Malaise. Breathing started to be difficult too; each breath was shallow and deep at the same time. I had no vigor left. It was ebbing away with every drop of sweat.

To the eyes of a normal person, this episode may seem contrived, that I am suddenly feeling this way on account of a simple rejected photo.

It isn't.

It isn't contrived. Only those who have experienced what I have experienced will understand.

## PORTRAITS OF THE WIND

To us nostalgiacs, it's pleasant how seemingly random objects and events can retrieve the memories of yesterdays. Although sometimes, it can leave you brittle, particularly when there is already a dark seed sowed in your life. This is the tightrope that I was talking about. A false move and you're done. And any negativity, however trite it may seem, is a hurricane wind atop the precarious thin string you're walking on. One moment, you're ecstatic; the next, the voracious beast of despair with glowing eyes is visiting you. Snorting. Stomping. Growling. Besides terrorizing you, through its glowing eyes, it evokes memories that you do not wish to remember, namely my mom's voice filled with sorrow.

"No!" I shouted aloud, "Shut up!"

The beast, manifesting the voice of my mom, said, "She's not coming."

I paced around my tiny living room, shaking, palpitating. "No, no, no, no. Please!" I begged myself. I pleaded to the beast living inside of me, "Don't do this!"

The beast gnashed its teeth, bit my heart, and burned it with pain. In another breath, the creature's sharp ivory horn ripped my heart open. To and fro, the beast of despair swung his horn, to and fro, prying a wider gap to fit its enormous body.

I dropped to my knees. The creature started towering over me with its foot stomping on my head. Its horn gored me, flipping me over, wanting to dig a hole in my eyes, despite me playing dead. It did not stop. It will not stop until it had its fill.

"Please... I don't want this again! Not again!"

"I'm really sorry, Xavi."

"No... please... stop..." I whimpered, pressing my hands against my ears, shielding it from my own thoughts.

The beast lowered its snout onto me. From its nostrils came a puff of mist tinged with the stench of winter rain and wet pine trees. Gooey saliva dribbled into my mouth as it whispered, "She's not coming. I'm so sorry."

A scream of agony raged out my mouth, hoping to silence everything. It silenced nothing.

I switched tactics. Over the tears pooling in my eyes, I strained to focus on Cola's face. Flashes of her smile, her laughter, her sweet voice, her tight embrace, and the fiery kiss cropped up in various beads of tears. Then the memories started fading out, sinking into the dark ocean under a moonless night.

"No! No! Cola! Please…"

I groaned as I gathered my strength to lift my body off the ground. With a sudden surge of power, I bolted for my closet and grappled my shoebox of hard drives. In an instant, I found Memory Bank 001, the hard drive with all of Cola's photos from the day we met.

"I'm really sorry, Xavi." This time it was my dad's low, raspy voice. I ignored it.

I dashed for my laptop on the dining table. It took me around ten thousand steps for what was hardly ten meters away. I hastily plugged the USB cable to the lap—

It slipped.

The hard drive slipped from my trembling fingers and plummeted onto the ceramic floor. It bounced three times with loud plastic clunks, breaking the casing into multiple pieces.

My stomach heaved at the sight of the splintering drive.

Articulate swearing accompanied my arms as it reached for the cracked hard drive. Preparing for the worst, I slowly and surely reinserted the USB cable to the laptop. It clicked into place. I fixated on the hard drive's tiny LED light, waiting for it to glow.

Please work. Please work.

Though tiny, the white LED light glowed to penetrate every dark corner of the room. The familiar whirr of moving parts came next, but it had the low rumbling voice of the beast.

"Click-click," the beast said.

Silence.

"Click-click."

Silence.

This was the sound of a dying hard drive.

"Click-whirr-crrkk—"

Infinite silence.

The drive, it's dead. With it, a million smiles drifted into obscurity. I prepared for the worst, but nothing can prepare you over the agony of loss.

I heard Cola through the beast: *"Never let me go…"*

# Chapter 12:
# Five Days of Rain

When dry, hot air from a large landmass rises into the atmosphere, it creates a low-pressure area that pulls in cooler air from the ocean over the land. The coalescence of warm and cold air creates moisture which leads to the formation of clouds. The more water vapor is in the clouds, the heavier it gets, and then condensation will start to occur. Rain. That's what I was staring at outside my window in Baguio City during the monsoon season of July 2009. Good 'ol nostalgic rain, adding more coldness to the freezing mountaintop air.

My relationship with Cola was infallible, and we were pros with the long-distance relationship. Though we wanted to be closer together, we both had unique job opportunities at that time after graduating. So, we decided to give our respective job opportunities a try for one year, even if that meant continuing to stay eight hours apart. By the end of that year, we'd assess who had the most miserable job, then he or she would quit and move closer to the other one. Within six months, she faltered. She said that the distance was not working anymore, and honestly, neither did it for me. So, I decided to end it (the space between).

I reached into my pocket and pulled out a small velvet box. I opened it, and six diamonds around a silver ring glinted with the dim, rainy light of the day. Six — one for each year that Cola and I had known each other.

I asked myself if it was too soon to ask her hand in marriage, but we've known each other already for six years, it should be okay, I thought. Besides, we were both employed now, and we're earning enough. So, when I asked myself, is this the right time? I answered:

the right time doesn't come to those who wait, the right time comes to those who try. The right time is not a day from now, nor is it the day before; the right time is always now. If things did not work out the way you wanted it, then try again until you hit the right time. If you wait, if you linger, that's when regret, remorse, and disappointment begin to nest.

"Are you sure about this?" Rodrigo asked me during our secret meeting at an Arabic restaurant in Las Piñas, a week before the heaven opened to shed its silver tears.

"Yes po. Hundred percent," I replied earnestly.

Rodrigo stared at me for a long time. He must be pondering the thought of giving away his only daughter to this man, whom he knew only as a kid six years ago. Evelyn was more emotional, though. Beads of sorrow and joy freely flooded her eyes when I expressed my intention to marry Cola.

"Thank you," Rodrigo said, now with palpable gentleness strewn within his bull-like voice.

The charred lamb kofta in my mouth turned into a chewy cardboard while I deliberated what Rodrigo meant with those two words. It can only be one of two things: one, "thank you, but no," or two, "thank you, we accept."

Rodrigo remained pensive for a long while, looking out the window of the diner we were in. He watched the swaying trees that danced with the humid wind as if trying to find answers from its rustling leaves. Evelyn gently laid her hand on his shoulder, softly bringing him back to the crux of the moment. He turned to her with a conflicted look, only to be reassured by her comforting glance. Finally, he turned to me with a stoic face.

"I always thought I will have to fight with Nicola over the choice of her boyfriend," he said, "I imagined it will be a thug or a womanizer, or someone I wasn't at ease with. But I never had that with you. You radiated ease and reassurance the moment we met. So, thank you."

The corner of my lips gently rose as I came to understand what he meant with his "thank you."

There was another long pause before Evelyn broke the quiet air. "Rodrigo and I were talking about you a few weeks ago. We knew this day would come, of course, we just didn't know when. But we were prepared, and we were ready. From the time I met you... I don't know how to explain it, but when we got to know you, I had the same feeling I had when I met Rodrigo; I knew he was the one. And now, I knew you are the one for our Nicola," she said, her eyes glinting with subtle tears. She reached out across the table to hold my hand. "Yes, Xavi," she paused to let emotions through her lips. "You have our blessing."

My mom, on the other hand, wasn't enthusiastic, as always. She thought I was too abrupt with my decision. "Give it another year. Give it another two years," she said.

"Mom, I made my decision the moment we shared the same love. I just waited for us to graduate and get a job, then I would propose," I firmly said.

She couldn't say no. How could she? I'm no longer living under her roof. I have graduated, I am employed, and I am independent. It was only her aging eyes that showed she was torn between leaving the past and facing the future of me having my own life.

Dad... Dad was dad. He was reposed, and through his wordlessness, he showed his love and support.

I closed the lid of the ring box and looked back out the window. The ruthless monsoon had been pouring for five days straight, only intermittently pausing with each moaning of the wind. There were no typhoons, only the southwesterly monsoon shedding tears over the changing season.

The plan was to have Cola spend her birthday lunch with both families at our house in Baguio. Then I would take her out for dinner at night. There were no restaurants planned. Instead, I would take her up to the peak of Mount Cabuyao where two large radar dishes stood. We would sit on the roof of my car and have our candlelight dinner there. Once we're full and merry, we'd lie down and stare at the infinite ceiling of stars, the same stars that stared down at us when we climbed up the Rendezvous rooftop. We'd be lying in opposite directions, so our heads will touch. I would not kneel like a moron when the time comes to propose. Instead, still lying down, I would take her hand, lift it above our face, then with the stars reflecting on the ring's lustrous surface, I will slide it on her finger. I have no speech planned; I will let the moment dictate my words.

"Why in Baguio? It's a weekday, I still have a lot of documents to encode. I can't just go. Why don't you come here?" Cola argued over the phone when I told her my plan for a family lunch on her birthday. The rest of the plan was secret, of course.

"I always come there!" I said.

"So? It's my birthday anyway!"

"What about the weekend?" I replied. "That way, you can spend part one of your birthday with your friends and coworkers, then we'll celebrate part two here in Baguio with our families."

The line fell silent for a second, then a sigh. "Fine. You always have the perfect excuse for us to be together."

"You don't like it?"

"I love it."

The rain hammering outside ruined my plan for a starry night. I had no Plan B. I thought I'd just wing it if things go awry.

I love the rain though. I can't fault it if it changed my plans. Rain brings with it a portion of tranquility through its low grey clouds and cold winds. It compels you to just sit down, stare out the window, and admire nature process its emotions.

I thought that maybe Cola and I could just stare at the rain from our porch while I take her portraits with the wind blowing around her. Perhaps, we could channel the children inside us and romp under the icy shower of Baguio City. We've never done that. It could be fun. Then I'll pop the question whenever our hearts are on their fullest.

The monsoon sneezed and blasted a flurry of raindrops onto my window. I glanced at my phone; the clock said 12:24 p.m. There were no updates yet from Cola, and they were almost an hour late. I was jittery with unease then, from worry.

"It must be the rain. You know how traffic slows to a crawl when it's pouring. Especially at the zigzags. And it's the weekend, tourists are flocking; traffic is the worst," my dad said to alleviate my tension.

"The subscriber cannot be reached. Please try again later," was what answered me when I tried calling Cola.

It was unusual for Cola to turn off her phone, especially when traveling. As a matter of fact, this was only the second time I was answered by the recorded message. The first time was when her phone really died on itself. But it could also be the rain messing with cellular signals, as it always does up in the mountains.

I sent her a message at half-past, then another at quarter past, then at 1:00 p.m. No answer. I tried calling her parents—couldn't connect either.

"Don't worry. Better slow and safe than fast and risky," Mom said.

"But the food is getting cold!" I said, attempting to reason with my increasing fretfulness.

## PORTRAITS OF THE WIND

Time wore on painstakingly slow. Every tick of the clock's thin hand was a thunderous roar in the chambers of my mind. From my bedroom window, I counted three thousand droplets dripping from the roof's gutter. I estimated about two hundred and fifty thousand leaves on the tree in front of our house by doing math on its leaves, twigs, and branches. I was also able to change the various settings of my 7650 three times.

"Have you heard anything yet?" my dad asked while he chewed the Italian pesto Mom painstakingly prepared.

I grimly shook my head.

They started eating when I gave them the go signal. I wanted us to eat altogether for lunch, but they were already famished. I, on the other hand, had no appetite for anything, not food, not TV, not even reading. I grafted myself onto a chair in my bedroom to wait.

The massive grey skies turned pitch black as the sun retreated behind the horizon and the earth's own shadow cast on the clouds above. With that, Mom started wrapping the food with cling film and stored it in the fridge. My dad recorked the wine and removed the glasses. The glass dining table, once adorned with orange china, colorful fruit basket, and an Italian pesto, was now slowly emptied. To me, each plate that was removed was replaced with mounting concern and distress.

"Don't remove all. Leave something for when they arrive," I said.

Mom left the calamari and covered it with a bowl. "Did you try calling again?" she asked.

"A hundred times."

The clock struck six. For four hours, I kept scanning old negatives with my prosumer film scanner. This killed, or at least sedated, the mounting anxiety that hammered wooden pegs onto my chest. Five hundred strips of color negatives from 2000 till 2006 passed through the scanner's light, digitizing each frame, giving immortality to its color and resolution. I've meant to do it since I bought the scanner five months ago, but I always didn't find the time. Now, fortunately, or unfortunately, time was available. I stored the digitized photos onto a hard drive I named "Memory Bank 001."

Again, I found myself waiting, and with it came a pang of hunger. I shuffled out of my room towards the glass dining table in the living room where the calamari patiently waited to be eaten.

"What??" a voice said. It came from the front porch.

I rushed towards the front door and swung it open. There, two figures stood by the porch, silhouetted by the loud rain. Dad's dripping raincoat flapped wildly as he held an umbrella over mom.

"What's going on?" I asked mildly as I bore through the merciless wind.

They glanced at each other restlessly, talking with their eyes, silently shouting their foreboding thoughts.

"Xavi, I'm sorry, but she's not coming," my dad said slowly with a cracked voice.

"What do you mean?" I prepared for the worst.

"She's not coming…" Mom said, her voice trembling.

"Why?" was my abrupt reply. It was a question with one word profoundly filled with numerous speculations.

"She… she's not…" Mom began fidgeting. A drop of tear glinted in the corner of her eye.

"There's been an incident, Xavi," Dad said feebly.

During the time I was digitizing the photos, Mom and Dad saw a flash report on TV. Kenon Road, one of the three twisting and winding access roads to the mountain city of Baguio, was closed due to a landslide. There were casualties. The report didn't say any names as the rescue workers were still clearing the debris and identifying the recovered remains. What was clear was that the landslide occurred around 10:45 a.m. Fearing the worst, Dad made a break to the Baguio Disaster Operations Center to ask for updates. He was given a detailed dossier containing twenty-six names based on identification cards and five who's still yet to be identified.

The report stated that a giant boulder eroded onto Kennon Road at Camp 4, blocking both inbound and outbound traffic. Due to the collective weight of the giant rock and the cars that were stuck around it, plus the softened earth caused by the five-day continuous downpour, the ground gave way in a ferocious mudslide. One passenger van carrying five people, two cars carrying two and three people each, and a provincial bus carrying twenty-one people were pulled by the avalanche of mud and were buried underneath. There were no survivors.

I remained unmoving against the assailing wind as Dad recounted what he learned from the disaster center.

Of the twenty-six identified names, three were familiar to my dad:

*Rodrigo Cueto (54), Resident of Barangay Dimalupid, Las Piñas, Metro Manila.*

*Evelyn Cueto (52), Resident of Barangay Dimalupid, Las Piñas, Metro Manila.*

Dad didn't continue. He knew I knew who's next.

There was a long silence. A ringing silence.

"And Cola?" I asked. I had to hear it. I had to know for sure.

Dad lowered his gaze.

"Tell me!" I stood still, rigid, fierce, acting as though I can stomach anything.

Dad swallowed excessively, remorsefully, before relaying the last name he recognized:

*Nicola Cueto (25), Resident of…*

My world turned mute. The alluring aroma of winter rain and pine trees changed into the rotten stench of death.

A heavy hand hammered my chest until it caved in, exposing my feeble heart to be trampled by a thousand rhinos, and then dropped into a lava of molten tears. It was infinite hurt and pain. Infinity plus one. My brain burned, every fold and lobe. Why was it her? What did she do to deserve this? I wasn't even with her. I should have been with her. I shouldn't have... I should... Oh god...

I felt sour with contempt, disgust, revulsion, all against myself. Why wasn't I with—

*"Hey, stranger..."* I heard her voice.

Instantly, a brick of pain fell on my head, and my trembling body plummeted to the hardwood floor. I tried to use my hands to stop me from hitting hard, but my arms had lost all its strength. Sprawled face down, joy leached away through the tips of my fingers.

*"I'm yours, and you're mine..."*

My stomach constricted in agony. Breathing suffocated me. My vision blurred in and out while I try to fight despair from taking over the better of me. I struck rock-bottom. I entered hell. I was so in shock that tears only came when my mind fully comprehended that she was in fact... gone.

I prepared for the worst, but nothing can prepare you for the agony of loss.

*"Never let me go..."*

Nicola was gone. My Cola. She, who brought light into my lonely soul. The hearty laughter, the amused side stares, the almond eyes, the scent of lilacs and lavenders, heaven's painting, my universe, my light, now condensed into none. The world had lost its brilliant beacon of golden splendor.

Cola. She's dead.

# Chapter 13:
# Complicated Grief

Cola's death had given me grief that kept on going over the years, only temporarily subsiding, and then flaring up again randomly. It didn't help that I have this penchant for the nostalgic and an aptitude for silence and isolation.

Born under thunder and rain, draped in slime, the creature with glowing eyes, the beast of despair and anxiety, has been dogging me ever since. Like mold and mildew, each sunless morning allowed it to thrive. It fed on my despair and excreted a heightened sense of mourning. It plagued me every day, preventing me from healing. Some days felt so long that I thought it would never end. Ending it did not end it.

Desperate to find some distraction from the insidious memory, I marched out of my apartment and let my feet take me to wherever they want, leaving the broken hard drive splayed on the floor. Minutes later, I found myself meandering into the red line of the metro. There was no destination, my body just felt like going there. I rambled invisibly among the crowd until I was inside the train.

The train began its interval stops. Move. Stop. Move. Stop. Again. Move. Stop. Move. Stop. It was tolling on me. The scores of people coming in, with their oblivious jeers and laughter, and clearly having no problem at all, bore more weight over my rising despair.

*"It's your fault,"* the beast berated me again.

I still tried to fight and keep my emotions in check though I knew I was a goner. I sought for distractions with the whizzing lights, the faces of people, the scrolling LED information board below the ceiling, but it was forlorn. A dark force was wringing my heart, flushing away all joy, all hope, until only nothing remains. Fewer than a second later, my throat seized, and out gushed a torrent of tears. I turned to face the corner to hide from unknowing passengers, and there, a familiar face saw me back. I abruptly twisted the other way.

Not a minute later, a hand touched my shoulder. It was neither light nor heavy. It didn't grip me; it didn't rub me; it just rested there. It landed in just the right way to convey a sense of unspoken understanding. In all its essence, it was comforting.

Tears in my eyes obscured the man. Though I didn't see his face, I can sense his empathy flowing through his warm and consoling palm that was resting on my shoulder. Was he a he, though, or was he a she? I didn't care. Frail and trembling, I just found myself burying my head onto that person's shoulder.

Two stops later, my tears dried up. I wasn't expecting my waterworks to parch so soon. I wanted to release more bitterness but there wasn't more. "Why?" I thought.

When the train doors opened, the warmth enveloping me evanesced as the person whose hand and shoulder became my saving grace exited the train. I peered out the window to get a glimpse of the person, blinking a few times to clear the sadness from my eyes. That's when the image of the person walking away became more evident and more apparent.

He was... she... A woman. She limped into the crowd, and the station's light glowed pink on her wavy crimson hair.

# PART TWO: LUMA

Now, close your eyes again and imagine this: you're panting hard, vigorously breathing in and out that the muscles around your belly begin to sting. Inside your rib cage, you can feel an intense pounding, like a wrecking ball trying to tear down the walls of your chest. Any moment now, without warning, your heart could explode from the intense stress you're subjecting it to, but you continue anyway. Would your face then chisel a grimace or any form equal to suffering, or would it sculpt a vibrant smile on your lips? For Luma, yes, her face would mold a grin of pain.

"Luma has a matchstick personality," that was how Luma's high-school teacher had described her.

"A what?" Luma's mom inquired.

"A matchstick personality. Someone who keeps starting something new, but never gets to the end of it. Like a match, when you strike it, it burns bright, then it slowly fades out before the fire reaches your fingers. It's the same with Luma. I've seen her over the years try different hobbies, join different clubs. None stuck with her."

Luma indeed tried several hobbies before discovering her craze. She attempted to love several unrelated things, ranging from piano to chess, to poetry, and to badminton. But can you fault a girl for trying to seek her passion?

Before finding the pursuit that held her interest, her life was an endless road of twists and turns with no definite destination. However, once she found something that spoke to her, she became unstoppable with one goal.

Is there something that you do, which you do because it's what makes you breathe? It's what makes you free? It took Luma until she got to college in her hometown in Ifrane, Morocco to find that elusive pursuit; that activity, the passion that allowed her to be limitless. It was an obsession that allowed her to be as free as the wind, soaring beyond the stars, and no one would bat an eye. It taught her to love and ignore the burning pain that her body would bestow as she pushed herself hundreds of kilometers into the unknown to discover the many treasures of nature. It might be compared to heroin for its addictiveness, excluding the adverse side effects. She became addicted to it. It was Luma and two wheels propelled by her own strength—she found cycling.

"Haram!" That's how Luma's father described cycling.

Haram is an Arabic term that means forbidden, mostly associated with religion, referring to something sinful, or something that is not permitted.

Luma had a difficult time growing up with a conservative father. She just couldn't do whatever she wanted. She always had to defend herself whenever what she wanted crossed the line between what was deemed moral and immoral in her father's eyes. And that's the keyword: "in her father's eyes," because haram was a word that her father liked to throw a lot, even though it wasn't something that his religion forbade. To him, *haram* is synonymous with *no*.

"Cycling is a boy's game! It's not very womanlike!" her dad reasoned out.

"Baba, you do know that many Muslim women are excelling in sports, right?" asked Luma.

"Sure, in sports that don't require you to ride a bike!"

Luma began to stutter. "Then, I'll be the f-first one!"

"No! It's haram!"

# PORTRAITS OF THE WIND

"You can't say h-ha… you can't just say haram every time you don't approve of something!"

"Just forget about cycling! Sooner or later, that little flame on the tip of your match would die down anyway, right? So why prolong our disagreement, stop it now!"

But her father was wrong. Luma was prepared to strike a thousand matches that will burn brighter and hotter to keep the fire alive. What her father was failing to understand was that Luma had fallen in love with cycling. And a bond held by love is never easy to break apart.

"How can you say the flame is going to burn out?" Luma's mom defended. "She's way past that matchstick thing! She's way past burning through the half-way mark! She's already winning races! You can't just forbid her. You know she's a free spirit! The more you push her into a corner, the more she spreads her wings!"

"Haram!"

Against her father's wishes, Luma trained hard for herself. She rode up the unforgiving gradients of Morocco, atop mountains that overlook the whole nation. She raced with pigeons, with cats, with dogs, and her own shadow. She rode in the heat of the desert, and under thunderous rains. Nothing stopped her, not even severe headwinds that reduced her speed to a child's walking pace. And with every peak that she conquered, her power increased two-fold. It yielded a lot of pain, and she loved every sting of it. It was glorious. It imparted her the feeling of superiority whenever her body would be drained of energy by the end of the day.

On two wheels, she saw the world as a linear smear, zipping past uncontrollably. To the bystanders, to the meager people on the side of the road, they saw her as a streak of color succeeded by a gust of wind. A crimson blur.

With gritted teeth, she spun her way to the top of every podium of every local race, to the ire of the many men she bested on the road. She became a celebrity among local cyclists and a familiar face to the morning people of Ifrane.

There is only one more hill left to ride before she can be the best in the world. It's a mountain that is said to be the killer of dreams: employment. After graduating, she had to follow in her father's footsteps and work in Qatar, where she could earn triple than what she would make in Morocco.

If only winning a few thousand dirhams every few months was enough to support her and her family, she could have stayed longer in Ifrane, maybe a year, to join more races and potentially be discovered. Luma joined the ranks of almost everyone in the world then: a dreamer who had to hold off on her ambitions.

Now imagine this: you've found your devotion, your fervent pursuit, but life itself seemed to be against it.

# Chapter 14:
# The Charmed Life, Sort Of

I placed my palms on the blackboard, stretched my left leg backward, and my right leg bent forward. I pushed down on my left foot, and instantly, the many fibers that formed my hamstrings twanged like guitar strings being pulled into tune. I vocalized with it, ah…

My muscles burned ever so slightly. And I love it! Especially when I walk, when I climb up the stairs, or when I stand. It brings with it a sense of satisfaction, an awareness that I haven't been laid back, that I am almost to the top of the mountain.

"Are you okay, Ma'am Luma?" a student asked.

I swung around to face my class of twenty. It's a mixture of races from all continents, meeting together inside a tiny classroom in Doha. All of them were staring curiously at me.

"Yes," I replied almost automatically. Without warning, my mouth opened wide, my whole body stretched on itself, and I let go of a loud, loud yawn. That felt good. "Please excuse me. I'm just tired," I told my students.

A student raised her hand. "If you need to take a rest, go ahead. We're okay," she said playfully.

The whole class murmured and nodded in agreement.

"You'd like that, don't you? Maybe next time. We have a lot to c… we have a lot to catch up on." I tied my hair into a bun and rolled my blouse's sleeve up to my elbow to show them I'm ready for business.

"Open your books to page—" What page is that again? I browsed my book and turned to the car-marked page: Page 105.

"Turn to page one h...h... h..." I took a breath, "one o... f... five," I finally said.

The whole class flipped through their book in unison. The fluttering sound of pages turning came in and went in a big swoosh. And then one by one, as each student reached the prescribed page, wrinkles formed in their forehead, followed by a single syllable word synonymous with confusion, "huh?"

"So, what is a Pythagorean theorem?" I asked aloud.

The students stared at me with most of their mouths slightly open, as if I have asked an obtuse question that chipped my credibility. I stared back steadily; one student per audible tick of the clock. Nobody wanted to answer.

"Anyone?" I asked firmly.

In a few seconds, everyone surveyed each other to see if anyone would raise their hand. There was one. Finally.

"Um... Ma'am, page fifteen is an introduction to trigonometry," the puzzled student said, smiling nervously.

The whole class, through their body language, agreed with the boy who answered.

I squinted at them. What the hell is he talking about? I went to check the book of a student in the front row. It was opened on page fifteen.

Page 15?

"Not page fifteen. One—" Oh, now I get it! Darn it! They missed the *O* in one-o-five. Sometimes stuttering can get really frustrating. Therefore, I decided to shorten the words. "T... ten five," I said.

The class frowned in confusion altogether. I heard everyone's thoughts say, *what?*

I tried again, "One h... h..."

This was one of the rare moments I wished someone would finish my sentence. But nobody did. They were all so polite. Yay! Lucky me!

They had known better now. Someone once innocently finished my sentence, and she incurred the wrath of Mrs. Wellbrock, our plus-sized Kiwi school principal.

"Do not finish someone's sentence! Where are your manners?! Don't you know that it's rude? You interrupt their train of thought. It's disrespectful. And it shows you're impatient!" Mrs. Wellbrock screamed with her irritatingly low voice to the innocent student.

But it's true! What's more frustrating than stuttering is feeling incapable when someone couldn't wait for you to finish your sentence. You'd absolutely want to smack that someone's face.

"One h…"

One of the students sitting in the front row slightly turned his ear towards me.

"h… hundred…"

His eyes broadened. I pointed to him earnestly, bobbing my head, and flashing my eyebrows.

"One hundred five?" the student said. Probably not sure if I really wanted him to finish the sentence, or not sure if he finished my sentence correctly.

"YES!" I screamed. Heck, that was awkward. My stuttering was uncharacteristically worse lately.

I turned to the blackboard and wrote, "Pythagorean Theorem." I paused. I glanced at the powdery white chalk I was holding. Then it hit me. Of course! I slapped my forehead. I could've just written it, and everyone would have felt better.

Sometimes I can be a real dumbass, am I right? Yep. I am.

# JANIX PACLE

***

The afternoon sun had dived into the horizon, and its warm golden rays splashed all over my empty classroom, making it ripe for the clock to fall asleep. I glanced up from the papers I was checking and relished the sight of the nostalgic hour. There were faint echoes of laughter and reverberating footsteps drifting from the corridors and into the room.

Again, my jaw muscles involuntarily contracted, and my mouth yawned. A relaxing pain traveled down my spine as my back arched inward, and my legs stretched outwards under my desk and beyond. 'Twas a magnificent yawn. It always feels like it had been a hundred years since a yawn such as this was made. But in truth, I yawn like this all the time. Just like in the morning, in front of class, remember?

A loud knock burst my bubble. My posture straightened and stiffened.

"Luma," Mrs. Wellbrock's head peeked from the doorsill almost cartoony, like spying on someone. "Could I see you in my office?" she asked.

I nodded politely. I didn't speak. I didn't have too. No need to waste valuable energy on speaking.

Walking together through the empty corridor towards her office, I let Mrs. Wellbrock take the lead. I stayed back about two, maybe three steps behind. As we walked, she kept glancing back to me with her mouth opening and closing. Clearly, thoughts were stuck between her teeth. I kept my head down, or up, or left, or right, somewhere, pretending not to see her suggestive attitude to start a conversation.

I'm used to silence. She isn't. Silence triggers chatty people to be awkward. Silence is their enemy, am I right? Silence is similar to an airplane ascending to the stratosphere. It pressurizes their ears until it pops.

We passed by our school janitress, who was mopping the hallways that were once trodden by hundreds of students just thirty-minutes ago.

"Good afternoon, Latha. All is well?" Mrs. Wellbrock bubbly said.

"Yes, ma'am," Latha meekly replied.

Latha then turned to me and merrily nodded, and I did the same. We understood each other without words being uttered. No need to waste valuable speaking energy with pleasantries. A sincere body language would always suffice.

The second we passed Latha, the principal gave me a knowing look. This time, she looked at me a smidge longer. With a deep breath, her mouth opened...

Since our school had a population of only around 700 students with 150 faculty members, information (or gossip) from the south easily ripples to the north faster than you can say fake news. Especially if you have a chatty-chatty principal, e.g. Mrs. Wellbrock. It was already a well-known fact that Latha's son is about to graduate college in Sri-Lanka; however, I don't recall Mrs. Wellbrock talking to me about that. So, that's what I expected her to say.

Nuh-uh.

She closed her mouth with an audible exhale. Her shoulders dropped a fraction of an inch, and we continued walking with hushed lips until we reached her office.

\*\*\*

Entering the principal's office, a sharp groove lined up my nostrils, akin to the feeling of peeling back the skin around your nails. I pinched my nose, but I thought that wouldn't be polite, so my fingers twisted and began rubbing instead, pretending my nose was itchy. Wellbrock had a humidifier at the corner of her room. Normal people would go with fruity or flowery scents, such as jasmine and apple. The principal chose bubble gum. Crap! The smell was so intense, it bordered between fragrance and poison.

"Hmm…" I feigned interest as I sniffed the putrid aroma. "Bubble gum?" I asked.

"Yes. You like it?" Wellbrock said while she arranged the many documents and books on top of her worn-out desk. "It's new! Studies show familiar smells help people become more comfortable. Hopefully, the students will feel more comfortable when they sit in my office, and we'll have a meaningful conversation when I'm reprimanding them." She giggled to herself.

No wonder Latha kept complaining about cleaning more and more bubble gums stuck under desks and on toilet doors. The school's head honcho was subconsciously encouraging students to chew bubble gum.

When Wellbrock finished arranging her desk, she clasped her hands together and rested it atop the table. She pouted slightly, looked up to the left, then back to me. "Did you know Latha's son is about to graduate college!"

"No!" I said with a faked surprise. Ha-ha! I knew that was coming!

Wellbrock continued, "Amazing, isn't it? Hard work gets you to places! That's what I keep telling the students. If you really want something, as long as you break your back over it, your sweat, it will open a lot of doors. That's common knowledge. Even if that means simply working hard to provide for your family while holding a mop and cleaning after some rich kid's vomit. Right? Now let's get down to the real business why I called you here."

Finally! Always with these long intros. Mrs. Wellbrock has this aptitude for softening you up before delivering the news. And speaking of news, another one of her many skills is being able to fill bad news with chocolate cream, then put a chocolate glaze on top of it. It is terrible news, but it's also sweet. So, when you sit in her office, you'll never know if you're about to get good or bad news until she spills it.

"The parents and students really find you an amazing character, which you are," she began. (That's the chocolate filling.)

"And some students even look up to you as their inspiration. Because you know, despite your stutter, you decided to confront it and become a teacher." (That's the glaze.)

"But lately," (There's the "but!" This is bad news, alright.) "some students are expressing their concern that you've been stuttering more. Is there something wrong?"

I shook my head, "No. Ev… All good."

"But you are stuttering more lately, aren't you?"

"Yes, but that's just because I'm tired."

"Tired?"

The Luma in my head started to ferret around for credible reasons. "Uhm, yes. Uh, as you know, the p… the periodical exams recently finished. There were a lot of papers to check."

"That was last week. You had the whole weekend to rest and whatnot."

"Yeah. No!" I chuckled nervously. "I've also been increasing my training load lately. I'm getting ready for the race next month. There will be scouts watching, so I need to be at my peak. It may be my ticket to the pro peloton."

"Oh," she said with hints of faint reproach. Her contralto voice switched to an off-putting high baritone. "I don't care what you do with your own time, just be sure that whatever you do, it doesn't affect your work. Especially because you're a teacher. You set an example to students."

Don't you think I know that? I didn't say.

"Just be aware of your responsibilities," she continued.

"It's either I chose the wrong career, or the wrong sport," I said jokingly. But with my stuttering, the humor failed to jump the fence.

Wellbrock's eyebrows almost became a straight line. "No, I don't think so," she said without any intonation, "It depends on what you want to achieve. But, in all cases, time management is always the key to success. I believe what you need is to have a better grip of your time. You do know many successful people in the world used to have a different day job, right? Hugh Jackman, for example. He was a teacher, and now, he's a Hollywood A-lister."

Yes, yes, I know. Again, I didn't say.

She slowly reclined on her chair that creaked under her weight. "Now, how about that. A teacher and a future Olympian, that right? That's another thing the students can find inspirational in you!"

I let a gentle chuckle loose through my bogus grin.

Inspiration? I have a long way to go before I become a real inspiration. I haven't even been in any major international races yet. Without trophies or medals, I'm hardly anyone. I need a win. I need to be successful. Then I can consider myself an inspiration. If I compete with the pros, then I'll be a real inspiration. And not an Olympian… a World Champion.

I stood up and bid goodbye.

"Also, try wearing some makeup from time to time. Especially red lipstick," Mrs. Wellbrock said. Her voice was now back to her jolly contralto. "Children are attracted to red lipstick. That's a fact, various studies proved it. It makes them more attentive."

I briefly stared at the principal's lips. It was so red, and shiny, and wet. Ugh! I shoved my hands inside my pocket to prevent me from shivering in disgust.

Excuse me, but I like the way I am. I don't need makeup, not for men, not for children, not for anyone. Makeup? Bleh! It's greasy, it's heavy, it's time-consuming, am I right?

# Chapter 15: Stationary Racing Bike

"Wally! Luma's here!" shouted one salesman as I entered Cycle City, my favorite bike shop across Qatar.

The smell of new rubber instantly glided up my nostrils when I walked down the shop's august corridors. Left and right, marvelous bikes, lustrous and gleaming, waiting to be owned, called me by my name. There were road bikes, mountain bikes, kid's bikes, BMX, folding bikes, and bikes that I don't even know what they're called because there are so many of them. This must be how heaven is, if bicycles were angels. Only unicycles were excluded from the shop. Those belong down in hell.

I know the shop inside out. I can navigate its tight corridors by memory. If I have to, I could directly walk to the section that I will be visiting. But desires are stronger than will most of the time, I think.

Every time I enter the shop, my feet would always halt on its own at each bicycle on display. And my fingers, through the mind of its own, will tap the carbon fiber frames and components, and my ears will be amazed at the light hollow (tok-tok-tok) sound it would create. Occasionally, a measure of awe would spread from my lips whenever I would lift the aluminum bikes and realize how modern technology can produce alloy frames that are at par, sometimes lighter than carbon fiber.

I would then glide my hand through the handlebar, along the corky, smoothly rough surface of the bar tape. And when my fingers are guided to the brake levers, my hand would squeeze it, always verifying if hydraulic is indeed better than cable-actuated brakes. And I'll tell you, yes... yes, they are.

Of course, I know all of these and the rationale behind all the technobabble. But still, I always find myself spending almost half an hour at the display racks every time I enter the shop. And that's solely from coming in. Leaving is another story.

Consider a dog chasing butterflies in the meadow: its tail wagging incessantly left and right, its mouth dripping in excitement as it jumps up and down the fields of dandelions. That's how I feel, free in paradise. It never gets old. If I had the money to buy all the bikes I see, I probably would.

I crossed the hall of bicycles (after fifteen minutes) and approached the workshop at the end of the store. No one was there except a familiar sound tickling my ears.

Tick-tick-tick-tick!

It was getting louder. The sound came from another room, way behind the workshop.

Tick-tick-tick-tick! Metal ratcheting against metal.

Like a mother who can tell apart the cry of her baby from a brimming nursery, I can tell whose tick that belongs to. And like a mother, I cannot wait to caress my baby.

The door opened. A limping man came out: Wally. Rolling beside him was the source of that sound: my yellow Giant Liv, glowing brightly and singing its heavenly melody.

There it is!

The sight of my bike always uplifts my mood. If I'm sulking, I look at my bike! If I'm lethargic, I look at my bike! If I'm going crazy, I look at my bike, and then I'll border between sanity and madness. For us cyclists, our bicycles are our pride and joy. If it weren't blasphemy, some would go and set up an altar in the name of their bikes.

"Hi Luma, how are you?" Wally asked in his thick Filipino accent.

"Good! How's... How's my bike?"

Wally gaily sneered at my bluntness. Less pleasantries, always direct to the point.

"Come, come." He gestured me to come behind the counter separating the showroom and the workshop. He touched and pointed to the various parts of the bike as he talked about them. "Cables, I changed. Also, I putting lubricant inside, so it's more smooth. Chain, still okay, but it's little stretch already. Maybe after 400, 500 kilometers, need change. Also, bearings, I make cleaning and put new grease."

I nodded as he spoke. I love talking with Wally. I understood his broken English, and he understood my broken words.

"Also, I discover this crack." He pointed to a tiny little crack on the seatpost where it meets the seat tube. It's almost microscopic, your nose would have to touch it to spot it. "I think, maybe, you overtighten the clamp," he said.

I ventured into my brain's archives, searching for the clamp. *La shayy*. Nothing. I don't remember doing it. "Do I need to replace it now?" I asked.

"It's recommended. But we can also observe only. During my time in the tour, my frame has crack for two weeks. No problem!" he replied.

The tour Wally was talking about was the Marlboro Tour, a multi-stage bike race around the whole Philippines. Wally rode professionally for ten years until he got involved in a massive pile-up at the fourth stage of the centennial edition of the tour. He broke his leg. The team paid for his treatment, and the leg got fixed. Unfortunately, he can't compete anymore. He can still ride, but he can't ride as hard as he used to. Then the passing time made his hair grey and his body weak. His dream was gone. Now, here he is at Cycle City, fixing my bike in exchange for an acceptable wage.

"You observe only," Wally continued, "If crack become big, then you replace. But if you have money now, better replace now. Better safe."

"How much?"

"Five hundred riyals, good alloy, but for you, need carbon. This is eight hundred to one thousand."

"One t-t-th... Okay. I'll just observe for now. Maybe next month I'll buy."

Wally handed me the bike and asked, "What's your power now?"

My chin rose involuntarily as I answered with alacrity. "Four-point-three watts per kg."

Wally snapped to attention. "Strong!"

Ooh! My heart leaped in joy. Someone complimented me honestly, and it wasn't a compliment of just because. It wasn't one of those fake compliments when people are trying to be affable. It was the real thing.

On my way out, I passed by the clothing section. An orange jersey caught my eye, singing to me. I took it from the rack and examined it. I checked the tag: *90% Polyester with 10% Elastane shell-mesh fabric for maximum lightweight and breathability.* I checked the price tag: *QR 1,200.00 incl. bib shorts.* Oh, hell no! Why is cycling so expensive?

***

The taxi arrived at my house in the Al Mamriya area of Doha. I didn't ride my bike home because as you know, my dad, my baba, might shun me for good, because haram, blah blah.

I stepped out and pulled out my bicycle from the back seat. People often wonder how bicycles fit in a car. The answer is simple: remove the front wheel and slide the bike in the back seat. The rear wheel stays on the floor, and the front fork sans the front wheel should rest on the seat. It will only take fifteen seconds to do all that. You don't need tools; it's all quick release.

As I got out and reattached the front wheel, our neighborhood's music welcomed me, music played with hammers, drills, beeping bulldozers, and thudding jackhammers. It arose from the metro's finishing touches, new buildings, sewage works, road works, and so on. Every few blocks or so, there is some construction ongoing. We live in a busy street. People imagine the word "busy street" as having a lot of shops, bright lights, and people walking and milling about. *Au contraire.* My busy street is the kind that has a lot of scaffoldings and heavy machinery. Our area is old and continuously renovated.

I remember the first time I arrived in this place eight years ago. Though faded brown, the door to our house was still intact. Now, it's no longer brown, it's turning grey, and thin strips of wood are peeling off. Inside the abode, the ceiling has cracks branching out from the corners. Baba said he would fix them, patch them, cover them, or something to that effect. He said that eight years ago. Now, it's still there, growing a centimeter each year.

For almost a decade, whenever I came home, Baba would always be already sitting in his 20-year old couch, watching his explosive action movies. The undertone of his Moroccan mint tea would blend with the jasmine and saffron fragrance of Ma's diffuser, reminding me of Ifrane. And at precisely 5:30 p.m., the tang of Ma's cookery would overpower the whole house, totally like the *hamour* she's frying now.

Ma came out of the kitchen and spotted the paper bag held in my left hand. "What's that?" she asked, jabbing the air with the ladle she was holding towards me. With the other hand, she wiped it on her traditional Moroccan house dress, which covered her body from neck to toe.

Baba gawked from his couch too. His brown shirt was unbuttoned, revealing the grey hair on his chest. Uhm, eww.

"New clothes," I replied to Ma with straight, clean words.

If you're wondering where my stutter went, well, it's more manageable at home. Academics say it is the result of my comfort levels being through the roof whenever I'm talking with my parents.

"It's from the bike shop?" Baba asked as he craned his twisted neck from the couch. As if the huge Cycle City logo on the paper bag wasn't obvious enough.

"Yes, it's from the bike shop, I bought a new jersey. Don't worry. It's not expensive."

Ma chuckled inwardly.

Baba rolled his eyes. "I'm not asking whether it's expensive or what. I simply wanted to know what you bought and where. Okay? Nothing more to that," he said.

"Okay," I said plainly and continued to my room.

\*\*\*

I was never fond of decorating my room. Back in grade school, high-school, and college, all my girlfriends had flowery decorations splashed all over their room. Not me. What I had in my bedroom was a bicycle wall hanger, to where I hanged my, you guessed it, my yellow Giant Liv, right in front of my bed. It is the only decoration my crib needs to be dazzling and pompous. I took a few steps back and drooled at the sight of the yellow bike hanging there.

Wow, woman! That's your "Lumamobile."

I took the orange jersey out of the paper bag. Yep, I bought the jersey. The whole kit actually, jersey and bib. I told you, leaving the bike shop was a different kind of story. It wasn't impulse, though. I really do need a new jersey. All my other jerseys were already a year old. They're still functional, but they're already a year old! And this was the last piece. With all these new meshes and breathable thingamajig, how could I let it pass?

My hands ripped the price tag from the jersey and tore it into pieces. I didn't have to give any instructions to my hands. They did it on their own. It's as if they knew the high number printed on it gave me a bad case of nausea.

I slipped into the jersey, zipped it up, and its cold fabric embraced my body. Rage filled me at once—the rage to ride outside. The jersey fits perfectly, molding onto my skin. I move, it moves. It produced no visible wrinkles, and importantly, it had no loose fabric that would act as a parachute at high speeds.

High speeds...

I can already see myself as a streak of color under the waning light outside. With adrenaline building up in my veins, I put on my cycling shoes and took my bike from the wall hanger. In less than five minutes after trying on the orange jersey, I was hastening out of my room and sneaking towards the front door.

Reverberating gunshots, zinging ricochets, and deafening explosions arose from the TV loudspeakers, filling the living room. I ducked, along with the characters on TV. But instead of avoiding bullets, I was trying to avoid my baba's attention.

Tick-tick-tick-tick!

My French-made freewheel ticked louder than all the racket on TV.

Tok-tok-tok-tok!

And the sound of my cleats rapped on the floor.

Baba's ear flinched with cat-like dexterity, homing in towards the sound.

Tick-tick-tick. Tok-tok-tok.

Baba spontaneously twisted from his couch, making me halt in my tracks. Darn it! I was only an arm's reach away from the door. I felt like a kid caught opening the cookie jar. Baba probably saw me as one too.

"Where are you going?" he asked firmly. By the expression on his face, it looked like he heard an explosion in real life.

"Out for a ride," I said with a discernable stutter.

"No, you're not." The words just rolled out from Baba's mouth. He didn't have to think.

I glared at my father as a contemptuous act of defiance. I did not want to get changed again without riding outside. That's as frustrating as being served ice cream and then taken away without even a single bite.

Thousands of words spiraled from my head, funneling down to my mouth to the tip of my tongue, but only one word came out: "Baba!"

"No. You know the rules," he answered effortlessly.

Ma walked out of the kitchen, still with a ladle in hand. "What's going on?"

"Your daughter wants to bike outside," Baba said, and he turned to me, "Why do you keep trying anyway? You know I won't change my mind."

"Ma, please?" I begged.

Ma spoke sternly over the loud TV. "Hashem, your daughter is twenty-six. Stop treating her like a teenager. She's old enough to do what she wants!"

"You know I'm not treating her like a teenager, Rabiya! We've been over this a hundred times! And then another hundred! You want to go over it again? I'm just being protective."

"Overprotective," I blurted.

Baba stood up. "So, you want to go ride in the dark with the cars going over one hundred beside you? Go ahead then! You know how people drive here; their shits are hanging out their asses and they need to get to the toilet ASAP! It's not safe!"

"I hate to say it, but your baba's right," Ma said.

Whatever.

Don't you hate it when someone gives you a valid reason not to do something, but the actual truth behind the reason is that they completely don't like you to do what you want to do? Am I right?

"But others do it!" I protested, pointing my finger to the invisible others.

"What's the purpose of us gifting you that expensive, direct-whatever-trainer, if you're not going to use it?" Baba asked.

He meant to say the direct-mount trainer, where you remove the rear wheel of the bicycle and mount the rear drop-out of the frame directly onto the machine. That way, you have something like a stationary bike, using your own bike. And it lets you train or race with others who are connected to the same virtual cycling app.

"I'm tired of the trainer, no!" I roared, almost yelling but not. "Every day I ride that! It's b-b-b-b-boring!" Oh god, my stutter is getting worse. Stress! "All I do is wait for the timer to reach zero while I stare at a white wall!"

"Boring? How much was that again? Four? No five! Five thousand! And you don't like it because it's boring?" Baba said.

"Hashem…" Ma said in a reproving tone.

"But isn't it worth it? You keep telling us about your power increasing and increasing. Don't you think you owe it to the trainer?" Baba continued.

"I know! But what's the use of a high FTP when y-y-y-y-y-you—" Oh hell! Stupid stutter! Mama and Baba patiently waited for me to finish my sentence. Yet their growing impatience manifested through his bouncing heel and her widening eyes. "—what's the use of having a high power when you can't ride outside!"

"But you ride on the weekends," Ma said.

Oh, Ma! Whose side are you on? I yelled in my mind.

"Yeah! Once in a blue moon, when there's no activity in school during weekends!" I said.

Ma snapped to Baba and persuasively raised her eyebrows.

"*La!*" he said firmly, shaking his head. "La! No. I already tolerated you, my daughter, a woman, to ride a bicycle. The agreement was you can bring your bike here, but you only ride with a group in the morning with girls! Not solo. Never solo. And only in the weekends. The weekends!"

"I'm freaking twenty-six!"

"And you're still my daughter! You can do absolutely whatever you want when you get married and move out!"

"What about the bike lane? She can ride in the bike lane," promptly suggested Ma.

"How are you going to get there?" Baba asked me.

"Bike," I said.

"No."

"You can drive me."

"No." Baba dropped back to his couch and faced the TV.

End of discussion.

My grip on my bike tightened. My teeth made grinding noises as they gnaw against each other. I was flustered. The image of me zipping past streetlamps hastily faded into the back of my mind as I considered my two options: one, storm out and ride; two, storm in and sulk. I chose option two. I am still living under his roof, right? Blah blah.

Like a child hating her parents, I immaturely stomped back to my room with Ma following close behind.

"That jersey looks good on you," Ma said encouragingly as she closed my bedroom door behind her.

With a cumbersome sigh of defeat, I dropped onto my bed.

"I need to ride outside if I expect to win the race," I said. "Biking outside is different. There are technical skills that I need to master which can't be done with the trainer, like pacing, and cornering, and training against the headwind."

"Well, you have the Friday group ride, right?" Ma said.

"But…" Ah, crap, I give up. Why am I still living with them? Oh, yeah, right! Economy! Freaking economy.

Ninety-nine percent of people I know in Qatar, and whose parents are also in Qatar, live with their parents. Arabs, Asians, Europeans, Africans, whatever. Hell, I even know of some who are married and have children who still live with their parents. It's all down to money-saving economics. People don't go to Qatar to start a life. I mean, not all, but mostly. People come here to work, right? Like me.

I squeezed my eyes shut in defeat then. And when I opened them, there, on the wall in front of the bed, my yellow bike glowed placidly. The sight of the beguiling beauty washed away a minuscule amount of contempt from my resigned body.

# Chapter 16: Red-Orange, Red-Orange

The wind kept roaring in my ears, roaring the sound of speed. I pushed the pedal hard, fast, like pistons in a V6. I bent low, ducking the headwind; my nose almost touching the handlebar, my back horizontal. I got aero and slick, piercing the wind with the ferocity of a bullet—a female bullet. Strands of hair sipped through the vents of my helmet like little blades of grass flailing in a storm. I'm a blur. I'm a streak. I'm the crimson streak: the red-haired lady who is unstoppable on two wheels.

Thirty-eight kilometers per hour, my wireless speedometer read. My power: 230 watts.

"Mmmm-mmmm-mmm!" someone shouted from behind.

Whut?

Sound waves don't travel forward well from the back of a twenty-man peloton what with hurricane winds blowing against it. It doesn't matter if you scream at the top of your lungs, it will only be distorted into a garbled gibberish. Besides, I wasn't paying attention to anything else. I stayed focused on keeping my power output within the bounds of my sweet spot.

Forty kilometers per hour, 243 watts, my speedo now read.

One hundred seventy beats per minute, my heart rate also read.

My fingers reached for the integrated shifter behind the brake lever.

Chak!

I pressed the shift lever that had the softness and responsiveness of a mouse button. A three-hundred-dollar mouse button. In the instant that it clicked, it released a cable slack of exactly 2.7

millimeters. At precisely the same moment, the rear-derailleur of my bike moved outwards with a louder mechanical grind.

Ka-chak!

The bike's ultra-narrow chain glided down from the fifteen-tooth cog to the fourteen-tooth cog, essentially shifting up to a higher gear.

I maintained the same cadence of 92 revolutions per minute, and my speed rose from 40km/h to 41.2km/h. My power held a steady 250 watts.

"Hey! Luma!" someone yelled brashly from my left. It was the ride captain, the person in charge of keeping the group ride organized. Though I cannot hear his breathing, his twisted face showed how much my tempo was toiling his lungs. "Slow down!" Deep breath. "You're..." Breath. "...splitting the bunch!"

I glanced over my shoulder: the group had been strewn into a single line. All riders were trying to get into the slipstream of the cyclist in front of them. Some were already disconnected from the train. Some appeared to be stopping to a halt even though they were simply slowing down.

"This is not a race! We're only here to have fun!" the ride captain continued to yell over the gushing wind.

I politely nodded and veered to the right. My pedals stopped turning, and I began coasting. My speed dropped exponentially. Now, the cyclist behind me took to the front and did the pace-making.

As I dropped back to the end of the train, the faces of mostly men possessed the face of a fat dog panting hard, tongue sticking out, after chasing the mailman for ten meters. Some of them gave me disparaging looks, critical of my speed. But the few women who rode with us gave me an eloquent congratulatory shake of their head, as if they're saying, *"you're stronger than most of the men here."*

As soon as I latched on to the last rider at the rear, the numbers of the speedometer dropped to 35km/h. That's the speed of a leisurely pace on a flat breezy road. I wanted to bang my handlebars in frustration, but I didn't want to seem like a jerk. I think most of them already saw me as one, right? So, I shook my head in quiet deference.

Serious cyclists are not so many in Qatar; therefore, there are not many cycling clubs around. Most of the cycling groups here are only out for a comfortable and relaxed ride. The group I'm on is a more serious one, with one caveat: to let everyone hang on, we're not allowed to exceed the maximum speed of 35km/h. That places me on a limbo. If I ride with this group, I am limited to a slower speed. If I ride with no group… well, well, well. You know what I mean.

"You're outside now, aren't you?" I said to myself. "What's stopping you from riding solo?"

The peloton approached a roundabout. The point-man extended his right hand towards the right, signaling a right-hand turn. He took the first exit, and the rest followed behind, making a long majestic snaking line. In a few hundred meters, they will be making a pit stop at a *baqala* (a small supermarket), which I don't need, for I have everything I need in my back pocket (food and all). This was my chance to go solo, I thought. So, I decided to split from the group and take the second exit, the path that leads to Al Khor, a 32-kilometer stretch of rolling terrain.

Perfect!

As soon as I exited the roundabout into the straight, I placed my forearms on the top of the handlebar and lowered myself into a time-trial position. I shifted to a higher gear again.

Thirty-five.
Thirty-six.
Thirty-seven.
Thirty-eight.
Thirty-nine.
Forty kilometers per hour.
My power, once again, a stable 250 watts.
Perfect.
I was in my zone. No one to stop me. I'm racing against my own shadow.
Pfft-pfft-pfft-pfft.
Ten minutes in, the faint intermittent sound of high-pressure air escaping into the atmosphere reached my ears.
Oh hell!
I stepped off the bike and inspected its wheels. Rear: still rock hard; front: tender as an empty bra.
I detached the front wheel and examined it further by running my hand around the rubber. "Ouchie!" I inspected the tire closer. A thin strip of wire protruded through and through. Without another glimpse, I can already tell that it came from the wire beading of a blown-out car tire. Blown-out tires are notorious among cyclists in the Middle East for causing ninety percent of punctures. I looked back at the road I traveled. Yes. Pieces of blown-out truck tires littered the tarmac. Darn it!
I reached to the back pocket of my orange jersey to get my puncture repair kit. I took out my phone, two energy gels, an energy bar, two salt sticks, and…
That's it?

## PORTRAITS OF THE WIND

The hairs on the back of my head stood and cascaded down my spine. I forgot to take my repair kit, and worse, I forgot to bring my cycling wallet. I had no money! Curses! Expletives! Profanities!

I watched the road in both directions. Only one car appeared every two minutes. No taxis. I checked my phone; it was only 5:30 in the morning.

Ugh! How will I get home??

Hitching came to mind. But my dad would freak if he would have learned that I had ridden with a stranger, in my sexy cycling outfit, nonetheless (accentuated curves and all). Darn it! That's one point for group riding and zero for solo. I had only one option left...

\*\*\*

The air inside Baba's 2004 Nissan Sunny had the odor of a unicorn's vomit (unexplainably fragrant). The car is well taken care of. Even after 15 years, there is no shake nor rattle in its engine. Food and drinks are a no-no inside the vehicle unless you want verbal torture. Yet there I sat, dripping salty sweat on the clean upholstery. Baba looks pissed, but I knew it wasn't about my sweat.

"Did the group leave you?" he asked.

"Y-y-y-yes," I answered.

He gave me a once-over and didn't say anything. I knew then that he knew the truth. My stutter had betrayed me. So, I confessed.

"Not exactly," I whispered.

"What happened?"

"I... I broke... I broke away from the group."

He glared without saying a word.

"It was the only way to improve my power. Train solo!" I abruptly said.

Baba groaned and faced the road. His eyes flashed the years of heated arguments we exchanged since the very first day I became a serious cyclist.

Baba is a Muslim and a very conservative, religious man. He wanted me to wear a hijab to cover my hair and an abaya to cover my body. He demanded me to go to the mosque every Friday and roost in a secluded area for women. He didn't want me to do "boy" things, and biking for him was for boys as cooking was for girls. Yet everything I am doing now was the exact opposite of his wishes.

I do pity Baba. He fought hard, and still fighting, to keep his traditions alive. But he married a Christian woman, so... well... he botched that one. Although, he succeeded in persuading Ma to be more conservative and don a hijab to cover her hair. But I...

Oh, I am not going to bow down. I am going to be who I say I am. I will wear whatever I want to. I will do what I want to. If I want to cover my hair, I will cover it the way I want it. If it's hot outside, I will wear the most comfortable clothes I can, reasonably. I respect Baba and his beliefs, and I hope someday he would also respect me and my own individuality.

Nobody spoke for the rest of the drive home. He knew we will only be going around in circles if we started arguing. We've been down that road so many times before, and we're both exhausted going over the same thing.

***

Four-point-three watts per kilogram, 4.3 watts/kg.

The screen of my smartphone reflected the massive grin on my face as I reviewed the cycling fitness app open inside of it. The app told me that I had raised my FTP, my functional threshold power.

That's the power I can theoretically hold for one hour, which was now 260 watts. Now divide that to my weight of sixty kilograms, then my power to weight ratio is 4.3 watts/kg.

That places my ability and strength at Category One, which is one category away from being a Domestic Pro. To get there, it's either I lose more weight or increase my power even more. Then, it will be the World-Class Category afterward, and I will be competing with the best of the best! I'm close. I'm close. I'm close!

I clenched my fist and punched the air after the nth time I ogled my new FTP.

"Ma'am, are you okay?" a student in the front row asked.

I glanced up from my phone. Everyone's faces said, "What the hell is she doing?"

I straightened to poise myself. "Yes. I'm okay. It's nothing. Co… continue your seatwork."

The whole class exchanged bewildered glances before going back to their work.

My legs stretched under my desk then, and the muscles surrounding my thigh became rock hard and bumpy. The familiar rewarding pain took over my whole lower body. It resonated the pain of progress, and it felt glorious. As soon as my body settled down from stretching, my mouth opened, and an enormous yawn escaped from my lethargic lungs.

The sun, white and fierce, shone through the windows and bounced soft and pleasing light from the floor to the ceiling, making me squint ever so slightly. My ears worked like a filter, sieving the familiar words of students discussing seatwork among themselves, and turning them into a collection of humming white noise.

White noise.

Afternoon light.

My vision had begun to haze.

Another soft yawn escaped my body. I swiftly covered my mouth and forced it close, but it was a futile attempt to stay awake. All my trainings and incessant workouts, they use up a lot of energy, and rest should not be taken lightly. "Train hard. Rest hard," as they say. But here I am, in front of a class.

I propped my head up against my palm and continued supervising the students from the comfort of my desk. I minded them, observed them, heard their murmurs, until nothing that I saw or heard registered in my mind. Gradually, everything turned into white noise.

The pupil's voices (white noise).

The gentle rattling of the air conditioner (white noise).

Dancing shadows on the floor (visual white noise).

Slowly, slowly, slowly, my eyelids drooped, and everything darkened as my window to the outside world closed.

Peace.

Quiet.

Rest.

Time stood still under my placid mind.

A loud knock.

My head slid off my palm, and I'm jerked back to the outside world.

A flood of noise came rushing into my ears, "Mine, momine, mangle, mamotenun, mm megeruj, mm megeruj." With a blink of an eye, the filter inside my ears broke, sending a gush of recognizable words, "Sine, cosine, angle, hypotenuse, Ms. El-Guerrouj! Ms. El-Guerrouj!"

I cleared my throat. "What?"

"Ma'am," the student closest to me pointed to the door, "Mrs. Wellbrock."

The principal was standing at the threshold with arms akimbo and a face that signaled discontent.

Oh hell.

"Ms. El-Guerrouj, may I talk to you outside for a moment?" she said in her low unsettling baritone voice. That's the voice of displeasure if you will.

The whole class glanced up from their work and watched me walk towards the door. A few of them sneered discreetly.

"M... Mind your work class," I said.

I closed the classroom door behind me. The door latch clicked, and Mrs. Wellbrock took that as her cue to begin.

"Let me guess. Training?" she said.

My eyebrows raised questioningly. "Sorry?"

"You were sleeping in class!"

"Was I? I thought... I thought I just closed my eyes." I rubbed my eyes.

"For a full fifteen minutes, according to your students. What's going on with you? You've been performing so poorly lately!"

I froze, glanced up and down, left and right, here and there, searching for a sensible response.

Nothing.

My mind drifted into space, floating away from Earth. I didn't know how to stutter my way out of this. "They are just doing seatwork," I said. I had no idea if those were the right words to say.

"You're not setting a good example, Luma. These kids look up to you. They admire you for becoming a teacher despite your stutter, and then you're going to sleep in class? You're betraying their trust," my principal said.

I lowered my head and looked at my feet. At that moment, I am no different from a student being reprimanded by the school principal. It reminded me of my high-school years.

"When do you train? In the morning or the evening?" she continued.

"Evenings."

"Don't you get enough rest."

"I do... sometimes."

"Explain to me. I want to understand why you always have red-eye at school."

I chuckled abruptly, "It's not d... drugs. Don't worry."

Mrs. Wellbrock's lips remained shut; her forehead wrinkled.

Oh, crap.

My edgy nerves became more prominent, and I began to stutter over my own stutter. "W-w-w... well, when I get home, I have to prepare for t... prepare for tomorrow's lesson. Then I do my training around 9:00 p.m. for one hour. Take a quick shower, then sleep around eleven. Wake up 5:30 then drive to s... go to school at six."

"Six hours of rest, isn't that enough?"

I shook my head. "It should be. But..." I explained that the physical toll of training plus the mental drain from school needs at least eight hours. The compounding six-hour sleep isn't helping either.

She pursed her lips with reproach. "What is with you and cycling? They're just bikes, aren't they?" she said.

I frowned and cackled at the same time over the ignorance of her comment. "Cycling is more than just bikes, more than sports. It's not even a lifestyle. It's an escape to a different world where you're fitted with wings, and you fly to wherever it pleases you. It's freedom on two wheels."

"But you're training for it. It's a sport."

"To me, it is, but also not. I'm training to fly higher."

She motioned dismissively, "Well, you better check your priorities. You're still working here, and it seems you definitely can't split yourself in two. If one isn't working out, you must let it go. Life isn't fair to those who force themselves into two things at once. It's either be excellent at this or be excellent at that. No in-betweens. Unless you hardly want to live a life."

I nodded at her dimly with respect.

What did she say? That was my first question when I returned to the classroom. The workouts over the past few months raked enough fatigue to make everything fall asleep, including my thoughts.

\*\*\*

My body shivered gladly at the touch of my frothy bed, which accepted my ardent leap with its soft, loving hug. Then it cuddled me between the cold sheets of the bedsheet and the comforter.

Ah! Feels so good!

I closed my eyes for a few beats and took a deep lingering breath.

*"Life isn't fair to those who force themselves into two things at once,"* Mrs. Wellbrock's voice echoed in my head.

My eyes jerked open.

Shut up, Mrs. Wellbrock. I'm not forcing myself. I'm just tired. I only need a longer rest.

A soft knock at the door saved me from Wellbrock's thoughts. It opened, and Ma's head craned over the doorsill. Her face gave me the impression that she had tripped onto a face powder, and her meteorite red lips betrayed her attempt to look kissable. Eww. Okay, sorry. I love Ma. But that makeup… ugh!

"Luma, we're going to a party, your baba's co-worker, or whatever, is having a birthday dinner. There's food in the fridge. Eat! Alright? You're already thinner than a supermodel!" she said, and closed the door.

Thinner than a supermodel. If she meant it as an affront, it didn't work. I took it as a compliment knowing that thinner means lighter, and lighter means faster on the bike.

I went down to the kitchen and opened the fridge, hoping maybe Ma cooked something scrumptious. What stared back at me was a tub of hummus, a grilled chicken thigh leftover from the other day, bottles of water, Long Life fresh milk, some vegetables, and no more. I checked the freezer, and a frozen beef tenderloin waved at me.

Okay...

I searched the internet within my smartphone for healthy steak recipes for cyclists. Hundreds of results came back, and most of them required tedious preparation. My stomach grumbled; it didn't want to wait too long. Fine. I'll take the grilled chicken thigh, please.

After heating my meal, I started with my daily evening routine. So, I ate, and while eating, I did some schoolwork. This time, I checked the seatwork that I gave in the morning. I planned for a lecture, but I was too drained to even consider talking, let alone stutter. Two hours later, my brain ceased functioning. If you checked two hundred and ten papers for seven classes with thirty students each, your brain would probably malfunction too. Ugh! And I still have to do my training. Double ugh!

Let's get sweaty then.

Today was threshold day: a grueling exercise of 2x20-minute threshold intervals. That means I must hold my power between 250 to 260 watts for forty minutes. My heart rate would then be around 165 to 175 beats per minute for the whole duration.

# PORTRAITS OF THE WIND

Uhm…

Yes, that's a lot of pain.

I considered if today can be a rest day instead, but the big race was coming up in a few weeks' time.

Uhm…

Zip!

Clack!

Lock!

Can't skimp on training!

My bike stood upright, glowing, while attached to the direct-mount trainer, whereas I glowed orange with my "little overbudget" jersey. We were glowing so bright that the darkness should be afraid of us.

Ka-chuck! Now the cleats of my cycling shoes are locked onto the pedals.

The training plan started with a warm-up of ten-minute easy spin in zone one, the endurance zone. Afterward, the real pain began. I watched the prompt on the cycling app from my smartphone rise from 150 to 260 watts. That brings me to zone three: threshold. Beside the prompt on the screen was the readout of the actual power I'm doing: 258 watts.

The app communicated its prompts wirelessly to the trainer. With the app's instruction, the electromagnets inside the flywheel increased in power, generating more resistive force against the power of my legs.

Eight minutes in, lactic acid began pooling around my quads. My legs burned. My lungs gasped for air as the demand for oxygen increased. My heart now pumped blood at 160 beats per minute and steadily rising. My skin took on a glossy shine, and a pool of sweat flowered on the floor.

The rhythm kicked in. A rhythm of cadence, a rhythm of power, a rhythm of breathing. This rhythm built a wall around my pain receptors and numbed me. I was invincible.

"Come on! Halfway there!" the app told me.

I pushed harder, faster, and—

My legs spun freely.

The force acting against my pedal stroke waned. The actual power dropped from 258 to 240. Then 230, 220, 210, 195, 185, 120, 80, 15. Despite the app still prompting the trainer to give me 260 watts, the speedo showed that my actual power was only at 15 watts.

What the hell?!

I stopped. A flood of pain signals rushed into my brain. I gasped and grimaced. I paced around my room, breathing heavily. I was breathing heavily from both catching my breath and keeping my temperament. I cannot afford to miss a training day! I banged my handlebar in frustration.

I rebooted the app. It connected with the trainer but adjusting the resistance setting did nothing with the actual resistance.

I restarted the trainer.

Nothing.

Only one more trick left to do…

"Have you tried turning it on and off?" the bored sounding customer rep said over the phone.

"Yes. Don't you think I did that? Three times I restarted."

"Ok, ma'am. Please keep calm. We'll solve this. Please, can you check the status light beside the power cable?"

I leaned over to check. "Yes, it's going on and off."

"What color is the blinking?"

"Red-orange, red-orange."

## PORTRAITS OF THE WIND

The line hummed for a while. I can hear the other guy on the line typing on his computer, possibly searching for the answer.

"Ma'am, I will give you an address to send the trainer for service—"

I interrupted. "What do you mean? What's wrong with my trainer?"

"Ma'am, red-orange means there's some internal failure in your trainer. We can't say exactly what it is until we look at it."

"How long will it t… how long will it… how long?"

"Depending on the fault, it may take anywhere from one to two weeks."

Darn it!

I threw my phone to my bed. All I could think about now was not reaching my full potential. I could already see myself finishing last, and it shook my body in disgust. I need to train. I need to continue the pain. But how? I can't ride outside, and my trainer is kaput.

I found an answer from my only friend in times of stress: my unjudging bed. I lay down slowly after I had changed clothes, and my body melted instantly into the mattress. Calm followed and draped over me. Then silence arrived.

Silence.

Too silent to be honest.

I glanced at my watch; only 8:00 p.m., yet everything was already deathly still. There were neither gun fires, nor explosions, nor Wilhelm screams, nor the sound of frying and clanging pans in the kitchen. Only my heavy breathing added life to the silence.

A truck roared past outside. It sounded like an old diesel engine, trailing off into the night. Then everything fell silent again. Too silent, even for the busy street outside.

I got up and strolled to the window. There and beyond, the empty street placidly glowed in amber under the towering streetlamps. Construction sites had fallen asleep. No sight of living beings anywhere. Even the dumps were safe from cats. It was only the endless road with its shiny black asphalt reflecting the moon's light back to my eyes.

"Luma..." the road called out to me. "Luma, come and ride the wind," it whispered.

I glanced at my bike, now hanging comely at my bedroom wall. Its bright yellow paint screamed at me, "Come on! Let's go! Nobody's home! Outside!"

I glanced back out the window, and I can already hear the tiny crunching rocks beneath my bike's thin tires. Without any hesitation, I found myself slipping on my half-finger cycling gloves, which in turn, through the mind of its own, grabbed my orange jersey, my bike, and my helmet.

Then, I was outside.

# Chapter 17: Screaming Legs

Whoosh! The still, cold night was disrupted by my immense speed, displacing a measure of turbulent air in my wake. A hushed whizz billowed from my deep-section wheels that greeted the hushed streets. Derailleurs, front and back, resonated reassuring grinding noises as I shifted up and down the high speed rotating crank. With every push of the pedal, my bike powerfully surged forward.

The night wind roared in my ears, "Faster! Faster!"

With a quick press of the shifter, the chain dropped to a smaller gear. My cadence dropped a few revs, but I easily adjusted to the new load. My speedo counted up: 38, 39, 40 kilometers per hour. It still felt slow.

I checked my power reading: 230 watts; I'm just in my sweet spot. I can still push it. I can go faster.

"I'll help you!" the wind said, who was roaring behind me, pushing me forward the open black road. "Faster! *Yalla!*"

I raised my output to 240 watts. My speed rose to forty-three. I felt no pain, or at least I didn't feel it sooner. An abundance of air quenched the thirst of my breathless lungs, who in turn supplied oxygen to my laboring heart.

"You're not pushing hard enough!" my heart said, who was still working at a low 155 beats a minute.

Under my saddle, some creaking noise arose (Kkrk! Kkrak!). I presumed it was originating from the crack in the carbon seatpost. It got louder with every kilometer I churned. Ignored it, I did.

I shifted up another gear. My legs now forced a fifty-three-tooth chainwheel against a thirteen-tooth cog.

Now, 250 watts, ten watts less than my threshold. I can still push it.

Beyond me, the road was ending, so I feathered the brakes and banked right towards an exit. I cornered so fast that I leaned so close to the ground, I could already smell the tar and asphalt of the tarmac I was tearing apart. As I straightened out, I was now on a ramp towards the freeway.

A brighter glow of yellow lit the road in front of me. Intermittent cars zoomed past, but I didn't care. The freeway's shoulder gave me security from the fast vehicles. I am safe aside from the tiny pebbles that vibrated my ride.

To my right, I caught a glimpse of a few cyclists with flashing headlamps. They were riding comfortably inside the wire-fenced bike lane. I could have ridden there, but the bike lane can only accommodate one cyclist going each direction, and its streetlights shone no brighter than a phone's flashlight. I wouldn't be able to go faster than my grandma over there. In the open road, I can be as free as the wind.

I checked my legs. "I'm okay!" it told me, "Go! Push!"

I stood up and stomped on the pedals. My bike danced left and right, following the beat of my thrusting legs. As soon as I got to speed, I sat back down and settled on the brake hoods.

Thirty-five.

Thirty-six.

I scraped, I pulled, I pushed the pedals into a perfect circular stroke.

Forty-one.

Forty-two.

Forty-three kilometers per hour; two hundred and sixty watts!

## PORTRAITS OF THE WIND

The road bent to the right, and the wind that was once helping me go faster slammed hard on my face like an invisible wall. The speedometer quickly rolled back to 40 km/h.

I switched to the drops and tucked my elbows inward to reduce my front profile and to be as aerodynamic as possible. That allowed me to bore into the wind like a hot knife through butter once more. I grinned, exposed my teeth, not from delight (maybe a little), but more because of the gratifying burn throughout my body.

Forty-four!

My speed returned but I had to exert more power than before.

Two-hundred and eighty watts!

It's harder now to stay on this speed with the headwind pushing me backward.

Two-hundred and eighty-seven watts; forty-five kilometers per hour.

My mouth opened, the size of a whale, scooping all the air it could take.

Two-hundred and ninety watts; forty-six kilometers per hour.

My heart rate reached zone five, the anaerobic zone.

"Stop! Stop!" my legs screamed, "Enough!"

"Slow down!" my heart shouted at 189 beats per minute.

Above it all, my soul whispered, "Focus. Listen to me. Listen to the music, to the drumming inside you, the whistling in your ear. Focus. Hold the pain. People will respect you and fear you with the amount of suffering you can take."

I found my rhythm.

In that instant, the roaring wind disappeared. The screaming heart and legs settled. Stars of the night sky were now zipping and zapping by beside me. I was flying. Serenity. Now my grin no longer signaled pain, it heralded delight.

I held forty-six kilometers per hour at 295 watts for about ten minutes until I saw the next exit that would take me back home. I didn't take that exit. I was so focused in my zone that the looming exit felt a tad bit too soon. So, I decided to take another exit two kilometers away which took me to the backroads towards home.

\*\*\*

As soon as I completed that exit, the seemingly endless amber wash of the streetlamps came to an end. I could see almost nothing, only the asphalt glowing blacker than the moonlit sky. The bike had no lights. I never expected to be riding at night. If I did, I would have bought one. Still, despite the blackness, I maintained a healthy resting speed of 35 km/h.

When my pupils adjusted to the darkness, the moonlight splashed dimly over the narrow and uneven road that I was riding on. Potholes and construction debris lay scattered everywhere. Left and right, scaffoldings, whose edges gleamed with the moon's light, acted as exoskeletons over half-built villas.

"Ow!"

My arms tensed up. My whole body jerked. The front wheel wobbled, and I fought it by wobbling the handlebar the other way. What the hell was that? Did I hit a rut or something? I looked over my shoulder. *La shayy.* Nothing. I couldn't see anything other than shadows beyond a radius of ten meters.

This exit might be a bad idea, I thought. Well, at least I didn't fall.

In the darkness ahead, the moon outlined a dark object littered on the road. When I recognized that it was a plank of wood, probably discarded from one of the construction sites, it was already too late. I was too close. I veered to the right in a last-ditch effort to evade the object, sending me careening off-road. The front wheel hit something again. A block of wood, a rock, an alien, I don't know. Couldn't see anything! The front wheel locked up, and the bike's forward momentum catapulted me, hurling me into the air, somersaulting, till I plummeted hard into a pile of building debris. Scraps of wood bounced and cracked all around me. Stars twinkled under my eyelids. Chaos reigned for a second, and then after another, the night's serenity resumed. The stars returned to the sky and everything fell silent.

I tried to stand up, groaning and whimpering in shock. "God!" I bellowed, holding me frozen between standing and not standing. Searing pain consumed my right leg and it extended towards my feet. I sensed warm and viscous liquid leaching down my calf. But it wasn't just liquid, there was something else, something hard, something…

I squinted and adjusted my leg to the moonlight.

Wha—what's that?

As I reached out my hand towards the object, my mind enumerated things that it could be: my bone, a piece of rock, a twig. But there was iron, and there were tiny rough splinters.

"Oh, God! What the hell!" I screamed.

I took my phone and turned on its flashlight function. The tiny LED light illuminated my thigh and continued down to a plank of wood, about the length of my arm, clinging on my leg, held by three large nails. Crap! The first two nails gored my calf. The third protruded from the top of my shoe and out the bottom of my feet. Worse, the nails were as thick as a pencil.

A bucket of fear washed over my body. "Oh no, no, no, help. Help! Help!" I cried.

Silence answered. It was an area still being developed. No one lived there.

I tried to remove the plank. "Mother of—" The pain crippled me, making me yelp helplessly while taiko drummers commenced pounding my heart. They weren't pounding a drumbeat of rhythm; they were pounding a clout of fear. And with every beat, a bead of tear rolled down my cheek.

I searched for Baba's number in my phone. But Baba would—no.

Instead, I dialed 999. I was about to press the call button when my mind pictured my father talking with the paramedics and doctors with a stern and condemning face. So, I put the phone away and I decided to pull the plank out myself.

Slowly... slowly... carefully...

It moved an inch, together with a deafening scream.

I squeezed my eyes shut, bit my lip, punched the ground, bit my lip harder, squeezed my eyes harder until white spots appeared, and I punched the ground again. But no matter what I did, nothing numbed the burning pain that consumed all my senses.

My chest began to tighten from fear and chaos.

I looked around in the darkness; still, nobody was there to help. I took many deep breaths and tried to pull out the plank once more. Do it faster this time. On the count of three: one, two, three— Flesh squished wetly as it clung to the rusty nails, holding on for dear life. A wet snap followed. More warm blood gushed out of the wound, freeing a million cries of agony.

Drained of energy, I fell facedown onto the ground and tasted the bitter earth. But I remained awake to the screams of my right leg. Specks of dust wafted into the air with every lifeless breath I made.

Once I regained a minuscule amount of strength, I yanked myself up and headed to my twisted bike. Pulling the bike up, the front tire fell limp to one side. The crash had unseated the tire from the rim. I thought about repairing it, but with a strong desire to get home, I just removed the tire altogether. Though unsafe and absolutely not recommended, the bike would still be rideable that way.

Hopping onto the saddle, I saw the handlebar facing the wrong way in relation to the wheel. O c'mon! I whacked it with my palm. It did not straighten it. Never mind, the bike would still be rideable that way.

I shifted to the lowest gear and pedaled forward, leaving a trail of blood leading into the blackness of the night.

"Come on! Come on! You're close!" I whimpered to myself. The elation of speed and strength I felt just five minutes ago was gone.

\*\*\*

I never thought I'd make it back home, but I did. All the way home, with each pedal stroke, every fiber of my body throbbed together with the wailing of my right leg, demanding me to stop. There wasn't a moment when I wished that my leg would just detach and fall. To add to the evening's horror, Baba's shiny white Nissan Sunny was already parked at the garage. Thank heavens, the lights were already switched off in the living room and in their bedroom. That meant they're asleep.

I inserted my key into the door, twisted it counterclockwise twice, and KABOOM! KABOOM! It made a noise as loud as Baba's bombs! I glanced back at their bedroom window beside the door; the lights didn't turn on. Good.

I held the silver doorknob. Cold as the color itself, it sent goosebumps unfolding from my hand, racing up my arm, then into my scalp.

I twisted the knob. I hoped for the best, even if I was expecting the worst. Best would be a dark living room; worst would be Baba still awake, glowering at me. My bladder almost went haywire just thinking about that.

The door creaked open. A moistened air of jasmine and saffron greeted me. Baba's TV sat quietly at the corner, and the kitchen was glowing jet black. With a soft and lengthy trembling exhale, I released the tension held up in my lungs. I was relieved. Nobody's awake.

"Fudgie hell!" I got too complacent about my parents being already asleep that I forgot my leg was injured. When I stepped in, I placed too much pressure on my right leg that I felt some of its tendons stretch and snap. I crumpled for a few seconds, then I soldiered on.

Tick-tick-tick— Crap! Ugh! Shut up you!

I swung my bike over my shoulder so the rear wheel wouldn't ratchet aloud. I yelped. Wrong move. The load only added agony to my already suffering leg. But I had no choice. I took a shaky step. And another. And another. And another. Until my hands latched onto the toilet door, and I rested my bike on the wall beside it.

Looking back at the unwitting living room with its dark, peaceful glow, that a few hours ago was bright and charged with excitement, tiny glints on the floor, sporadically tracing towards the door, caught my attention. Moonlight from the windows revealed its color: red. Then, in an instant of a gasp, I recognized them. I checked my leg. It was drooling blood. Lots of blood.

"Oh no!" were the first words my mind tossed. *Oh-no* not because of how much blood I lost, but *oh-no* because of the blood strewn on the floor.

## PORTRAITS OF THE WIND

Without turning on the lights, I hobbled into the kitchen and tightly tied kitchen towels over my bleeding leg, one on each wound. I didn't know if the towels were clean or not; it didn't matter anyway. Then, with a big roll of paper towel, I wiped my blood trail, merely with my phone's light to guide me in the dark and cold living room.

\*\*\*

The bathroom light flickered on.

I took my helmet off and faced the mirror. A battered Luma stared back. I've got a gash on my chin that hinted on scarring. The scrapes on my arms and elbows bring to mind paint that had been sandpapered away. And my orange jersey that once sang to me was now in tattered ruins. There were holes the size of bullets all over the fabric, and lifting it exposed more deep cuts on my skin. I paused and stepped back, trying to see the bigger picture. Aside from my tattered cycling kit, the mirror revealed a body that had fallen into a box of knives. Cuts and slices and bruises, all oozing scarlet fluid, carved my entirety.

I perched on the edge of the bathtub and reached down to the reddened, warm towels. When I untied it, I clearly heard squishing and tearing flesh, although no sound really came from it at all. A soggy mess of dirt, skin, and blood covered the cloths and the three fleshy holes in my leg.

I opened the bathtub's faucet. A waterfall came roaring from the tap, pulverizing the already shattered peace inside of me. With one swift move, I slid my leg under the running water, and it felt like a thousand silver needles began pricking my wound. My hands moved barely in time to clasp my mouth and capture the escaping scream.

A stream of brown and red—earth and blood, circled down the drain.

Could I have avoided all this if I just took the first exit?

I began swaying. Nausea and lightheadedness were bludgeoning me to black-out. But I fought it. I fought it by opening the shower to rain down icy teardrops on my face.

When I had cleaned everything, I retired for the night, sapped of the vigor I once possessed an hour ago. I am defeated. Even my bed that used to embrace me without bias couldn't comfort my pain now.

With another glance on my wounded leg, now covered by three tightly wound gauze, my soul was sucked out of me. I fell asleep.

*** 

I smelled the scent of morning leaves and fresh oranges that wafted in the streets. The sound of two-stroke engines, muted whooshes of intermittent cars, and Moroccan music captured my ears. Tourists and residents came in and out of buildings whose pointy roofs touched the clouds. Guffaws and spright chatter echoed under the cloudy skies of Ifrane. The scarf around my neck flapped gently as I pedaled leisurely along the city's sloping streets.

That was the dream I desired when I slept. A comforting and pain-relieving dream. Instead, only blackness filled my sleep. Infinite darkness stretched beyond what I can see, or what my mind can imagine. There was nothing in my dream but burning heat rising from beneath my feet. The pores on my forehead shed droplets of sweat as the scorching winds grazed my face. Snakes with the eyes of pain slithered and coiled around my leg, striking it with their fangs, piercing my skin, and injecting poison that seared my veins. The heat increased, sizzling my sweat, and then…

## PORTRAITS OF THE WIND

My eyes burst open and a gush of breath escaped my mouth. Thousands of tiny angry men began thumping and thudding inside my head. I groaned, the first of a series of walrus grunts. I tried to stand but my whole body felt wrong. I was thirsty. I was light-headed. I was nauseating. I was burning. I was feverish. I was sweating. I felt like dying. And my leg, my frayed leg, it was both numb and stinging at the same time.

With the light of the breaking dawn, I removed the gauze. I was still half asleep, but when I saw what I saw, I awoke.

Green and foul pus covered the bandage, but that was just half of it. The whole lower leg turned insidiously red and black. Prominent black shiny blisters swelled around the puncture wounds. Some were even leaking rank and cloudy viscous fluid. When the malodor traveled to my nose, my stomach heaved and forced out whatever was left inside it as a vomiting projectile onto my bed. Fear began blurring my vision then.

I strained a whisper, "Ma... ma..."

That probably wasn't the best idea, I thought.

I grabbed my phone and saw it was only 4:25 a.m.

I dialed 999.

A sedate female voice on the other line said, "999, what's your emergency?"

"I... I..." Fudge! The fever was disabling me. Talking itself was physically draining, now add stuttering to that— hopelessness clawed its way up from my feet. Even my heart had begun stuttering. "I need an ambulance... p... please."

"Alright, ma'am. What's your address, please?"

"Villa 19, street 32, zone 10."

"What's the problem, ma'am?"

"I don't know. There's something going on with my leg. Please send an ambulance!" I gagged loudly as my stomach heaved again.

"Are you vomiting, ma'am? What's happening to your leg, ma'am?"

"Please! Just send an ambulance!"

"Yes ma'am, the paramedics are on the way. But if possible, please, can you stay on the line while I get some necessary information from you, so the paramedics would know best how to treat you immediately."

"Please, no sirens, no lights. Okay? I'll wait outside." My feet touched the cold tiles of the floor. They shuffled forward, inching painstakingly, towards the door.

"No, ma'am. Please don't go out. Stay where you are, the paramedics are coming to you. Can you tell me about your leg, ma'am?"

"It's... there are blisters. Big blisters." I heard a faint siren from the distance. "Please, tell them no sirens." My stomach heaved once more, and my throat burned as it gave way to the bitter bile that my stomach puked.

The siren stuttered louder.

I continued shuffling towards the door. I saw my feet do a hundred steps, but I hardly made it a meter away from the bed.

"Please... my p... my parents..." I whispered as the last of my strength left my body.

Without warning, I fell, cheeks over the warm bile on the cold floor. The last thing I saw was red and blue flashing around the walls. Then, there was a loud knock on the front door. Everything else after that became a muffled gargle of voices.

# Chapter 18: Freedom on Two Wheels

My love for cycling started in college. Yes, I had ridden bicycles when I was a lot younger, but that was it. It was no more than just playtime. When I was growing up, Baba always wanted me to become a girly-girl with tutus, Barbies, and whatnot. I never really cared for it. I actually enjoyed playing with dinosaurs more than drawing colorful rainbows. In high school, he even complained about the way I look.

"Why aren't you putting on makeup? Girls your age are already experimenting with makeup. Look at your ma! She's so beautiful with makeup on!" my dad would say.

I wanted to reply, "Why, how does she look to you without makeup on?" But of course, I didn't. I just took all the mansplaining in my gut.

Unfortunately, we're not very rich, so my dad had to accept an irresistible offer as a construction foreman in Qatar. Right after my graduation in high school, he boarded a plane en-route to the land of golden sand.

Enter the recession of 2008. Prices everywhere skyrocketed; however, salaries remained the same. My mother wasn't working then. She never had since the day I came out into the world. Baba had requested her to be a stay-at-home wife. So, both of us had to think of ways to avoid getting broke. I considered the little things such as restraining myself in buying *maqouda* every day or laying low on the shawarma, you know, little things. I also started walking to school. It was only four kilometers away anyway. And with Ifrane's yearlong sweater-weather, the city's rolling hills were a breeze to walk.

One morning on the way to school, I walked past a girl about my age. She had her bike turned upside down on the side of the road. She was doing something with the chain, which I didn't understand back then. I glanced at her, and she caught my eyes.

"Hi, sorry, hi. Could you lend me a hand? It's a challenge to fix chains on the road solo," she said. She constantly glanced at her watch, and the way she spoke like an auctioneer, it was obvious that she had to be somewhere quick.

I approached her.

"Can you push this while I fix the chain?" she pointed to the derailleur cage. "There's a spring in it that keeps tension on the chain. If there's no chain on it, it pulls itself backward," she explained.

"What happened to the ch-ch-ch—"

"The chain?" She interrupted.

Ass.

"I was grinding up the hill, then it snapped. I bought this and installed it only last night. I think I didn't lock the pin properly," she continued as she held the two ends of the chain into a portable tool. With the help of a tiny lever, she screwed the bolt that pushes the link in place. After a quick snapping sound (TACK!), the chain was whole once again. "You can let go now," she said.

I withdrew my finger from the derailleur cage, and the chain dangled in tension.

The woman flipped the bike over and hopped on.

"Thanks for your help. I'd be completely late for my class if you hadn't come along," the woman said. Then she pedaled up the crest of the road without looking back.

I looked at my grease-soiled finger, then I looked back from where I walked. A thought entered my head: The hill is not that steep. If she can bike up it, why can't I?

# PORTRAITS OF THE WIND

I wiped the grease off my finger with the bottom of my long skirt, but it didn't come off. That little grease left a lasting mark in my life.

***

"What, are you serious? Haram!" Baba yelled over the speakerphone. I can still hear the faint hammering and drilling in the background that drowned the sound of his voice.

Mama listened beside me.

I knew it was a bad idea placing an overseas call to my father and sharing my intentions of buying a bike. But Ma insisted, because, you know, money, am I right? I need extra money if I want to buy a bike.

I defended my position to Baba. "Yes! It's a good investment! I don't need to ride buses or taxis. And I can go wherever I want with minimal effort!"

"La! No! I won't allow it!"

Ma interrupted, "Hashem, why not? It's not a big deal. How much is a new bike? About a thousand dirhams? It's just a one-time investment, and she'll be using it for a long time."

"Rabiya! You're too lenient with your daughter! No is no! It's not only haram—"

I interrupted, "It's not haram! Many women here are riding a bike! Muslim or not! Some are even part of lo... part of local teams! I even met one! And if she can do it, why can't I?"

But Baba ignored me. "—it's also dangerous to ride outside with those fast cars whizzing by you!"

"Baba! Are you forgetting we're in Ifrane! Cars here are not tangled in an endless spaghetti! You're thinking about Casablanca or Marrakech! This is the Switzerland of Morocco!"

"Come on, Hashem. Don't be too stern with Luma, will you? Let your daughter have the life she wants," Ma said.

"Habibi! Why do you keep teaching your daughter to defy me?"

"I'm not teaching her—"

"She's not wearing hijab; she's not going to salah; and now you want me to allow her to go around town on a bicycle like a boy? Haram!"

"Oh, c'mon! You always say haram when you don't approve of something, even if it's not really haram!"

"It's not just me. Cycling is not very womanlike! She can lose her virginity from that!" Baba's argument was met with derision and a burst of incredulous laughter from me and Ma.

"Are you serious? But you let her ride a bike when she was a kid!" Ma said.

"That was when she was a girl! Now that she's a woman, it's not proper anymore! That's haram!"

"You know you're not making sense, right?" Ma said.

"I don't care. It's haram!"

"I don't see what's wrong. We're not even in Saudi!" I said.

"Yet Saudi laws apply to my household! Rabiya, your daughter… she's a woman now! Let her do woman things!"

The conversion of sound waves into electric signals and back to sound waves again made Baba's voice shrill and irritating.

I spoke with a suppressed scream, "Like what? Vacuum? Do dishes? Stay at home?"

"Eventually! Yes!" Baba said.

I gripped the phone tighter. My head heated up in anger, and my mouth precipitously spew words that I had no control over. "God, Baba! Don't be such a ch... ch... chauvinist! Are you just forbidding me so you could atone with your god for marrying a Christian woman?!"

Ma snatched the phone from my hand and pressed it against her ear. "Hashem, *omri*, this is enough. She's a grown girl, and she can do what she wants. Alright? Time will come when she will be deciding for herself. Rather, start it now than later. Okay? Goodbye now. We don't want to hold you up from your work." She hung up and said to me, "Why did you have to say that?"

I pursed my lips and avoided eye contact by looking at the inclined road outside our house. I knew what I said was wrong, but still wrapped in rage, I wasn't sorry for what I said.

"Luma, you know your dad. You know how religious and traditional he is—"

"Yeah, why did you marry him?"

"Because I love him. I accepted him for who he is. Listen. He's not as strict as you think he is. With how you defy him, others would have already disowned you. Besides, without him, there won't be you."

"At least you won't have a daughter who's stu... sta— oh goddamn!"

"Relax Luma. I chose this kind of life because of him. You don't have to choose the kind of life he is imposing on you. You've defied his traditions once; I'm sure you're gonna do it again."

My lips made a lopsided smile.

"Don't smile. It's not a compliment! It's just a statement of fact. All I want you to know is, whatever you decide with your life, your father is always going to oppose you if it's against what he believes. But he's gonna adjust to it, and everything's going to be alright. If the love your parents are giving you is genuine, then forgiveness is always there, and acceptance will follow, no matter how much they frown upon you. Do what you please, and I'll handle your baba." She whispered then, "And believe me, Luma, after five miscarriages, the love we have for you is as genuine and pure as the sun that gives us warmth."

A tear escaped from the corner of my eye, then Ma laid her consoling arms around me in a tight embrace.

Neither Mama nor Baba specifically mentioned that I can buy a bike, but I understood Ma's point. The very next day, I was already riding a bicycle to school. I only had to be extra stringent with my expenses for a couple of months or three, because obviously, I didn't get extra money from Baba.

***

I rode to the first hill from our house with the mountain bike that I bought from the mall. It had six gears in the back, which I had no idea how to use. The salesman who sold it to me had no clue about it either. He told me the bike should be suitable for Ifrane because it was a mountain bike. He also showed me a sticker on the bike saying *18-speed*, so it must be a fast bike. In all its essence, the bike was a mall bike. A "mall bike" is a derogatory term used for cheap pretentious bikes.

As I got to the foot of the first hill, the pedaling became progressively tough. Gravity kept working its magic to pull the bike back downhill and slow me down. So, I stood up and started stomping on the pedals. The shifters called to me, but I never listened to them. I never knew who they were, that they were supposed to be my friend. Halfway through the hill, my legs hardened to stone, and my chest thumped violently. I couldn't push the pedals any longer, no matter how much power I drive it down with. My lungs screamed. My vision blurred and darkened, turning the sunny day into a hot, sweaty night.

As soon as I stepped off my bike, I puked. Then with whatever strength I had left, I shuffled to a nearby tree and rested underneath the cool canopy.

The sudden effort I gave in climbing the hill without prior training was causing me to faint, and I fought hard against the urge of my body to pass out. I breathed deeply and exhaled tersely, quickly, swiftly, in a bid to race against my collapsing consciousness. Ten minutes later, my effort to sit under a tree paid off. Everything came back in focus, and everything was restored. My breathing returned to normal, and blood recirculated inside my brain.

That didn't matter, though, 'cos I walked the rest of the 3.8 kilometers to school, and my bike walked beside me. When I got to class, I was sweaty and reeking sour of puke.

On the way back home, it was different. The sun started to hide its face behind the horizon, and it got darker and colder— well, that was the only difference. I still walked. And the bike walked with me.

As soon as I reached home, I started doing research about biking uphills. The first website I opened said I should use my gears. It said:

> *Smaller chainring plus bigger cog helps you go up hills; that's called low gear. Bigger chainring plus smaller cog enables you to go faster on the flats and downhills; that's called high gear.*

I stopped and reread the whole paragraph again.
Okay...
I studied my bike, all those levers, and gears, and everything.
Oh...

I was enlightened.

The website I visited was a trove of information about cycling. I also learned about proper seat height to help my leg push the pedals more efficiently. Who would have known there was such a thing? More importantly, I learned about proper bike sizing. Yes, the seat height is adjustable, but that's just one aspect. What's important is having the right frame size for my height and reach.

After a quick calculation, I found out that based on the lengths of my inseam, trunk, arm, thigh, suprasternal notch, and overall height, my bike should have the following measurements:

Bike size: small with a top tube length of 520-530 mm

Stem: based on the top tube, between 80-90 mm

Saddle height: 67 cm

Ideal weight: between 49 to 57 kg

Yes, there is also an ideal weight if I want to become a professional cyclist.

Armed with this information, I pulled out my mother's tape measure and started measuring the mall bike. And then...

Well, there you have the first reason why you should never buy a bike from a department store if you want to be a serious cyclist. All the measurements were off, aside from the obvious fact that it was a cheap, cheap bike. After tinkering with my bike, a bug called "upgradiditis" got into my bloodstream. (Upgrade-di-ditis, get it? All cyclists have that.) What's that, you ask? Oh, just a simple illness that causes us to buy more stuff for our cycling addiction.

The following morning, equipped with new knowledge and an adjusted saddle height, I set off the front door with confidence. As soon as I got to the foot of the first climb, I engaged the friction shifters to a lower gear. The pedaling loosened up. What was once like scooping frozen ice cream became stirring a milkshake. My legs still burned, and my lungs again gasped for air, but they didn't try to make me faint. Plus, the euphoria I got from going uphill numbed all the pain. I was actually passing people!

When I summited, looking back down gave me a sense of a high (pun intended). Pure ecstasy. And this was just the first hill. More hills swelled before the school, which means more of euphoria and ecstasy to come.

After the teeth-gritting climb, the bone-shivering, adrenaline-inducing downhill run arrived. The bike's knobby tires shrieked while chomping the asphalt at seventy kilometers per hour. Tapping the brake levers made the brakes squeal like an angle grinder as two rubber pads press against the aluminum rims. In the beginning, the thought of going downhill at speed scared me. But when I learned to let go of the brakes, OMG! I banked right; I banked left; I zoomed forward into the tunnel of speed. The velocity seeped into my veins, giving me another dose of ecstasy over the ecstasy from climbing. Ecstasy squared. If this is the stuff that gets pumped out from a falcon's heart, then I am one of them now, gliding over the chergui winds.

When I was a kid, bicycles were just for fun. It wasn't about speed nor strength. It was simply about playing and laughing and feeling the wind brush against your face. But when I rode to my university, the meaning of bicycles wholly changed. Sure, I used it for transport. It made life more animated, yeah, sure. But on top of that, the hills of Ifrane woke something inside of me. That something (I didn't know what) transformed me to become more competitive and more passionate about this sport. Perhaps, it was the pleasure of the pain.

Every day became a new challenge. Every day, I raced against the Luma from yesterday to climb the hills faster. Cycling became my drug, and true to the term, like a certified crack addict, I searched for a more potent high.

First, I got a buzz out of the hills en-route to school. Then I savored the hills at the back of our house. Weeks later, I found myself touring around the whole province of Ifrane, riding up and down its undulating hills and mountains.

Gradually, my mountain bike lost its capacity to give me highs. That's when I turned my attention to the road bike, or more commonly known as a race bike, or a racer. It has bars that bend inwards into an inverted *C*, so the rider has three positions: one for resting, one for climbing, and one for bowing from the wind. It has ten gears in the back which lets you choose the best cadence for the climb. It has thin 23–25-millimeter tires that minimize road friction. Overall, the road bike has a narrow front profile to help you slice through the wind.

The road bike was my next hit. It was my new heroin. But, of course, like everything in the world, there was a catch. Its price-tag: Two-thousand United States dollars.

Oh, hell no… (oh, hell yes!)

I dedicated ninety percent of my monthly allowance to save for it. That meant I really had to obey my one-shawarma-rule. I kept the seed money in a jar and regularly watered it with my monthly allowance until it got filled to the brim.

A year and a half later, I acquired my heroin, my yellow roadie, the Giant Liv. The full cycling gear: tight jerseys and padded shorts, gloves, helmet, and clipless shoes followed the next day.

Riding a racer did satisfy my urge for a while. After six months, I was already blowing past other cyclists in my route, including that woman whose chain I helped fix. I got hungry for speed. I hunted for local races, joined them, and pounced on the trophy. Soon, regional competitions weren't a high enough. I needed more, more pain, more suffering, more wind, more hills, and at the top of the mountain, more ecstasy. I needed more of those agonizing yet pleasurable concoctions to inject into my senses.

I switched my attention to national races, where I had the chance to be discovered and become a pro. But by the time I had been training for the big races, I graduated from college, and... well, you already know what happened next.

Luggage. Bike box. Plane ticket. Passport. Zing! Land in Qatar. Become a dreary worker whose hopes and dreams are caged in a box tucked away from reality.

Baba knew about my dream of being a pro cyclist. He knew it, and he did not support it. It was haram. It was against his will. So, if I want to live the dream, I must work hard, train hard for myself, and hope that someday I will catch a break. Working in Qatar was just a temporary setback, or so I thought.

If only I had the resources to exclusively focus on training since college, I probably would have already been drafted by a team somewhere.

# Chapter 19:
# It Only Felt like Minutes Ago

I sprinted, stomped on the pedals, gritted my teeth till I crossed the finish line in a photo finish. Barely two millimeters and less than a hundredth of a second separated me from my opponent.

I stood on a podium, accepting my trophy. Apart from that, they awarded me the coveted Rainbow Jersey, and I wore it with pride. It is a white jersey with a band of Olympic colors (blue, yellow, black, green, and red) printed across the chest. That is the jersey given to new world champions.

Confetti rained down from the sky, and flashbulbs blinded me. The mob cheered as the announcer said my name, "Luma El-Guerrouj! The new women's road race world champion!"

My hands rose triumphantly and waved to the ecstatic sea of faces in front of me. My ears captured their exultant screams.

A camera flashed. Beep! I saw Ma's face, teary with joy. Beep! The confetti cannon erupted with a plume of glittering dust. Beep! A high-speed crash. Beep! Dark. Beep! Moonlight. Beep! Blood. Beep! My legs. It hurts! Beep! Sirens. Beep! My ma's harrowing cry: "Luma!" Beep! A calm voice: "she's going to be alright." Beep! Wheels squeaking. Beep! Beep! Beep! Beep!

My eyes flickered open, and a burning white light struck my pupils with lightning precision. After a few more bats of my eye, my iris woke up from its slumber and adjusted to the blinding fluorescent light. The smell of bleach and disinfectant tickled my nostrils, and the putrid chlorine-like smell of iodine drove me to cough and gag.

Beep! My head strained to face the right where the sound of the beeping was originating. I saw a blob of colors: yellow, black, blue,

# PORTRAITS OF THE WIND

red, and green. I stared at them for a while, long enough to recognize some green digital numbers. There was another dry beep. Beep! I recognized what I was staring at: a vital signs monitor. A hundred beats per minute, it read. Impossible! My resting heart rate should be fifty beats a minute, especially when lying down.

I tried to sit up. Something tugged and pinched in my arm. An IV tube.

The clear silicone tubing led to a transparent bag hanging above the vital signs monitor. I squinted as I tried to read the name on the bag: Levofloxacin. What the hell is that? Then it dawned on me. I'm in a hospital! It took me that long to figure it out. I must have been heavily drugged. Then everything came rushing back: the speed, the wind, the crash, the wound, the blisters.

The blisters!

My body sprang up, and my eyes abruptly locked on to the blanket covering my legs.

I paused.

I didn't know for how long, but long enough for horrible questions to arise. I can see my left leg rising like a mountain draped under the hospital's weighty wool blanket. Over my right leg, there were no mountains; it was... flat. Flat as a quiet ocean. There must a mistake or something. With a swift motion, I lifted the blanket up and away. Then there, looking back at me was...

Nothing.

Pulling the blanket backward more, it exposed the dreaded sight of dreams being crushed. Oval-shaped and covered with bandage, spotted with brown stains, my thigh wagged at me. My thigh. Only my thigh. There was no leg attached to it, only a stump. I felt my soul being sucked out from my anus. A tsunami of emotions washed over me. Fear, anxiety, panic, alarm, confusion, dread, horror, came crashing down my chest and drowned my lungs. My leg!

I screamed so loud that my own ears stung. I wanted to stand. I wanted to run and flee the horrible sight, but how? How?

Mama and Baba rushed to the room, and like a lost child, crying and sobbing, I stretched my arms towards my mother. She sat beside me and gave me the tightest hug I had ever felt.

Baba went back out of the room without touching me.

"W… wa… what's going on?" I bawled.

Ma never let go of her tight embrace. As tears rolled down my cheeks, Ma's hug became tighter. I knew it was supposed to be comforting; however, only the sour sensation of fear embosomed me.

"It's gonna be okay," she whispered.

Baba came back with a man in a lab coat. The doctor looked young despite his graying hair. I got embarrassed for being hysterical, but judging by the flat emotion on his face, it had to be an everyday sight. He looked at me and his shoulders broadened with a deep sigh. I knew that sigh. That's the sigh of *here we go again*.

The doctor said to Baba, "Maybe I should come back later."

My dad nodded.

"P… please! No! Why?" I screamed with incredulous fragility.

My dad nodded again to the doctor signaling him to leave, and the latter did without hesitation.

"Shh, it's okay, it's okay," Ma said, rubbing my back.

"It's not! It's not! It's not okay! I'm missing a leg! Why? What about— oh god!" The thoughts of bicycles, races, world championships, now faded into obscurity. I sobbed once more, softer this time, while I burrowed my head on my mother's shoulder. She stroked my hair like she used to back when I was trying to fall asleep as a child.

## PORTRAITS OF THE WIND

I struggled to speak. Only a desperate whisper came out. "Why? Why did you c... c... why did you cut my leg?"

"You should rest more—" Baba said.

"No!" I lifted my head and faced my father. "I want to know now. Call the doctor back! Please."

"Are you sure you want to do this now?" he stolidly asked.

I nodded dimly. I still wept, but it was subdued now. There was no sound, only tears, and every sob came as a crashing wave, eroding the breakwaters of my heart.

I understood then, people who cry silently are those who are wrecked deeper by anguish and grief. Infinite heartaches rain down on them and sink them in a flood of bitterness and despair. And with strengthless arms, they drown in their own misery. They vanish into the shadows without a squeak.

The doctor came back and sat on one of the chairs for visitors. The sight of him sitting down tells me he brought grave news despite his emotions being as eloquent as a plank of wood.

He cleared his throat and spoke, "First of all, what happened?"

My mind wandered back to before the accident. Everything still felt like only minutes ago. I could still feel the gusts of wind over my face as my legs pushed hard on the pedals.

I looked to Ma, to the doctor, and then to Baba. Then I looked down with a hushed terror over what's left of my destitute body.

Ma placed her arm around my shoulders. She didn't say anything, but her arms spoke to me, saying, "It's okay, you can tell us the truth."

Still looking down, staring at the weaves of the hospital blanket, I spoke, explained, stuttered, and then hesitated to continue. Any moment, my dad's angry sharp voice could erupt and kill the air, but he remained dormant. I took a deep breath and kept looking down, avoiding my baba's stabbing eyes. With a shaky voice, I continued, "It was dark. I hit something and I... I crashed into a pile of wood. Next thing I know, there is a wooden plank with nails sticking to my leg."

"Oh my god," Ma said, horrified. Her warm arm slid away, sending growing chills on my shoulders.

"Why did you disobey your dad?" Ma continued.

I turned to my mother but saw a total stranger. Why is she suddenly questioning me now about my defiance from Baba? She had been on my side ever since, and now, suddenly, out of nowhere? Why?

"Why didn't you call us sooner?" she followed through.

I shook my head. "Because Baba..." I glanced at him. He had no anger in his face, nor grief, nor sadness, nor pity, nor dismay. His face conveyed the blankness of a white sheet of paper. He was stolid. He only stared back at me, patiently waiting for me to continue.

"I didn't want to—" I started sobbing once more. I longed for Ma's arm to wrap around me again, but she remained miles away, and my shoulders remained barren and cold.

Baba looked away, still without emotions.

The doctor caught Baba's side glance and took it as a signal to continue. "So, what happened was, because of infection, you developed gangrene. Gangrene is when the tissue dies... your flesh. Now gangrene has different types. What you developed was gas gangrene. To explain in the simplest term, your wound was infected with a certain bacteria, which is normally found in the soil, that releases toxins causing tissue death and generates gas at the same time. This was the foul smell and the blistering. Your test results also showed a low blood count. I'm assuming that's because of the puncture. You've lost quite an amount of blood, and this may have affected your body's ability to fend off the infection."

"How long was I out?"

"A day," the doctor replied dryly.

"But why did it happen so fast?" Ma asked.

"Commonly, symptoms begin to show anytime between six to forty-eight hours. If not treated immediately, it will develop into, well, what happened to your leg."

Ma turned to me and cried with condemnation, "Why? Why?"

What did she mean why? Again, Ma doesn't usually do that. In fact, she had never given me that level of condemning tone.

"Now, now. Please. Now is not the time for blaming anyone. It happened, though unfortunate, it already happened. What's important is we have stopped the spread of the infection, and you're safe," the doctor said.

"Couldn't you have saved my leg?" I asked.

"In your case, I'm afraid amputation was the best course. Your muscle tissue suffered severe necrosis. Even if we have killed all the infections, the necrosis would continue to spread unless we cut it off. Now, we're administering a dose of broad-spectrum antibiotics to kill any remaining bacteria."

"So, what's next? How long does she have to stay here?" Baba asked.

"We'll continue observing her for another week or two. If all is stable, you can go home. Then you can start the therapy once your wound is completely healed. Usually, that's anywhere between one to two months."

"Thanks, doc." Baba stood up and shook the doctor's hand.

The doctor regarded me with solace. "Don't worry, people do adjust quickly to this. There are some support groups available if that would help you feel better," he said, and left.

Only a blank stare was given back. How could this doctor possibly say something patronizing? Doesn't he know how important my legs are? Now what? One leg! One useless leg! I'm ruined! I... I haven't even reached my peak! Now I'm a pathetic amputee!

"Why? Why? Why?" My mother started crying hysterically. "Why did you have to disobey your father? Why didn't you listen? Now you're... you're—"

She looked at me in never a way she had before. Prior to this, she only regarded me with encouragement and fragility. But there she stood now with a fierce glowering gaze. Her voice grew ragged and sharp, puncturing me like the three huge nails once more.

"Your father was right! You shouldn't have picked up cycling in the first place! I was wrong! This is my fault! I enabled you! Hashem, I'm sorry. I'm so sorry, this is my fault! This... this... our daughter... this is my fault! I encouraged her to disobey you."

"Ma!" I shouted in pitiful protest. I shouted the one word that bore the weight of all those things I wanted but couldn't say: *You're my mother! You should be empathizing with me right now! You should be making me feel better! Where was that shoulder I was crying on minutes ago? Shut up! Shut up! Shut up! You're making me feel worse! Shut up!*

"Rabiya, enough." Baba crashed into my mother for a tight embrace to comfort her alarm.

"It's not right! It's not right!" Ma continued. She's now really getting into my nerves.

"Quiet now. It's not the time to start blaming," Baba continued in his stoic manner.

"But Hashem! Our daughter! I raised her! I nurtured her. I took care of her like a fragile glass. I never let any scratch on her when she was young! She was our perfect baby! My baby! I should have known cycling is so dangerous." To me, "I saw the races you watched. I saw the horrible crashes, the pileups. I got scared, but it also seemed like an impossibility since you were so happy!" To Baba, "I should have known better. I should have listened to you! Now she's going to be miserable. She's dismembered!" To me, "Why didn't you listen?! Why did you have to be so stubborn?!"

It's incredible how someone you trust can unexpectedly turn on you on a dime. She hugged me tightly just a few moments ago, giving me comfort, and bracing me courage, then, like a prowling jaguar in the dead of night, she jumped out of nowhere and buried her razor-sharp teeth into my jugular. She wasn't anymore the mother I knew who raised me. Who is this woman? What is she doing here? Where did this monster come from?

I twisted to the panels behind my head. There was a yellow button to call for a nurse, and there was a red button in case of emergencies. Guess which button I pressed.

An alarm blared outside our room. I could hear the commotion of nurses scattering and scampering there. I listened to their alarmed yet controlled voices: "Room 411, room 411." The door in my room swung open. The sound of the alarm shrieked. It was soft yet loud enough to stun the hysteric woman in my room. Then, there at the door stood two nurses engulfed in confusion. They brought with them a crash cart with a defibrillator and other items used to revive a crashing patient. But they saw no crashing patient, they stared at a patient who was keenly grinning back at them.

"I want to rest. I want to be alone. P… please send them out," I calmly said.

The bewildered nurses turned to my equally bewildered parents.

"Luma!" Ma yelled in protest.

Before another word was spoken, the older of the two nurses went to the panel on my headboard and stopped the alarm. "Please, our patient needs to rest. Please come back another time," the nurse said to Ma.

That nurse instantly became my hero.

"We're her parents!" Mama yelled unrestrainedly.

"Ma'am, please keep your voice down. We're in a hospital."

"I don't care! You can't push us away!"

"It's the patient's wish, ma'am. If you don't leave, we'll be forced to call security on you."

"Come on, Rabiya," Baba said, pulling Ma gently by the arms, "Come along now."

Mama gave me a final pathetic woeful glance.

Baba, on the other hand, briefly gripped my remaining leg. It felt like a hug. In that moment, our eyes briefly met before he disappeared into the long hospital corridor. But his eyes said nothing. Or maybe it was nothing because I couldn't see beyond his gaze since my vision was dimmed by brittle tears.

After they left, peace descended upon the room. But was it peace?

The air conditioner's hum became more prominent in the newfangled silence, yet it wasn't silence. There was peace, but it wasn't peace. It was an unnerving stillness, like the calm before the storm. With a blink of an eye, my whole life flashed before me: my dreams, my hopes, the wonders of the unwitting yesterdays. I saw the finality of it all at the bloody stump where my right leg was supposed to be.

Lying back down, despair rose, oozing from the blackness of the night, into the cracks and gaps and every recess of the room. It ascended gradually, steadily. Then I felt, or hallucinated, a cold liquid touch my arms, my leg, and my back. It lifted me up from my bed and floated me lifelessly towards the ceiling. Then from the depths of this dark sea, thousands of hands wriggled their way up and grabbed hold of my desolate body. With one easy tug, I sank into the darkness of despair, to the depths where not even light can reach. I drowned helplessly without a fight. My life was over.

I am finished.

Now I want to sleep for a thousand evenings. For it is in sleep that I experience triumph and live the realities I seek. That's where I have control over my life; I have the ability to restart. Yet when I wake, the ghosts of departed dreams begin to chase me around my prison called life. They are unrelenting and unyielding, a breathing nightmare under the morning sun.

# Chapter 20:
# Life Sucks

Seriously, life sucks. I wish there were a fast-forward button in life so I could skip to the good part. Or maybe a rewind button so I could go back in time and change things. Crapitty-crap-crap assholes!

# Chapter 21:
# Use It or Lose It

Use it or lose it. That's the mantra of sports training. A day, two days, three days; this is how much rest is recommended for athletes. During this period, the body repairs the muscles damaged by training, and then it adapts to the new workload. But rest for too long, your training reverses. Often times, you lose fitness faster than you gain it.

After seven days, the amount that the heart can pump blood is significantly reduced, usually by about twelve percent. So, it must work slightly harder to maintain the same workload you could easily manage before.

After two weeks, your maximum oxygen intake or VO2max declines by twenty percent, which will ensure you pant readily and accumulate lactate faster.

After three months, the heart's walls lose their muscular thickness, and you become progressively weaker.

Of course, I had no way to test all these theories given that I only have one flipping leg. It was only through my fitness app that I knew I had been losing strength. The app showed that my cumulative training load had dropped to nil during my three and a half months of inactivity.

"Ma'am," a student called, his voice rising towards uncertainty.

I glanced up from my smartphone and nodded to the edgy student whose arm was raised half-mast.

"Why are we watching 'A Beautiful Mind?'" he asked.

My swaying stump stopped. He disturbed me. Not good, little boy. Not good. "Nash is a math g-g-g-g-g-g… math g-g-g-g…

genius!" I can see from my students' physical responses that they were all having a harder time understanding my worsening stutter.

My stutter got worse at home and at work, and I didn't know why. It just happened. It just happened, like what happened to my leg. Life enjoys smiting you with its arbitrary injustice. There is no explanation for everything. Sometimes things happen "just because." That's how I think my stutter got worse. And the worse my stutter got, the greater my urge not to speak anymore. And since I still must teach, I resorted to film showing.

I screened all kinds of films: cartoons, dramas, documentaries, and anything that had maths in them. Hell, "Baby Einstein" was on my list too if I ever exhaust all the good films.

"Yeah, but how is it related to trigonometry?" the student followed up.

The class slowly turned their attention from the TV towards me one by one, like a domino toppling the next. All of them hung waiting for me to say something academic.

My ears heated up, red with annoyance, and in that quick instant, my mouth spurred the words that were only supposed to be screaming in my head: "Shut up, will you! Just watch the goddamn film, ungrateful sod!" No stutter. Oops. I froze, but unapologetic, and with a glowering stare.

The poor student sunk in his chair, humiliated. I might have been a little too harsh, sure, but I didn't care, because afterward, an envelope of suspense descended upon the class that killed any attempt to speak their minds. I love it.

Halfway through the film, a loud knock broke the wholesome tension I crafted with my glare. The door opened without me saying anything. There could only be one person who had that power in the whole school and... not now! Not again!

## PORTRAITS OF THE WIND

The principal's face peeked through the door, then her low voice stabbed the air of tension. "Luma, can I see you in my office?" She spoke cautiously with a little smile as if she were talking to someone very fragile.

Heat stained my cheeks at the sound of her faux-compassionate tone. I'm not judging her. Well, maybe I am. Because every time someone looks at me or speaks to me like I'm about to break, it only shows a blatant attempt to be politically correct. Dickheads. Don't baby-talk me. I'm a grown-ass woman.

I reattached my prosthetic leg to my stump (I usually take them off whenever I sit for long periods to let the muscles around my right thigh relax and take a breather). After tightening the strap around my thigh, I stood up and wobbled, almost losing balance. I don't think I will ever get used to this new leg. And I will never get used to the sorry eyes that followed me while I limped towards the door.

\*\*\*

Mrs. Wellbrock and I walked alongside each other through the long empty corridor. As always, I would delay a few steps to let her advance and take the lead. But whenever I slowed down, she also slowed to match my pace with her hands stiffly clasped together. I don't know if this was a conscious or an unconscious effort from her, but it broadcasts her readiness to catch me. Ugh! Argh! Gah! I'm not a toddler!

Once more, the gut-wrenching, devil's breath, bubblegum scent of Mrs. Wellbrock's office stuck up my nostrils. I belched. I gagged. My stomach heaved, and my throat spasmed as soon as I stepped through the doorway. Maybe because the smell reminded me of a chipper life of innocence or something similar. Meh. Who cares? I just hate it, and it keeps making me gaaaaag.

"Are you okay?" asked Wellbrock as we sat.

I pointed to the humidifier and scrunched my face.

She pressed the off switch and said, "It might be hormonal change because you know…" She pointed to my leg.

My face contorted to perform a sincere smile. Every line, wrinkles, creases, and muscles of my face twitched. It didn't want to smile; it wanted to frown and scoff and… ugh!

"How are you feeling?" she asked.

"I'm f-f-f-f-f-f—" darn it! "Fine!"

A pause visited us for a time. Wellbrock steadily kept her eyes on me, studying me, examining the movement of my eyes as it danced in and out of her line of sight.

"Did you hear," she began, "Latha already applied a visa for her son. So, when he graduates—" She stopped short upon seeing me unintentionally roll my eyes.

Again, like in the classroom, I thought I was only doing it inside my head. I never knew some of my internal monologues were already spurting out the spout. Wellbrock then collected some papers on her desk and stacked it. I guess to unconsciously "collect" herself too, after getting steamrolled by the eye-roll.

"Alright," she said. "Listen, I received some worrying concerns from the students. They say that since you returned, you never taught. All you do is show movies. And believe me, I knew it was something to worry about because the complaints came from the students themselves! Them who don't like lectures!" She chuckled dimly. I didn't. "Are you sure you're ready to teach again?"

"Of course!" I nodded, turned my head to the side, and avoided eye contact.

"Why aren't you teaching then?"

I cocked my head back towards Wellbrock. "Yes, I am!"

"Then why are you just showing films for the past four weeks? What will they learn from that? Like now, for example," Wellbrock stretched a hand towards the direction of my classroom, "what's that? 'A Beautiful Mind?' That's about schizophrenia! What is that got to do with mathematics and trigonometry?"

"Th... they c... they c... could..." oh hell! Goddammit, freakin' assholes! Lay off the stutter, you dimwitted oaf! Meanwhile, the principal kept looking at me expectantly. Darn dang dammit! "They could learn from his passion for math," I splurged.

"Nonsense! Why aren't you teaching? I don't see the fire in you anymore. All you do is brood behind your desk."

Yeah. Whatever. Since my leg got excised, I have been living in criticize-ville over at harangue-nation where the citizens kept telling me I'm no good. Worse, all roads there only lead to a cul-de-sac. There is no way out. And my stutter, ugh, that's the annoying neighbor. It seems I will be in it for the long haul. For life! Oooh, this is getting old so fast. Darn it!

Wellbrock continued to talk, and I tried to mute the words entering my ears by focusing on the wall behind her.

"Do you remember your work interview?" she said, "The first time we met. I asked you why you wanted to teach. And you said you wanted to challenge yourself to overcome your stutter. That is so brave! The kind of example you are going to be! But right now, I'm not seeing the same brave woman who sat before me. Look, I know something terrible happened to you, and obviously, it's making you depressed—"

My head sprung back to her involuntarily, my stare sharp and true. "I'm not depressed!" I shouted. No stutter. "I'm angry!"

"I apologize. But there, you see my point. You visibly have issues. And for the benefit of the students and for your sake, I don't think you should be working at this moment. You should be doing something else, like maybe recovering."

Irritation took hold of the better of me. "But, keep me busy, right?! That's what everybody tells me. Mental health basics! I need to keep myself occupied to quickly recover!"

"That's true. I give you that. However, the school, the classroom is the wrong place to do that."

"What do you suggest? Go out biking?!" my shrill voice bounced around her office.

"No. Luma, please quiet down. I just wanted to tell you that you need help—professional help for you to cope with your depression."

I jolted up; the chair slid backward. My voice came out jarring and piercing, "I'm not depressed! Why do you people think that?! Do you think I look like someone who wants to cut herself more after my whole leg was cut? I'm not someone who's pining, moping, and dragging her body across the floor! What makes you think I'm depressed? Do you think that helps me?"

I began to pace and wobble around.

Wellbrock stood up as well. Her arms extended cautiously towards me. "Okay, okay. Take it easy," she said in a whisper-like tenor.

"God! Why don't you people look at me like a normal person?!" I said, pacing back and forth faster and flailing my hands to the rhythm of my speech. "Why do you have to treat me differently? I saw the way you held your hands in attention! Ready to catch me if I fall! Why? Because it makes you feel better that you can help?!"

"Luma, calm down. Forgive me. I wasn't thinking. Fine, you're not depressed. Can we sit?"

## PORTRAITS OF THE WIND

I dropped to the chair and gripped the armrest with hulk-like power. In, out, in, out; my lungs rushed to collect my breath.

Wellbrock studied me before proceeding to articulate her next words carefully. "Okay, listen, the board of trustees and I decided… it wasn't an easy decision, but we know it's for your own good… we decided to give you an indefinite sabbatical. You know, for you to be able to find your footing," she coughed awkwardly, "for you to be better again. So you can get help… not for depression… but to help you put a smile on your face."

She lingered to let the words sink in. She studied me, probably wondering how I was taking the news, but she only received an angry glare from me. "Um…" She awkwardly blinked and continued, "I also know that you need this job as much as anyone, so, because we want to help, you will still be paid half your salary for up to six months during your absence. Then when you're better, we'll welcome you back with open arms." She smiled cautiously, a little self-conscious, lips quavering minutely.

"Is that why you called me here? Why didn't you start with that in the first place! Why do people always have to talk too much? Be direct to the point!"

"Luma, please, this is for your own benefit. You need to get better."

I sighed. "Again, I'm not depressed. I'm angry. At the world. At life." I sighed again, hoping sighing will help me vent myself (it doesn't).

"You can come back tomorrow to say goodbye to your students, especially the seniors. Tomorrow will be the last time you'll see them, unless you get better quickly," Wellbrock said.

"I'm fine. I don't need the sab… the sab… I don't need the break."

"Luma…" Wellbrock paused for dramatic tension, "it's not a request." Darn it!

# JANIX PACLE

\*\*\*

No work and no play makes Luma a dull girl. This missing leg had me stuck within long, monotonous, and unstructured days that stretched into weeks, and probably more. I have been in the house for... however long, and I couldn't picture myself doing anything. I imagined walking in the park to kill time, but really? A walk in the park with a missing leg? How was that supposed to help me get better? I did try cleaning the house to distract me. But how many times can you do that before getting bored? Apparently, two times were enough. The problem is, you do it because you want to forget, and the more you try to forget, the more you remember.

Sometimes I just wanted to sulk like that girl who stared out the window for three months after her ass got dumped by a glittery vampire. But, no! I'm not gonna do that, because I'm not depressed! I'm angry! And I'm more upset when I see that yellow bike hanging on my wall. I should sell that.

"Yes!" I shouted, "I should sell it. Maybe that will help me feel better. Yes!"

I took the bike down from the wall hanger and examined it. Aside from some scratches on the paint, the twisted handlebar, the wobbly front wheel, the scuffed derailleurs, and the bent drop-out hanger, it was still in a rather good— Okay, so maybe not so good condition. Still, if I fix everything, I would be able to sell it at a good price.

I hadn't touched the bike since that ill-fated moment months ago. I forgot how I would always get giddy whenever I carry the bike with one hand despite having owned it for years. Holding it now brought back memories of riding up and down the hills of Ifrane, and memories of me sprinting and winning races, to the exultant roar of gathered crowds.

## PORTRAITS OF THE WIND

The nostalgia gripped my throat into a chokehold, and the hairs on my arms stood up like dying grass revived by the rain. "Stop it!" I wriggled my shoulders, shrugging all the feelings off. I have no time for stupid memories.

I took a dishwashing soap and a sponge and started cleaning the bike on the bathtub. I first pointed the shower head towards the frame to rinse off all the dirt that was still stuck in its corners. Then I started scrubbing. Not too hard though, otherwise, I risk damaging the paint job. With each gentle yet forceful wipe of the soapy sponge, it revealed the bright yellow paint that once made me fall in love with this bike. A final hosing down restored the bike to its shining glory.

At the floor of the tub, brown dirt streamed down sinuously towards the drain, where it circled for a moment before descending into the blackness. The sight looked familiar, horribly familiar. I took a leaden breath. Just then, three invisible rusted nails stabbed my chest repeatedly. I took another deep breath and visualized something else. Anything. But grief and loss had latched on to me. Ugh! Fine. Screw it! Come at me, motherfingers.

Scores of doctors and scientists have dissected and studied the heart. They've seen all its chambers; how it pumps blood through its arteries. Hell, they even know how to bypass the heart, or replace it with a mechanical one. Yet, with all the scientific advances involving the heart, they still couldn't tell where heartaches are stored. I'm willing to pay billions even if it only cost a million to surgically remove heartaches. Yeah, right. I don't even have thousands. I'm a "nillionaire."

Once I had repaired all that needs to be repaired, I looked at my bike once more and examined it deeply: its shiny curves, its narrow chain, and its super-thin cables that pulled the brakes at 80 km/h downhill. It used to be a part of me. Now it simply stood in front of me, no different than a regular bike. Then I saw the front wheel, the wiggly wobbly untrue wheel.

Oh, man...

\*\*\*

I reached the bike shop using the newly opened metro.

Getting around now seemed like a daunting task. Take that morning for example. I hailed a taxi in front of our house, opened the door, got my ass in first, and I pivoted into place, pulling my prosthetic leg over the door's edge. Turning to face the driver, I saw his eyes were affixed to my feet where a portion of the titanium pylon peered out in between the shoe and the bottom of my pants. He then looked at me, then looked at the pylon again. What's the matter, curry man? Haven't seen legs of steel before? He looked at me again with an unpaintable face. Oh, for heaven's sake. Ugh! I got out of the car and slammed the door.

Why do people stare? What are they thinking? Don't they know that their gazes methodically poke more holes into someone's already bullet-ridden confidence? Especially kids walking or playing on the side of the street, their innocent curiosity sprinkles salt into the wounds that time couldn't heal.

At least in the metro, people are busy, people are clamoring. When they glance at my gait, it stops there. It's just a glance. No judgment. It doesn't matter if I had to hobble-wobble all the way from my house towards the station. I'll choose that a hundred times over prying eyes. A-holes.

Inside Cycle City, everything remained the same as before, as if I hadn't lost a leg. Upon entering, the scent of new tires took shelter inside my nostrils, and the sight of new bikes on the display racks... well, they did nothing. I expected some of these bikes to call me by my name, hailing me to marvel at their glory, like they used to. This time though, they just stared at me like the inanimate object as they are. There was no magic dust floating. There was no awestruck wonder amazement at each fancy component. It merely is a tight corridor that I must limp through and be careful not to topple any of the bikes on display. I didn't stop. I hobbled straight away to the workshop.

There, Wally was tinkering over someone else's bike. "Luma! Long-time no sees!" His eyes shifted to my limping leg. "You got accident?"

I chuckled and nodded. I didn't say anything, I just gave him the front wheel.

He examined it with a brief glance. "Is it because of the seatpost?"

Oh yeah, I forgot all about the seatpost. I assumed if ever I would get into an accident, it would be due to the seatpost breaking. But life is as random as chaos itself. What you expect is not always what you'll get.

"No, it's not the seatp... seatpost," I said.

"Ah, but you okay? You are limping, no?"

I nodded rapidly. "How long to finish that?"

Wally motioned to his full workshop, "I have too much customers today. Maybe tomorrow. I call you if it's finish."

I agreed.

Wally bid me farewell, pivoted, and with my wheel, he limped away, like me. I watched him for a few steps, then I held my breath.

"Wally?" I said.

He turned around and waited while I formulated my words carefully.

"How did you cope with your accident? Do you hate retirement?" I asked.

"Why you ask?"

"I just wanted to know. Because you're a pro. Or was a pro."

"Of course. I think anyone who is forced to retire is not happy. But it don't matter now. Retirement bring me closer to my wife and kids. I'm happy. You know, Greg LeMond was forced to retire also. Maybe you should ask him." He let out a chuckle.

"But LeMond was already a World Tour pro. You were still in the nationals. You could still have graduated to world-class if it weren't for that crash."

"It's all behind me now. It's past. I don't think of it. If I keep thinking of it, I think I will be depress. You're right. I can be world-class. Maybe. I'll never know. Life is not fair. Some are born to succeed, while others are born to watch others succeed. It's okay. I'm happy now."

"But... what did you do to be happy?"

"Nothing. I just move on. Forget the past, look at tomorrow," Wally said with a tight smile. "I need to work now. I have many work to do." Then he disappeared behind the workshop's back door together with my mangled wheel. "I call you when it's done, okay? Maybe tonight, maybe tomorrow!" he said aloud.

*"Some are born to succeed, while others are born to watch others succeed."*

I shriveled as Wally's words echoed in my head. That scared me. That scared the living hell out of me. Pictures of what could have been started flashing in front of me. And out of the darkness, a ghostly cold wind suddenly brushed up against my right leg.

My right leg! It ached, only there was no leg. In its place was a rod of titanium pylon that kept me from falling to the ground. But it throbbed, and it twinged like it was punctured by three large nails again, piercing my skin and gushing a river of blood.

I wanted to run from the thought, but I can't, I can only limp. And limp away I did, scuffling, shuffling, like a walking dead.

# Chapter 22:
# The Lyrics of Melancholy

The train ride home from Cycle City dropped my mood from angry to foreboding. The train had nothing to do with it. The metro was actually faultless. It's new and smelled new. People kept to themselves, and a tranquil aura circulated through the air conditioner. But during the ride, a sickening feeling of no tomorrow squirmed in my gut, as if a meteor was beelining for Earth, and we could do nothing but watch the fireball burn brighter until it burns us.

I kept my mind occupied by looking at all my social media accounts. But instead of finding a distraction, it showed me posts about the successes of everyone, from my childhood classmates to my college friends. They boasted of job promotions, achievements, and fulfilled ambitions. Social media clearly didn't help me. If anything, it helped me become more miserable and more inept. And worse, the targeted sponsored posts appearing on my feed were all about cycling.

Crap. I should stop looking at my phone now.

I got off the train at Al Mamriya station, a ten-minute walk from my house. I scanned my prepaid card on the turnstile, and it subtracted only two riyals from my account. That's a considerable saving. Typically, the taxi would cost around twenty-five riyals between Cycle City and home.

Thinking of Cycle City, Wally popped into my mind. Wally and then Greg LeMond, and all the other cyclists who retired too early. Where are they now? What are they currently doing? How did they manage their retirement?

## PORTRAITS OF THE WIND

I pictured myself googling them while I sit in my dark and bleak room where the aircon spews death. Okay… Maybe let's not google them then. Maybe the library is a better place to do research.

I headed back to the turnstile, ready to scan my prepaid card and board the red line to the library. But an *idiot*, who had trouble scanning his card, slowed me down.

In front of me stood a plus-size wooly Asian guy in leather shoes, black pants, and blue polo under a black jacket. He seemed smart in that outfit, but as they say, do not judge a book… if you're not a judge. Ha! Shut up Luma! Yeah, I think my humor is suffering too. Anyway, this wooly Asian was testing the patience of the people behind him. Worse, I also got agonizingly uncomfortable. Standing still on a prosthesis is not as easy as it looks.

A full minute had passed, and this nitwit still kept on swiping his card over the wrong place. I groaned and snatched his card. I swiped it over the right place with one swift motion of my disgruntled arms. A loud beep followed, and the turnstile opened. The idiot dashed forward without thought and, upon crossing the barrier, he spun around to thank me. I gave him back his card while I pursed the corners of my lips.

You can easily tell when a person is new to something. They fumble and flounder around like idiots. Well, I understand that. I was the same when I rode up the hill without changing gears.

Inside the train, now that I decided not to look at my phone anymore, I watched the other passengers looking at theirs. Knowing as how I might give the impression of a perv, I observed the travelers discreetly through the reflection of the car's tinted windowpane. In the silent oblivion of everyday life, some of the commuters found amusement from their "world-in-your-hand" devices, laughing and giggling, while some of them simply enjoyed what they saw in solitude. Unsurprisingly, a lot of them were deadpan.

At the sight of their delight and boredom, I found my fingers tapping ceaselessly on the windowsill. They itched to do the same, to pick up the burning phone in my pocket, and then scroll and scroll; like this and like that. But I resisted the urge. I kept my attention to the black tunnel and the lights that whizzed by. Light, dark, light, dark, light, dark, light— a phone rang. I impulsively turned my head.

The guy reclining at the opposite side immediately answered his phone, embarrassed about his loud ringtone. Beside him—OMG— I saw the wooly Asian man, sat with indifference, wedged between two unsuspecting travelers, under the bluish-white glow of the train's LED light. He had this unkempt beard that he probably thought suited him. It was a little too patchy though, like a badly mowed lawn to be qualified as a beard. He smiled and nodded at me; I briefly did the same.

A few minutes later, the train reached my stop and I wobbled my way into the library.

\*\*\*

BOOM!

I whirled around, spooked, and saw nothing. I only heard laughing teenagers from afar as more booms echoed across the space. It's probably some jackasses impressing other jackasses by backfiring their cars.

Then, under the setting sun, a hundred yards from the station, I caught the lonely figure of— There he is again! The wooly Asian! We must be going to the same place.

## PORTRAITS OF THE WIND

I was about to acknowledge him, but my stump got pinched. So, I grimaced and adjusted the cup. When I glanced back at him, he was standing still, looking up to the heavens, or something like that, in a contrived fashion. Weird guy.

As soon as I approached this magnificent library, the automatic swinging glass doors revealed the massive staircase of bookshelves.

Oh hell!

Literally hell. I forgot about those staircases. To access the upper shelves, you must climb what looks like a hundred steps. Sure, the library had wheelchair access, but that zigzags into a kilometer too. Okay, maybe not a kilometer. It's only going to feel like a kilometer after you shuffle your prosthesis up the winding ramp that stretches into a... kilometer.

First thing's first. Before I waste my time and energy going up the stairs, I need to ensure that I will be visiting the right place. For that, the digital catalog is the right place to ask.

I typed *Cycling*. In one second, the little tablet mounted on the kiosk returned the location: 2.211B. Beside it was a small button labeled Map. I clicked on it, and an animation of a line, starting from where I stood, pointed me to the right shelf.

Holy hell! It's up at the topmost level. Crap! My fake leg cramped even before I took a step.

I had two choices: the zigzag ramp, or the straight staircase. The ramp was longer, but the stairs required more effort. Darn it! I never used to think about these things before. (Oh, the things we take for granted!) I took the stairs anyway. They were shorter. Though they required more effort, they were indeed still shorter.

Huff... huff... one more step... huff... argh... whew!

As my plastic feet landed on the umpteenth step, my legs, they burned. Not the lactate ecstasy I previously so desired, instead, they truly burned. They burned as my lungs burned. It was a dull searing pain.

I reached the topmost level and checked the labels on the entrance to each row of shelves until I saw *Sports*. Ah, finally. I lumbered into the narrow strip of bookshelves, scanning the racks for anything related to cycling. My fingers ran through the spines of books: hardbound, leather, and paperback. Each unique texture gave me a sense of curious buzz.

I saw books about cooking, recipes, cooking, native dishes, cooking, one hundred foods you need to try before you die, cooking. My left brow lifted towards my scalp. I was confused. These are all about cooking!

I went back out to where I came in to double-check the row's label. When I emerged from the shelves and into the lung-burning staircase I—

What the hell!

The wooly Asian man stood frozen in front of me, whiter than a bleached ghost. I spun around twice, perplexed. Could he be staring at someone else? You wish. Only me and him stood there at that time. I opened my mouth to ask him if he was okay. But before I could say anything, he held up his left palm gesturing *stop*, and his right hand palmed his chest like saying he means no harm.

Luma confused. No, Luma flummoxed.

Then he scuttled away towards the digital library without uttering any words.

What a weird guy! I knew he meant no harm. I mean, even if he didn't speak, his aura sang the lyrics of melancholy.

Okay...

## PORTRAITS OF THE WIND

I turned my attention back to the row's label. It still says *Sports*, but below it is a small arrow that pointed to the left. You had one job, whoever designed this! Great work! These little things really irked me now.

Once again, I ran my fingers through the spines as I scanned the books. The books were about baseball, football, basketball, formula one, cycling, cycling, cycling… Ah, perfect.

I skimmed the titles: "Training with Power", "The Economics of Professional Road Cycling", "Art of Cycling", "Getting Started with Cycling", and "Competitive Cycling". I looked up, looked down, and then looked towards the end of the shelf; all were about cycling. Darn it! That's a lot.

I took a gander at all the cycling books, taking my time to read all the titles. To my dismay, there were no books about Greg LeMond. Sure, there were books about the cycling greats: Merckx, Hinault, Fignon, but none of them really mattered; they all retired happily.

Another title caught my attention: a biography about one of the cycling greats from the '90s. And he was forced to retire early.

Right, this must be my book.

I had placed my finger on top of the spine and about to pull it out when I remembered one crucial story about him: he OD'd with cocaine because of depression.

Depression? Noop, not my book.

Surprisingly (or maybe not because he is still famous), a whole row was dedicated to cycling's biggest fraud. I guess after coming back from cancer, he wanted to prove to himself that he can still be a champion, even if it meant doping. Does that resound to me? Not entirely. Even if I do all kinds of doping, how can I be a champion with one leg?

Out of curiosity, my hands grabbed one of his many books, and my fingers flipped the pages over and over on its own accord. Then they stopped randomly, instructing me to skim the text. There, I found a phrase from one of the cyclist's interviews: *"I'm not scared of crashing and breaking my bones... I'm scared about losing."*

I choked on the last word. Like instinct, I slammed the book shut before it does any damage to my being. Too late. A tear had already escaped my eye, landing on the book, which I quickly tossed back onto the shelf without thinking.

From the shadows, in between the cycling books, that massive sensation of dread and despair crept out and swaddled me.

I should have taken that first exit. That thought sizzled inside of me.

My hand groped for another book then, quickly and randomly, while grief smeared my vision. I opened it arbitrarily, to any page, anywhere, to get rid of that rotten image of despair in my head. What I saw next was page after page of vivid images of people riding their bikes, in races, or alone in open roads.

"No..."

I riffled the pages right after the other, persuading the book to show me something else, but it only taunted me, reminding me who I'm not, who I will never be.

Within a breath, I started moving, arms clutched over my stomach, away from the cycling books. Tiny beads of woeful sobs landed on my arm, on my hand, then on the floor. I escaped into the night then, shouldering on towards the metro, dodging glances from strangers. But it didn't make me feel any better. Outside, people seemed so happy, full of life, giving me the sensation of drowning against a world overflowing with toxic positivity.

## PORTRAITS OF THE WIND

I was alone.

I was hopeless.

I will never amount to anything now.

I wish I were really drowning for that would be a thousand times better than this. Wally's right, others are just born to watch others succeed.

# Chapter 23: Incontinence

The wheels I brought to Cycle City didn't come back for another three days. It didn't matter though, I wasn't looking for it, unlike before where I become restless when I miss a day of training.

Now, I tried to stay away from the thought of cycling altogether. And not just cycling, I tried to stay away from everything. It was a new concept for me. Aside from my desperate breathing, most of the time, only loud silence echoed in my room. No phones, no social media, no internet, nothing. You know why, right? How can a recovering junkie move on when she's always reminded of the thing that made her high?

Movies once used to be my escape. You'd think it's a no-brainer. You'd think it would assist me in my journey to acceptance. How, though? How can I move on when I can't even focus on the movie? Instead of seeing the moving pictures on the screen, I would see my own frustration. That's why I stayed away from inspirational, romantic, and every uplifting, morally rich films. They are full of rainbows and crap, reminding you to persevere because you will always achieve your dream. Yeah, right. Assholes. So, I was limited to horror, to suspense, to mystery, and thriller, being that they're the only ones who don't have any morals to impart.

Sometimes, when I find no suitable movie to bore me, I resorted to counting how many cars per hour passed my window. Later, I would categorize them by the brand and color. Then I would do some averaging and calculating the mean per hour. Pathetic, but at least math did distract me.

## PORTRAITS OF THE WIND

When I'm fed up with life outside my window, and no horror movie would scare me no more, I would find myself staring at my stump. I would stare hard at it, toiling over the "mind over matter" crap, channeling all my energy into growing my leg back. It's stupid, yes, but believe you me, I would do anything to get my leg back. I'm willing to trade one of my kidneys, a part of my liver, or my breasts if in return I could have a fully functioning leg.

It was only when I received a call from Wally that I remembered I brought the wheel for truing. Honestly, I didn't want to take it back anymore because, you know, that meant I must walk through a corridor of crack and heroin. But if I wanted to sell the bike, I must endure it, right? So now, the dim yellow bike was whole again, hanging on the wall in front of my bed. Now I can sell it. Or should I?

A part of me doesn't want to split ways with it and say, *till I see you again*. It had been my friend for nine years—a part of my life—and letting it go just felt plain wrong. But on the contrary, a part of me just wanted to get rid of it. It was an emblem of the past that housed the pinnacle of my dreams, or rather, the beginning of my dreams. Now, the bike only reminded me of who I will never be. It evinces agony. It's an impediment to my own happiness. It's the source of my anger. See? I don't need help. I know what I'm doing.

Still, I found myself asking: am I so sure that letting go of what used to bring me happiness would bring me happiness? (Stupid, no?) Am I so sure that I can no longer ride a bike? Maybe, just maybe, if I could feel the wind on my face once more, if I could just coast effortlessly on two wheels again, then maybe, just maybe, I could glide over all the anguish festering inside of me.

Only one way to find out.

Tick-tick-tick-tick!

I rolled the yellow steed out my room. My left hand rested on the top tube, the other rested on the bars. A familiar feeling.

Tick-tick-tick-tick!

The familiar sound surged a million joules of energy from the bike, up my arms, and into my face, tickling my lips to form a tight smile.

I kept my eyes on the front door that kept growing as I got closer with each stride. I didn't realize that I was already in between walking and running. It didn't even feel like I had prosthetics on.

The door opened, and the cold breath of the winter desert touched my skin, shrouding me in delight. Another familiar feeling: freedom.

"What are you doing?" a voice yelled from behind, from the darkness, if you will. The voice hit me like a punch from nowhere, almost knocking me down.

I whirled around with startling dexterity. The excitement I had popped, the anticipation—gone. Coming from the kitchen, emerging from the smoke, ladle in hand, Mama marched with scalding red eyes. "Are you seriously going to ride your bike?" Her tone made it clear that it wasn't a question.

I nodded; a tiny one, a mere minute movement from my neck. I continued to the door.

"No! After what happened, you're seriously going to ride your bike again?! Look at you now! You only have one leg!" Ma said.

Her voice drilled into my eardrums which halted me right between the threshold. Cold breeze from the outside mixed with the warm blood filling my ears.

"And now you're going to ride it again?! What's wrong with you?! Do you want to lose another leg?! Do you want us to go through that horrible experience again?! The nights at the hospital?! The therapy sessions? Watching you learn to walk again was depressing enough! Stop being a stubborn girl!"

Fury upwelled onto my face. My forehead wrinkled. My brows dived. Rage enlarged the veins of my temple, my neck, and my eyeballs. My vision blurred, but not blurred. I can still see, but I didn't comprehend what I saw. My ears have gone deaf, but not deaf, I can still hear but only garbled noises. Hell, my missing leg was also enraged.

I hobbled back into the house. The door slammed behind me. It was loud but wasn't as loud as the Luma screaming inside my head.

Bending forward, my hands grappled the Liv by the down tube and the top tube. With a heavy grunt, I stood back up and willed all my muscles to lift the bike over my head. I smashed it back onto the earth.

It bounced twice across the floor, where my wounds cried blood months ago. I expected the bike to break into pieces, but it didn't. It only thudded softly and whimpered like a homeless puppy. Unsatisfied, I found my left leg stomping on it with immense force. The resin that held the carbon weaves of the frame started to crackle and pop. I stomped more. Harder. Harder! It made loud muted cracks, like twigs snapping under a blanket, bones breaking under the skin. I stomped more. More! There were more cracking, more popping, here and there. Pieces flew up and hit my face! I didn't care! I inched forward and my prosthetic leg got caught between the spokes of the front wheel. I stumbled and fell to the floor. It didn't stop me. I grabbed my prosthesis and started using it as a weapon against my bike. I smashed, swung, and smashed! My mother yelled, but I didn't hear her. I can only tell from my peripherals that she opened and closed her mouth with force. And when my breath ran out, I stopped.

After the dust had settled inside the prison house, I found myself sitting amidst the broken pieces of my bike. Yellow and black bits were sprawled all over the floor. Pieces that used to be solid now exuded carbon fiber strips. What used to be whole, now lay into a hundred thousand desuetude pieces that couldn't be mended.

I took a piece of the wrecked frame and brushed away black fiber dust to reveal what used to be the chainstay. "H… how am I going to sell this now?"

"Oh…" Ma said.

I produced a wooden face. Absolutely no emotion, nothing at all. No anger, no pain, no guilt, no regret, not even emptiness. I was simply catatonic; only breathing for the now.

Ma looked away. She couldn't look at me, not when I lay legless amidst the fragments of my joy. Without a word, together with her ladle, she walked back to the kitchen.

***

"It's only been one week," said the confused Wellbrock.

I shrugged. I'm back in the bubblegum room. That's how the students describe Mrs. Wellbrock's pretentious office these days.

I wondered if Latha was keen cleaning Wellbrock's office, what with the smell that reminded her of all the gums stuck on the toilets, floors, and under the chairs.

I really detest going into Wellbrock's office. I attempted five times merely to knock on her door. When it opened, I had to force myself through the doorstep. To sit down, I had to let go of my will to live.

It wasn't my idea to come here so soon. But a woman in my house insisted that I do something with my time instead of moping around (which I wasn't, you know that, right?).

"What makes you think you're better now?" a man's voice asked.

## PORTRAITS OF THE WIND

Oh hell. It was a yuppie Englishman biting the tip of his pencil and bouncing his knees. He analyzed me, examined my body language, my posture, where I look when I answer truthfully or falsely.

I scrutinized him too. The nametag on his shirt pocket says *"Jerome."* A black necktie evenly divided his white short-sleeve shirt, which is tucked under his baggy black pants. His spiked blonde (and bland) hair brings to mind a withering lawn. And aside from the old-man specs that obscured his baby blue eyes, he appeared to be fresh from college.

Why does that attire look familiar? Oh, right. Mormons.

I stared at him steadily. I didn't blink, but he kept blinking. I believe my sharp stare made him uncomfortable. Then after some time, his eyes darted away, breaking the Bifrost between our gaze. Yessir, he's too young to be an experienced professional.

I grimaced to my principal. "Are you sure Jerome needs t... needs to be here? This was supposed to be like a girl talk."

"I invited him to assess you if you're really fit to come back," Wellbrock said.

"But he's a student counselor," I protested. "Does he even have any experience with grown-ups? Look at him! He's still on a pacifier!"

Jerome abruptly took the pencil out of his mouth and cleared his throat. "Psychology is a big part of counseling, you know," he said. "I graduated with a bachelor's in education and a master's in psychology. I even treated a few cases under the supervision of psychiatrists during my master's. In the school setting, we're the first line of defense before referring students to external psychologists or psychiatrists. I think I am more than qualified to assess you. So, back to my question, what makes you think you're better now?"

"What makes you think... what makes you think I'm not?" I replied with a rising tone.

"Let's keep our wits to ourselves, shall we?" Wellbrock said.

"Well, for one, your temper still needs management," Jerome said. Later, he eyeballed my messy crimson hair bun and my wrinkled T-shirt and pants. "I am not acquainted with you that well, but I've seen you walking…" He stopped, bit his tongue, cleared his throat, wiped his mouth, all the while turning a little red, but he stuck with the word anyway. "I've seen you walking around, previously, around the campus, the corridors, so I know how you normally look on your good days. This…" he motioned at my attire, "doesn't look like your good days."

"Of all people, you should know better than judging how people look!" I said.

"I'm not judging. I'm merely stating the facts of my observation."

"You're also still stuttering more than usual," Wellbrock said.

Jerome acknowledged Wellbrock and said, "Would you say that's because of what happened?"

I started yelling. "No! That's because I'm angry! I'm angry! I'm angry when people think I'm not okay! I'm fine! I just need to come back! I need to be distracted!"

"Distracted from what?" Jerome asked.

"Everything! It seems like the whole world has gone against me! Everyb… b… no one won't listen to what I'm saying!"

"So, you're not okay?" Jerome said.

My ears flushed red once more as rage engulfed me. So, I took a deep breath to maintain my composure. Meanwhile, my hands displayed the building fury by gripping the armrest of my chair and scratching the leather padding.

Jerome caught the sight of it and said, "Alright, let's take it easy now. Breathe in. Breathe out. Relax…"

I remained rigid on my chair. Veins bulged around my neck as I ground my jaw against each other. Don't tell me how to relax! I know how to relax! I wanted to shout. I wanted to scream. I tried to speak, but my mouth only opened and closed like a fish out of water.

Jerome kept tapping his pencil on the notepad. He never wrote anything. He only observed me. I glanced at Wellbrock, and she gave me a gentle smile, perhaps a little broken.

"I quit!" I said.

Wellbrock and Jerome fell back, "What?"

"If you don't let me c… come back, I quit," I said.

The sound of my voice ricocheted against the walls and bounced back into my ears. I heard myself.

Oh crap! Holy hell! No!

I quickly retracted, "No. I take that back. I'm sorry. Don't fire me. Please…"

At a loss for words, I took a breather for a few seconds while squinting beyond the walls of the bubble-gum room. I rewound my memory to a few seconds ago, then to a few hours ago, then to a few days, then to weeks, then to months… "I'm just tired. Seriously, I'm tired of all these," I said as I slouched and lowered my head.

Wellbrock's hand extended across the desk and towards mine. "Don't worry, we're here for you. However, we can't let you come back to work yet. I hope you understand that." She gripped my hand tighter, "You need professional help."

I did not respond. I just kept my head down in quietude, keeping the floor open for anyone who wants to talk.

Jerome decided to speak first. "I can refer you to an excellent psychiatrist if you want. He's helped hundreds of patients already. Successfully."

I wanted to scream I'm not depressed, but I lost the oomph to do it. I just wanted to keep my lips together. Speaking, stuttering, and convincing them that I don't need help saps the life out of me. I just wanted silence.

"Here..." Jerome slid a business card across the desk and directly into my line of sight.

On the top, it read: *Dr. Raju's Clinic, Mental Health, and Counseling.* Then on the middle of the card, it read: *Dr. Raju Khan, Consultant Psychiatrist.*

"There's no harm in trying..." Wellbrock said, "If you really want to come back, you'll get the help you need."

I didn't respond. I kept my head down.

"Are you listening?" Wellbrock continued.

I glanced up. I sighed. I thought about refusing, but the urge to keep my lips shut remained strong. The only sound that I expelled was another loud sigh together with my neck squeaking as I nodded.

"Good. So, will we expect you to visit Dr. Raju?" asked Wellbrock.

My shoulders dropped—an imperceptible act of defeat.

Darn it!

***

Shhquweeeeeeee! That's the sound of a dried-up marker giving its last drop of ink to slash another date on my calendar.

I went back to the fifties now. I don't use apps, phones, or even my own laptop for the reason that they make everything in life so fast, which is good for the rest of the world, but not for me. I needed things to be slower, otherwise, with the technology these days, I would run out of things to do before I could think of another.

## PORTRAITS OF THE WIND

For example, the calendar in real life: make a mistake – put white ink; blow and watch the ink dry and crack, then write over it. Wrote too soon while white ink wet? Clean the tip of the pen with tissue paper; put on another white ink; blow and watch the ink dry again; make sure it's dry by lightly tapping it, and write over it. But with the calendar app, you make a mistake? Delete! All is done before you could ruminate why you deleted it in the first place.

Technology also impelled me to stay within the dreary white walls of my house. Movies? Thousands are available for streaming. Millions more if I search through the pirate bay. Buying stuff? With a click of a button! No need to leave the house! But leaving the house is exactly what I needed. I've had enough of the darkness from the white walls of this bleak house. It disgusts me. The air reeks of dead and rotting dreams.

Realizing that I was already pacing endlessly around my room, I took that as a sign to get outside and breathe something else. I took my jacket and headed out towards the metro station to board the red line into nowhere. I had no intended direction. I just followed my feet wherever they went, wherever they felt good.

\*\*\*

"West Bay," the recorded female voice announced.

The train doors opened, and the noise of the station wafted into the train. I groaned and got out. I passed children who were screaming and crying, smelling like farts. Underground, their noise echoed a million times, infuriating and searing my brain. I was about to cover my ears, but I stopped for I don't want to look like— well, whatever I would have looked like to passersby. So, I limp-sprinted towards the exit and out into the quiet open city.

But it wasn't quiet at all. Cars, busses, horns, jackhammers, planes, all harmonized together into an orchestra of metal. My feet betrayed me. Instead of taking me somewhere that would soothe my anger, they took me to where it was hellishly exasperating.

I stomped my foot. The fake one. Luma irritated. Luma angry. Angry at noise. Angry at feet. Angry at missing leg. Darn it! Why am I talking like a caveman? Ugh! I stomped my foot again. I wanted to grab my prosthesis and start hammering things with it. Thankfully, I still had an ounce of sanity left and was able to control myself. Instead, my fury manifested through the sweat that started beading on my forehead, even though the weather was a wintry twelve degrees centigrade.

With clenched fists and jaw pressed against each other, I decided to trudge towards a mall beside the station, bitterly. Maybe over there, tranquility would be present.

The mall's door slid open for me, and the air-door above blasted warm air, creating a curtain of wind over my head and slicing it. God! Why is everything so irritating!

I kept walking and walking, looking for a restful place to stretch my leg. Food court? No, too deafening. Restaurants? No, I'm not hungry; also, noisy. Why are there so many people in malls?!

Unawares, I found myself queuing at the box office. Why not? I thought I'd give horror movies another chance to scare the melancholy away from me. Then a kid bumped me.

"Darn it!" I growled.

Unfortunately, there was a kid's movie playing, so there was a handful of loud, misbehaving children milling around. Some of them were jumping up and down, some were squealing, while some were darting in and out of the queue. A few of them kept bumping me, banging my leg. You know, these children are playing with fire around my super-volatile blood. If I were a pufferfish, I would have already puffed into a ball and pin them with my spikes.

Another kid crossed in front of me, slightly grazing my prosthesis. I growled once more with gritted teeth. At the same time, the queue inched forward, so I also step—

What the hell?! Something went dripping down my left leg, inside my pants. It was unpleasantly warm and cold at the same time. It was warm on my thigh, and it gets colder down my feet.

"Ma! She pee-pee!" a kid on another queue shouted and pointed at me. A million eyes swiftly turned to me, stinging me.

I looked down. Some kind of yellow liquid was pooling under my feet. And it bloomed outward as the bottom of my pants poured out more yellow liquid.

Imitating a school of fish evading a hungry predator, the people around me shot outwards. They stared at me, gawking, goggling. Some were repulsed. The children sneered. I was mortified. Humiliated.

Normally, logically, I would have already bolted to the exit, but I was paralyzed. My feet didn't want to move, pitting me against the oglers. Phones were out, darn it! Flashes, selfies, and recordings were going on, causing tears of embarrassment to stream down my face. Great! More liquid oozing out of my body!

When the peeing stopped, my feet relaxed and listened to my brain. The muscles in my thighs started contracting and stretching to make the movement of walking. My stump lifted my fake leg and ordered its first step... *splosh!* It stepped on the pool of urine.

My god!

The liquid produced a loud sloshing sound and sent tiny yellow projectiles all around. People grimaced in disgust.

The hell to all of you!

I ran. I limped. Away. Anywhere! Leaving a trail of yellow blots on the floor. Back to the metro. Back to the red line. Back home to where the dead dreams lay… where I lay.

I didn't know what happened. It happened. It just happened! I spontaneously peed in public and there was nothing I can do.

Maybe I need help. Maybe I do need help.

# Chapter 24:
# A Flicker of Light

The fading afternoon light was framed through the windows, casting its yellowing white light onto the gloomy people seated around the waiting room. Some of them were reading a magazine; most were on their phones. I... I watched them. It's becoming a habit of mine, people-watching. I'm not exactly proud of it, but I wasn't exactly averse to it either.

Watching and pondering what's going on in the life of these people, their issues and whatnots kept me occupied. I wondered how many of these people are needing help. Are they depressed, or tired, or angry like me? Did some of them spontaneously pee as well? Or did they do something else that merits them to seek the help of a professional?

I checked online; what happened to me was called urge incontinence, a type of urinary incontinence where the bladder leads an insurgency and says, "Screw it! I don't want to hold your urine any longer, you bitch!" Then it opens all the taps, and the beer colored frothy liquid drains down the side of your legs. One cause of this is depression. But I am not depressed, and the doctor will be confirming that.

The split air-conditioner swiveled, blasting its cold, dry air towards me, sending chills throughout my body. Really? It's twelve degrees outside, and they have their air-conditioner on? I intuitively placed my hands on my vajayjay, hoping there won't be any insurgency happening. Thankfully, my bladder cooperated.

A loud thin plastic clack reverberated in the quiet room. I glanced at the wall clock. The hour hand that I've been watching since three in the afternoon pointed precisely at the number five. At this point, a slender Jordanian female staff on plainclothes came into the waiting area.

"Luma El-Guerrouj," the staff announced coldly.

I stiffened. I kept staring at her while I deliberated if I should really be doing this. Oh, to hell with it. I stood up and said nothing. I followed the staff towards a room where there were more staff. This time, they were wearing scrubs.

The clinic's nurses took my vitals, then they drew a vial of blood (don't ask me why), then they took my weight. They used a vintage mechanical scale, where you had to slide blocks end to end to balance the weigh-beams. I paid attention to the counterweight moving from 60, 61, 62, 63. It still wasn't balancing. It continued to 64, 65, 66, then it stopped there. The beam held its balance.

Sixty-six kilograms.

I stared at the number incredulously. In doubt, I tried to move the counterweight back, and instantly the weigh-beam leaned towards the left. I moved it back to 66, then the balance held once more. My brain couldn't grasp the numbers. I lost a leg, and I gained six kilograms? I've been gaining weight since that stupid accident? That means, my power to weight ratio would have dropped from 4.3 watts/kg to— Oh, what the hell! It doesn't matter now, does it?

I punched the scale. I punched it with a force so immense that my knuckle bled. "Ow!" I said furtively.

The nurses and stuff spun towards me, studied me, and went back to doing their work. Nobody showed any signs of panic or distress. I guess they're used to patients causing a scene. I pursed my lips, trying not to look embarrassed, and asked for something to wipe the blood from my fist.

A little while later, the Jordanian staff then escorted me up the staircase and led me to a room full of books, expensive-looking trinkets, and framed certificates. Sitting behind a marble-top desk, a balding Indian gentleman greeted me. A red necktie went over his bright yellow polo, and his blue coat was hanging over the back of his expensive-looking office chair. On his desk was a nameplate that read, *Dr. Raju Khan, Consulting Psychiatrist.*

Raju glanced at me as the staff handed him a brown folder. "Please, have a seat," he said while gesturing to the leather cantilever chair in front of his desk. Then he waved to the staff as the door closed behind her, and now we were alone.

"So, tell me, why are you here?" he asked.

Raju opened the thin brown folder that was handed to him. It only contained three pages. The first page had all my personal information that his team took from me:

DOB: January 26, 1992
Status: Single
Height: 5'5"
Weight: 66kg
Eyes: Brown
Hair: Red, wavy.

The second and third pages were blank ruled sheets under the clinic's letterhead, waiting to be scribbled with Raju's notes. I glimpsed at the other folders over at the side of his desk. A stack of pages, maybe close to fifty, were sandwiched in each folder. Those patients must have really lost their screws. Crap. Am I gonna get close to that?

My eyes drifted back to Raju, who stayed looking at me, waiting for me to answer. But I was waiting for him to tell me to lie down on the couch and start talking while he listened inscrutably.

I looked around, there was no chaise lounge (or what is more known as a therapist's couch). There were only the regular two-seater and two single-seater couches arranged around a small glass coffee table at the other end of the room.

He gave no instructions to move either. We stayed in our places. He was reclined on his leather chair, making him look superior, and I was rigid on a cantilever chair with cold metal armrests.

"What brought you here?" Raju followed up.

"The…" I stuttered again. God, I wished people could just read my mind. I thought I will have the strength to speak once I'm in front of the help, but obviously, I can't.

Frustrated, I yanked a blank page from the brown folder, my folder, under Dr. Raju's hand. Then I took a pencil from the coffee mug on the corner of his desk.

With my lips sealed, I started writing, "I need meds."

"Why?"

"They said I need help."

"Who?"

"Everyone. The school, my parents."

"What are you experiencing right now? How are you feeling?"

I bent down, unlocked my prosthesis, detached my leg, and placed it nonchalantly on the table. Raju flinched backward, a little disgusted, or maybe surprised. I wasn't sure. He was literally taken aback. I bet he didn't see that coming.

"Okay… Please, you can put it back," he said while recapturing his poise.

I reattached my leg.

"Did something also happen with your," he motioned over his mouth, "talking, speaking?"

I shook my head, keeping my lips pursed, and I wrote, "Do you think you can help? Help me get better?"

"Maybe. But I still don't know how you feel and what you're experiencing."

I rolled my eyes and scribbled loudly on the page. Then I shoved the paper in front of his face. "ANGRY!"

Raju lifted a brow, shifted his gaze towards me, and studied me like he's done this a million times and I'm the millionth and one. "Are you willing to be helped?" he asked.

"Can you grow my leg back?" I wrote.

Raju looked at me steadily and said, "Therapy only works for those who want to get better."

Obviously! I sarcastically nodded. Why do you think I voluntarily went here?

"Can't you just give me meds? For my anger and incontinence," I jotted.

Raju cocked his head with interest and said, "Incontinence? Really?"

"Meds. Please?"

"I can't give you any medicine. I still don't know to what extent of help do you need, or how rooted your anger is. We hardly started. More sessions will follow to observe your progress. You told me you're angry; so, tell me, where is this anger coming from?"

Again, I detached my leg and slammed it on Raju's desk.

"Okay, I understand. I know what you mean, but what I wanted to know is the why. Why are you angry? Some people get sad because they lost their limbs. Some people sulk and retreat into the darkest place they could find whenever they lose something or someone. But you're angry. Every depression is different. Yours might be manifesting in anger and incontinence."

"I'm depressed?" I wrote incredulously.

"I couldn't say... But you could be, maybe. It's difficult to assess in just one meeting, but some indicators say you could be."

I furiously wrote. The pen's tip dug trenches on the paper. "I'm not depressed! I'm angry!"

Raju sighed and said, "Alright, listen, let's first start with lifestyle changes. Keep yourself busy—"

I chuckled ironically. I wanted to tell him that I had tried, and then the school slapped me with an involuntary time out.

Raju kept going, "—Try something new, get into a new routine. Challenge yourself. I know this sounds silly given your depression, but do have fun! You might say it's not fun anymore; don't listen to yourself, that's only the depression talking. Do it anyway!"

I wanted to write: *They tell me you're one of the best mental doctors, but don't you think I've done all this? Don't you think I did all these, and none of them worked, that's why I'm here? Everything you said is easily found on the internet! The internet could have been a better doctor!* But I didn't write that. Instead, I wrote, "What if it doesn't work?"

"We'll see... When you're comfortable enough to talk about what's making you angry, then we'll have more to work with. For now, that's all I can prescribe you."

I let out a loud exhale. To the window, I watched sparse clouds come and go from view, while the tip of my pencil hovered over the now wrinkled white sheet.

I gawked for a long time. How long? Long enough for thoughts to circle round the planet.

Raju waited patiently, unemotionally. Through my peripherals, I can see him shooting back and forth between me and my writing paper with an interval of two breaths.

I didn't know what I was looking at outside the window. But in the stillness, I heard a little piece of me that was still crying. A piece that hasn't stopped crying for a while.

When I looked back at the paper, I saw the words that I needed to write. It was already written, and I just had to trace them with my pencil.

"I'm angry because my leg is an integral part of my dreams," I wrote.

"Alright, what is your dream?" Raju started writing on his pad.

"To become a professional cyclist," I wrote. The idea now appeared to be a billion light-years away as I scribbled them down on the paper.

"I see... why did you want to become a professional cyclist?"

"It's the sport I love!"

"Obviously, but why?"

My blood started to boil again. "What why? There's no why. It just is!"

"Luma, there is no 'it just is' when it comes to our decisions. Everything we do, the things we like, the paths we choose, are all predetermined by our inner needs and desires that are reared from our childhood. It might be that we were repressed that's why we chose this thing, or maybe we were abused so we resorted to this. Do you understand? Athletes don't excel just because; they excel for many reasons such as unconsciously trying to be better than what they don't seem to recognize—"

The phone rang. Raju picked it up and nodded. After a few seconds of "yeses" and "uh-huhs," he looked at me. "Alright, I'm afraid that's all the time we have for now."

I lurched forward from my chair and hurriedly scribbled on my paper. "That's it? I don't think we even got somewhere!"

"Yes, we did. As I said, there are more sessions to follow. We'll dig deeper, and we'll try different things to give you relief. We can't rush this. Depression is like a wound that heals over time. You can't force it to heal. It needs proper attention and care. For now, try what I told you. Have fun!"

I wobbled down to the front desk, flabbergasted. I've been doing what Raju exactly told me, or at least I think I was. I got even more flabbergasted when I saw the bill.

Oh, my god! A thousand riyals for one hour?

"What's your insurance?" the Jordanian staff asked.

I shook my head.

"Okay, will that be cash or card?" she continued.

I gave her my debit card, inserted it into the machine, and I entered my pin. A few seconds later, I received a message on my phone saying that a thousand riyals were deducted from my account.

"When would you like to have your next appointment?" she asked.

For a thousand riyals?

"No need, I'm all better now! :)" I wrote with the pencil and paper that I took from Dr. Raju's office.

***

The metro station by Dr. Raju's clinic was surprisingly empty. Or maybe it was empty because it wasn't rush hour yet? Whatever. What's important was nobody's there. There were no loud voices, and no people bumping against you.

I got to the turnstile and scanned my card. The scanner's friendly green glow flashed hostile red. That meant I didn't have enough credit on my metro card. But that didn't concern me as much as the embarrassingly loud alarm reverberating in the void of the station (BWONK-BWONK-BWONK), accompanying the flashing red light on the turnstile. Just then, all eyes shot to me.

I froze and closed my legs tightly, paralyzed in place. Oh hell! Please don't pee! Please don't pee!

Thankfully, my bladder held. When I was a thousand percent sure that me bladder did hold my pee, I hobble-wobbled to the ticket booth and gave them my prepaid card. The teller held it up questioningly, waiting for me to say something. I wanted to speak, but again, the urge to keep my lips together remained strong. So, I slid a fifty across the counter.

"Do you want to recharge?" the teller asked.

I nodded.

A few minutes of limping later, I got onto the train heading south.

I swayed with the tender rocking of the cab as the train gently started its journey of multiple stops towards my station.

My ears captured the familiar muted low rumble of the train's wheels as it whooshed beneath Qatar. There was also the continuous subdued chatter between the passengers in various languages. There were Arabic, Hindi, Filipino, Korean, Singhalese, Chinese, Malay, English, German, French, Dutch, Spanish, and more which I don't recognize. Qatar forged itself to be a cauldron for various cultures to come together.

I also observed the interior lights subtly flicker. The lights did not turn on and off like what they do in horror movies, but it had a very subtle flicker, a gentle pulsating of light and dark that is invisible to a crowded mind. You only see it, that very little throbbing of light, when you focus and tune out the rest of the world. A silent mind unlocks a whole universe within the visible world. Go ahead, try it.

With silence, I can observe the mundane beauties of the world like that little plant I spotted on my windowsill. It was an innocuous sight: a tiny plant with one white flower thriving on a patch of dirt built by one, or maybe two, perhaps three decades of strong winds. Or that pigeon I saw outside my classroom window, whose feathers fluttered with the wind as it rested on the corner ledge of the other building's rooftop. It was a sight directly from a surrealist painting as a sea of blue skies engulfed the bird.

Why haven't I tried silence before? Why have I chosen to challenge my stutter and become a teacher when I can work in an office without people disturbing me. What if I had worked in an office, like an accountant for a small company, where I would have started work at nine instead of half-past six in the morning? That would have given me more time to rest after training. Probably, I would also be training in the mornings instead of the evenings. Yeah, what if? Would I still be in the same predicament?

Oh, shut up... What ifs are used by the frustrated, by the losers, by the failures, and by the manqué.

Darn it. I'm one of those!

The train changed tracks. A loud and thick mechanical thud followed the sudden jerk of the cab. It was totally unexpected. Though I was sitting, it still threw me off balance and I fell sideways to the seat beside mine. As I collected myself, I caught a glance of another innocuous sight. Although I don't think innocuous is the right word to describe what I saw.

Brooding only a few seats away from me was Mr. Wooly. The Asian. The plus-size wooly Asian.

His hair looked like it had been stroked a thousand times by a trembling hand. Wrinkles and dirt stains adorned his clothing. Has he been rolling on the floor? How long has he been sitting there?

The train swayed and Wooly started looking around swiftly. He glanced here, there, up, down, as if trying to look for something.

## PORTRAITS OF THE WIND

When he didn't find what he had been looking for, he released a river of tears. It was like a dam opening its floodgates. His face was dry, and with a blink, it got soaked in salty tears. A gentle sobbing and sniffling followed next. The sound was weak yet perceivable over the gamut of banal noises inside the train.

The other passengers gawked at him curiously. When he caught the gaze of one, he abruptly diverted to my direction, and his eyes accidentally found mine. Not another second later, he deflected towards the window and covered his face with his feeble hands.

With that split second of eye contact, I got to see beyond him, beyond the façade that we call the body. Through his tears, I was able to peek into his soul, giving me a glimpse of someone familiar, like looking at a mirror. I saw someone who's in pain, who's drowning in a sea of despair, and whose lungs breathe only grief and sorrow. I didn't know what was going on with him, but somehow, I saw myself.

He curled into a ball of agony while the other passengers discreetly pulled out their phones to record him. My feet started walking towards him then, slowly and cautiously. I was drawn to him. Is it because we're living in the same dark universe? Is it because I empathize with him? Is it because I am him? I have no answer. All I know is, there are moments in life that you meet someone whom you will be involuntarily drawn to without reason—beyond comprehension. Like a star slowly pulled into a black hole, we were two stars heading into the same void.

I sat beside him, and without a word departing my mouth, I laid my hand on his shoulder. An orb of energy instantly left my body through my hands. I didn't know what that was too. I just accepted it as it was.

He glanced at me, then he precipitously buried his head on my shoulder. There and then, a jolt of vigor entered my body from that spot. Incomprehensible, but it felt right. It felt safe. I think he experienced it too because not long after, his sobbing stopped while his face remained succumbed on my shoulder.

People stared at us. I understood it must be a peculiar sight. Public displays of affection are frowned upon in the country. I didn't know if this counts as a PDA, but through their optics, it might just be. But to hell with them! I didn't care, and I shielded Wooly from the passengers' judging gaze. I stared back at all the people whose eyes were upon us. I stared, I glared, until they found it uncomfortable and thus looked away.

"Al Mamriya Station," the train announced.

Still with no words uttered, I gently pulled my shoulder away and exited the train without looking back.

What was that? What the hell was that? It felt good!

For that brief moment, I wasn't weeping inside. Instead, I was listening to a symphony that I haven't heard before. It felt like life was back in its proper place, but only for that moment. It was only at that moment that I forgot— I was missing a leg. It was only at that moment that there was no anger. It was a moment that I wished would last a lifetime. And as I walked further away from him, the foreboding darkness started coming back, as if I was voluntarily walking away from the light and into the night.

Out of the blue, as I approached the turnstile, three taps landed on my shoulder. I spun around and saw...

Wooly.

# PART THREE: TWO NEGATIVES

For the last time, imagine this: pain, frustration, anger, all of life's negativity has devoured your vim, all is lost, dragged into an abyss not even anglers dare to wander. And there, deeper into the darkness, you see a faint flicker of light. Would you still fight your way up to the surface? Or swim deeper into the light?

At six in the evening, people of different backgrounds swarmed the Al Mamriya station like ants. All of them moving in and out, each in every way. No one stopped except for the mandatory pauses at the turnstiles, in the ticket booth, and behind the platform's yellow line. Thousands of footsteps and cackles of soft voices pooled into one loud cacophony of noise.

One man diverged from the horde of indifference: Xavi. He was running, emerging from the stationary train, piercing the throngs of oncoming passengers. His silhouette approached a limping woman: Luma.

"Excuse me…" he said.

Luma turned, saw Wooly, and then speechlessness sewed her mouth shut. Another incomprehensible jolt of energy overwhelmed her, like a sudden rush of vigor and life that roared from an eternity away. Just like inside the train.

She found herself poring over his face, particularly at his sunken eyes glimmering in the same way that hers did. She thought he had a sense of familiarity lurking within him, a dark splendor, a sense of sanctuary, a kind of comfort in knowing that someone shares the same despondent universe as hers. Yet she was paralyzed as if his voice had the power to turn her to stone. All she could do was to feel the clock tick by.

"Um... thank you," Xavi said before he also froze in time, uncertain of what's next.

Up close Xavi saw more details in the woman's face. He saw bags underneath the lady's crystalline hazel eyes that seemed to collect all the tears she wasn't allowing out. Charming little freckles, which looked like sprinkles garnished on a cupcake, sprinkled her face. He admired those pale pink lips that were pursed tightly in either confusion or thought. He followed the sharp jawline that curved down towards the scar under her chin, slightly obscured by a yellow scarf. She has an unapproachable charisma, spellbindingly flawed, snobbishly magnetic. Just like Col—

Now back to her eyes, her puffy eyes. There, words seemed to be trapped under a pair of glossy orbs, like a child staring out the window, determined to play outside, but committed to staying inside. He knew that feeling, the feeling of wanting to say something but the mouth is unwilling. "What is it?" he asked solemnly, "You okay?"

Luma had the urge to speak and tell him everything. Her throat and her tongue began the motions of speaking, but her mouth seized. In a second, she walked away.

Xavi hurried after her through the oncoming crowd and asked, "Wait, are you going home now?"

Luma nodded, keeping her eyes forward.

"Can I at least walk you home?" Xavi continued, "That's the least I can repay you with, for your shoulder."

Although stumped, Luma maintained her pace while entertaining questions in her head. Should she say no to the man who was bawling some moments ago? Or say yes to a stranger? And that peculiar ball of energy tickling her senses didn't help either. It only raised more questions about that particular ball of energy itself. She had no answer. So, she gave Xavi a look that was neither approving nor disapproving.

"I'm Xavi, with an X," he said, and then later realized that it was an absolute step away from his character to be talking with strangers. Nevertheless, he had the urge to do it.

Luma stopped walking. For the third time, she tried to speak, and for the third time, her lips remained glued together. If only eyes had a mouth to speak. Oh, wait! From a folded piece of paper, soft and moist from the sweat in her pants, she wrote, "Luma," and held it up to him.

Looking at the movement of Xavi's eyes, Luma saw what he was reading through the thin paper that was rendered translucent by the station's bright lights. He first read her name, then his eyes moved to the top where it says: *Dr. Raju's Clinic, Mental Health, and Counseling,* then he read a word with thick lines, written by a heavy hand: *ANGRY!*

Luma got embarrassed when she saw Xavi was reading this. Within a split second, she crushed the paper, shoved it back to her pocket, and without glancing back, she tramped away like a humiliated child.

On the escalator leading to the streets above, Xavi, attempting to settle his unspoken debt, stepped in front of Luma and offered his hand. It was the politically right thing to do given her limp, he thought. It gave him the sensation of being a proper gentleman. However, when he saw Luma's wrinkled forehead of disapproval, he felt like a boor. Self-conscious, he took a step back and accidentally grabbed hold of the moving handrail, propelling him up, bumping Luma's shoulders.

Luma wobbled and lost her balance, but with cat-like dexterity, she grabbed hold of the handrail too, preventing what could have been a horrific situation, possibly where her prosthesis is left on the bottom while she is on the upper floor dragging her legless body like a zombie.

Luma glared at Xavi and gestured for him to back off. She wrote, "I'm fine, I do this all the time."

Xavi's face warmed with blood that turned him tomato red.

No one spoke afterward.

\*\*\*

Outside, walking home, Luma kept her head straight, only looking at the road ahead while trying her best not to limp too much. Beside her, Xavi kept looking up to the heavens, to the darkening blue sky, and sometimes to the amber streetlamps that bathe the streets in orange-yellow. Luma checked him through side glances, checking what his hands were doing. Was it doing the same actions that her principal did, always ready to catch her when she falls? No. Xavi's hands were in his pocket. She appreciated this, then she turned her eyes back on the road.

The wind blew. Luma tightened her scarf. Xavi closed his jacket. They gave each other a meek smile and then eyes back on the road.

From afar, the scene looked simple: the neighborhood empty, two people walking, footsteps crunching, no voices, only the sound of distant cars and jackhammers filling the air. They kept glimpsing at each other, checking if the other was okay with the deafening stillness of the night. Both turned their heads one after the other, missing each other's gaze by a breath. Occasionally, their eyes would meet, and they would smile silly as if saying, *"I'm fine,"* then eyes on the road.

## PORTRAITS OF THE WIND

They turned a corner and passed a garbage dump. A cat jumped out, startling the pair. They laughed, but only briefly. Xavi wanted to say something, opened his mouth, and this time it was him whose words got stuck between his teeth. Still, no words departed any of them since leaving the station. He looked forward then, eyes on the road.

The wind blew once more, stronger this time, ruffling Luma's crimson hair. Her hand swept the flailing strands automatically and tucked it behind her ears. Xavi saw this and it reminded him of someone from the past. He gawked. When Luma caught him staring at her, he smiled; she smiled too. Next, both eyes were on the road.

Ding-ding! A man on a bicycle passed them – a supermarket delivery boy. Luma's attention got piqued. She watched the man turn the pedals until he became smaller and disappear around a corner. That brought a look of mild sadness on her face. She took a deep breath and turned to Xavi, smiled tight-lipped, ready to say something. After a few steps, eyes on the road.

Silence is always a welcoming friend to sadness. Both knew something was dragging each other into a downward spiral, and both knew that for now, walking together in silence was the only remedy. They knew that showering each other with uplifting words would only do more harm than good. To the miserable, to the bereaved, unsolicited encouragement is not unlike pouring cold water to burning oil. One may think that's helpful, but all it does is flare up the fire that's already blazing out of control.

A final turn led them to Luma's gateless compound. Still with sealed lips, she stopped in front of her house, took her writing paper, and wrote, "Thanks."

"Thanks," was also Xavi's reply.

Luma extended her hand, Xavi shook it, and then they parted ways.

When they turned their backs on each other, moving away into the starlight, they both smiled with puckered brows as more questions filled their heads.

# Chapter 25:
# Emotional Cacophony

Rabiya wiped the sweat off her forehead precipitated by the hot steam rising from the iron clasped in her hand. She pressed hard on the wrinkled clothes; more hot steam arose.

BOOM!

A loud explosion rattled the household. But Rabiya wasn't fazed by the startling sound. Her head placidly lifted, switching her stare from the wrinkled clothes to the wrinkled man on the couch. What if the TV wasn't invented, she wondered, what would Hashem be doing other than watching? BANG! More mechanical sounds of explosions zinged around the room. She shook her head—an imperceptible shrug of forgiveness. She was back to ironing.

A moment of respite from the explosions came when the lead characters stealthily escaped the bad guys. During this moment, Rabiya heard a voice from the outside. Like the characters in the movie, she treaded stealthily towards the window and curiously peered out from the tiny slit between the curtain and the windowsill. There, under the pale moonlight, she espied her daughter smiling sweetly at a bearded flabby man. Worse, it seemed like they were holding hands. Rabiya felt a pang of something, perhaps jealousy, that made her edgy and apprehensive.

Rabiya stood at the front door, which moments later, delivered Luma right in front of her. "Who was that?" she asked with a foreboding tone.

Luma squinted questioningly.

Hashem swiveled around from his couch, "What's going on?"

"Luma was holding hands with a boy outside!" Rabiya said without turning away from her daughter.

Though surprised, Hashem didn't say anything. He just stared, the way he usually does since Luma's accident. It was a blank stare filled with meaning and also filled with none. It was only a steady gaze of two aged pupils locking onto Luma.

"Well?" Rabiya asked her daughter.

Luma smoldered red with fury, looked up, closed her eyes, took a deep breath, and held it.

"Who is that boy?" Rabiya asked again in a flat but biting tone. The same tone she held since the day of the missing leg.

Her daughter opened her eyes to the ceiling, sighed loudly, albeit scornfully, and stomped derisively towards her bedroom, displacing cold air in her wake. There was nothing said.

Rabiya watched Luma hold the edge of the latter's bedroom door, ready to slam it. Mid-motion, Luma stopped and looked at her mother…

What would be more infuriating to an already agitated person? Calmness… a cold, misplaced, emotionless calm.

So, instead of slamming the door, Luma held the doorknob and slowly pushed it all the way to the doorsill. It creaked softly, gently. When the latch bolt went into the strike hole, the supposedly humdrum sound of a door's click exploded violently inside Rabiya's ears, almost knocking her down.

Rabiya screamed to her husband, "Did you see that?! Do you see how your daughter defies us?!"

Hashem scoffed, "You taught her that."

"But she was holding hands with a boy!"

"Relax."

"How can I relax! She was with a boy! Holding hands! That's haram!"

"Oh," he chuckled, "you care about haram now? Let it go! I'm sure if it meant something, Luma will be honest with us."

"Honest? Like the day she snuck out and lost a leg?"

Hashem sighed and dwelt for a moment while words to refute or support Rabiya roved in his mind; however, he was already exhausted with the years and years of imposing his will to no effect. Without saying another word then, he turned back to the TV and continued to enjoy the gunshots and explosions.

\*\*\*

Luma sneered as she took her ears off her bedroom door. It left a fresh ear smudge on the cold surface, indicative of the little acts of defiance against her mother, the bullying warden in her prison home. And little acts of defiance, such as not greeting her, not eating the food she prepared, staying away from home for as long as possible, were how Luma repaid her mother's irritating guilt trips and constant rebukes.

*"I'm sure if it meant something, Luma will be honest with us,"* Hashem's voice rung in Luma's head while she removed the prosthesis off her stump.

Yes, it meant nothing, she assured herself. However, only a few minutes later, she wasn't so sure anymore for she knew, somehow, she had been gravitating towards Xavi since the moment she saw tears of misery stream down his face. She also took note that the anger consuming her waking life wasn't there when they walked home. Bewilderingly, the annoying pinch that her prosthetic cup would usually make was absent too.

"Why?" she asked herself.

Luma lay down on her bed and stared at the concrete ceiling, picturing on its rugged surface the events of the previous hours, wondering if what she experienced, that energy, was normal or was it also a part of depression. She considered going back to Dr. Raju to ask, but she straightforwardly rejected the idea (too expensive).

All night, before she would sleep after midnight, her mind ran some thoughtful analyses, wary of the curious thrill she felt about Xavi.

\*\*\*

*"Luma,"* the name resounded in Xavi's head. He ignored it. Instead, the super bright lights of the corridor, which lead to his apartment, annoyed him more. Has it always been like this? he thought. It has. It was only his mood that previously projected dimmer lighting into his reality. He got to his apartment door then, unlocked it, and swung it open.

*"Luma,"* the voice in his head said yet again. Then he realized that it was, indeed, a voice. It was a woman's voice. But whose voice? He never heard Luma spoke, so he had no allusion to what her voice would sound like.

The voice was the work of man's powerful supercomputer, the brain. The sound he had been hearing was the voice chosen by his mind subconsciously, filling the gap between soundless words and a woman's face. It was how his brain thought Luma would sound like. It was "hearing by substitution."

*"Luma."* The voice sounded familiar, awfully familiar. He scanned his brain, the conscious part, by browsing the collection of faces and the sound of their voices, trying to find a match. Was it Mom? Sis? Sherry? Mia? Joie— he stopped, startled.

## PORTRAITS OF THE WIND

He stood frozen at the threshold of his unlit apartment. Over there on the dining table, reflecting the pale blue moonlight, he caught the sight of the hard drive. *The* hard drive. And on the floor, silhouettes of the hard drive's shell traced into the shadows.

It's just a hard drive, he thought. That's what the eyes saw, but what *he* saw was the miserable sight of a million memories lost to oblivion.

SNORT!

Xavi's ears fluttered. Not his physical ears, but the ears inside his mind, his subconscious. He heard the beast of despair. It stomped and growled, gradually revealing itself, trotting out of the darkness.

At the imaginary sight of the beast, Xavi sunk against the massive weight of the discord of horror, terror, and panic. He felt himself standing under a looming cloud of doom, and over at the distance, the glowing eyes of the beast were glaring directly at him.

SNORT!

He felt a pinch on his chest. Just then, he knew that the creature was already stampeding towards him, over the moonless, indigent meadow of his soul. If he didn't do anything, he knew he will curl up into a ball once again.

Quickly, without thinking, Xavi grabbed the hard drive and tossed it to the trash. Off the floor, he picked up the tiny pieces that once was a complete object then hurled them to the bin together with the drive.

He glowered at the trash bin, breathing heavily, waiting for the insurgency of emotions to subside. But instead of calming down, pain bloomed in his bones, weakening his knees. Even when it was already in the trash, he couldn't stand seeing the hard drive broken, he couldn't stand imagining the fragments of Cola's memories gone.

With a surge of strength, he picked up the whole trash bin and ran out of the apartment. He made his strides as wide as he could, as fast as he could, one after the other, footsteps echoing, racing against his beast.

Xavi reached a narrow door. The hinges squealed at the speed that he hurled it open. And then there was another door, a smaller one, of hammered steel. He opened it and caught a whiff of foul odor. A garbage chute.

In one fell swoop, he tossed the drive, trash bin included, down the abyss of the metal tube. The bin clanged and banged as its destitute contents began the long drop towards the darkness. A loud thud followed, and a plume of silence arose from the bottom of the chute. It's gone. There was no sight of the hard drive at all, including his trash bin. Now, only Xavi's breathing could be heard throughout. It gradually slowed down. Getting rid of the hard drive seemed to be working.

Then, Nicola's face materialized in the white walls of the bright corridor. Instead of uplifting his state, it brought the poisonous memories of loss. And just like that, the beast of despair was once again hot on its heels, making Xavi ran back to the apartment with all the speed he could muster.

Xavi screamed in terror. He kept seeing Nicola's face on the walls, on the floor, on the ceiling, on the TV. He jumped into bed, head down, and covered his head with a pillow. Nicola still showed herself there, in the darkness of his eyelids, where tears began to seep through uncontrollably.

"Saving grace!" he told himself, "Think of your saving grace!"

The female voice spoke, *"Luma."* It had a morphine effect on his choking emotions, calming him down within one second. He imagined her face. *"Luma."* Those hazel eyes. *"Luma."* That wavy crimson hair. *"Luma."* Those freckles. *"Luma."* The scar on her chin. *"Luma."* The limping. *"Luma."* She says she's angry. *"Luma. Luma. Luma."* He imagined his face on her shoulder. He imagined himself marching down the streets quietly with her. *"Cola."*

Nicola's face burned through like a raging wildfire, scorching Luma's film reel that was playing under his eyelids. Xavi growled and screamed, trying to fight the strength of his beloved's memory.

It was futile.

There was no more Luma, only Nicola now, who smiled sweetly. It was the smile that he loved so much, the smile that always gave him shivers of glee. But now, the same smile was drowning him in a sea of anguish, and he couldn't get rid of it.

Xavi pressed the pillow harder against the back of his head and loudly pictured the other woman. *"Luma... Luma... Luma..."*

Irony. Weeks ago, he aggressively buried Luma's image and actively exhumed Nicola's. Now, he pined for the opposite.

***

Saeed Bin Yousef stood in the corner of Al-Zubara Contracting's conference room, watching the replacement photographer, Bilal, prepare multiple strobes, umbrellas, and softboxes. He wondered if Xavi had the same equipment, would his photos be less dark? More impressively, Bilal wasn't alone. Two assistants accompanied him. They scuttled around with laser focus, setting up the equipment with marine-like efficiency. Two light stands rose to the ceiling, lifting photographic strobes the size of a medium printer. With the command of Bilal, the assistants set up softboxes to fit the two strobes. Another two strobes, softened by umbrellas, were set up facing the background. There was also a foamboard held by a clip on a stand facing the chair where the subjects will sit. Little by little, the conference room that once held critical meetings slowly became a sophisticated studio.

Bilal approached Saeed with a questioning look. "Mr. Saeed, how would you like the photographs?" he asked.

"What do you mean how?" Saeed replied. He didn't know how to answer Bilal. It was one of the rare moments where Saeed's answers were less than ten words.

"Like, how? Do you want it dark or light, moody or bright?"

"With all these lights, will it still be dark??"

Bilal extended an arm towards the window. "Even with the sun, I could still make it look dark."

"Weren't you briefed by Xavi? Just make it bright and cheerful."

Bilal shook his head. "Who's Xavi?"

"What do you mean—" Saeed looked towards Xavi's desk. His photographer was not there. He checked his watch, it was 11:00 a.m. "Who reached out to you?" he asked, scraping the skin under his ghutra.

"David… something. Someone from marketing."

Saeed nodded. He knew David. That stubborn David, who doesn't listen to instructions, not even those superior to him. He detests David publicly because of the latter's stubbornness, but secretly because David was chattier than him. Talkies hate other talkies like thieves hate thieves.

"Are you all set anyway?" Saeed asked Bilal.

"*Aiwa*. I'm just waiting for the brief to lock the look."

"You went here without knowing the brief?"

"La. I was told that I will be briefed on site."

Saeed was once again stumped.

"Where is that Xavi?" he asked himself while storming out of the conference room, phone clutched between his fingers.

## PORTRAITS OF THE WIND

\*\*\*

The high-pitched polyphonic melody of the old Nokia 7650's ringtone tore the stillness of Xavi's bedroom. A subtle *brrr-brrr* accompanied the tone as the phone vibrated atop the nightstand.

Xavi wasn't moved even though he was awake. He was motionless in bed, looking up the ceiling with bloodshot eyes from crying and lack of sleep. In fact, he hasn't slept. He stayed awake all night battling his inner beast who growled and rumbled, ready to charge at the faintest whiff of weakness.

The beast only lowered its head and went to sleep when Xavi sang a lullaby to the tune of Luma's name. Luma. It was a relief, but at the same time, it felt wrong. Wrong that it wasn't Nicola who was able to shut the beast. Wrong that he had to think of another woman's face.

Luma.

Nicola.

His chest squeezed within itself as somber thoughts scuttle around his head. The sliver of peace that worked up Xavi's body vanished.

The phone rang again, pricking his eardrums with the irritating melody. He twisted his body towards the nightstand and grabbed the phone. He checked the caller-ID. Dammit! "Yes, Mr. Saeed." His voice crackled due to the nightlong of suffering.

The voice on the other line also didn't sound positive. "Xavi, hi, good morning. Where are you?"

"At home."

A long pause followed. The dead air dragged on with Saeed breathing heavily over the line, while the cursor in Xavi's thoughts blinked, waiting for an input from its user.

"Didn't you arrange for a replacement photographer?" Saeed sternly asked after a few long breaths.

"I did. I gave David a few options."

"Why did you give it to David? I told you to arrange it yourself."

"I'm sorry. I wasn't feeling well yesterday."

"How are you feeling now?"

"I'm a little better," Xavi said as he sat up.

"Good. Because I need you here. Please speak with the photographer and make sure he understands what we need. I already spoke with him, but I want you to follow through. Give him the photographer to photographer language."

Xavi hesitated. He strongly wanted to decline, but he has a penchant for not saying no however eager his tongue may be.

"Sure. I'm coming. Give me an hour," Xavi said.

"The photoshoot is scheduled at one o'clock! Can't you come earlier?"

"Sure, half an hour," Xavi said, and sauntered into the bathroom.

The sorry sight of himself on the toilet's mirror produced a sigh wielding the pressure of a million bars of madness. The tear-stained, wrinkled, soiled, and sour from sweat garments from yesterday were still clothed over him. His hair was standing stiff and the beard on his chin looked more like an untrimmed pubic hair. Such a deplorable human being, he thought.

With a quick wash of his face and a change of clothes, he went out of the apartment, locking away the yesterday yet bringing with him the stench of the past.

\*\*\*

## PORTRAITS OF THE WIND

Voices, phones ringing, printers, more phones ringing, and more voices added to Xavi's chaotic mind as he sat quietly, smoldering, staring blankly at the imageless monitor at his desk. Inside him, these sounds stirred an intense resentment towards the outside world.

"There you are!" Saeed said loudly, coming out of nowhere and patting Xavi on the back.

Xavi flinched when Saeed's stodgy hand landed on him, as if Saeed's palm contained the opposite magnetic polarity that Xavi held. They repelled each other; their energies did not match.

A half-baked smile strenuously covered Xavi's face, masking the irritation brewing inside. The flinching was obvious enough, though.

"Something the matter?" Saeed asked.

Xavi merely shook his head before standing up and asking, "Where's the photographer?"

"At the conference. Come on, let's go." Saeed fixed his ghutra before heading out into the maze of cubicles.

Xavi followed his boss through the narrow spaces and corridors leading towards the conference room.

Please don't talk. Please don't talk. Please don't talk, he thought.

"So, this photographer, Bilal…" started Saeed.

Dammit, Mia! Xavi bit his lower lip in an effort to remain stoic.

Saeed continued, "He's setting up all these huge lights with all these huge umbrellas. I think you will be impressed with his equipment. He's also taken photos of many heavyweights, politicians, celebrities, even the royal family themselves. I think you will like the guy. He's excellent. He also has this charisma with him that exudes professionalism." He ended with an approving nod.

"Have you seen his work?" asked Xavi after taking a minute to register his boss' barrage of words that could be condensed into one concise sentence.

"No, but I'm already impressed. He even showed me some of his works and…"

Oh god, please stop talking! Xavi nodded to all the worthless noise coming out from his boss' mouth while he gradually increased their pace in an attempt to get Saeed out of breath. It did not work.

By the time they reached the conference room, Xavi's ears had been bleeding from all the bullets of words that were shot at him. Usually, he would gingerly take it all in, but today wasn't a gingerly day.

"Xavi," Saeed extended his palm, "meet Bilal."

Bilal shook Xavi's hand and said, "So, what did you do wrong for me to mop up your work?"

Asshole, Xavi thought while looking Bilal in the eye and shaking his hand.

"So, what do they want? How do they want their portraits?" Bilal asked. "What's the brief?"

Xavi scanned the conference room: four strobes, two on softboxes, two on umbrellas, pop-up background with a blue brushstroke pattern, polyboard for a clamshell bounce, a medium format camera. Alright, impressive, sure. He rolled his head to Bilal, "Bright and cheerful."

Bilal and Saeed waited for a continuation. When no additions came to Xavi's words, Bilal and Saeed exchanged confused glances.

"That's it?" Bilal asked.

Xavi nodded.

Bilal faced Saeed, "You told me that already," to Xavi, "you didn't have to come all the way for that."

"Well," Xavi looked to the side, and then up the ceiling, trying to piece together fading words from only a day before, "they also said they want it to be dynamic, youthful and indicative of a bright future."

"That's the same thing... bright and cheerful!" Bilal said. "Alright, nice meeting you. I'll finish setting up, and I'm ready in fifteen minutes." He walked towards his strobes and started moving them to the positions he preferred.

"So, what do you think? Impressive, no?" Saeed asked Xavi.

Xavi gave an unconvincing look. "Yeah, sure."

"You're not impressed. Why not?"

Xavi shrugged, shook his head, rolled his eyes, and looked at the wall, looking at nothing in particular at all.

Saeed grabbed Xavi's arm and dragged him out of the conference room. "Xavi, I'm sorry I even asked you to come here. Obviously, you're not okay. If you need anything, like someone to talk to, I'm all ears."

"I'm fine. I'll be at my desk," Xavi said.

"You can go back home if you want to."

On his way to the cubicles, Xavi replied, "I'll be at my desk."

\*\*\*

Thud! Thud! Thud! Thud!

Xavi turned towards the window where, over the distance, two jackhammer excavators ripped the earth open.

As quickly as the sound had traveled his ears, thoughts stirred inside, that after twenty-five years, Doha still haven't— Oh god no, he abruptly shook his head. Xavi remembered being down the same path weeks ago, reminiscing how he got here, how he started his school life, and how he met... Cola!

The suppressed emotions started to cascade anew. The hair on Xavi's arms stood. He began to quiver, but he was twenty steps ahead. He rushed towards the conference room before any more signs of breakdown manifest externally. He dodged glances and voices, here and there, until his hand grasped the door handle and swung the conference door open.

"Xavi!" Jaber Al-Zubara extended both his arms in welcome, "Glad you could join us. You see..." Jaber swept his palm across the room, "This is what I'm talking about. Big lights, professional. Bright and cheerful. Not dark and somber."

Shut up.

Xavi grinned, showing his teeth, eyes blinking twice.

FLASH! FLASH!

Bilal did some test shots. The strobing lights gave Xavi brief cracking headaches. FLASH! Headache... gone. FLASH! Headache... gone.

Dammit! Xavi pulled Saeed out of the room with urgency.

"What's going on?" Saeed asked as he closed the door behind him.

"I need a leave."

Saeed was first stumped but quickly realized the desperate look on Xavi's face. "Yeah! Yeah! Of course!" he said in a concerned and supportive way. "How long do you need?"

"Indefinitely."

"Indef—what?" Saeed's ghutra almost fell as he jerked his head back. "You know that's impossible," he added while straightening his headdress.

"How long can you give me then? Four months? Three months?"

"Not even a month! You already cashed your vacation leave. I can give you days, I'm afraid, based on your sick leave."

"Days???"

"You know the policy. Three days a month for sick leave."

Xavi's face withered, but it came off as a mean stare to Saeed.

## PORTRAITS OF THE WIND

"Hey, I'm not the villain here. I want to help you, but it's company policy. You can take a leave, but it's going to be unpaid."

"Fine! I don't care! Three months, unpaid leave."

"Three months? Xavi, listen to yourself. That's as good as signing your own resignation letter."

"Just give me something!" Xavi started to look increasingly desperate, his face turning milky sour. "I need to clear my head for some time!"

"Alright, alright! One month. I'll harangue human resources to give you a paid—"

"I don't care if it's paid or not. I just want a leave."

"Listen first, will you? I'll make sure you get paid for the first month of leave. Then after that, you get another month's leave, but that one is going to be unpaid. If you need more, I can try to cover for you, but I can't guarantee your safety with human resources. Do you understand that?"

Xavi nodded, a tad bit relieved. He thought Saeed was going to put up a fight, but it turned out to be a scene from a Hayao Miyazaki film: no villains, only misunderstood good guys.

"Alright," Saeed said. He studied Xavi briefly before saying, "Go home."

Xavi breathed a sigh of relief as he walked out of the office, away from the loquacious Saeed, the jackhammers, and straight into a haven of peace, or so he thought.

# Chapter 26:
# What Could Have Been

Luma opened her eyes and found herself in a dimly lit white room. The single fluorescent bulb gave an electrical hum, thinly illuminating the desk that she sat from. Piles of binders and folders, stacked head high, untidily cluttered the table. One document laid open; it was a profile of Julia, the champion of the race that she was training for before the accident. It contained biometric data and some handwritten remarks which she could not read. What she grasped clearly, though, was the power profile of Julia: 3.8 watts/kg. Luma abruptly laughed, knowing her power used to be higher than that.

She rotated on her seat, taking inventory of the place while rubbing her arms for warmth. Behind her, on a column of shelves drilled to the wall, were lustrous blobs. She narrowed her eyes and focused on the blobs. They became clearer for just the least bit before becoming blobs again. Whenever she squinted, the room stretched longer. The closer her eyelids touched, the further the wall slid away. She growled.

By their blurry shapes, she can only assume that the blobs were trophies, medals, and other memorabilia proudly displayed in a place that tasted like sweet, acidic green apple. Wait, why does this room taste familiar? Wha— why does this room even taste like something at all?

Luma rapidly opened and closed her mouth, making a slurping sound as she imitated a snake flicking its tongue, tasting the environment. Her forehead wrinkled when she recognized the taste. Energy gel? It tasted like the energy gel, a green apple citrus blend, that she consumed back in her cycling days.

The door opened, and a man in a yellow polo shirt, black jeans, and running shoes lolled onto a seat behind the desk across Luma. He had a pointed nose, square face, gelled hair, Slavic cheekbones, and blue eyes. He looked strikingly familiar.

The man took a folder under the pile of documents on his desk. Luma's eyes followed his thick fingers as it pinched the folder's flap and swung it open. When she switched focus from the fingers to the contents, her backbone cracked as it snapped straight. Her brows arched upward in interest. And like a curious cat sniffing a new toy, she leaned forward to look at the document that caused her to jolt. Paperclipped to the top of the folder was a picture of her, donning a smile that was still full of promise and hope. At the bottom of the page, an encircled written note read, *4.3 watts/kg Category-One.*

Holy hell! What the hell?! Luma glanced back up to the man and faintly recognized him. Is that the ride captain? A rush of anticipation struck Luma, not sure for what or of what; she just knew it had to be good. After all, the man appears to be impressed with the data he's reading from the folder.

Doha's national cycling team was relatively new. They didn't have many riders, given the little attention cycling receives in the country. But they are trying their best to recruit nationals or even migrants who're willing to represent the white and maroon flag in UCI (International Cycling Union) sanctioned races.

The current national team directeur sportif, a former Slovenian pro cyclist, hosts family cycling events, organized stage races, and crafted a strong social media presence in order to promote cycling in the country. The current director also happens to be the ride captain, who kept shouting at Luma to slow down during the weekend group rides.

When she recognized who the man is, she stiffened in curious excitement. Only one question protruded in her mind: why would a team director have a dossier on her?

The man kept nodding at the document and giving impressed glances at Luma.

"Luma, you know why I keep telling you to slow down?" the man said, and clasped his hand together atop the open folder.

Luma nodded. "It's not a race; we're there to have fun." She abruptly pursed her lips, surprised that she didn't stutter.

"Exactly. Now, you will have the chance to shine and demonstrate the pinnacle of your potential. I want to put you on the national female squad. If you perform well, I can put you in my continental Slovenian team, then you're just one step away from the World Tour."

Luma held her breath. She wanted to scream in joy, but she only managed an excited giggle.

"Unfortunately…" The man paused for an uncomfortably long time.

Luma's smile waned.

"You only have one leg."

"Holy hell!" she scowled.

"See, if you look back there…" The man pointed to the shelves.

This time, Luma saw the items clearly. Every trophy and every medal bore her name. Every photo was of her crossing the finish line with arms raised high in victory.

"That's all the trophies and medals you could have won," the man continued.

Luma's heart plummeted to the floor with a muted thump.

"And see that little framed paper with your signature on? That's the first contract you would have made as a world pro. You were supposed to compete with the likes of Marianne Vos, Annemiek Van Vleuten, and Pauline Ferrand-Prevot. But now, you can't because you have one leg."

Luma stepped towards the shelves and examined closely the photographs of the what-could-have-been. The pictures that, with each breath, crumbled to dust.

"Luma."

Luma did not respond. The shelf of would-haves and could-haves drew her closer, calling the moth into the light.

"Luma…"

Still no response.

"Luma… … …"

Luma felt a stream of air on her nape. She turned and— The man's nose touched hers. "Don't wake up!" the man said in a raspy voice.

"The hell!" Luma yelled. At that point, blinding whiteness consumed her vision whilst she felt her shoulder being pinched.

After the blinding light receded, her brain registered a wave of familiar sights such as the wall that used to carry her bike, the calendar with many black slashes, her lifeless leg laying on the floor beside the bed, and a pair of feet. Wait, whose feet are those?

Luma looked up, and there, her mother's angry gaze wielded a thousand spikes aimed at her, coercing her to lurch upwards from bed. "W… what… what are you doing here?" she asked, and clamped her teeth upon realizing that her stutter had returned.

"Awake now, your highness?" Rabiya asked.

The dream quickly resurfaced in Luma's mind. It was a terrible dream, but she couldn't tell which one was worse: continuing a bad dream or waking up to a nightmare. Sometimes, she wished things could all end in a blink of an eye.

"Do you know what time it is?" Rabiya added.

"Time for you to leave me alone?" Luma scowled.

Rabiya tramped towards the dresser and took the first object that stood out: a clock in the form of a bicycle, fashioned from copper. Afterward, the clock spun in midair and landed with a plop on Luma's stomach.

"It's time for you to start working again!" Rabiya declared.

"I'm still on the school's payroll Madame Rabiya. It's called a paid sabbatical."

Rabiya said scathingly, "Oh, look at us! We're so rich! Oh, the money, how can I fit it all in my purse? Thanks to you and your selflessness, and your aptitude for heeding your father's wishes… we're broke, goddammit!" She started yelling. "Don't be so indolent, Luma! You're earning just half! It's not enough! You need to start working again! Otherwise, we'll all be living off the streets!"

"Trust me. I would if I could!" Luma said. She hastily attached her prosthetic leg, locked it, stomped passed her chaotic mother, and escaped towards the peaceful living room.

"Why not? Because the school… the school thinks you're depressed? You're not depressed!" chuckled Rabiya.

Luma stopped walking. Was her mother beginning to understand her?

Rabiya laughed with high scorn. "You're faking it! You can't fool me! I don't believe in depression! Depression is overrated! Depression is what people say when they don't get what they want! Kids who lost in video games are depressed! Depressed this, depressed that! Half the world is depressed!" She said with finger quotes.

Blistering heat branched throughout Luma's body from her head to her one leg. Boiling blood roasted every cell inside her body. Her scalding fingers brushed up her wavy red hair and pulled them outwards while growling and roaring, sanity hanging by a thread.

## PORTRAITS OF THE WIND

"Argh! You think depression is fake?! If I don't look depressed to you... you..." Luma stuttered non-stop that she slapped herself just to make her tongue stop sputtering like a garden sprinkler. She drew in a sharp breath and continued yelling, "You're the one who's driving me madder! You're a vacuum sucking the life out of me! You used to be by my side! Now you're pushing me away! What kind of a mother are you? I don't even know you anymore!"

Rabiya equaled her daughter's high decibels, "I'm not pushing you away! I'm simply reprimanding you for your stupidity! Your carelessness! You're reckless! I want you to understand that what you did was wrong! A thousand-fold wrong! You hurt us badly! Me and your baba!"

"You think I don't know that?! You think I don't know?!" Luma arduously took her leg out from under her shorts and threw it with all her might to her yapping mother. At once, Luma lost balance and collapsed onto the floor like a ragdoll. "I will live with it for the rest of my life!" she yelled.

Guilt rose from Rabiya's feet to the top of her head. It was heavy, pushing her down. Her feet shuffled just to keep her balance. Meanwhile, her contrition transformed to shame, but she fought it. Her face remained cruel, and her eyes continued beaming pride. Afterall, she is the mother; she should be the one showing who is right or wrong, not the other way around.

Rabiya wanted to yell something, say something, anything to defend her side, but her mind became a howling chasm of guilt and shame. It immobilized her. She was only able to watch Luma crawl towards her to collect the prosthetic leg that landed beside her feet.

Luma spoke as she attached her leg once more, "I think if I move out, would that please you? And Baba?"

Rabiya watched her daughter as the latter got to her feet. "Maybe you should," she said. The words fell out of her mouth effortlessly, without thought.

Luma honed in on her mother's unblinking eye. Without another word, Luma disappeared into her room and reappeared a few moments later wearing pants and a jacket. Reeking of hatred, she wobbled past her mother, who was still glued to the same place, straining to hold a frown made strenuous by tears and quivering lips.

*** 

With a gentle click, the front door closed behind Luma.

Hoping to receive the gift of tranquility, Luma raised her head to the heavens and inhaled its breath. The heavens gave her something else, though: anger and resentment… again. This drove her madder, and her feet began walking briskly, as fast as they could, aimlessly, stump pinching, to wherever. With each step, she subconsciously punched the walls that she passed by. Step, punch. Step, punch. Blood.

A car whooshed past.

She cocked her head, watching the car disappear into a corner. What if she stepped in front of that car? Will that shut her mother up? Will that prove to her that Luma is depressed and angry?

She stopped, looked at her now bruised and bloody fist, then to the street.

Another car zoomed past.

She exhaled a stream of nervous thrill as she stepped to the edge of the curb. Let's do it, she thought.

The sun gradually felt cold on her skin. Her muscles shook and quivered, and her mouth dried up.

Another car whizzed by.

Her ears now only heard her thumping heartbeat.

Another car drove by. And another.

Cold sweat collected in her pores the moment she closed her eyes.

She expected bikes, wind, and ecstasy to flash in her mind; those long-gone emotions that had burrowed into the depths of the earth. But none of it turned up. There was nothing except the face of her mother, shouting at her, screaming at her, unloving her. Shut up!

"Goodbye, mother."

She heard a truck. By the sound of it, it was a big one: a lorry, an eighteen-wheeler with powerful diesel engines. The sound got closer. Louder. Roaring. Whistling. She started screaming inside, in her head, to numb her, everything. She willed her lungs to take a deep breath until it stung. Bikes and wind exploded in her mind; although it wasn't of ecstasy, it was the disastrous crash. Bursting with anger, she took a step onto the road.

The truck's horn blared.

Everything happened so quick.

Warm wind with the smell of diesel slapped Luma's face, pushing her back to the safety of the sidewalk.

"Crap!"

She waited for another car.

"Let's try again…"

Whoosh! Her feet remained still.

"Aargh!" she yelled to the heavens. She yelled to the walls around. "Dammit!" Her fists began jackhammering the wall there until red blots appeared on its white paint. When her knuckles had begun to crack, she stopped and winced. She leaned her forehead against the wall to catch her racing breath.

"Am I not yet brimming with fury?" she asked herself.

She wondered how much more pent up anger, how much more dissing from her mother would push her to step beyond the curb. One more day? One more hour?

She observed all the people in the streets, in the cars, the kids playing, and the adults busy with their own thing. They were all oblivious to her failed attempt. She wondered what were they thinking about at that moment, where were they headed? What would they do if they lost a leg too? Is it worth losing a life over? Is it? Is it?

A voice inside her said, "Seriously, you need help, you legless bitch."

"Fine," she whispered laboriously. "Crap!"

\*\*\*

The box-like three-story villa of Dr. Raju's clinic loomed above the others in its surroundings. Luma marveled at the clinic from the other side of the road.

The other villas were a measly one-story structure, housing beauty salons, and spas. Unlike the others whose walls were painted dull white, the clinic boasted a façade of black marble tiles and gold-tinted windows. If gangsters blinged-out their cars to display their purported wealth, Dr. Raju blinged-out his building to flaunt his. To Luma, it either indicated Raju's success over his long career, or along with the Mercedes G-Class SUV parked in front of the villa, it indicated his lavish price tag.

Luma looked left and right, crossed the road, got to the clinic's entrance, and then stopped short of the door, hand gripping the handle. The sight of a thousand-riyal per session bill drifted across her mind.

Dr. Raju, who was talking with his receptionist, glanced up to the front entrance when the light coming from the glass doors was blocked. There, he saw a woman clasping the door handle stiffly and not moving. She looks familiar, the doctor thought. When he had paced to open the door for this dazed woman, she fled, limping, into the streets there.

"Look, Dr. Raju, I don't have anything against you. I want to get better. Trust me, I do. It's either I die now, or I get better. But you charge diamonds for your ear!" Luma mumbled to herself as she hastened away from the clinic and went running to the neighborhood of paltry-looking villas. "How will you get better then?" Luma stopped at the thought, her lungs throbbing to catch her breath. "Darn it!" she howled.

*"Do something different, get into a routine, keep yourself preoccupied, and have fun."* Luma recalled all the tips that Dr. Raju told her for conquering depression alone. I'm doing all of that, aren't I? Am I missing something?

Luma continued wandering the semi-residential, and semi-commercial neighborhood. She thought profoundly and dug for clues inside her muddy mind for what might be hindering her progress to betterment.

Fifteen hundred meters passed, an increasing mechanical roar unnerved sleeping birds on the trees there. It sounded like an angry V6. In a split second, Luma's hair flew forward after a black sedan whooshed past her. Its brakes squealed, and its tires screeched as the vehicle came to a halt a hundred meters away from her. The passenger door opened, and a toddler around the age of four stepped out. A yelling mother followed closely.

"Slow down!" the mother howled to the prancing child.

The boy disappeared into a villa whose blue and yellow gate swallowed him. Next, soft yet distinct noises of laughter and joyful screams wafted through the distance. The sounds that traveled into the canal of Luma's ears piqued her interest, and she found herself treading towards the villa. She didn't know why she was suddenly drawn to the noise of jovial screams; she just was.

She mouthed what she was hearing, "Laughter, and joyful screams." Then, like a veil pulled out from the top of her head, she understood what those words meant. Fun? The three-letter word reverberated in her mind. Is that why I'm still angry? I just need to have fun?

Luma continued pacing towards the villa, and the sanguine noises kept getting louder and sharper, with enough decibels to push any teacher in a classroom to the edge of their sanity. Fortunately, she wasn't in a classroom, and she wasn't a teacher at that moment. At that moment, she was a trapped soul in a deafening cave of misery, looking for an escape.

The A3-size nameplate mounted on the concrete fence read: *Kabayat Day Care & Nursery*. She peered through the small slit between the metal gate and the wall there. Even with its millimeter-wide gap, she could see the precious figures of little children.

Kids of various races and ethnicity played together. Some were on the playground. Some were scampering around playing tag. Some were facing an easel, painting.

Painting? The word lodged in her mind.

The kids who were holding brushes and drawing colorful strokes on the canvas became the center of Luma's attention. There were five kids painting, arranged in a line at the porch, and none of them showed signs of sorrow. Only glee and delight were the emotions that radiated outwards from their innocent faces. She could do that, probably, she thought. She reasoned that that activity could be an outlet, a medium, where she could dump her emotions and free herself from her leaden burden. And it doesn't need two legs.

## PORTRAITS OF THE WIND

Luma took out her phone and googled for paintings. She searched for paintings that expressed the tenor of their artist's emotions. It returned too many results for only two artworks resonated with her: The Scream by Edvard Munch and The Blue Room by Pablo Picasso.

The former spoke to her resentment and anger with its striking darkness underneath the manic combination of colors. She heard the voiceless screams of anguish that each brushstroke expressed. And the two men in black chasing the deformed screaming person made the hair on the back of her neck rise to its roots. To her, the black-clad men were agents of unrealized dreams and unfulfilled ambitions, trying to wreak havoc on a person's soul.

The latter, Picasso's sad art, spoke to Luma's feelings of dread and despair—the feelings of helplessness and loneliness. There were no sharp corners on the painting; everything was curved and rounded, almost melting, redolent of her life.

In that artwork was a naked woman standing over a basin, bathing. On the wall behind the naked lady hung a portrait of her wishful past, and it was taunting her nakedness, taunting her present decrepit self, where tears are lost in a pool of rancid water beneath unsteady feet. Luma identified with the lady at once, with the loneliness and the haunting of the past.

What aroused her interest more was the hidden image behind the colors of The Blue Room. Only discovered in 2014, beneath the sad artwork of the woman was an unknown portrait of a man resting his head on his hand. The painting was depression underneath another depression. She thought that it mirrored her life. Probably. Maybe.

"I could definitely paint my feelings," she told herself, "I'll be the female Van Gogh. Instead of a missing ear, I have a missing leg."

Pleased at the thought, and with a renewed sense of adventure lined with uncertainty, Luma charged to the nearest bookstore.

# Chapter 27:
# A Tangent in a Universe of Lines

Six p.m. It was getting busy at the red line metro station again. Amidst the multitude of faces impetuous to get home after a busy day was a limping woman, lugging an easel and a bulky plastic bag. She waited for the next train behind the painted yellow line, and like any society, except maybe Japan, unruly commuters stepped ahead of the yellow line in a shot to secure the best spot inside the train.

The blood coursing beneath her skin was now as volatile as rocket fuel. A single rogue spark can trigger a catastrophe, and there, in the form of rowdy travelers, was a furious tinder. Even more infuriating, the unruly mob raised their heads high, acting superior. Grr... Luma fumed internally. In a bid to stabilize her threatening rage, she pressed her lips together until it formed wrinkles while she waited long-sufferingly for the next train to arrive.

At precisely three minutes, the doors of the next train slid open. Luma stayed put, allowing the passengers to detrain. To her dismay, the other commuters pushed against the outbound travelers, creating chaos of people bumping against one another. Her anger reached a critical point right there.

"Dickheads!" Luma swore aloud. "Let the people get out first!" she added.

No one listened; the horde elided her. Furious, she held her easel tighter by the leg, gripping it like a bat. A desire was mounting to use it as a weapon to pummel the divergents into submission. But that would be too scandalous, she thought. Instead, simmering with outrage, she pushed through the lawless grains of people and surreptitiously swung her easel left and right. It hit someone. Who?

She doesn't care. It hit someone again. Who? Who cares? It hit someone once more; she giggled maniacally. She swung the easel left and right until she boarded the train. Unbeknownst to her, the corner of the easel's horizontal frame, the part that holds the canvas, got caught at the edge of the train's door.

"Doors closing," the female recorded voice announced, "Please step away from the doors."

Luma felt the easel being yanked from her. Thinking she was being mugged, her veins popped one after the other. Rage oozed out her body. She clenched her teeth, and with a low growl, she whirled around with lightning speed. Fire consumed her, ready to decimate the criminal into smoldering ashes. Then, like a tsunami over a campfire, fear drenched her rage. In place of a mugger, she saw in horror the easel about to be crushed between the train's sliding doors. (That was the first second.)

Her mind pictured many scenarios of what might happen. She heard stories of people's legs or arms getting stuck between train doors only to have them freed at the next station. That was a best-case of what could happen. Panicking minds always think of the worst.

She visualized the part of the easel sticking out will break apart, splintering, and hitting some critical part of the train's wheels, causing the train to stop, irreparable, in the middle of the tunnel. Upon investigation, the authorities will find out that her carelessness caused the disruption, then be apprehended and fined thousands for all the line's unexpected delay.

Many more horror scenes played inside Luma's mind as the train doors— A pair of hands wedged in and pried the doors apart. These same hands then thrusted the easel inwards with cobra-like agility before the doors slammed shut.

Silence.

Luma was stunned. (That was the second second.)

The train, unwitting, gradually inched forward. Luma grabbed hold of the pole closest to her to keep her balance. Intuitively, she peered out the window to see who those heroic hands belonged to. She spotted the same hand waving at her, getting smaller together with the receding platform. Her eyes tracked it from its fingers to its palm, to its arm, to the wrinkled blue polo shirt, to the wooly beard.

Wooly Asian!

Luma scoured her memory bank for Wooly's name.

"Xavi!" she remembered. She waved back in gratitude. Too late. The train already entered the tunnel before she could raise her arm. (That was the third second. Everything happened in only three seconds.) Now, for some reason unknown to her, as the train disappeared into the dark tunnel, she felt a golf ball lodge in her throat.

"Al Mamriya Station," the autonomous female voice said. The doors opened, and Luma aggressively fought her way through the unmanageable inbound passengers. Get out of the way, bitches! She swung her easel left and right once more. Her easel was Moses' staff, and the people were the Red Sea.

There was a small café just before the escalator leading up to the city. Hurriedly, Luma scanned her metro card on the turnstile and sped to a seat at that café. With a quick mental math, knowing that the trains are only six minutes apart, she surmised that Xavi would walk out of the turnstile approximately seven to eight minutes, barring any mishaps.

"Ma'am, can I take your order?" a voice asked twelve minutes later, breaking Luma's fixated gaze at the outgoing commuters. A waiter stared at her with a look that says, *"you have to order if you want to sit."* Well goddammit! Luma picked up the menu waiting for her at the table. The cafe sold cakes, tea, coffee, cookies, milkshakes, and chocolates, and the price tag was also expensive.

"Water!" Luma said audaciously.

"Anything else?" the waiter lingered for a while.

She shook her head without looking at him.

With an imperceptible scoff, the waiter left and punched-in Luma's single order to the POS system.

Luma checked her watch. How long has it been? She couldn't tell. It felt like an eternity, at the same time it only felt like a second. Tipping her bottled water side to side, she realized that she had drunk three-quarters of it already.

Where are you, Wooly? Did I miscalculate? Am I also bad in math now? Darn it! Wait a minute, why am I even waiting for you? Luma chuckled as she took a crumpled bill from her pocket, placed it on the table, and left.

Luma hobble-wobbled home past the streets of cloud nine. Though she was limping, in her mind, she was skipping. The sight of Wooly, even just for an ephemeral second, threw the livid events of the morning with Rabiya into the outer rim of her memory. She kept wondering, each step of the thousand steps home, what is that peculiar energy she keeps experiencing?

Why? Why? Why do you make me feel this way? There is one thing I'm sure of, it isn't love. Love is cycling; cycling isn't Xavi. But why?

She reached home, opened the door and...

It wasn't astonishment that froze her, it wasn't shock, it was indignation. The morning's rage returned with an uproar. For there, twisted on the couch, was Rabiya and Hashem staring at her. Her father showed indifference, but her mother, god her mother, she was scowling, steaming, glowing redder than molten steel in a furnace.

"I thought you're moving out?" was Rabiya's greeting to her daughter.

Luma did not respond. She flounced into her bedroom and let the door slip from her fingers into a moderate slam. Cloud nine was gone; she's back to the prison home.

In her room, still fuming with righteous anger, she set up the easel and the canvas. She picked up the paintbrush and… nothing. She had lost her will to paint. Was it her fury? Was it her matchstick personality?

The female Van Gogh. What a joke, she thought, and then she pondered about moving out, or just really stepping in front of a truck next time around.

\*\*\*

Xavi woke up to birds outside the window that sang melodies with the gentle breeze. After the dreary events of the previous days, their songs were a welcoming sound to his exhausted soul. His limbs extended outwards, and a measure of mirth percolated throughout his body accompanied by a gaping yawn. He took in the new sparkling day and inhaled the splendor.

Xavi proceeded to the kitchen, opened the freezer, and took out a box of "the breakfast of champions" (chicken nuggets).

The tiny ice crystals clinging to the nuggets' skins sizzled over the hot oil, and their pale white coats turned golden brown. His lips pursed atypically while a whistle of delight harmonized with the frying meal. Ten minutes later, he loafed across the dining table with a plate of rice and golden nuggets. Every bite of the crunchy nugget released more saliva in the corners of his mouth. He has been having nuggets since he was five. Almost three decades later, his taste buds still haven't had enough of its crumbly goodness.

Xavi momentarily stared at the beautiful nugget that he forked. No thought came to mind, not even a brush of the ancient yesterdays. It was one of those moments where you find yourself staring at a piece of the present, like staring at the clock for a long time without realizing that you are watching time itself. And as he lifted the nugget to take a bite, he remembered Nicola; so quaint in her Filipiñana attire, propped up in The Philippine School clinic's bed. She was holding a fork with a piece of chicken nugget on its end, waving it to his mouth.

A smile crept on Xavi's face, and it was of pleasure, a sudden burst of merriment. "Ha!" A sanguine scoff unconsciously escaped his mouth too. Confusion directly followed.

Dazed, his head swiftly turned about towards the living room, his bed, and the kitchen. He scanned for the beast of despair, searching for its glowing white eyes, waiting for it to start stampeding towards— It was nowhere to be found! It had no place to hide either, the room was bright, sunny, and shadowless, with visible specks of dust hovering through the rays of sunlight. He chuckled once more.

"I'm… I'm okay?" Xavi asked himself, thinking how staggeringly fickle emotions can be. A week ago, he was gradually descending in a desolate pit of despair, with the world turning black, and his body struggling even to get out of bed. Now, he's back in dry land for no perceptible reason.

The screenwriting class once again rang inside Xavi's head, how everything should be tangled in reason. But the truth is, things do happen without reason, and those who try to find a single thread of purpose in the fabric of life will only drive themselves mad. Life itself, sometimes, is too unbelievable even for fiction.

Or is there actually a reason? Xavi asked himself.

He retraced his steps leading up to this moment of effervescence. He thought of the few days where he was caged in the dark with his beast, without any hope of freedom. And in a seemingly random moment, an angry girl named Luma comes up to him and offers her shoulder.

Crying over the woman's shoulder felt right, though he can't fathom the reason why.

On another day, yesterday, he took a long walk after getting off work early to clear his mind. And when he got into the station to board the red line home, he caught a glimpse of Luma once more. At that moment, he experienced a brand-new crushing pain in his chest after he missed the chance to ride with the woman. It wasn't a crippling pain; however, it wasn't a measly mosquito bite either. The pain lingered, compelling him to pace around, pivoting every five steps or so, irking other commuters. It was the kind of pain brought by an ephemeral enchantment laced with a sting of disillusion, a sort of visceral hurt you get when you meet someone new and the moment is seized by the fleeting passage of time. It is the sorrow of experiencing a single tangent in a universe of intersecting lines, or in his case, two souls pulled apart by a departing train without even given the chance of a touch.

"Wait a minute... no! Is it you, Ms. Luma? Nah. It can't be. There's only one woman who can bring me joy, and that's Cola," Xavi said with muted severity while looking at the whole piece of chicken nugget that's still clinging on the fork. He stared at it, searching for a reason within its crumbly crust, picturing the gentle, almost imperceptible pull of Luma's gravity.

"Well, there's only one way to find out." Xavi, at last, took a bite of the poor nugget. "Wait, are you sure?" Xavi chewed, savoring the mouthwatering flavor. "Yeah, why not? There's nothing wrong with it, right? I just want to know who she is, why she is. Right?"

# Chapter 28:
# Rules of Serendipity

Qatar's red line is one of the busiest routes having direct access to the center of Doha's business district. Every day, the silver bullet moves a hundred thousand strangers from a small desert town all the way to the jungle of West Bay by Doha's edge. There, tall trees are made of concrete and glass, and metal birds roar beyond the cloudless skies.

On the fourth hub from the south, a thousand faces blended in innocent serendipity. Travelers frolicked unwittingly in the universe's game of passing destiny. In the Dictionary of Obscure Sorrows, they had named this very phenomenon "the moments of tangency."

From the cobalt morning to the glittering night, eyes saw eyes, shoulders brushed shoulders, people met people randomly like a silver ball in a giant pinball game. It is unbiased, impartial, and nonprejudiced, just as the first law of serendipity dictates: ***Those who seek shall not find; those who do not seek shall find.***

Every day, a man with a wooly beard rode the red line train. He rode it faithfully from five to six in the evening during the height of the rush hour. He had no direction and no destination. He boarded the train with only one objective in mind: find Serendipity. Serendipity, who accidentally brought him comfort in the days of his dejection. Serendipity, whose name echoed sporadically in his mind's ear. He was curious. He was keen to meet Serendipity again, just to prove if Serendipity was, or wasn't, indeed, exhuming the gaiety that was once buried under the weight of five million minutes.

If he failed to see Serendipity in the train, he would wait on the platform, watching every face, close and afar, looking for Serendipity's recognizable wavy red locks. To him, Serendipity had no voice, but her shoulder spoke louder than any mouth can bellow.

In between the moments that he didn't search for Serendipity, he occupied himself in learning a different language. It was a language that maybe Serendipity understands.

One thousand one, one thousand two, one thousand three, he trimmed his beard. One thousand four, one thousand five, one thousand six; six days that felt like a thousand each, he would watch and wait, and wait, and wait, and wait, and nothing. He knew where Serendipity lived, but he thought he'd instead leave their meeting in the hands of destiny rather than looking like a stalker, prowling behind the blades of steel grass on the floor of the concrete jungle.

The second law of serendipity states: ***Two faces of the same coin will never meet eye-to-eye.***

On the other side of the coin, on another thunderous speeding worm, a limping woman searched for her Serendipity. She doesn't know who Serendipity is; all she knew was Serendipity gave her a peculiar ball of energy—a vigorous vivacity of joie de vivre. Serendipity imparted to her a verve that made her somehow, weirdly, bewilderingly, astonishingly, richly smile. It was almost the same kind of energy bestowed to her when riding on two wheels. She wanted more.

Serendipity flummoxed her. One side of her saw Serendipity as an ugly disheveled man, who wore pubic hair on his chin. However, the other side of her stared out the bedroom window, peering into the starlight, and waiting for Serendipity to trudge up to her doorstep and deliver to her that vim of life. Other days, she would go to the platform for a moment thinking that maybe, just maybe, the hands of fate will be kind to her, and she will be gifted the chance of a glance. But Serendipity was never there. There were only a thousand faces, blank faces that carried no weight. Was she slow? Was she too quick? Was she early? Was she late? She'll never know because Serendipity always took another path.

The third and last law of serendipity decrees: ***Don't be lazy. Go write your own destiny.***

On the seventh day, at 5:00 p.m., Xavi was watching the forward accordion diaphragm that connected the train cars together. He paid attention to its breathing motion as it extended and distended with the metal worm's momentum. When the train passed a curving track, the cars temporarily misaligned, revealing in the forward car— The wavy crimson hair! She was sitting in the same row, behind the bellows. The track straightened. As briefly as it had appeared, the hair disappeared.

A bolt of anticipation hit Xavi. He leaned forward on his chair as far as he could, hoping to get another glimpse of the hair. His stomach touched his knees. His bottom approached the edge of the seat. He turned his head, turned ninety degrees, and there on the other side of the accordion, he saw the upside-down image of Luma.

Finally! Incredulous emotions filled Xavi. Finally! He remained in a stooped position for a minute before Luma caught a glimpse of him. When she did, he snapped back up and blood abruptly drained from his head. He became lightheaded, not only from the lack of blood in his brain, but also from his bursting exhilaration.

On the other side of the bellows, Luma saw Xavi in one second, and in another, he was gone. Her heart started to race. She kept her gaze locked to where Xavi appeared. A minute later, he still did not reappear. She lowered her head, eyes on her fingers, slowly turning them, looking at the unpolished nails. She thought of what she just saw: Xavi was strangely more groomed; the pubes on his chin were trimmed into a tidy stubble.

## PORTRAITS OF THE WIND

The corners of Luma's lips rose imperceptibly as images of Xavi staring at her flashed with each beat of her heart. Try as she might, she was having a hard time denying that his face had enough lumens to pierce the darkness of her world. She hoped that this time, though, their meeting will be more than a passing moment.

The bellows between the two cars gently pulsed back and forth. The train softly bounced at its own speed. Luma checked again if Xavi was there, still, he wasn't.

The train passed a light mounted on the tunnel's wall. Luma caught the glow briefly on the other car's window, opposite where she saw Xavi. It was such a blur. There! And then gone. The instant the tunnel turned black, an image on the windowpane appeared. It was Xavi, looking directly at her reflection. Again, Xavi looked away, embarrassed, but Luma kept his sight.

The train shook, like driving over a speedbump at high speeds. Xavi monitored the window again, and there, once more, they found each other through their reflections. Then both turned away.

Their eyes danced with the symphony of light and dark. Light swoosh! Darkness, reflection. Both glimpsed at the same time. Both turned away at the same time. Light swoosh! Darkness, reflection. One looked and watched the other. Light swoosh! Darkness, reflection. The other looked and watched the other. Light swoosh! Darkness... reflection... SQUEAL! The brakes engaged. The train slowed down steadily as it arrived at Al Mamriya station. The doors opened, and the windowpane that was once alive with glances is now a regular window again.

\*\*\*

The pair stood still a train car apart. Outgoing passengers brushed against them, and incoming travelers filtered their gaze. Half a minute later, the train departed, and they were alone in a platform that smelled like sweet winter.

The man was awkward; immobilized. The lady was— just the least bit the same. The announcement of the next arriving train broke their muteness, and Luma cordially pointed towards the exit with an eloquent stare. Their bodies twisted and turned. Their feet started trudging, forward and diagonal, towards an invisible point beyond the turnstile. Their paths converged twenty steps later and they continued walking together.

They wandered once more with lips sealed under the glistening stars. Cold breezes ruffled their hair.

Over the distance, Xavi saw a small corner restaurant. He turned to his companion, waved at her, and gestured a language of hands. His lips mouthed inaudible words, and his face was intense as he tried to communicate his message across.

Xavi had formed a letter *C* with his right hand, and he moved it up and down his chest like he was stroking his esophagus with the cupped hand.

Luma furrowed her brows. She didn't understand what he meant.

Frustrated with his failed attempt to sign language, Xavi improvised. He stopped walking, raised his right pinky, tapped it in his chest, and rubbed his stomach with the same hand in a big circular motion.

"What?" asked Luma with a short burst of amusement. "What are you saying? I'm not deaf!"

Xavi was thrown back. "Wha— I thought you were mute. I thought you knew sign language."

Luma laughed. "No, silly wooly man!" she said.

"But..." began Xavi. They continued walking again while he looked down and watched the ground scroll beneath his feet. He thought of the few passing meetings with her where she didn't speak. He was sure, he thought, she was mute.

"I just didn't want to talk because of my severe stutter. Why?" Luma giggled, "Did you study sign language for me?"

Xavi watched her lips. "Stutter? Like how?"

"Like when I talk! I stutter!" She stopped abruptly and placed her hands over her lips. Her thick brows arched and dipped. Her eyes shot everywhere, rapidly, before landing back to Xavi with a look of astonished incredulity.

Both fell quiet. The wind gently howled. The date palms rustled.

She glacially pulled her hand away from her face, showing the quivering lips underneath. "H... hi... Hello? *Halo? Hola? Marhaba?* The quick brown fox jumped over the lazy ass. I mean dog."

Xavi chuckled.

Luma sniggered in delight and then jumped up and down. "I'm not stuttering? I'm not stuttering! Oh my god!!"

Could it be possible that a person's sheer presence alleviates another's ailment? Perhaps. Even placebos have been documented to cure Parkinson's disease.

After her ecstasy returned to normal levels, she faced Xavi, overjoyed and panting. "What was that you wanted to sign to me?" she asked through her curved lips.

"I'm hungry. Do you like to try Filipino food?" asked Xavi while pointing towards the corner of the street where a small ramshackle restaurant stood.

Luma thought for a moment before yelling enthusiastically, "Why the hell not?!" Without any prompt, she started leading the way towards the restaurant. Something new! she thought.

The cyclist, the teacher, the lady with the wavy crimson hair, who was brooding months ago, was now filled with vigor for the unknown.

"Come on, Wooly! Let's eat that Filipino food!" yelled Luma over the distance.

***

Warm steam billowed from the kitchen towards the restaurant floor, sending the sweet and pungent aroma of garlic, vinegar, butter, peanuts, and coconuts, fanning everywhere. It enveloped the cramped room of five tables with barely a space to pass in between. The door opened, quickly evaporating the Southeastern kitchen odor onto the cold Middle Eastern winter outside.

Twelve pairs of eyes, customers and staff, turned and gawped in awe at the rare sight of a foreigner entering the humble restaurant. Even rarer, a Filipino man accompanied her. It is usually the other way around—a Filipina with a foreigner.

The two unlikely new friends found a table, the only empty table, near the toilet. They shuffled sideways along the restricted space, bumping their butts to the weathered tables and customer's backs.

"Why are they all looking at us?" softly asked Luma.

"I think they know you've overcome your stutter. They're proud," replied Xavi, his voice congratulatory.

She playfully punched Xavi's arm as they had lazed in at their chosen table.

The waiter approached with the menu.

Luma skimmed through the choices and scanned for recognizable items from a list of foreign names. "Sinigang na Baka", "Lumpiang Gulay", "Bistek Tagalog", "Tapsilog", "Longsilog", "Tosilog", "Bangsilog."

What the hell are these? she thought. She softly asked Xavi, "Do you know Filipino food?"

Xavi nodded and took the task of ordering a selection of food for them. The waiter leaned in, turning his ear towards Xavi who spoke in his native Filipino tongue. The waiter double checked the order in his mental notepad, squinting, looking up, and reading the list of items written in the air. When Xavi was satisfied, the waiter left and shouted the orders in the kitchen.

Rock music then blared without warning, adding to the cacophonies resident to a small ramshackle cafeteria. Luma noted that the sound was coming from the video karaoke near the kitchen door. A few seconds later, a patron's discordant voice started shrieking out from the speakers as she sang the lyrics displayed on the TV. It would have been annoying, save for the fact that the patron's overconfidence made her more entertaining.

Luma turned back to Xavi. "You're Filipino?" she asked loudly over the discorded musical notes.

"Yes!"

She shook her head in surprise. "Oh! I thought you were Indonesian, or Malaysian with your," she motioned at his beard, "It's shorter now, but still, I don't see many Filipinos with a wooly face."

"I know!" replied Xavi, with his head raised high. Unexpectedly, or maybe it should already be expected from him, words had gone from his mind. So, he suddenly found himself fascinated with the singer with a discorded voice. For days, he was looking forward to meeting the girl with the wavy red hair, and after just a few minutes sitting with her, he got dumbstruck.

Luma bit her lips at the abrupt silence. She's used to silence, she loves silence, but this silence was restless. She had the strong urge to talk and to exercise her unstuttering lips, however, like Xavi, words elided her searching mind.

After a few breaths of the moistened air, Luma looked left to the other customers joking around; she looked right towards the TV with the label *videoke*, and she looked up to the ceiling fan that had gathered years of oil and gunk. She kept looking around, everywhere, seeking for a topic to open a conversation.

After a long while of thinking, searching, and formulating words, a question finally came out from one of the two people sitting by the toilet.

"Where are you from?" Xavi asked.

"Morocco."

"Ah. Luma from Morocco." He nodded excessively as his mind went blank again.

The waiter came and served the food after another off-key song. Xavi served Luma a cup of rice, poured a soup of *sinigang* over it, and then sprinkled some beef chunks on the side.

Luma took her first taste of the sinigang (a sour beef stew of sorts), taking a sip of its zesty tamarind soup. Her face soured pleasantly as her taste buds absorbed the delicious, zingy flavor of tamarind, guavas, and beef. It was *lutong-bahay*, Xavi explained, a staple food in Filipino houses.

The delectable lutong-bahay seemed to soften their stiff tongues. After a few bites of the chewy chunks of beef and a few sips of the soup, their mouths began to pour out words after words, like they were intoxicated with the sourness of the sinigang. They talked about their country, their work, and their childhood. They spoke of Xavi's ugly beard and Luma's artificial red hair. They indulged in conversing, sometimes with long sentences, and sometimes with few words. They spoke until their plates were wiped clean, their drinks were refilled, and twelve discordant songs were sung in the background.

While waiting for the dessert, Luma caught a distinct sound ascending from the other table. A customer was watching a replay of the 2019 Tour de France in his phone, at the stage where Egan Bernal, the youngest tour winner at 22, snatched the leader's jersey from a Frenchman. She gawked at the tiny screen. A negative thrill quaked in her bones, a kind of electrifying joy that pulled her down instead of up. She wanted to look away. She moved her head, but her eyes stayed put.

Xavi noticed Luma's mouth unhinge slightly while her breathing slowed and shallowed. Her fingers were also subconsciously scratching the color off of the blue vinyl tablecloth. "Are you okay?" he asked under the loud music.

Luma took a deep breath, held it for a second, and released a long sorrowful exhale.

"Luma?"

She pulled her hand away from the table, leaving tiny white streaks where her nails plowed. "W... wh... what?" she answered casually.

Both were stunned off guard. The stutter, was it back?

"Are you okay?" asked Xavi, even softer and slower.

Luma looked to her left, back to the faraway phone. In a second, she averted her gaze to the next table's food in a bid to distract her mind from eliciting the emotions that have never visited her for a while. She turned to Xavi; her tongue contained the words, but her lips stuttered in silence. She exhaled, forcing all the frustration through her mouth.

Xavi waited patiently, smiling, and looking away whenever their eyes met.

She appreciated that, but it also pressured her to sputter. "What…" she paused, breathed in and out, and continued, "What were you crying about last time?" No more stutter.

It was Xavi who paused this time, again, out of words.

Luma held up her palms in surrender. "No. My bad. Sorry. It doesn't matter. Don't answer that," she said.

"No, no, it's okay, it's okay. I suppose you have the right to know what type of tears fell on your shoulder." He smiled lopsidedly, sighed, and looked away. "Those tears were a decade worth of caged grief."

Luma furrowed in intrigue.

"I have… um…" Xavi bowed his head, spooned the left-over rice on his plate to one side, and said, "Well, the doctor said I'm suffering from depression." He paused again and spooned the rice to the other side, and said, "Had it for ten years now."

"Oh, wow," Luma said softly in disbelief. In the back of her mind, she considered that it might be the reason why she felt such energy with him; they had the same negative aura emanating from their cores. Perhaps only the depressed would understand how she felt.

"Well, I had my ways of managing it," Xavi continued.

"Meds?"

He abruptly shook his head. "Oh, no! No! Medicine will make me forget. I don't want to forget. I didn't even proceed with my therapy because I fear that I will forget."

"Forget what?"

Xavi seemed brooding for a time, which prompted Luma to wave a hand and shake her head.

"It's alright, forget it. We don't have to talk about it," she said.

"Her name was Nicola," said Xavi. Shivers ran in his arms. "We met here in Qatar as students. She was… we were supposed to be married now, I think. God knows. She died—" he choked, "She died the day I was supposed to propose to her in the Philippines. We were together for six years. Supposedly sixteen years now if she had said yes."

Luma exhaled a breath of empathy. "Oh, hell. And you, after ten years? You must really love her."

Xavi's lips curved proudly while his face remained bleaker than the night's winter skies.

"Did you go to the shrink voluntarily?" she asked.

"No. I was forced to. Well, because..." He was about to spoon the rice again, but he pushed his plate away. "Never mind. That was stupid. I was stupid. I wanted to be with her. I wanted to join her; if you know what I mean." He briefly shook his head. "Stupid."

Another man picked up the microphone over the videoke station. He started singing. He had the confidence of the previous patron, but he was more out of key.

"And that's why I came back here," added Xavi, "I read somewhere that familiar places can sometimes help people with Alzheimer's. I thought it would be the same for grieving."

"Was that recommended to you? Coming back to familiar surroundings?"

He shook his head, "No... it was my own medicine. Sometimes it helps; most of the time, it doesn't. Sometimes, the source of one's pleasure is also the source of one's grief. So..." He shrugged and let out a long thin exhale. For ten years he didn't find anyone comfortable to talk with. But now, here she sat, listening to him, unjudging, no encouragements, just lending an ear.

The dessert finally came. Xavi immediately dug into the soft, Filipino leche-flan, hoping its rich sweet taste would overpower the bitter memory.

"Thank you," she said.

"For what?" he asked, chewing.

"For talking to me. For trusting. I mean, we only met. Granted we've met before, but we only actually begun talking just now, and you willingly opened up. I think that's brave."

"Did it change?"

"What?"

"Your first impression of me. What do you think of me now?"

Luma leaned back, crossed her arms, tilted her head, and scoured the chubby wooly man. "That beard really looks ugly on you," she said with a straight face.

Xavi snorted, almost choking on the flan. He wasn't expecting her to be too direct.

Luma giggled and said, "Well, since you've been so honest with me, can I show you something?"

"What's that?"

Luma scanned the surrounding. A new set of customers already occupied the other four tables, and all of them were facing away from the pair. She checked the man at the videoke: also back turned towards them. Satisfied that no one was looking at them, she gently pulled out her prosthesis and nonchalantly brought it up to the edge of the table, playfully sliding it left to right while humming to the tune of *Jaws*. At the climax of the theme, Luma flailed her fake leg around up high like a jumping shark.

Shock painted Xavi's face. His wide-open eyes followed Luma's leg as it moved around the table and then back to her stump.

"What do you think of me now?" asked Luma.

Xavi thought of a competent and funny quip, and what came out was: "Still beautiful." He pursed his lips inward, surprised at the words that blurted out.

A pulse of red heat came in and went over Luma's face.

"So, what happened there?" Xavi quickly asked, averting from his awkward comment.

"Have a guess."

"You wanted to be a flamingo?"

"You're bad at banters, aren't you?" she mused.

"Yeah," he said proudly.

"Well, I was also stupid. I was training for a race, 'cos I'm a cyclist. And so, yeah, long story short, I got into an accident. And guess what, I think God found the story of my life boring, wanted to give it a twist ending, so they cut my leg. And now all my dreams, my ambitions, they're gone. You know what's worse? I'm always reminded of it because I have to carry my missing leg around. Know what I mean?"

"Is that why you're angry?"

Luma looked at him, confused. How would he know that she was angry? Did someone finally understand her?

Xavi waited for an answer. When she only replied with a bewildered look, he added, "That's what you wrote, right? At the paper? From the psych clinic?"

"Oh, the paper..." She stared at her flan for a while whilst thinking. "Wouldn't you believe it; anger is also a form of depression. Anger!" She scoffed. "So here we are, two depressed people, eating flan at a Filipino restaurant." She took a bite of the flan.

"How're your sessions going?" he asked.

"Oh, no, no. Like you, I didn't continue. They really have a great way to cure your depression."

"Oh?"

"Yep. I got cured right away upon seeing my first bill," she chuckled.

He laughed, "Yeah! I know, right!"

The howling man at the videoke finished his round.

"So, how are you coping with your... thing?" Xavi asked after watching the man who sang take his seat.

Luma shrugged. "I'm still discovering things. I'm still a neophyte. It's only been less than a year. But I am trying new things. The shrink said it would help to ease the agony. Do something fun, he said." Then with earnest conviction, Luma tossed her spoon on the table and pointed to Xavi. "Hey, wait! Maybe we could paint together! I bought all these painting materials, hoping to try something new, but I haven't done anything yet! Maybe we could paint our depression! You think that's gonna be fun?"

Xavi considered it, "Sure. But you know what's really fun?"

Luma slightly turned her ear in attention.

"When was the last time you sang?" Xavi pointed to the waiting microphone under the TV.

Luma shook her head. "No!"

"C'mon! You experienced the food, it's time you experience the pastimes!" He stood up, pulling Luma.

"No! No! No! No!!!"

Xavi shoved the microphone into her hand. "You'll be great, I promise! If not, it doesn't matter; you'll sound exactly like the rest of them!" He pointed to all the people in the restaurant, who were now curiously looking at the foreigner with the microphone. "Try new things, right?"

Xavi grabbed the song book, flipped the pages with excitement, and chose a song for Luma. He punched in the song number in the videoke device, and to Luma's surprise, "Drop Dead Legs" by Van Halen appeared on the screen.

"Too soon?" asked Xavi, sheepishly.

Luma playfully gave a mean look and then a soft laugh. "I don't even know the song!"

"It doesn't matter. Just follow the melody."

The song's electric guitar riffs and heavy rhythmic drumbeats started. Women with long thin legs started marching behind the white lyrics. A few beats later, the color yellow scrolled over the white words, signifying which lines to sing.

"Sing!" Xavi elbowed Luma while nodding his head with the drumbeats.

Luma started singing softly, trying to match the melody of the MIDI track.

"Louder!" Xavi yelled as he leaned towards the microphone and started singing off-key.

Xavi himself had never done this before. He doesn't sing, and he didn't dare to sing in front of a crowd. And he never, in his entire life, imagined he will be singing with a girl inside a tiny corner restaurant. But here they were, two faces of the same coin, having fun and enjoying, singing loudly, out of key, and carefree.

The patrons and staff clapped their hands to the beat, cheering and laughing at the two persons making fun of the moment. Minutes later, the song ended, and the gathered lot cheered and applauded. Another minute later, everyone was back to their own lives like nothing happened. But to the two persons who just sang, it was a huge moment. It was the genesis of a bond being strung together in the web of time.

***

The lights of the houses across the streets of Al Mamriya started turning off one by one. The stars glowed brighter in the deep of night. Under the amber glow of streetlamps, the pair trudged the empty streets in beautiful peace. Their encounter was no longer a moment of tangency; it was now a tangible parallel that they can draw together.

Unlike the first time they walked home, this time, they weren't dragging bulky cases of burden. No pain bothered their hearts nor her leg. They only carried huge smiles in their hearts and on their faces, unconsciously thrilled about the sparkle they unwittingly share.

Xavi and Luma savored the moment. They reveled in the chill of the winter night whose air was fragrant of a blooming bond capable of soothing ailing souls. Each step that they took echoed across the vast silence of their universe, and it was a step to a different kind of tomorrow. A tomorrow that none of them know what kind, only hoping and trusting that it will be an excellent chapter to their unfolding lives.

# Chapter 29:
# When the Wind Whispers

Luma wiped the sweat off her forehead from the cold heat of the sleepy Arabian winter afternoon. She bit one side of her lip and glanced at the peaceful green scenery of rolling hills sculpted by man. Over the top of the sloping green grass, children with a cupful of young vigor ran up and then rolled down resembling ants romping around its mound. She studied every color of the view yonder her sight: the greens of the trees, of the grass; the blues and whites of the sky; the greys and blacks of the city beyond; and the greenish-bluish hue of the ocean by the bay. Then she looked back at her canvas, it was still blank. She didn't know where to begin. She turned to the man to her right, Xavi, draped under the dancing shadows of leaves above their heads. He projected focus as he sketched over his own white canvas.

The wind blew, tickling and rustling the canopy overhead.

Xavi glanced at Luma, then at her blank canvas. "Hah! So much for something new!" said Xavi, who yawned thoroughly at the lazy passing of the afternoon sun.

Luma turned back to her absent painting. She considered the shadows that lay upon her canvas as it filtered through the leaves above. Maybe she can draw that instead. Still uncertain, she took a pencil and drew the shadows anyway. As soon as the pencil's smooth tip landed on the rough canvas, everything else faded into a level of quietude. The sounds of the kids screaming and laughing, the planes roaring above, the sea crashing into the breakwater, all gone.

CLICK!

Luma turned to the man pointing a DSLR to her face. "What are you doing?"

CLICK!

He lowered the camera and reviewed the photos. "I'm bored," Xavi said matter-of-factly.

"Are you done painting?" Luma asked.

"Yep." Xavi showed his canvas full of squiggly lines and splashes of color.

"What the hell is that?"

"Abstracts," Xavi said effortlessly.

"What's that? Is that supposed to be how you feel?"

"Nope. I don't think so. They're just colors and lines. I have no idea how to paint... nor draw."

"But you're supposed to paint what you feel."

"That's what my camera is for. As a photographer, I don't take just photos. I take photos to capture what I feel."

"Alright," said Luma, her voice intrigued. She dropped her pencil and twisted to Xavi. "How do you suppose you capture what you feel with pictures?"

Xavi's face beamed with enthusiasm as he began to formulate the words to describe his passion. "Lighting, motion, sound."

Luma reeled backward. "Sound?"

"Yeah. Visual ears. You hear sound through the photos. I'll show you." Xavi positioned himself three-quarters to Luma's front. He peered through the camera's viewfinder and centered her in the frame. "Please look to the front, or look to the painting. Wherever. Just don't look at me," he said.

Luma faced the man-made hills.

## PORTRAITS OF THE WIND

Xavi pursed his lips and started whistling. He whistled from a high note to a low note in continuous bursts, imitating the whistling calls of bushmen.

"What are you doing?" Luma asked.

"I'm calling the wind."

And as soon those words came out, the wind blew a mighty gust, whipping Luma's hair around her head. She laughed at the coincidence… or the sorcery.

CLICK!

Xavi showed Luma the back of the digital camera. On the tiny preview screen, she saw herself, hair floating with the wind; face half-smiling, half-laughing; and children playing in the background, frozen in time, under the golden rays of the afternoon light.

"What do you hear?" asked Xavi.

She pouted and shook her head.

"Look again closely. Observe everything," commanded Xavi.

She looked again, and then again, on the same things she saw before.

"Try harder," added Xavi.

Luma squinted, and she saw the same things again, only this time, the longer she stared, the more august the tenor of the image became. The photograph transported her to the past, to the age of ancient days, despite being captured only seconds ago.

"Children, laughing, trees, leaves…" she laughed, "I hear them!" She laughed again at the majestic discovery of visual hearing.

Xavi smiled with an *"I told you"* face.

"Darn it, that's more interesting than paintings. I knew I shouldn't have bought all these! Stupid impulse!" she added.

Xavi shrugged. "Eh. Never know what we like till we try."

And he was right; it took Luma until college to find cycling. An impulse purchase will not suddenly change her interests. Her only regret was it costed her money.

"So, going back to capturing your own emotions through pictures, does that," Luma pointed to the camera, "my picture. Does that capture your emotions?"

Xavi brought the camera's screen closer to his face, scrutinizing the photograph again. A second later, he nodded confidently.

"Really? How can someone else's portrait capture your own emotions?" asked Luma.

He leaned over to her and showed the preview again, "See the smile, the wind blowing your hair? That's how I feel."

"You feel like a smiling wind?" she blurted with a laugh.

"No... yes... something like that. Okay, if you see almost all my pictures, there's always some kind of wind involved. Because for me, the wind, they encapsulate all the emotions in the world. They came blowing from the day the Earth was formed, brushing all the creatures with its breeze and taking with it every person's emotions and lifting it up to the clouds, then back down to earth, as an epitome of every laughter, every tear, every pain, every anger, every suffering, and every triumph.

"A picture of the wind will speak to us in many ways, just as it whispers in our ears all our secrets and all our worries and regrets. The wind knows what makes us smile and laugh inside. If you believe in a god, then the wind is God himself. It is His gentle hand, caressing His creation." Xavi sat upright, a little empowered by his own thoughts.

"What did you have for breakfast? A typewriter? First time I heard you speak a whole paragraph," Luma said.

"No, hotdogs… and nuggets. But seriously, when you ride your bike, what do you feel when the wind touches your skin?"

"Excitement. Pain. Delight."

"Exactly. Ever wondered why sometimes, we stare out blankly at something when the wind tousles our hair?"

Luma shook her head.

"That's the wind whispering to our ears," continued Xavi.

"What do they whisper?"

"Whatever you want to hear. Whatever you want to feel."

"So, let me get this straight. The wind, when you take a portrait of the wind, you take a portrait of your own emotions? Is that what you mean?"

"Exactly." He nodded.

"So, that picture you took of me, what emotion did it capture?"

"The nostalgia of today," he said simply.

Luma scrunched her face to show her skepticism.

"Look, pictures are like paintings, or music, if you will. Photographs, paintings, music, art in general, it has a surface meaning, the most apparent emotion. But it also has a deeper meaning, which is more subjective. To me, the portrait I took of you is about the nostalgia I feel right now, but to you, it may mean something completely different."

"Okay…" she slowly replied.

"That's why when I take pictures, as much as possible, I want the wind in it because the wind is a blank canvas. As I said, the wind whispers whatever you want to feel. So, in my pictures, it literally whispers what you want to feel or hear."

"If you say so, mister," Luma said, a little unconvinced.

The canopy above them started rustling. The wind blew ripples into the leaves, flowing to the twigs, then to the branches until the whole canopy swayed. Luma looked up to the tree, took a gander for a long while, deep in thought, whilst listening to its mellow crackle.

Xavi nudged Luma. "See, now you're getting it!"

She chuckled, leaned back to the trunk, and kept her stare at the dancing leaves with the knowledge that it might have been the same wind that brushed the earth a billion years ago. Xavi joined too. In a while, their breathing synchronized without them knowing it. They were breathing the same air and exhaling the same emotions.

Five minutes later, a loud roar of rushing water charged their ears. Over the distance, numerous nozzles on the ground shot water upward, creating columns and arches of rushing water. The children atop the hills dashed towards the fountains and whizzed under the roaring waters where they frolicked, laughed, and got wet.

Luma stood walking, leaving the now forsaken easel and canvas. It had served its purpose; now, it can be forgotten. A few meters later, she spun around and yelled over the distance, "Aren't you coming?"

Xavi replied aloud, "What are we doing?"

"Let's see how well you can capture emotions!"

Intrigued, Xavi took his camera and ran towards her, towards the enormous dancing fountain. Tiny rouge sprays of cold water began touching their skin as they get closer. Xavi stopped, wary of the camera getting wet. But Luma continued marching, removing her shoes before the glimmering columns of dancing liquid. She treaded on dry grass that transitioned to wet tiles underneath the fountain. There, beneath the arches of crystal waters, where screaming and laughing children whizzed in and out, Luma's spirit soared.

Xavi got confused. Was he supposed to take photos of her? Or was he supposed to take more photos that captured his emotions? He didn't know. He was simply agog at the sight of Luma getting wet and carefree. Then she peered through the waters and motioned at him to come.

Capture the emotions. A lightbulb lit up above Xavi's head. Now he knew what she meant. Capture emotions. Not by photographs, but by seizing the ephemeral seconds of life.

Xavi laid down his camera, removed his shoe, and leaped into the cold pillars of water.

Their joyful screams and laughter merged with those of the little children, whose parents watched, in shock and delight, the sight of two adults who played with their little ones. They jumped in and out, up and about. They played tag, chased, got chased, and were tagged. Their lungs bristled with delight, and their voices of glee reached far and over the steep slopes of the man-made hills.

"Children only! Please, children only!" shouted the Kenyan security guard, jogging from his outpost, gesturing for them to leave. It was too soon. Their shadows on the ground haven't even changed their lengths.

The pair escaped to the crest of the yonder hill to continue their joy. The security might have stifled their screaming mouths, but their screaming hearts continued to laugh as they lay down over the rugged green grass, atop the tiny mountain. Little puffs of clouds scrolled over the vast expanse of the golden sky. Underneath the heat of the waning sun, the pair lay still, hoping their clothes will dry before the night rises to steal the light.

"I think we should totally do something else," said Luma. "No more of that painting nonsense. A five-year-old can draw better leaves than I did."

Xavi lurched upwards, using his elbows to hold him up. "You know what?! I think you should teach me how to bike!"

Luma propped herself up. "Are you saying you don't know how to ride a bike?"

"Yeah," he nodded animatedly.

Luma giggled, "What did you do when you were a kid?"

"Take pictures."

"Pfft! That's stupid."

"Come on! What do you say? You're a teacher! Teach me, Ms. Luma! Pretty please!"

Luma turned back to the sky where the earth's umbra started to form. To the sky's right, the sun began to hide, taking away its warmth and leaving a cold twilight ceiling. To its left, the night sky unveiled its stars, letting it sparkle and breathe across the ether. She felt spellbound at the marvelous expanse of the converging day and night, inducing her to lie back down onto the grass to get a better view.

"No," she answered Xavi, whispering.

"Why not? I thought you love bikes?"

"Not anymore."

Xavi stopped talking. He saw in Luma's eyes a little fire that burned and then died. He lay back down too and waited for a moment to see if tears will pool over the windows of her soul. There was none. There was only a slow and deep rhythmic breathing content of the present.

"What about photography? You want to learn that?"

"Uh-huh. Sure," said Luma, softly. "Something new…" She closed her eyes and became quiet. Her body relaxed, and peace worked up her soul.

Xavi switched his gaze heavenward too, to the pulsing stars, to the same stars whose light were no different from a rooftop nearly two decades past. His eyelids closed wearily. Slowly, slowly, his body relaxed. And then there was silence among the city noise. The children were gone; the cars were gone; the sea was gone.

"Luma," whispered Xavi, eyes closed.

"Yeah?" she answered softly, also eyes closed.

"Are you sleeping?"

"No, are you?"

"No, what are you doing?"

A peaceful wind breathed a tranquil breeze upon their quiet face.

Luma whispered softly and gently, "Listening to the whispers of the wind."

\*\*\*

Luma yawned aloud inside a café at Doha's old souq; already lethargic even when it was still ten in the morning. She counted the coffee residues in her empty mug, wondering if the coffee was low in caffeine, or was it the way Xavi explained in excruciating details the parts of the camera that was bludgeoning her to sleep. Her eyebrows arched upwards like a frightened cat, straining to keep her leaden eyelids from closing. She focused on Xavi's mouth that kept making the motions of talking. But she heard no words, only the obscure ramblings of a man trying to enthusiastically explain his avid craze.

"You see, this is the shutter dial." Xavi pointed to the little knob on the top of the camera. "This controls the shutter speed."

"Uh-huh." Luma nodded, feigning interest.

"It's either you let your aperture dictate your shutter speed," he rotated the aperture ring on the lens back and forth, "or you let your shutter speed dictate your aperture. But!" he fervently interjected, "Your aperture and shutter speed will be dictated by the ISO. That relationship is what we call the triangle of light."

She let out an amused chuckle and said, "That sounds like an Illuminati crap!"

"No! Listen, this is important! If you want to take good pictures, you need to understand the theory."

"Why not use auto?"

Xavi sighed. "Because there's no auto. This is a manual film camera."

"Manual?" asked Luma. She ogled the black and silver casing of Xavi's camera. "How old is that?"

"It belonged to my father. Now, why do you think it's called the triangle of light?"

"Some men in dark robes and hooded masks thought it's a cool name?" She smirked.

"Dammit, Mia! No!"

"Who's Mia?"

"Not important!" He let out another sigh, trying to get back on board his train of thought. "It's called the triangle of light because the light dictates your ISO, your aperture, and your shutter speed."

"Uh-huh," she said, peering out the café's arabesque window as Xavi continued to talk.

The sun was beating down the archaic Arab streets and buildings of the old *souq*. In keeping with the peculiar characteristic of old Qatari neighborhoods, the souq had cobblestones for its pavement, and its boxy buildings were intentionally rough plastered. Vaguely, it reminded Luma of a famous scene from Indiana Jones when the hero was in Cairo. Just like in the movie, the vendors were barking their faux-antique merchandise on the streets. Policemen were wearing 1950's uniform, dawning khaki vests, and white ghutra while galloping down the cobbled streets on their white stallions. It was a market that elicited the past, uniquely tailored for tourists.

Bored and impatient, now enlivened by the sight outside, Luma said, "Can we start shooting now? The sun looks perfect for your Illuminati triangle."

"No!" loudly objected Xavi. "You only get thirty-six shots. Each shot should be near-perfect, if not perfect."

"Oh my god! Why do we have to do it in film?"

"Because! You need to learn the basics! Even if you have the best digital camera in the world, if you don't understand the simplest rules, you'll get bad pictures. That's why there are many so-called photographers today who depend on photoshop! Because they think they have a camera, they think that they're Ansel Adams already!"

"Lame. Teach me outside. You're a boring lecturer." Luma grabbed the camera from Xavi's hands and marched out.

\*\*\*

Xavi crossed the threshold from the shadowy vintage Arabian café to the bright vintage Arabian streets. He swiftly turned looking at the living, breathing, colorful, and dazzling sights and here and there, sounds of the distant past. It was the perfect place to capture images, he thought. So, he reached for his camera while composing the frame in his mind: old buildings, horses, and old men in traditional clothes. But his hand found no camera. Luma had it, he remembered.

"Xavi!" shouted Luma over the distance. She was standing in front of a table of antiques with the shopman holding his smile. "Why is it blurred?"

"Dammit, Mia!" mouthed Xavi. He paced towards Luma and grabbed the camera. "Because you have to focus it! See... like this!" His fingers held the lens and rotated the focusing ring side to side.

Luma peered through the viewfinder again, framing the shopman together with the antiques afore him. She dialed the focus, pressed the shutter, and a satisfying mechanical click followed. She tried to take another photo, but her finger pressed an unresponsive trigger. "That's it? The film all used? I only took one shot!"

Xavi rolled his eyes in disbelief. Without taking the camera from her hands, his thumb gripped the film advance lever and swung it outwards. A loud ratcheting sound cracked as it pulled the film to the next frame. "You have to advance the film," he said in as calmly as possible, but his muscles were tensing up.

"Ho. Ly. Hell. This. Is. So. Tedious! No wonder they invented digital cameras! You can't even review your pictures!" Luma said. She then began to trek deeper to the old souq, scanning for a new subject.

"No! No! No! You don't understand! That's the beauty of film cameras! It's a time capsule of memories—"

Luma took a photo of a Turkish ice-cream vendor. She advanced the film and took another shot.

"—You wait for a long time before looking at your photos!" added Xavi. "It is what makes film sweeter and more gratifying than review-and-delete! You savor the past! You hold an actual memory!"

Luma clicked another shot, this time of the open square deep inside the old souq where throngs of tourists roamed about. She advanced the film. CLICK! Advance. CLICK! Advance. She saw a small girl on a bicycle with trainers attached and tassels on the handlebar. CLICK! CLICK! CLICK!

"Stop! Please! Don't waste the film!" shouted Xavi.

"I'm not wasting the film. I'm taking photos," she said.

"You're not even thinking of your shots! You just keep clicking and clicking!"

"No, I'm not! How would you know? I'm the one holding the camera."

Xavi pointed to the shutter dial and said, "See, you're on thirtieth-a-second! And your aperture is 2.8! On broad daylight! Your photo will be as bright as the sun!"

Luma growled and pushed the camera onto Xavi's chest, the latter grabbing hold of it with two hands. "Maybe photography is also not for me," she solemnly said, then walked away.

Reacting to Luma's sudden change of vibe, Xavi also changed his tone to be friendlier. "Where are we going?" he asked.

She didn't answer. She just kept strolling, weaving through throngs of tourists and locals, her feet navigating.

"That's a good subject!" Xavi pointed to a porter resting inside a wheelbarrow on the sidewalk. He glanced through the viewfinder, adjusted the settings, then offered the camera to Luma. "Want to take a photo?" he asked.

The crimson-head ignored him and continued advancing into no place in particular. They turned left into a roofed corridor full of fragrant spices. They turned right into a car-wide corridor teeming with colorful textiles. They pivoted here and there, pirouetting along empty and cramped corridors, alleys, and streets, wherever Luma's feet allowed them to be.

Xavi had set the camera to each beautiful sight, stopping, then going, then stopping, wanting to take a photo. But the woman he tailed kept disappearing into the thick crowd, lost in thought.

When the path ended into a decaying wall, a genuinely decaying wall, not a man-made antiquity, Luma stopped. There was nowhere to turn but back. But she didn't turn around just yet, though. She just stood there, facing the wall, unmoving. She pondered and deliberated what she had seen fifteen minutes ago in the square.

It was a girl, a child full of innocence, and she was riding... a bike. Luma remembered taking the girl's picture as the latter pedaled in circles, ringing the bell, tassels flailing, in the middle of the square. Now, this naïve girl cycled around in circles inside Luma's mind, laughing without pretense, unintentionally taunting her.

Bicycles. It tried to wreak havoc in her mind anew by reminding her who she won't be. She had two options: fight it, or flow with it.

Standing a few steps behind, Xavi spoke with caution. "Luma?"

Luma whirled around, bearing eyes so bright and fiery. "So! You still wanna learn to bike?"

Xavi nodded and said, "Yeah," with uncertainty.

"Great! Do you have a bike?"

"No."

"Then, how do you expect to learn? Imagination?" She chuckled and marched deep into the square of the old market with her friend following behind.

Is she okay? Xavi asked himself but didn't bother to ask her. Instead, he shrugged it off to the same fickle-minded emotion that they both share.

\*\*\*

The stoic voice of a Moroccan's late news presenter occupied the El-Guerrouj living room. Politics, current events, showbiz, and a few selected bites from international wires, were all part of the late evening news, including a new virus that migrated from Wuhan, China. Rabiya listened intently to the updates of the country that she departed a decade past.

Meanwhile, Hashem's head bobbed up and down, and his eyelids drooped to the presenter's soothing voice. His wife nudged him to force him awake, futilely at that. As long as there were no explosions, the workers inside Hashem's brain responsible for keeping him conscious would shut down his entire system. To Hashem, loud explosions kept him awake; everything else was white noise.

The front door opened, an explosive sound in the monotonous living room. Hashem awoke. Together with Rabiya, they whipped towards the door.

Luma entered, nodded (an impassive gesture to make her presence known), and marched towards her bedroom.

Hashem studied his daughter as she walked towards her room. He knew there was something different about her and it kept growing every day, he just couldn't point a finger at it. She wasn't smiling, her gait did not change, and her posture stayed the same. She was no different than before, but she was definitely different in something. He thought that it could possibly be her aura, which was blooming something new.

When his gaze reached Luma's bedroom door that shut with a peaceful click, Rabiya emerged from the corner of his sight, wrinkled red in fury.

"Did you see that?" asked Rabiya.

"See what?" he asked.

"She's coming home late! It's 10:30!" She pointed to the TV. "The late news is almost done, and she's just coming home?"

"Yeah, so?" asked Hashem in a stolid tone.

"What's wrong with you?!" said Rabiya. "You used to be so tough on her, and now you just let her come home whenever she wants? Did you lose interest in your daughter because she lost a leg?"

If the loud door awoke Hashem, Rabiya's piercing tone was the caffeine to his sleeping brain. "What are you talking about?" he asked, his voice now sharp and alert as he sat upright. "Can't you see she's starting to glow again after how many months of brooding?"

"She could be with that boy!"

"That boy! That boy! Don't you trust your daughter?"

"After what happened? No!"

"But what if 'that boy' is indeed making her feel positive about herself? Maybe he's the new bicycle or something that's giving her joy. Are you going to stop her?"

"Are you saying she's riding him?" she roared.

"Habibi! Listen to yourself! You're not making sense!"

"No, you're not making sense! Go talk to your daughter and let her learn about the morality of going home late, especially with a boy!"

"How do you know it's the boy?"

"Then go and find out!"

Hashem met Rabiya's reason with a derisive shake of his head along with his diaphragm that distended with a deep breath. Without even completing the cycle of his deep inhale and exhale, Rabiya yelled at him.

"Well? What are you waiting for? Go!" Rabiya said as her finger pointed towards Luma's room.

Hashem let out his exhale with a faint scoff. He smirked and nodded before standing up and strolling glacially towards her daughter's bedroom.

Hashem stood frozen by the bedroom door. His right hand had formed a fist as he raised it at eye level, ready to rap at the wooden door in front of him. Right there, before knocking, he considered Luma's new air and glow. Would he be standing yet again between whatever is causing her happiness and his own beliefs? Or rather, this time, his better half's beliefs.

Beliefs. He chuckled inwardly, albeit shamefully. He knew he lied when he used religion as the reason to forbid Luma from cycling. He thought religion was the most plausible, the most probable reason to persuade her daughter, like him.

Looking back to his younger days, fifty years ago, he remembered that his parents extensively used religion as the means to get whatever they want, ranging from simple household chores to life-changing decisions.

A perfect case in point was when Hashem introduced the first Christian woman he loved, Mahta, to his parents, who immediately gave her a wag of the finger. Not because Mahta was a Christian, no, but because she came from a poor family. He didn't realize this, of course, until the day he introduced another Christian woman, Rabiya.

"She's a fine lady," his dad said.

Later, his parents started condemning Rabiya too, the moment they knew she was cut off from her family's wealth for getting engaged with a Muslim man. Not a penny would be spared in her name.

"She's a Christian!" they argued then.

But Hashem fought for her; he defended her. Nonetheless, the more he upheld his position, the sterner his parents' disapproval came to be, and religion was the only catspaw for their condemnation.

And what good did that do? He chuckled. He married Rabiya anyway. He remembered the feeling of breaking free, of getting his way the stricter his parents became. Then, with a loud voice inside his mind, he exclaimed, "My God! I am my parent's son. And what good did that do?" He thought of Luma, how she must have felt with all his prohibitions, using religion as an excuse.

Hashem's fisted hand remained suspended in mid-air, the knuckles inches away from the weathered surface of the wooden door.

He was still in a moment of indecision when— He cocked his head. His ears shot towards the door.

A sound delicately escaped through the gap between the door and the floor. It had a melody. There were pauses and beats, crescendos and decrescendos. The music was weak, but Hashem's aged ears picked up Luma's humming of a pleasant tune. The melody lightened him. So, in an instant of a breath, he clicked his tongue and turned away.

He will never get in Luma's way anymore, he thought, a supporting father now he will be.

As he pottered towards Rabiya at the couch, he considered many credulous reasons to convince his wife to let this night pass and let their daughter be. He knew it wasn't going to be easy. A long night awaits.

# Chapter 30:
# Two People Walking on Mars

There was visceral awe and wonder of just the least bit as Xavi walked the narrow corridor of Cycle City. His eyes laid on bicycles that he knew Luma likewise inexorably laid eyes on. He wasn't that much interested in velocipedes, but he can't help and marvel at the multitude of breeds that were on display. He saw bikes with flat handlebars, while some with curving inverted *C* handlebars. Some had skinny tires, while others—fat and knobby. There were small bikes with tall seats and some big bikes with low saddles. He turned around, a full 360 degrees, perplexed at the choices he had in front of him.

"Hi, how can I help?" asked a staff who approached Xavi with a manner of wobble in his gait. He wore not the shop uniform of turquoise like the others wore, but a white shirt with the words *Team Philippines* written on it.

"Hi po," Xavi switched to their native Filipino tongue. "I'm looking for a bicycle."

"What kind?" asked the staff.

"I'm not sure. My friend told me to come here because you have a wide selection of bicycles," said Xavi, his gaze roving. "I think you might know her, she used to come here a lot. Luma?"

The staff's face lit up in reverence. "Yes! Luma! How is she? I haven't seen her for a while. I think she's still recovering from the sprain or fracture from her accident."

Xavi pouted. Clearly, the man didn't have the full story, and Xavi questioned himself if he would break the news to the man. But he knew better not to. Personal news belongs to the person itself; to divulge or not rests on no other but to the person itself. So, he replied with a simple, all-encompassing, "Yeah," with a rapid nod.

The man waited for more information about Luma while blinking in the lingering moment. When he sensed there wasn't any more coming, he proceeded with the sales talk. "So, what exactly are you looking for?" he said.

Xavi chuckled with embarrassment. "I'm new to biking," he let out another self-conscious snicker, "in fact, I don't know how to bike. I just need something for starters."

"Great!" the man said, "You are going to learn by yourself, or Luma's going to teach you?"

"Luma." Xavi nodded.

The man put his hands together with a loud clap. "Let me show you what we have!" He began walking towards the section of entry-level bikes. And on the way, he started talking about the girl whom he revered. "Such a sweet girl, Luma. And strong too! She's on her prime to be one of the strongest here in Qatar. She's even stronger than most men. I tell you if she didn't miss the club championships... Oof! She'd win that, and she'd probably be selected as a wildcard for a continental team. That's why she was so primed for that race; scouts were there! I just hope she recovers quickly and gets back to her regiment as soon as she can."

They reached the entry-level bikes. The man continued talking about Luma as he pulled out a bicycle to show Xavi. He talked and talked, briefly about the bike, but more about Luma. What would have been a brief purchase of a two-wheeled machine progressed into an hour of chitchat about a girl and her bike.

Xavi listened to the limping man who spoke significantly about what the cycling world holds for someone so focused and dedicated. The man expressed how cycling is the world's toughest sport, that cyclists ride up mountains for six hours a day, over twenty-one days in the Grand Tours.

He articulated his reverence for the heart and sheer will of racers who, after a crash, still propelled their bloodied and tattered bodies towards the finish line, while the world's most famous football players dived over the slightest elbow rub.

He spoke in length about world-tour teams, tours around the world, famous multi-stage races, world championships, and children who pedaled in their backyards who are now written in history books under the heading of "cycling greats."

The man proudly said Luma could be this, and she could be that; she would be this, and she would be that.

All the words the man spoke lit up a spark in Xavi. A spark with the same intensity that briefly flared in Luma's eyes, and now it's in his soul. A spark that would light a tinder and then rage into a blazing fire—not about him, but about her.

But first, he needs to learn how to bike.

*\*\**

Tick-tick-tick-tick!

The sound flatly reverberated through the arching chambers of the underground train station. Luma recognized the sound, turned towards the escalator, and sighted a man with a surgical mask who was covered lightly with brown dust, nonchalantly rolling a bicycle by his side. She squinted and then recognized the eloquent eyes above the masked mouth. Xavi. She peered more. This time not at the face but at the training wheels protruding out the back of the adult mountain bike he was rolling.

"Seriously?" Luma asked the approaching Xavi, letting out a gentle laugh. "Training wheels? What are you? Five?"

"Don't you need training wheels to learn? That's why it's called training wheels, right?" defended Xavi.

"Training wheels are used by overprotective parents on their fragile little children. You're a grown-ass man! You don't need training wheels!"

"But what if I crash?"

"Crashing is part of the learning process, you nitwit."

"Didn't you once use training wheels?"

Luma smirked and raised her chin. "No!"

"Let's take it step-by-step for me, alright?" Xavi said, and headed to the turnstile. "By the way, it's super dusty outside. Do you think it's a good idea to go to the park today?"

"Don't chicken out now."

"I'm not chickening out. It's really dusty outside!"

"It's just a little dust. I trained even through sandstorms!" she said sarcastically.

Approaching the turnstile, the pair held up their prepaid metro card to scan it.

A staff came rushing from the ticket booth, shouting, "No bikes allowed! No bikes allowed!" He held up his hand, waiving off the pair.

"What? I thought bikes… it's allowed, right?" asked Luma.

"Yes ma'am, folding bikes and kids' bikes. But full-sized bikes are not allowed."

"But… ugh!" Luma dug her fingernails into her hair and raked it.

The pair glanced at each other in dismay. With a resigned slump, Luma and Xavi sauntered towards the escalator and to the streets above.

As soon as they stepped out, a rush of dusty wind greeted them and slapped their faces with the coarse hand of the winter shamal. It was a colossal sandstorm. The streets were transformed into a Martian avenue, glowing crimson red as the round white sun peered through the thick earth wafting in the atmosphere.

"You train through this?" Xavi yelled over the overpowering winds.

Luma answered by rolling her eyes as if saying, *"obviously not this kind of sandstorm."*

Xavi slipped his surgical mask back on to block the fine dust from entering his lungs. Done, he saw Luma fashioning a niqab out of her long yellow scarf. She wrapped it around her head and across her nose and mouth. Now, only her eyes showed. And within those celestial eyes, Xavi sensed his own heart throbbing wildly like he was about to meet God.

"So, where to?" Luma asked loudly through the raging wind. "The sandstorm is worse now than it was before I got here."

Recovering from her entrancing gaze, Xavi quickly wagged his head. "Should we still go to the park?" he asked.

"Of course not! Unless you want pneumonia!"

Xavi nodded and jogged towards the taxi stand.

"What are you doing?" Luma asked aloud.

"Getting a taxi! We're going home!" he yelled over the increasing distance between them.

Luma called him back and spoke firmly, "We're not going to the park, but we're not going home either!"

\*\*\*

Under the red glow of the crimson sky, Xavi and Luma roved across the streets, looking for a safe place to temporarily take refuge from the furious dust. All the way, the public watched them through windows, or through cars, or through the thin slit of the niqab over the women's eyes. They weren't judging stares or anything resembling disapproval, they were more about curiosity. What the hell are these two doing outside on a storm like this?

Luma glimpsed at Xavi. She giggled at the sight of a man rolling his bicycle beside him. A bike that had training wheels attached. She laughed once more.

"What's funny?" Xavi asked.

"Do you know the fable of 'The Man, The Boy, and the Donkey?'"

He nodded, "Yeah, vaguely."

"I think that's why all the people keep looking at us."

"Hmm, yeah. I guess so," he responded while his mind wandered to the fable.

"And you're the donkey." She artificially chuckled, thinking how corny her joke was.

Xavi giggled anyway and thought of a quick banter. After ten steps, he was still thinking of a banter. He got awkward then, feeling sorry for his non-quippy head. So, he turned to Luma and said, "Wally also says hi!"

"Wally?" Luma got wide-eyed between the opening of her niqab. "How is he? I haven't seen him for a long time!"

"He's okay. He said a lot of good things about you. I don't think they know about your condition yet."

"There!" Luma yelled and pointed to an apartment building. Without looking at Xavi, she dashed and crossed the road, effectively changing the topic seamlessly.

The pair escaped into the corridor of the apartment building, where dust seeping through tiny gaps in the main entrance covered the floor. The hallway only had ten meters of space before it led to a staircase to the upper floors. It will do, Luma thought, at least their lungs were safe from the storm outside.

"Alright, so are you ready to learn?" asked Luma.

"What? Here?"

"It's better than nothing. I mean, you walked with your bike all the way from your house to the station. Wait, did you actually walk your bike from your house?" She smiled sheepishly.

He nodded with hints of embarrassment.

"Unbelievable!" She slapped the back of her hand over his shoulder. "You have training wheels on!" She laughed. "You could have ridden it!"

"It's embarrassing!"

She shook her head in a teasing way. "Just get on your bike, please!"

Xavi mounted the bike. Even with the training wheels on, he wobbled in fear as he pedaled the full ten meters of the narrow corridor.

"Holy hell, you're hopeless!" Luma snickered.

She adjusted the training wheels, lifting it a little higher so it wouldn't touch the ground. "Try now," she said.

Xavi held the bike. Unlike when the training wheels touched the ground, the bicycle now leaned to the left or to the right. A twinge of fear worked up his arms as he swung his left leg over the frame. He climbed to the saddle, and as he expected, the bike tilted to the right. He felt his manhood, his thingy, shrink in fear.

Luma chuckled. "Get on with it, you Filipino chicken."

Xavi started pedaling. He leaned towards the left to counteract the sideways tilt, but his bike remained slanted to the right.

"Balance the bike! Force it upright!" shouted Luma.

"I am!" Xavi shouted back. As he kept pedaling, his arms kept trying to thrust the bike upright.

"Balance it! Turn the bike to counteract the leaning!"

Xavi reached the end of the corridor, still twisting the handlebar left and right. "Nothing's happening!"

Luma marched to him. "Because you're not moving, twat!" Irritation had seeped through her voice as she tried to grab the handlebar to turn the bike around. But instead of the rubber grips, her palm landed on top of Xavi's hand.

Luma brashly slid her hands to the grips, feigning innocence. But her reflex didn't match the electricity that arced between their skins. Moving with the speed of light, curious electricity branched out from their hands to their bodies and then to their faces. If any of their cells were still sleeping, they're awake now. Before she knew it, an inescapable warmth had already enamored her face, and he, equally so. Trying to look unfazed, Luma pulled the handlebar and swung the—

Music arose within the captivating electricity between them, an enchanting music that added more warmth to their bodies. It came from nowhere, and then there it was, tickling their ears with a melody that pressed their faces to redden even more.

"Ahem!" an unseen person cleared her throat.

The pair turned and saw a woman in her forties peering out from her apartment, giving them a mean look. That's when they realized that the music roused from the old woman's place. A second later, when the woman's glare got across to them, the door slammed with an echoing force. The music stopped, but the magic wasn't gone, only half gone. The other half lingered in the depths of their souls, even putting more oddity to the peculiar energy they already share.

Xavi stepped down from the bike. "Am I angering you?" he asked with a low tone, trying to mask the subtle quiver in his voice.

"I'm used to stubborn students," Luma replied in a straight timbre.

"How can I learn with such a short runway?" he griped, waving his hand at the corridor.

"It doesn't matter if the path is long or short. What matters is your willingness to embrace fear and learn. Try again!"

Xavi raised his hand like a student in a classroom.

Luma raised an eyebrow in response like she did in a classroom.

"I have a question," said Xavi, "Why don't you try to ride again? I mean, I see people on Facebook who ride with one leg, and they get a lot of likes and hearts."

Luma's face crumpled. "Likes and hearts don't mean anything. They don't grow your leg back. Just get on your bike."

"Maybe if you could show me how to ride, maybe I'll learn faster?" he said sheepishly.

"No. Get on your bike!"

"Come on." Xavi pushed the bike to Luma, his childish toothy grin getting more prominent.

"I said no!" she shouted whisperingly. "Do you want to see an angry teacher?"

Xavi wiped the smirk off his face. "Sorry," he said before getting back on the bike and started pedaling again. This time, the bicycle slanted wildly to the left. "Whoa," Xavi yelled and stepped down.

"Tsk!" Luma clicked her tongue. "You won't be able to balance the bike if you keep permitting fear to take over your mind. You must trust that you can do it, that you can move forward."

"It's not as simple as you say!"

"It is, if you wash away all the anxiety! Fear always has a louder voice than guts. People are more attuned to hearing it than hearing the soft voice of courage. But if you really want to move forward, you must listen to that tiny voice of audacity and filter out the rest! Now get back on the bike and believe that the bike will keep you upright!"

Xavi took a deep breath of courage and mounted the bike for the nth time. He pushed the pedal, and again, the bike tilted to the right and then swayed to the left, then to the right, and then to the left. He dismounted, swung the bike around, and then tried again. He persevered going back and forth the ten-meter corridor. By the end of the day, when the storm calmed down and became breathable, he still walked the bike home.

# Chapter 31:
# Figures on a Silver Mist

"Holy hell!" muttered Luma aloud. She had been trying to open a pack of flour but accidentally ripped it apart. Now, she had a white mask over her face. To her dismay, it wasn't only her face that got covered in powdery white. The cup of unbeaten egg, the opened kilo-bag of brown sugar, the bowl of chocolate chips, all the ingredients she neatly laid out atop the dining table were now draped under a thick dust of white, including the wooden table itself and the kitchen floor.

Painting did not appeal to her, hence, this time she thought that maybe baking would be her distraction. Try something new, as Dr. Raju once said. So, why not? Besides, the internet said that the activity can be meditating.

"Darn it! Darn it!" her voice was shouting now, and it resonated across the void of the living room towards the bedrooms. A low growl accompanied her displeasure as she swept all the flour-soiled ingredients to the trash.

"What's going on?" asked Rabiya as she stepped across the quiet space of the living room. On the threshold to the kitchen, she stopped. Her eyes expanded, as big as her gaping mouth, upon seeing the white powder that covered everywhere. "What did you do?"

Luma answered coldly and gently, "D… don't start now, Ma."

Rabiya's voice remained high. "What are you trying to bake?"

"Cookies."

"Heh?" Rabiya remained at the threshold and observed her daughter scuttle around the kitchen while veiled with pastry flour.

Luma started to feel tense, possibly from the presence of her mother, who scrutinized her every move, from scooping flour from the heap that fell on the table, to screwing up the simple act of cracking eggs and splattering it all over her arm. Perhaps the most stressful of all was her mother's look of disdain whenever any ingredient was poured (flour, sugar, baking powder) because Luma only used her eyes as a precise yet not precise unit of measure.

Rabiya spun around to leave but then caught a glimpse of something peculiar. What is that doing there? Amidst the white mess, the cracked eggs, and the utensils covered in white fingerprints was a yellow box. "What's that?" she asked, pointing to it.

"Baking powder," answered Luma.

Rabiya scoffed, gave a lingering look of ridicule, race-walked back towards the master's bedroom, cackled loudly, then slammed the door.

Luma scoffed too. What the fudge was that about? Whatever.

As she began the forceful motion of whipping the raw cookie batter, her vacant eyes drifted to the yellow box sitting on the table. She tilted her head in curiosity, reading the small label in blue that says *Corn Starch*. CORN STARCH?! Alarmed, she hurried to the cupboard and swung it open. There was another yellow box of the same brand sitting there, untouched. She took it and read the small label, also in blue, that says *Baking Powder*.

She growled. She growled in anger and frustration. And then she growled again after emptying the contents of the mixing bowl into the trash once more. She growled louder at the thought that she had to start everything over again. Each growl led to a louder growl. And it angered her, even more, when she knew Rabiya was probably listening, giggling, and gloating inside the master's bedroom.

## PORTRAITS OF THE WIND

On the other side of the neighborhood, about a kilometer west, is the old plot of The Philippine School, where an apartment complex that housed Xavi now stands.

A loud sigh was the first sound that escaped the photographer upon waking up from a good night's sleep. It had been eight days since the winter shamal started covering the streets, the porches, the cars, the leaves, and the heavens with a thick layer of crimson dust. For seven days after Xavi and Luma parted ways, he can't help but be a little empty on the tank of happiness. Now, he thought, upon not seeing a ray of sunlight beaming through his window, that tank of happiness would be completely drained.

For the past few days, he had tried going out for photo-walks to give his dopamine a boost, but the weather wouldn't let him. He played hours on end his PlayStation, but it never delivered satisfaction. Television and sitcoms refilled the tank of happiness for just the least bit.

Something was missing, something that had got something to do with the renaissance of his gaiety. He knew exactly what it was, but he was terrified to consider precisely that. He didn't want to meet with joy for no reason. Watching movies together was taken into consideration, but it might be construed as a date. Going out for lunch was also considered, but again, it might be interpreted as a date. Besides, with the weather raining dust, he knew she would only take a rain check. He mulled over more reasons, but he didn't want to seem to be the guy looking for a date. He let go of another sigh and sauntered towards the kitchen.

The pair of still sluggish hands sloppily stacked white loaf, gouda cheese, turkey ham, pepperoni, salami, gouda cheese, and another white loaf. The sandwich went into the microwave, and the minute counter started ticking down. While waiting, his eyes wandered out the sole window of his apartment and saw the vast ocean of buildings that are resting steadily beneath grey skies.

Grey skies!

The final particles of dust had settled. The crimson mornings were gone, replaced with nimbus clouds.

Good enough, he thought. His head swiveled towards the wall where his bike leaned, and a smile curved over his face. Finally, he thought, he had a valid reason.

Luma sighed with relief at the sound of the oven door closing. She peered through the panel and wished good luck to a dozen of her creations that were about to go through the journey of baking. Just then, her phone rang. She glanced at the caller-ID, and the corner of her lips rose a tiny fraction of an inch. But what her demeanor didn't completely show, her voice expressed wholly with its euphoric tone. "Wooly!"

*Leggy* came to Xavi's mind. Thankfully though, he had the common sense to quash the thought. Instead, he said, "Hi," with lips stretching towards his ears.

An electric hum followed their pleasantries. Xavi blinked. Luma blinked. Xavi breathed. Luma breathed. Both waited for the other to say *the* words for which they didn't exactly know what. Perhaps these words were "missed you," or "spend more time," or "together." But these words only floated in their minds like a leaf drifting over the vastness of the Pacific. They thought these specific words were only exclusive to long-time friends.

"The weather looks good now," said Xavi.

"Yeah, yeah," she replied, without even looking out the window.

"Maybe you can finally teach me to ride?"

Luma abruptly said, "Of course!" with glee.

"I'll bring my car so we could go to the park. Do you want me to pick you up?"

There was a long pause.

"No, no. I'll meet you there. In two hours?" she said as she swept her left foot childishly left and right over the marble floor.

"In two hours. Alright, I'll see you then!"

The microwave beeped right after Xavi had hung up. Glancing over the ingredients still on the countertop, he decided to prepare a sandwich for Luma, for breakfast. He took a loaf, placed the same sequence of elements on top of each other, heated it to melt the cheese, and enclosed it in a zip-lock bag.

"This looks familiar," he whispered to himself. He began looking around his studio apartment as if seeking answers from its four corners.

One spot caught his attention. It was close to him in the kitchen. He took the three steps to get there and stopped. Subconsciously, he held up the sandwich close to his chest, breathed in deeply, and then gently, as gentle as an unsure decision, he dropped the sandwich to the bin in that corner there.

***

Xavi parked his car at the designated parking lot of the park. Across the distance, he spotted Luma, sitting under the tree where they attempted to paint, serenely listening to the cold wind of the grey noon. He pored over her for a little while. Without him knowing it, as the minutes innocently ticked by, his hands gripped and ungripped the steering wheel, his pupils dilated, and his bouncing knees synced with his racing heart. He remained uninterrupted beholding her until a thunderclap slapped his ears, and an arcing tree of lightning flashed in the sky. How long was he staring at her? Something pinched in his chest that bloomed into a twinge of disgrace. He chuckled over it, though he had a faint understanding that it was the shame of knowing that maybe he was developing something new for another woman.

"HAH!" he exhaled aloud, dispelling whatever kind of concoction that affection and shame had stirred inside him. A minute later, he removed the bike from the rack attached to the boot of his sedan. In another minute, he was walking the distance towards Luma, under the deepening grey clouds.

A sudden rush of cold blood surged throughout Luma's arms, and the tiny hairs on the back of her neck rose at the sight of the wooly man's bulbous silhouette over the distance. The familiar yet unfamiliar energy whelmed her, similar to a shower of ten billion cold drops of water, trickling down her head and sending icy spikes all the way to her feet. Luma swallowed. She looked away and then looked back again; Xavi was still far away, walking his bicycle across the bermudagrass. She looked down at her feet, and then at her fingernails, and then back at him; still, he was far away. She tittered, giggling at the awkwardness of the long walk. And then, their eyes met.

She never knew—or does anyone ever know when to begin eye contact when you see someone walking towards you? Perhaps half the length of a football pitch? Or an arm's throw away? Or maybe, at a whisper's distance, where you could already sense each other's soul? But when their eyes met, with yet ten thousand steps in between, they found it hard to look away. Their gazes were locked in an elastic seal; they can look away, but it will always snap back to their eyes.

At last, Xavi took the final ten steps towards her.

"Hi…" said her.

"Hey…" said he.

## PORTRAITS OF THE WIND

The pair stood in front of each other and adjusted their jackets against the chilly breath of the ominous weather. Within those seconds, they waited for the other to say the words that none of them dared to say. But none of them said anything, inadvertently prolonging the seconds of no words. Thankfully, a rolling thunder cracked, giving their minds something else to think about. Both gazed heavenward. There, electric flashes exploded in the sky, lighting the clouds with a wash of silver.

"Ready?" Luma said, ignoring the warnings of rain from the heavens.

"Yeah! Yeah!" he replied.

None of them commented on the weather.

"Still with the training wheels?"

"Of course!"

"We're in the grass now! It won't hurt if you fall. Remove those damn wheels!"

He crinkled his nose. "Maybe next time."

"Filipino chicken!" Luma said. "Alright, mount."

Xavi mounted. And then, right at the moment he gripped the bars, the clouds started to cry.

The first drops of rain felt like a child sprinkling water over them. A second later, it felt like mung beans being thrown at them. Another second later, the drops were the size of kidney beans with the weight of little pebbles.

Without a second thought, Xavi dismounted and called Luma to go to his car. Luma pulled her jacket over her head, then together with Xavi, the pair advanced to the blue sedan. One was hobble-wobbling and the other half-running.

Cars left the parking lot one after the other until Xavi's blue sedan was the only one left peering behind a fence of silver mist. Over the wet green grass, two figures silhouetted against the glimmering shower briskly strode and splashed their feet. Their sonorous laughter had enough loudness to overpower the sound of the hammering rain.

Xavi did not know whether to run ahead to the car and come back with some sort of umbrella to cover Luma, or to carry her all the way to the car. But in the end, he stayed beside the woman who was stealing Nicola's memory away. The hundred steps of bermudagrass felt yet again a thousand-fold. But in a good way.

# Chapter 32: Cookie Balls

Hashem's white sedan screeched to an abrupt halt in front of their house. The vehicle's seatbelt instantaneously locked, preventing the two passengers from launching forward over the dash. Within a second, the tranquility of the pouring rain returned, now accompanied by the sound of an idling four-cylinder engine and a pair of windshield wipers rising and falling with a breath in between.

After reeling back from the hard braking, Hashem and Rabiya gawped at the blue sedan parked in their spot. Intense fury instantly doused Hashem's body.

It wasn't the first time that someone else took his reserved spot. The last three incidents were from his stubborn shisha-addict neighbor who always partied every weekend. Instead of telling his guests to park a few meters away outside the compound, the shisha king instructed his guests to park at Hashem's space. The first time it happened led to a heated argument. The second resulted in keying the guest's paintwork. The last time was deflating the neighbor's car. This resulted in the neighbor escalating the complaint to the landlord, which led to the neighbor himself to be evicted given that the landlord and Hashem had known each other since the first time the compound was built.

"Take it easy, omri!" said Rabiya to her husband, who was now walking towards the doorsteps of their new neighbor.

Rabiya observed her husband let out his parking rage to the man who had been their neighbor for only a year. Because of the rain pattering loudly over the tin roof of their car, she couldn't hear what her husband was saying. She could only surmise from the rigid pointing of fingers and the bulging veins on her husband's neck that a lot of shouting and expletives had been discharged.

Despite being visibly shocked, the neighbor remained calm. He waited for his turn to speak, and when he did, he spoke gently and with grace.

Hashem got pacified at the calmness of the man. That is always the surest way to bring an angry man's blood to simmer—calmness. Shouting begets shouting; calm begets calm.

After exchanging a handshake, Hashem turned around to face his spouse with a puzzled look. He shrugged his shoulders, said nothing, and walked directly to their villa's door. The keys in his hands jingled as he inserted one into the keyhole and CHUG! It wasn't locked. The turn of the key readily opened the door, subverting his expectation of a double lock. As the door swung wide, he was smitten. Smitten with the relaxing aroma of butter, sugar, and flour.

Copper-colored memories filled Hashem's curious mind as he walked towards the smell. It was reminiscent of his young days in Ifrane, where he helped his father in their failing bakery.

He didn't announce himself or call out to her daughter; he just trod cautiously, expecting just about everything and absolutely nothing. And there, in the kitchen, his uneven expectations were once again subverted. For there, sat around the tiny dining table, was Luma and a bearded man wearing a too tight shirt and jogging pants for his chubby shape. Are those... are those Luma's clothes? he thought. Seeing the Ifrane University logo printed on the pants, yes, his thought was confirmed.

"What's going on??" The shrill voice began piercing everyone's ears.

Hashem expected those words would come from him with extreme fury. But again, those were only his expectations.

The shrill voice belonged to none other than Rabiya, who continued her tirade, "Luma! What is this?! Who is this man?!" Her voice was louder than the thunderclap outside.

The pair at the table stood up. One was obviously nervous, as shown by his attempt to pull down the short blouse to hide his belly button. The other, she stood with visible indignation.

"Hi, I'm Xavi. I'm Luma's—" Nobody looked at him for his soft voice couldn't match Luma's loud stutter.

"Would… would… could you not shout in front of my friend?" scowled Luma.

Xavi was stunned to hear Luma stutter over her own parents. He didn't know what to do then.

Rabiya yelled back, "No! I will not lower my voice! You have defied your father and me for the last time!"

"How? How is this defiance?!"

"I think I'll just go," said Xavi softly, as he took a step towards the exit.

"No! You stay! Your clothes are still in the dryer!" shouted Luma.

"It's okay, I'll just come back for it."

"No!"

Rabiya started to let go of a barrage of sharp words towards her daughter, intending to deliberately wound her into submission. Luma didn't back down. She too had her own arsenal of explosive words that launched rapidly into the growing conflict between them. Their throw of words increased exponentially with each argument; when the mother released five, the daughter retaliated with ten. Fewer than a minute later, the kitchen was filled with the piercing voices of the oppressor and the oppressed.

There was only one thing Xavi thought of doing at that moment: to melt and disappear between the grouting of the marble floor. Hashem perceived this and draped his arms over Xavi's shoulder. Together, they marched out of the kitchen.

"What's your name, son?" Hashem asked.

Xavi replied with his name as they continued across the living room. There, Rabiya and Luma's blaring voices still reached and ricocheted.

"So, please explain to me, why are you wearing my daughter's clothes?" asked Hashem in a controlled and stolid tone, as he tried to be in contrast from the verbal warfare in the kitchen.

Xavi explained from the very beginning, starting from when they first met on the train, to Luma's comforting presence, to the photography lessons, and to the bicycle lessons. He spoke about the expected but unexpected rain. And that instead of driving home wet, Luma invited him to their house to dry his clothes and have some of the cookies she baked.

"Cookies? Hmm… I knew I know that smell," he said softly with a low, placid voice. "And how were the cookies?"

"It was okay."

"Don't you like it?" Hashem constricted his arm around Xavi a little bit, just enough for the boy to rethink his answer.

"No! I mean, yes! They're good! They just didn't look like cookies, though. They were more like balls. Cookie balls!" Xavi smiled anxiously.

"Cookie balls, you say. Interesting." Hashem extended his free arm towards the doorknob, turned it, and swung the front door open.

The soothing noise of the winter rain filled the living room, but it didn't soothe anyone at all. It only joined the loud argument over the kitchen, adding more earsplitting decibels to their already stinging ears.

"Have a good rest of the day," Hashem said while gently nudging Xavi out of the front door using the arm draped over the boy's shoulder.

Xavi was shocked. He's still in Luma's clothes. He spun around, about to protest—

"I'm guessing that's your car?" Hashem pointed to the blue sedan.

Xavi nodded and grinned sheepishly.

"You're in my space," Hashem said, showing his full set of teeth, and then closed the door.

\*\*\*

Hashem smirked at the way he threw Xavi out (it was a proud dad moment). Now, what's left to deal with was his wife and daughter. He closed the door, turned around, and then Luma stomped out of the kitchen. His smirk shrunk.

"I've had enough of this! I'm d... d... I'm finished!" she said as she clomped across the living room towards her bedroom. "P-p-pray that I find a new place immediately, otherwise I'll sleep in the streets tonight!" She slammed the door, for real this time, with a loud wall-shaking bang.

"I don't have to! You have a new boyfriend already! Go sleep there!" Rabiya howled as she emerged from the kitchen with the look of an exhausted warrior.

"He's not my boyfriend!!" roared Luma from inside her room. Her voice remained commanding and energized.

Hashem turned to his wife and asked, "What's happening now?"

"She wants to move out. Let her. I don't care. She wanted to move out since the time you don't want her to bike. Now, let her! Go!

I don't care! She's a grown woman! Why does she still have to live with us?" Rabiya's voice showed signs of faltering.

"I don't understand you," Hashem shook his head gently, "when she was whole, you showed her a mother's love. But now that she needs the same mother's love and more, you... I don't know what you're doing."

"I want her to know how painful it is! For us! To see our baby hurt like that." She choked on her words. Tears started to pool on her fiery eyes that extinguished the same fire. "It's wrong and I want her to know that."

Hashem remained placid and stoic, "Oh, she knows, she knows. Is that how the kind of mother you're going to be now? Always going to deprive mother's love?"

"No. I don't know. I know it's wrong." She started sobbing. "But she's my masterpiece, and someone came and ruined it. And it's her who ruined it. She did it to herself. And I want her to know, that it's— oh, god! It's me, isn't it? I'm prolonging her grief. But I can't stop it! I can't stop. I don't see her being sorry. Hashem, am I... am I a bad mother?" Tears fell freely now. "You have to stop me being this way. Stop me hurting our daughter!"

Hashem walked towards her and threw his arms around her.

"I love her. I miss her. I miss her laughter. I miss her hugs. Please don't let her leave. Please tell her I'm sorry," begged Rabiya in a low, trembling whisper. "It's just too painful what happened. But I love her! She's my baby! I don't want to see her this way. But I can't stop being devastated! I'm devastated! Help me, omri! Help me become a better mother to our beautiful daughter..." She dug her head into her husbands' shoulder.

Hashem rubbed her back gently. "I know, I know."

"Talk to her, please."

## PORTRAITS OF THE WIND

"I will." Hashem tightened his embrace and gave his wife a peck on the forehead. "Stay in the kitchen. Drink tea to quiet yourself. Eat the cookies that your daughter made. That boy said it was good."

\*\*\*

Hashem opened the door to Luma's bedroom moments after he had knocked. There, he realized that his daughter wasn't joking around. There was an open suitcase atop Luma's bed that was already half full. He studied his only child move hastily back and forth between her closet and the luggage. She folded the clothes rapidly, some she rolled, and some she threw down the floor. The way she packed wasn't the way an emotional person would do impulsively. She was meticulous with the clothes that she stuffed into the suitcase and the clothes that she threw down. She's really moving out, he thought.

"Is there anything I can say to stop you?" he said with a quiet voice along with a subtle, sympathetic smile.

Luma returned it with a stern shake of her head.

"Can I at least try?"

She did not respond.

Hashem glanced at the now empty wall where the yellow bike used to hang. "It's my fault, you know…" he said softly.

She continued selecting and stuffing clothes into the suitcase.

"I let my own prejudice, my predispositions, get in the way of your happiness," Hashem said. "I shouldn't have held you back. Imagine where you could be right now. You know your ma told me about that race you were training for, that championship, where scouts would be present.

"I know how you feel about cycling. Trust me. I also know how to ride a bike. I know the feeling of the speed, the acceleration. It's all nice and addicting. Sometimes I would sneak out in the evenings before bed because my dad wants me to help in the bakery after school, so in the evening, I'd climb down my window then go ride downhills with friends. Sometimes I'd crash, get scraped. A friend was even sent to hospital when he went too fast around a corner and crashed on a wall. Then when I came back home, my parents would be waiting for me with sticks or hangers in hand, giving me more bruises on top of my scrapes." He giggled. "I guess I forgot about all those feelings."

Hashem paused to monitor the suitcase that was gradually getting packed. It seemed to him that Luma wasn't paying any attention, but he continued owning up anyway. "If you blame me for what happened… well, I deserve that. I wish I could turn back time and change everything. I just wanted to preserve…" He hesitated for a few breaths and whispered, "Haram," which had a punching effect in his gut.

The word also seemed to punch Luma as her head jerked sideways microscopically.

Hashem continued, "You know, despite all the gunshots and explosions from all the movies I watched, I learned a little something about storytelling. It's that in the end, there is always something that motivates the character to do something. Movies have it like, the parent had a bad experience or something that he doesn't want his children to experience, or something to that effect. In my case, you could induce, or probably because I always say it, that I forbade you from cycling because of religion. Haram.

"But the truth is… the truth is, that's all just a façade to complicate something basic. You're my daughter. That's the real reason. It's stupid. I don't think it even sounds valid at all."

Luma stopped packing, faced the cabinet, stilled.

"Your mom told me earlier that you're a masterpiece." His voice began to show traces of quavers. "Which you are. You're our only child. You're a gift from God. We waited for five years, after many attempts and miscarriages, to have you. And then you came, so chubby with a full set of hair, black hair. Not this red, crimson or whatever you want to call it, hair.

"When I first held you, I whispered in your ear, 'May God give you the success you deserve.' And He was giving it. You kept getting stronger and faster every day. And I stopped you. I was the devil because I failed to see that cycling was the success you seek."

His lips began trembling. "Because, you're our only child. You're our precious child. I didn't want to see you get hurt like I did, like my friends. I wanted to make sure you're far from danger. I wasn't lying when I said I was being protective. And because of me…"

He took a deep breath and worked his eyelids double time to try and stifle the tears that were about to fall. "I'm sorry. It's my fault. I was proud of you. Secretly, I was, and still am. But now, what happened… Forgive me. It's my fault. No parents want to see their child's dream crushed. Especially because of my own selfishness. I never wanted to see your dreams crushed." His eyes let go; he sobbed in visceral pain. "I'm sorry. I'm sorry. It's my fault."

Luma sighed and lowered her head upon hearing her father's sniffing and sobbing. She listened to his words. Even if she wanted to ignore them, her mind kept comprehending each verbal sound his father uttered.

"And your ma, she loves you. She's just handling your loss in a different way. She's angry too, you know, just like you, angry at herself. Angry at the same thing. Angry at the disappointment that's now taunting us. And the boy, he had nothing to do with it. He just happened to be in your mother's line of sight. I'm actually happy that you're happy. If it was because of that boy, I don't care. I want you to be happy and animated again. We love you. You're our only daughter. I'm sorry. We're sorry. Forgive us." He sobbed on his palms.

Luma slowly turned to her father. Upon seeing the streaks of tears in his face that he desperately tried to hide by twisting away, she also let go of her own river.

"Baba," she whispered.

Hashem turned back around with a face covered in sadness.

Sobbing, Luma ran to him. Her arms extended like sunflowers reaching for the sun. It was an unconscious decision, an intuitive action. It was the pull of her father's honesty that compelled her to dart towards him. And as she ran the five steps in between them, murky memories flashed in front of her: memories of childhood and innocence filled with unconditional love. After the five steps which felt like five hundred, she threw her arms around her father in a resonant embrace.

The father and daughter cried, they sobbed, and they wept for sadness, for happiness, and for love. It was an embrace many years overdue that they had already forgotten how wonderful, and how healing it felt. They were both hungry for it, for that love that they held back from each other since Luma had the will to decide on her own.

"Forgive us," whispered Hashem with a quivering voice.

Luma pulled her baba deeper into her hold.

He understood.

It took a little while before their tears dried up and their sobbing subsided. It was their moment of profound togetherness, after all. They were both surprised at how hatred kept them apart, but a single hug broke the twenty years of cold hearts.

"So, you're staying now?" Hashem asked.

"I… I'll hold packing, but I'm not removing the clothes that are already in it," Luma said.

Hashem sighed.

"Baba, I'm twenty-four. Soon, I will still have to move. It is time you guys let me go."

"When do you plan on moving out?"

"I was planning maybe tonight," she said sheepishly and chuckled.

Hashem grinned softly. "Then we have a new reason to be hard on you again. Forbid you from going out."

She smiled. "I'll start looking for a place, but when I find one, I'll move."

Hashem nodded. "What about your finances?"

"I'll be okay. I'll find another job if the school still won't take me back. Will you be okay?"

"We'll have to look for an even cheaper place now. Probably a studio apartment or something like that. Or maybe I'll retire. Let's see. Who knows? You're old, you're moving; we're old, and we also have to move on."

Luma smiled with profound sincerity.

Hashem gently bobbed his head and switched his gaze to the clothes on the floor while quietly pondering what just had transpired. He was gratified, for sure. He furtively yearned for his daughter's love for hundreds of months, and now, here it is again.

It reminded him of the first time he held her, the time when an abundance of love cascaded from his soul, through his arms and into the innocent child that he caressed. A thirst was slaked. He was overjoyed, not just on the surface but also deep within. It was a kind of joy that was lost with the passage of time. And like all things lost that had been found, he will now hold on to it and forever cherish it.

In a breath of a second, Hashem stood up and headed for the door. He stopped at the threshold. His fingers lingered on the doorsill as they calmly tapped to the tune of joy. He turned to Luma, said, "Alright, I'll let your ma know," and left with a smile.

# Chapter 33:
# A Collection of Passing Memories, Leaving a Trail of Misery

The white blouse and the white jogging pants lay strewn on Xavi's bed while he stood motionless, staring down at it. Unmoved by the cold air touching his naked body, he examined the clothes, wondering how these tight clothing for Luma's physique had fit his body. There were tears in the stitching and some signs of stretching in the form of waving in the fabric. Did I do that? he wondered. He looked at the logo printed on the black jogging pants: Ifrane University. He doesn't even know where that is. He frowned, at the clothes, at the thought that he wore another person's clothes. It was his first time, and he didn't know how to feel about it.

I didn't even wear Cola's clothes, he whispered in his mind. "Oh God, Cola!" he said aloud.

He forgot about her for the past few days, and for the past week, and vaguely and barely over the past few months. Not her thought, not her face, but the emotions that he kept in a tin can, which he opened every now and then to relive her memory.

"Cola," he whispered the name and pictured every letter in his mind. C–O–L–U–M— "Fudge! No!" he exclaimed aloud. "Cola! Nicola! N–I–C–O–L–A!" He repeated it, faster now, "N–I–C–O–L–A." Then even faster and faster and faster. "Her face. Think of her face! Her rich smile. Her wrinkled nose when she smiles!"

The cold air now shivered him, so he put on some clothes. His own clothes.

He kept thinking about her. Luma. Scar on the chin. Wavy crimson hair. Hazel— no almond eyes. Fudge! No! No! Stop! Wrong person! Stop!

Guilt seared his brain. He got terrified and mortified that another woman may be replacing Nicola in his head and in his heart, which now didn't fan the same fire as it used to ten, five, three, one year ago. The flame that he kept ablaze for years, where is it now? What happened to it? Questions and terrifying cloudy answers rang in his head. Even more frightening, the beast!

No, the beast of despair didn't show itself. He tried searching for it, but the beast that he now considers family is nowhere to be found. And is that because of Luma?

He went for the shoebox in his closet, instinctively looking for the item housing all his memories. Then he remembered: the hard drive itself was now just a memory containing more memories of days long gone. Panicking, he reached for his phone, the 7650, sitting quietly on a corner under the shadow of the falling rain.

The keypad slid downwards; the screen lit up. With the little joystick, he navigated to the Messages app, then to the saved messages folder, and to the only text message in that folder. The name of the sender: Nicola Cueto.

He opened the message:

*"We're now at the foot of Kenon road. See you soon! I love you like chocolates! P.S. Never let me go! xx"*

It was a simple message with only nineteen words, but it being the last message from Nicola, it was the one he decided to keep, especially the last four words.

He stared at the message, waiting for something. For something. But nothing. Nothing. Nothing came except the trickle of gentle nostalgia from the yesteryears. He was hoping to experience the immense desire to jump into a nauseating wormhole and come out in 2009 to change his future. But nothing. He hoped that the beast would help him do it, but it was docile. There was nothing around his studio; it was still, aside from the shadows of the gentle rain.

Ironic how when Xavi wants to welcome despair with open arms, it wasn't there. He could imagine it; he knew the feeling, but he was not feeling it.

*Luma.* The voice echoed in his mind.

Wait…

That voice! Now he realized whose voice his brain substituted for Luma when they met. *Luma.* It belonged to Nicola! Then there, in the middle of the room, Xavi froze.

Now he was experiencing something. Something that could consume a person. It was working its way from the inside and eating its way through, like a parasite consuming its unwitting host. He had known this feeling before, from inside the train, inside the library, and inside his car at the park this morning. And now, the feeling came back with greater severity. It wasn't despair. It was guilt. Guilt and shame, poisoning him. Guilt and shame that his mind allowed Nicola's voice to be used for someone else's—to a woman, nonetheless. Guilt and shame for breaking a promise. A promise to never let her go. The guilt felt heavy, bone-cracking, suffocating.

Palpitating, he slumped onto his bed.

The phone in his hand vibrated, followed by a loud melody that broke the room's jittery peace. Xavi glanced at the screen; it was Luma. He took a deep breath and let the phone ring for a while, staring at the name, Luma. In his mind, the name now resembled half the face of its namesake and half the face of Nicola.

Incapacitated from guilt and shame, he was not able to act upon the ringing phone. And like a paralyzed person, only his eyes moved.

His eyes traced the angle of the L, curved with the U, then slid down the M, and landed on the A.

The phone stopped ringing. A minute later, a message arrived: *Hey wooly, can I ask for a favor? Can you help me look for an apartment tomorrow? If it's okay to drive around? Say, 10am? No need to pick me up at my house, let's meet at the station. Thanks! I'll bring your clothes.*

Xavi typed on the tiny alphanumeric keypad: *S–U–R–E*

It took him five minutes to decide to type a reply, and now, his finger hovered, with mounting indecision, over the send button. He bit his lips. Thoughts, thoughts, and more thoughts of Nicola, Luma, the past, the present, the confusion, the beast, everything, and anything filled his head.

He exhaled, closed one eye (the side that didn't want to see what's going to happen next), and his trembling thumb hit send.

***

Luma waited at a bench by the entrance of the metro station. She was wet from the knee down, and the water dripping from her pants pooled around her feet.

The rain still hasn't eased from the previous day's outpour. Clouds roared, and flashes of white electricity continued charging the air as the sky cried overnight.

The news was active with stories and photos of flooding all over the country. In some lower parts where the land dips into a basin, the water level had risen knee-deep due to a lack of drainage infrastructure. Cars were stranded, some by bad luck and some by stubborn drivers. The government worked tirelessly, dispatching water pumps within troubled areas to siphon water off the road.

Luma thought of calling Xavi and having her picked-up instead. It should have been the practical decision, but she decided otherwise, opting to brave the rain with an umbrella and a thick skin. She played it safe; the shouting and the yelling from yesterday were still fresh. Even though Luma had already exchanged half-hearted pleasantries with Rabiya in the morning, she still didn't know how her mother would react to the sight of Xavi anew.

Luma glanced at her hundred-riyal gold quartz watch: 10:01 a.m. This made the clock inside her mind tick upwards, the clock that counted the tardy minutes of someone who should have already arrived.

To twaddle with time, she counted the colorful people entering the station. Throngs entered in blue, yellow, red, and brown raincoats. Some came with ballooning umbrellas, some with flowery prints, while some with solid colors. A thin pool of muddy rainwater at the entrance materialized, caused by these defenses against the rain, and it was spread by soggy footprints that traced towards the turnstiles.

She glanced at her timepiece once more. Fifteen minutes had passed, and still, there was no sight of the Wooly Asian passing through the gate.

Bored, she shifted her attention to her muddy shoes. She observed how her left foot had been soaking wet, while her right felt completely dry, despite beads of water dribbling down the titanium pylon of her prosthetic leg.

Eleven a.m.; still no Xavi. She sent a message.

\*\*\*

Xavi was already awake at eight. He cooked his breakfast, ate his breakfast, and flushed yesterday's breakfast down the toilet. At 8:30, Xavi was done showering. At 8:45, he was clothed and ready to leave. At 9:00 a.m., he had already been twirling the keys of his car around his index finger for a full fifteen minutes.

He continued twirling his keys while staring at a random spot on the marble floor. The question of whether he should meet or not with Luma decked his face heavily. The fear of angering Nicola's memory also complicated his indecision. He kept twirling his keys until it flew off his fingers when his cellphone rung a message from Luma: *Are you alright? I hope you didn't get stuck in the floods!*

He did not send a reply.

Xavi had decided to stay home in order to ease the guilt that persisted eating him inside-out. Yet, when he went to pick up his key that fell by the door, he unexpectedly found himself locking his apartment involuntarily from the outside. His unconscious action surprised him, but the fact that he didn't fight himself from leaving his abode astonished him even more. The next thing he knew was he was starting his car and switching on the windshield wipers. Then, he heard the engine roaring as he drove away into the rain.

\*\*\*

Seven minutes after Luma had sent the message, Xavi sauntered into the station, dragging a pessimistic burden. From afar, Luma pondered his air. It all seemed familiar, reminiscent of their second and fateful meeting on the train. He had those familiar brows that dipped in sadness, sagging towards his sullen eyes that avoided conversations by engaging the floor or faraway planes. The resigned slump of his upper body also signaled his desire to collapse onto the infinite coldness of the floo—

A scurrying person, trying to catch the next train, had whacked Xavi's shoulder by accident. Xavi thrusted forward, almost losing his footing. An "excuse me" or "sorry" should be expected, but the person ignored Xavi and continued towards the platform. Not even a customary glance was made. It didn't matter though, the wooly man remained impassive and locked on a single thought.

Luma continued assessing Xavi, paying attention to the invisible yet visible ticks of a despondent heart. She also took note of his voice that said in a low tenor, almost a whisper of sadness, "Sorry, I'm late."

Luma playfully tapped Xavi's shoulder, hoping to elicit some form of brightness over his darkened mood. "Are you okay?" she asked softly but optimistically.

"Car is over there." Xavi pointed to the parking lot and walked. He didn't commit to any pleasantries, no *hi's*, nor *hellos*. Only a blank stare that neither said anything definite was given.

Moments later, the two front doors of the blue sedan slammed shut one after the other. The rattling keys were inserted into place, and with a swift and decisive twist, the ignition started and the car grumbled to life.

Xavi pulled the seatbelt, locked it, and asked, "Where are we going?" The metallic drops of rain on the car's roof almost drowned his dispirited voice.

"I'm getting my own apartment!" Luma said with a volume that stabbed Xavi's ears.

"Oh, nice. Where?" He tried to show some verve, but his sullen eyes remained under the shadow of its socket.

"That's where you come in! We'll drive around and look!"

"Okay," he said. His shoulders dropped unwittingly together with a leaden exhale.

Xavi's right hand plunged over the gear lever, pulled it to reverse, and the car jerked into gear. Looking only at the rear-view mirror and the side mirrors, he released the brakes, and the vehicle started creeping backward. Pebbles crunched as the tires rolled over them on the wet tarmac.

Luma continued watching Xavi and his subdued emotions. "Wait," she said.

The car stopped halfway off the pocket.

"Are you sure you're okay?" she continued.

Xavi feigned a smile, said, "Yeah," then he frowned and said, "Of course!" and then he smiled again, saying, "I'm okay!"

Luma watched him rub the sides of the steering wheel with his palms. Something was obviously bothering him, and she debated whether to keep probing him or not. Alas, she decided that sometimes, silence is the best cure for miseries. She faced front, kept one eye on Xavi, and said, "Okay… Let's start at Suba Al Sara South. I've seen some ads over there."

\*\*\*

In the following minutes after the car had inched away, nobody spoke. Xavi drove steadily over the wet roads, guiding the vehicle through a thin layer of rainwater, whereas Luma quietly watched beads of raindrops draw lines on the window next to her. It was only the sound of the squeaking wipers sweeping the rain that filled the quiet atmosphere.

The *500 Meters* exit sign to Suba Al Sara South came into view. Luma turned to Xavi, assessing him. He made no indication of changing lanes and kept speeding in the fast lane. Luma thought that the rain did reduce visibility, but it wasn't enough to prevent seeing the signs nor the fast-approaching ramp to the right. She turned her attention back to the approaching exit, now only a car length away.

"E-e-exit! Exit!" Luma screamed, pointing to the mouth of the ramp.

## PORTRAITS OF THE WIND

Xavi pulled the steering wheel hard to the right. The wheels turned at an angle and their fast speed caused the car to hydroplane. The sedan violently spun, veering in circles in the middle of the freeway. Other cars blared their horns and zoomed past their swirling vehicle in one streak of color. That's all they saw; everything outside the window became thin lines that stretched into infinity. With quick thinking, Xavi counteracted the spin by steering to the left and to the right, hitting the brakes, and feathering the gas. The wheels locked and spun. The ABS and the traction control automatically powered on or off at the behest of the car's computer brain trying to regain control.

Two, three, four revolutions around itself, the car stopped at the outer lane facing the wrong way. For a brief instant, for a breath, everything became calm, until the jarring sound of Luma's shriek pierced the silence. She was screaming at the distressing sight of a fast oncoming SUV, flashing its blinding-white xenon headlamps.

Xavi thoughtlessly hit the reverse and careened towards the shoulder. The SUV swerved the other way, missing them by a hair.

"What the holy hell!" Luma scowled. Her nostrils flared with every laborious pant. "If I want to die, I want it quick! Not like this!"

The engine continued to idle. The wipers continued to sweep the falling rain.

Xavi whispered, "Sorry," with a face as pale and dark as the colorless clouds above.

"I don't want to lose another leg, man!" she said.

Xavi took a minute to collect his breath, and when the road was clear, he steered the car to face the right way.

Xavi took the next exit to Suba Al Sara, but it wasn't to the South, it was to the North. So, he navigated the backroads, trying to look for a way back to the south. After kilometers of turning here and there, their vehicle remained inside the endless maze of the North.

The sweeping wipers, the incessant puttering of the rain, and the pressing weight inside his chest had caused Xavi to be disoriented.

Another kilometer had passed. They're still lost. No one had spoken. Not even glances were exchanged. Only the stunned silence, which transformed into a stifled concern, filled the hearts and minds of the disjointed pair. Within the next minute, the fretfulness caused Xavi to pull over.

"Sorry. I'm so sorry," Xavi said while looking down across the steering wheel to his shaking legs.

"What's going on? Seriously? You're not okay!"

Xavi's lips remained shut while his diaphragm expanded broadly and contracted deeply with each inhales and exhales.

"Are you having another breakdown?" Luma touched his shoulder. He flinched.

"Forgive me. I can't do this," he said without looking at her.

"Okay, sure, it's fine. Let's go home."

Xavi shook his head. "No, I mean, I can't do this," he waved his hand across the space between them, "us."

Luma reeled backward, blinking thrice. "I beg your pardon?"

"I miss her."

Luma frowned harder, unsure of what he was precisely driving at.

"I feel guilty, you know," Xavi continued. "I mean, I was able to keep her in the center of my life for ten years, and now, I... I don't want to replace her. I'm scared. I don't want her gone from my life!"

"Nicola?" she asked dubiously.

"Yes!"

"Who's replacing her?"

Xavi turned to Luma. He didn't say anything, but from the way his contrite eyes stared, he meant her.

Luma reeled backward once more in one incredulous motion while waving her hands. "Whoa, whoa, Xavi, no, wha… what are you saying?"

"I tried to put on a brave face when she died, but even then… I'm weak. I always drop to my knees at the faintest whiff of her memory. I love her. And I miss her. And you, I tried to justify us, but you are not her. She's my light, my life, and you're trying to push her away."

"The hell, Xavi! I am not!"

Xavi whispered, "No you're not, but whatever way you look at it inside my head… you are."

Luma ignored Xavi's response. "Me?!" she roared, and backhanded Xavi's chest. "Me?! Who said anything about me replacing her?"

"I'm sorry, but that's what it looks like. That's what it feels like. Everything we do, it's…" He lowered his gaze. "I can't be friends with you anymore. Last night, I felt like sleeping for a thousand years, if you know what I mean, if only to smother the guilt in me."

Anger slowly ebbed through Luma like hot water melting away the tranquility of an idle ice. She was perplexed. She has been angry since the time of the accident, but never at Xavi. This was the first time, and it was ungodly.

"Y-y-y-you—" Luma punched the dashboard so hard that Xavi thought the airbag would deploy. "You don't say that to people! You don't say that! You just don't! Not even to your bestest friend! How thick can you be?! You're a moron! If you don't want to be friends, just disappear! Don't formulate stupid reasons about me being a replacement for your dead girlfriend! That's unfair! You unearthly sob!"

Xavi ate his lips.

"She's been dead for ten years! And you still, you still… God! Move on! Move on! Instead of moping and brooding and sulking for ten years! Get a life!"

Xavi waved his hands around. "I'm wrong, alright? I know that. But what can I do? This is how I feel. What do you want me to say—"

"Don't say anything! Get into a balloon and float away—"

"—I'm sorry if it came out wrong—"

"—it did come out wrong because it is wrong!"

"I'm depressed, okay? I make bad decisions when I'm depressed—"

Luma chuckled darkly, "No! No! You can't say you're depressed to get out of a jam! That's not good enough! It's not good enough! You can't use it as an excuse to get you off sticky situations! You know what you're doing even if you're depressed; your mind doesn't suddenly shut itself down. You're still aware of everything, you just can't accept the fact that she's dead, and you're projecting it into the world! Why don't you try thinking of other people's feelings first when you do something, say something? Think about how they'd feel. You can't? Because you're depressed? You're an a-a-a-asshole! That's what you are!" Luma removed her seat belt, unlocked the door, and got out.

"Where are you going?"

Luma did not answer. She slammed the door and allowed the rain to spit on her clothes. In another blink, she was already soaking wet, rushing away from the car.

Xavi stepped out into the shower too. "Where are you going? I'll drive you home! It's raining!"

"I have my umbrella!" Luma raised it as she limped and splashed away, but she didn't use it. The umbrella remained clutched in her hand as she hastened off into the distance.

"Come on! Don't be stupid! I'll bring you home!"

Luma whirled around and bellowed, "Exactly! I'm trying not to be stupid! Only a stupid person will ride with you after you dumped her ass like that! You want us to end, right? Whatever this is between us? I'd like to think it was a unique friendship. A collection of kindness between two grieving people! I thought it was something that would help me get better, that someone would help me overcome my anger! I thought maybe it will help you too. Two people breathing anger and depression found each other to build each other again. But no! You think I am a replacement for some dead girl! Well excuse me, I'm not replacing anyone! Because I am not a replacement!"

"Forget it, okay? Just come on, I'll drive you home!"

"No! The last time you drove me home wet, things didn't work out either!" Luma turned her back to Xavi and stomped away.

The flood got deeper the further Luma floundered into it. It was only ankle-deep when she first waded through, now it was already half up her shin. She struggled to walk with her real foot, what with the water's weight pressing down her feet. Now, with her prosthetic leg, the effort matched that of dragging an anchor from the bottom of the sea. A few more steps later, her leg detached; she tipped sideways, then sunk into the flood.

Xavi hurried to her to hold her up.

"Asshole! Don't touch me!" Luma yelled. She shoved Xavi away, who was once again stunned at the strength of Luma's rage manifesting in her muscles.

The legless woman hastily reattached her leg and walked towards a higher ground where she pivoted left to an apartment.

"Where are you going?" inquired Xavi loudly, hollering over the distance.

"I'll wait here for you to leave! Go! Go and be with your dead girlfriend! Brood in darkness! Go! Sleep for a thousand years! Or make it ten thousand. Make it a million years if you want to! I don't care!" She disappeared into the apartment building then.

Xavi stood for a moment under the rain, dazed and confused, hoping for something positive, whatever it may be. But alas, the winds only whispered sorrow, and with it, the cold and heavy teardrops of the sky soaked him in dense desolation and grief.

Splash, splash, splash.

Heavy footsteps waded through the floodwaters. Xavi knew what it was. Once more, conflict reigned in his mind. Should he welcome it now? Or fear it?

Splash…

Over there, in the middle of the street, the beast stood, slimy and enraged. It got bigger now, twice larger than it used to be. It was despair, grief, pain, sorrow, heartache, guilt, remorse, and all malaise, of the past, and of the present, all melded into one hostile ugly being. And over the distance, it stood like a dog staring at his master. Except that the creature was the master, and Xavi was the dog.

\*\*\*

Eager to wash away the grit, mud, and the memory of that morning, once Luma got home, she jumped right into the shower still with her clothes on. As the showerhead released a warm stream of water, she closed her eyes and let the freshwater trickle down her lips.

*"We can't be friends anymore…"*

CRACK!

She punched the wet tile of the bathroom wall. It wasn't the tile that cracked, though.

Luma winced in agony as her knuckles bled hot boiling blood. The aching was immense, but it was better than… she didn't know what. Surely the tore skin, the cracked knuckles, and the warm blood took over the hurt and pain from that morning. The pain from that morning, what exactly was that from?

She knew she was angry. Why? At what Xavi said. Yes, but why?

Is it because of the idea that Xavi sees her as a replacement, or is it because he is the replacement to her missing leg? Is it that she sees him as a new friend, a confidant, the face of the same coin? That behind all the misery is a beautiful person, breathing the same melancholic oxygen as she is, and staring at the same dark side of the moon at night? Opposites attract, but similarity feels home. And she certainly felt at home, more home than home, around Xavi. And now, he, like her bicycle dreams, is gone. Is that why?

Her head bowed down, and her lips blew the water cascading over it. A thin layer of mud circled down the drain. She stared at that for a second, for a moment, and for however long she wanted to.

Everything on earth will pass, she thought, like that mud circling down into obscurity. It will all pass. You would, I would, your girlfriend did, my leg did. That's what life is: a collection of passing memories, leaving a trail of misery.

# Chapter 34:
# To Sleep a Thousand Years

"Is this the strongest?" Xavi asked the pharmacist.

The Egyptian pharmacist nodded.

Xavi scanned the pharmacy, looking for nothing in particular. He just took inventory of all the medicine bottles displayed on the shelves for no reason whatsoever. Then, he looked back at the pharmacist and said, "Okay. I'll take it."

The pharmacist briefly studied Xavi's disheveled look, from the wet hair, to the soft tears, to the wet and muddy clothes. He grabbed the pill bottle from Xavi and said, "Wait, I'll change this."

The pharmacist went to the medicine cabinet behind his counter. His head rose to look to the top left, actively reading, skimming to the right, then going back to the left one row under, and then to the right again. He read all the labels, column by column, and row by row. "Ah, here it is." He pulled out a bottle from the drawer and then gave it to Xavi.

"Is this the strongest?" Xavi asked.

The pharmacist pretended not to hear Xavi. Instead, he gave instructions on how to drink the pills. "Once, after food and before sleeping. Okay? After food. Otherwise, your stomach will hurt."

Xavi tried to smother his forming smile by pouting and biting his lips. "Okay," he replied.

One minute he was paying by card, and then the next minute, he was strolling calmly, under the rain, towards his idling car.

***

## PORTRAITS OF THE WIND

**July 2010. Baguio City, Philippines.**

Xavi had been battling his depression for weeks after the fateful event that claimed Nicola's life. He suffered greatly like anyone who had lost a loved one. It fell like an iron yoke around his neck that could never be shed.

He denied her death and accepted the blame. It was his idea, after all, to spend her birthday atop the country's summer capital, Baguio City, nestled high in the clouds.

He bargained, pleading to the gods of his father, to the gods of his forefathers, and to the gods of the gods to bring back Cola, but no one answered.

Then he dipped into a solemn reflection and isolation. Where, inside the hollow halls of his heart, the beast of despair started to take shape and mature, sucking him to the fourth stage of grief: depression.

A year later, on the exact month that Nicola died, grief struck Xavi anew. But he didn't fight it; he accepted it. No, this was not the fifth stage of grief which is acceptance and moving on. What he accepted were the words that his mature beast whispered to him.

Depressed, disheartened, and hopeless, Xavi walked fifteen kilometers from his hilltop house down towards Kenon Road. He set afoot when the weather was bright and sunny; three hours later, the clouds had hung low, causing the whole city on the mountaintop to become damp and ghostly. He emerged from the thick fog like an apparition underneath the white mist. His face was dark, eclipsed by the hoodie of his thick sweater. Underneath the soft shadow of the towering pines, he meandered on and on, head down, eyes on the floor that scrolled beneath his feet.

When the surface of the road changed color from faded grey to neo-black, he stopped and examined his immediate surroundings. The new black tarmac was not longer than twenty-five meters. Newly poured concrete coated the hillside above, safeguarding it from any unwanted landslides. If nobody knew what happened over that place a year before, no one would have guessed that thirty-one people had died there on the spot.

Xavi grunted as he lifted himself onto the foot-high concrete crash barrier hugging the side of the road. On stepping up, he saw the long drop to the ravine below. He felt his insides turn over. To calm himself, he took a deep inhale, then he accepted the inevitable.

He closed his eyes. He breathed in slowly and held it. The rumbles of passing cars silenced, and he only heard his heart beating with the wind. Flashes of Nicola's heavenly face, her arresting eyes, and her contagious laughter appeared together with the phosphenes that floated behind his dark eyelids. He took a step and then inched and inched forward until half of his feet were hanging over the cliff. He exhaled submissively, letting go of all his past reservations. His shuddering lips steadied, and slowly, serenely, formed a smile. He lifted his right foot over the drop and waited for his body to tip forward.

This wasn't therapy. This wasn't forgetting and moving on. This was freedom from the limitations of life. This was freedom from malaise. Nicola was up there, down there, somewhere, and he was damn ready to join her.

With one fell swoop, he fell to the ground. Not forward, but backward. Back to the neo-black tarmac. He opened his eyes expectantly in hopes to see the woman he yearned for. But first, a blinding white light seared his retinas. He turned his head to the side where it was darker, allowing his iris to adjust faster. In a few blinks, he recognized a pair of shiny leather boots blocking his view. A pair of hands pressed on his cheeks and yanked his head to face the front, towards a highway patrolman mouthing words that he couldn't understand.

For a second, Xavi was confused. And then, as if despair weren't enough, another torrent of torment washed over him. His lungs tightened; he gasped; he drowned in agony when he realized that he remained breathing in the world that he wished to leave.

\*\*\*

**December 2019, Al Mamriya, Doha, Qatar.**
Single leg crossed at the bedroom floor, Luma gently blew a spoonful of *harira* soup that her mother cooked. Traditionally, it was prepared with tomatoes, lentils, and chickpeas. But her home chef mother had put her own twist by adding a thin layer of cooking cream, creating a coarse and smooth taste on the tongue at the same time. A quaint favorite.

Luma continued to blow on the steaming spoonful. When she brought the spoon closer to her lips to feel its temperature, the lentil's earthy scent traveled up her nose and whetted her appetite. In that instant, her jaw unhinged, released saliva, and her mouth swallowed the soup then. A spoonful of warmth traveled down to her stomach and then bloomed outwards to the tips of her fingers. Luma felt good. The coldness and wetness from the livid morning were washed away with tenderness. She forgot how her mother's cooking tasted like, and a sip transported her back to the innocence of childhood.

"There's more in the kitchen," a voice said.

Luma glanced up from the floor and saw Rabiya's head peeking into the room with an awkward smile. Luma nodded to her vibrantly. She knew what the soup meant. And with a tiny sip from a single spoon, she was ultimately accepting her mother's unsaid apology.

Acceptance, though seen by many as a weakness, is acknowledged as leading to peace by the strong.

Watching her daughter consume the soup while sitting on the floor, Rabiya recalled the sights from bygone years. They were memories when the sun was golden, shining its warm rays into her daughter's bedroom in Ifrane. In the middle of that room, sat on the floor, receiving all the bright orange rays of the afternoon light, was a six-year-old Luma, sipping a soup made of lentils and chickpeas. They were scenes teeming with the abundance of a mother's love towards her innocent child. And now, tonight, twenty years later, Rabiya was looking at the same scene, feeling the same mother's love once more.

Rabiya walked away, gratified. They understood each other despite no words being uttered.

Luma's phone chimed. She glanced at the glowing device beside her bowl of soup.

There was a message from Xavi: *I'm sorry. I am finally finding peace now. Thanks for everything.*

She shook her head, wondering if these words were his way of apologizing.

She typed a simple reply, which to her meant an ounce of forgiveness: *Stupid wooly man.*

Her finger hovered over the screen for a moment, considering if she should hit send. Instead, she locked the phone and set it aside. Let him suffer a tiny bit longer, she thought, they'll shake hands after the soup.

She took another sip of the harira, then she froze, spoon on her mouth, her head down, but eyes straining up towards the ceiling. "What did he mean 'thanks for everything?'" she inaudibly asked herself.

***

## PORTRAITS OF THE WIND

Amidst the dimmed light of his apartment, Xavi sat at his couch with a sealed bottle of sleeping pills clutched in his hand. To his right side, lying quietly, was his 7650. He dawdled for a long while, whilst glancing at the bottle and the phone from time to time.

Thoughts raced inside his wailing mind, thoughts of all the past that now haunted him. It haunted him for he knew, though he denied, he was feeling a certain something for someone new. The only question, for now, is: Is it only friendship, or is it more?

What he was sure of was that the lady with the crimson hair made him forget all the pain of the past. That she made him hopeful for a new day. That she made him enjoy the little things, like riding the train, or eating sinigang, or running under the rain, or lying wet on the grass, or laughing heartily like innocent children over the simplest fun. In all its essence, she ignited a glowing flare of euphoria in his blackened world. She made him happy... and that felt wrong.

It felt wrong that he even had entertained the thought of another woman, whatever label it may be. It felt wrong that a new wave of delight consumed him, while his dead girlfriend was... dead. It felt wrong to even think of anyone else. It felt wrong to be happy.

Now, he can correct everything.

He looked at the bottle in his hand. There were fifty capsules inside the plastic container. He figured it would be enough to put him to sleep for a hundred thousand years, or maybe more. He would be living inside his dreams where he could repeat the past and mold it to the present he desired. The pills were the only way out of life's misery that doesn't involve brutality. It grants eternal rest in a peaceful way.

CRACK! The bottle's seal broke as he twisted the cap off.

"Fifty pills, a hundred thousand years."

He held the bottle to his mouth, and with a series of gulps, he downed all fifty pills.

In the ensuing seconds, harmony and fear staged a battle inside of him. The hairs on his arms and legs stood in nervous audacity, whereas his breathing slowed down. His muscles relaxed; however, his stomach twinged. Misery and anxiety groped their way up his skin, but he knew it will pass, like everything on earth will pass. He simpered, he frowned, he jerked a tear. This is really happening now, he thought, this time it's for sure.

For the last time in his breathing life, he scanned his room. He looked at the window, beading wet from the torrential rain. He looked at the dining table with his lifeless laptop on top. He looked at his bed, who accepted his decrepit self without prejudice. He looked at the floor, where the Memory Bank's intestine once laid. He looked at his camera, which took all the beautiful memories that will all die away with his last breath. He looked at the digital art hanging on the wall depicting a rhinoceros with glowing eyes. Lastly, he looked at his 7650 that still contained the final message of Nicola.

Xavi picked up the phone, navigated to the message, and then deleted it. It hurts, but he knew he had no use for it anyway. He was finally meeting her, after a decade apart, separated by a cosmos unknown, which now he will travel within a blink. To hell with the living world.

The phone's screen went dark, and his own reflection stared back at him. He averted sharply, unable to sustain a final glance of his dark and dreary face.

His mind fell quiet then, and in the stillness, he heard Nicola whisper, *"Never let me go..."*

"There will never be a moment I'm not with you," he mumbled, "I promise."

"I'm sorry. I am finally finding peace now. Thanks for everything." Luma began mouthing the words as she read Xavi's message over and over, so it felt like the words were coming out from her mouth. "Thanks for everything. I am finally finding peace now. Thanks for everything. I am finally finding peace now."

She exhaled with a brief chuckle, laughing at her paranoid thoughts.

She laid down the phone again and continued slurping the soup. But the soup didn't taste as good as it did a few minutes ago. Luma lost her appetite. Her taste buds stopped working as jitters rippled outwards from her gut. Xavi's message had drilled a hole deep inside her mind that numbed everything, except fear.

Thanks for everything. Peace. Finally.

"Why does this make me feel uneasy?" she asked herself aloud.

"What's that?" shouted Rabiya from the kitchen.

"Nothing! Talking to myself!" she replied.

A minute later, Luma mouthed Xavi's message once more. "Peace. Peace. Finally. Peace. Thanks for everything."

*"I had the strong desire to be with her... If you know what I mean."* The words regurgitated back from her memory. She remembered Xavi's sullen face, back at the ramshackle restaurant, as he expressed those words to her.

"What did he mean by those words?" she asked herself.

*"I felt like sleeping for a thousand years."* She froze. The room's air suddenly felt cold on her skin.

"Holy... hell!"

She grabbed her phone and muscled her way to the bed, leaving the prosthesis on the floor. She opened Xavi's message and replied: *Hey! No biggie! It's alright! Wanna talk?*

Send.

Luma sat at the edge of her bed and waited for a reply while flicking her thumbs against each other. The clock ticked aloud. Every passing second was anxiety on top of another, building and rising to become a stockpile of fear. Five minutes in, still no reply. Luma reread Xavi's message once more. She lingered at every word, at every letter. Ten minutes, still no answer. Maybe he's busy or something, she thought.

She typed another message: *Woolyman! Sorry for everything I said. I didn't mean any of them. It's just the heat of the moment...*

Send.

Fifteen minutes after the last message, Luma was now pacing around her room. The bowl of harira was still on the floor, untouched and coagulating.

One hour had passed. Luma decided to throw the soup secretly down the drain and wash the bowl to tarry with time.

"Do you want more?" Rabiya asked.

Luma shook her head.

Two hours. Luma walked about her room once more with the phone pressed against her ear. There was a ring. And another. The line automatically cut off after sixty seconds of no answer. Five minutes later, another try. Five minutes later, redial.

Three hours after she had received the message, she grabbed an umbrella, hobbled out their house, and stood under the rain outside their gateless compound. She looked left. She looked right. The neighborhood never seemed so vast and endlessly dark until now. The few lampposts, whose amber glow made dancing raindrops glitter in midair, struggled to light the streets.

She knew Xavi lived within the area, but within the area could mean a hundred meters, or a thousand, or five thousand meters. Where should she begin?

Luma braced against the onslaught and shouldered through the rain. She let her feet lead the way, turning corners without heeding, wandering aimlessly through ankle-deep floods. Luma's small umbrella shielded nothing except her head. From the neck down, the wind and rain besieged her. But she soldiered on, rounding corners she had never been to, to neighborhoods that she never saw. Turn here, turn there. She looked back; nothing looked familiar. She was lost, scared, worried for both herself and Xavi. With her cold hands shaking with panic, she tried to call Xavi once more, and like the previous fifty times, there was no answer.

She continued wading deeper into the dying light, alone under the tempest of a changing season. Each step felt like a step in the same flooded and bleak place. Still, she kept floundering forward until she saw two lights approaching her: a cab.

She slammed the door.

"Where we go?" the driver asked.

"Huh?" she responded. The hammering rain was more deafening inside the cab than it was outside.

"Where do you want to go?" the Pakistani driver reiterated.

"Just drive, I'll tell you where."

The taxi drove off, further into the center of the submerged neighborhood. It was the only vehicle driving around within the endless urban maze. They had driven past houses, parked cars, and flooded streets, and they drove past them again until they all became too familiar.

She did not know where to go.

Hopeless, Luma opened her social media account for the first time in six months.

*X–A–V–I,* Luma typed in the search field. A relief! Xavi came second to the top result. He looked noticeably young in his profile picture, and he had a girl beside him.

Is that Nicola? she thought. A beautiful girl indeed.

She clicked on Xavi's profile. She clicked on it with such force that her finger caused a ripple of white light to appear across the screen.

While the smartphone uploaded instructions and downloaded data through the internet, she could suddenly hear everything around her: the muted roars of water splashing outside, the driver's earphones softly playing deafening music, and the explosive tick of her quiet wristwatch.

Xavi's profile loaded, and behold…

His account was private.

"Darn it!" she growled. Then she remembered something from the back of her head. It was a long shot, but at least it was something. She leaned in and gave the taxi driver directions. Within a minute, the streets of Al Mamriya were empty once more.

# Chapter 35:
# The Beast of Despair

It was night in the jungle. The moon's pale blue light filtered through palm trees and acacia trees that towered under the cloudless skies.

Among the thick brush and tall plants, a man with a wooly beard emerged. His pupils adjusted quickly to the darkness and witnessed the threatening sight of the jungle at night. Here, insects sang, and animals howled invisibly beyond the trees.

The man continued in solitude, deeper into the dense, dark, and humid jungle. Fear crept up his legs with every step. And with every step, his bewilderment grew. He was hoping to be in a familiar place, but his fifty pills brought him somewhere else.

He heard a low growl that caused birds to disperse into the night sky, flying onto the clouds that started to obscure the moon. His heart began pounding like inharmonious timpani played by children. With it, a million glowing eyes had lit up and peered at him from the trees, the bushes, and from the ground. For every loud drumbeat of his chest, an eye would open.

THUMP. A new sound thundered. It wasn't Xavi's heart. THUMP. It was loud. THUMP. It shook the earth. THUMP. It signaled death. THUMP. Pebbles and loose rocks rattled with each stomp.

Xavi squinted to see what's behind the trees, whose leaves fell from their branches with each thunderous step. After a few more stomping and low rumbling... silence. Even the wind dared not to whisper.

He swallowed in fear.

The infinitely small sound of his gulp rippled across the waves of grass towards the blackness of the trees. A hefty snort answered, like that of a bull preparing to attack its matador; but it was heavier, lasting the equivalent of two human exhales.

THUMP! SNAP! CRASH! Two tall acacia trees snapped at the bottom of their aged trunks. They fell with a mighty shake, trembling the still forest. The million glowing eyes that flashed on Xavi streaked away into a blur of white. Then out of the two fallen trees, the giant creature emerged.

It had a massive body, standing twenty meters high over its meter-wide paw. Its belly bulged on the sides. Over its snout grew two horns of ivory, the tallest of which towered at two meters high. It had eyes that glowed ghostly white. It was a colossal rhinoceros, the embodiment of Xavi's beast of despair and malaise, and now of guilt too. For a moment, it stood its ground as it stared down at the measly figure draped under its moonlit shadow.

Xavi recognized his beast. "Dammit! Why are you here? What is this place?!"

The beast roared, louder than a tyrannosaurus rex, then it sprinted towards Xavi.

"Holy Mia," he whispered.

Without hesitation, Xavi whirled around and ran in the opposite direction, skidding on corners, sliding on mud, and jumping and ducking logs and leaves. He sweated profusely, freely, with sweat as cold as ice chilling his blood. He ran as fast as he could, but still, he could feel the beast breathing down his tiny body. There was no way out. Everywhere and everything was the jungle; everything was dark. He kept running, faster, like the wind, through tiny gaps between the trees.

# Chapter 36:
# Race against the Hourglass

"There! Stop there!" the fretful passenger yelled to the taxi driver, pointing to one of the towering glass structures in the concrete jungle of West Bay. The taxi stopped. The passenger dashed out, ignoring her change.

Soaked by the rain, Luma perused the building's directory by the foyer. It's a long list. Her finger guided her eyes through the multitude of offices listed in the 40-story building. On the row of the twenty-first floor, she saw *Al-Zubara Contracting*. The office timing read, *9:00 AM to 5:00 PM*.

She checked her watch. 4:47 p.m.

"Dick!"

The lobby had six elevators, and none had readouts of its current floor. They only had an arrow pointing up or down that lighted up when a lift was ready to accept a passenger. Luma waited blindly for one, glancing at the time, counting the minutes.

One minute had passed, she pressed the call button again. In two minutes, she called once more. Three minutes, four minutes, Luma was now heedlessly pacing around the elevator lobby, unintentionally drawing a line of muddy footprints on the marble floor. Five minutes—DING! A door opened, and she was heading up to the twenty-first floor.

The numbers on the floor readout display ticked upwards slowly. Or perhaps it was only her sprinting mind that made the outside world feel drawn-out. Still, it didn't help that the lift stopped at almost every other floor, only to be asked by denizens, "Going down?" At every instance, she pointed up with one hand, and with the other, she pressed the close-door button repeatedly. Every time the elevator stopped, she felt a drop of hope leach out her bottom. It's 4:55 p.m.

The twenty-first floor arrived. Like a horse with blinders on, Luma burst out of the elevator and stormed into— She stopped. The floor had two offices. One had "FilmChow" on its nameplate, probably a production company, and the other had "RenderFarm Productions" on its nameplate, another production company. Ugh! What the hell! She entered FilmChow.

"Wh-wh-where's Al-Zubara Contracting?" she asked.

The FilmChow receptionist shook his head.

"What floor is this?"

"Twenty," he replied.

Luma swore and cussed so fluently that the receptionist there almost shrunk beneath his desk.

She checked her watch; 4:57 p.m. She hobble-wobbled to the elevator and pressed the call button. Of course, none came immediately. Her wristwatch ticked; 4:58 p.m. Crap! Luma burst into the stairwell and dragged herself up towards the twenty-first floor.

Panting, she threw open the twenty-first-floor stairwell door, sending mighty echoes booming all around. Her muscles were strained and tense and frail altogether as she limped, scurried, and dragged her prosthetic leg towards the unsuspecting Slovakian receptionist of Al-Zubara Contracting.

"Hi," Luma said brashly while catching her escaping breath.

The receptionist looked at her watch and then back to Luma with false sincerity. "May I help you?" she asked with traces of annoyance; it was closing time after all.

Luma perceived the irritation on the receptionist's face, but she ignored it. "I'm lo... lo... looking for... looking for Xavi!" she said aloud.

The receptionist sighed and looked down at her directory of phone extensions and then looked up to the ceiling with a wrinkled forehead, thinking. She paused consciously, deliberately stretching the time, waiting for the seconds to reach zero. Then, after a long beat, she turned to Luma and spoke slowly, "Ah! I'm sorry, but Xavi is currently on leave."

Luma got aggravated at the sardonic manner of the receptionist, and she overtly showed her effort to stay calm. Tapping her fingers on the counter, she nodded readily and replied, "Yes! Yes! I know! But can you give me his address?"

The receptionist widened her eyes and then blinked twice. "Sorry ma'am. We don't give the private information of our employees," she said, and checked her wristwatch. Not a second later, she closed her workstation, tidied up her desk, and locked her drawers. It was closing time, finally.

Luma got triggered. With a stern shrill voice and fisted hands that banged the desk, she yelled, "Please! He might be in danger!"

The Slovakian reeled backward, surprised at the visitor's sudden change in volume. Embarrassed, she tried to keep her poise by keeping an unpainted face. She eloquently brushed her golden hair with her pink-polished fingernails and said, "We can't give out the private information of our employees."

"Is there someone I can talk to then?" Luma asked firmly.

The face muscles of the lady behind the reception started twitching microscopically. Luma knew that that meant the receptionist was being either convinced or rattled by her decorum.

"Uhm... All the managers left already," the receptionist said.

"Then please! Give me his address!" the limping lady shouted firmly at the top of her lungs. No stutter.

The receptionist froze, stumped. For a length of a breath, she didn't know how to react.

"What's going on?" a rich voice said from deep within the office.

The two people at the reception glanced towards the voice, and there they saw an old man in white thobe locking the door to his glass office.

"Mr. Saeed! I... I thought you left," said the Slovakian, stunned and surprised.

Saeed walked towards them. He straightened his ghutra and kept his gaze steady at the lady who's dripping wet. "How can I help you?" he asked sincerely and concernedly.

"I... I... I need to find Xavi... I... I..." she forced an exhale.

"Relax, take your time," said Saeed.

Luma shook her head, "No! I need to find Xavi! I think he's in danger!"

"He's what? Why?" he asked. He then instructed the receptionist to call Xavi.

The receptionist, now also concerned, readily obliged.

Luma continued, "He's depressed, and I think he's done something stupid!"

"I knew it!" Saeed gloated to himself while his brain flashed memories of Xavi being sullen within the workplace. "I knew those eyes were depressed!" he said through his gritted teeth. "Like what? What stupid thing can he do?"

Luma shook her head, "I'm not sure, but I know he has a history of s... suicide!"

A long pause arose as the words sunk into the registry of the receptionist and Saeed's brain.

Suicide. It is such a familiar word. Sometimes it is so trivial that it could easily slide out your tongue. You read it in the newspapers, you hear it on the TV, yet when you learn that someone you know contemplated suicide, it feels completely unreal.

Tick-tock, tick-tock. The wall clock above their heads reaffirmed the urgency of the situation.

The receptionist replaced the handset and said, "He's not answering."

"Have you tried his cellphone?" Saeed replied.

"That's his cellphone."

"Damn!" Saeed grabbed his keys and pointed to Luma. "You, come with me, we're going to his house! And you," he looked to the receptionist as he ran out with Luma, "you don't speak to anyone about this! We don't know anything for certain yet."

"Yes sir!" the receptionist replied as Saeed disappeared with Luma into an elevator. Then she wondered, will they reach the ground floor seamlessly, or will there be how many stops in between?

\*\*\*

The Lexus SUV of Saeed weaved in and out of traffic, sometimes skidding due to the rain-soaked tarmac. Its horn blared constantly. Its blood-warming xenon headlights flashed against the strolling cars on the fast lane.

Luma held on to the edge of her seat and on to the door handle to keep herself stable inside the luxury roller-coaster. After a kilometer of lacing the traffic, the inevitable rush-hour jam at the Doha Corniche slowed their quest. Not even multi-million-dollar road upgrades could quell the swelling cars in the capital's asphalt veins.

Saeed hit the brakes and pressed the horn. "Hemar!" he yelled aloud. "If only it's not illegal to ram cars, I'd do it without thinking!"

Luma kept her eyes on the long way ahead. She heard Saeed, but she couldn't look at anything else apart from the road crammed with motionless cars. Craning her neck, she traced the endless wave of glowing red taillights, hoping to see an end to it. It had no end. Knowing that they were losing the race against the hourglass, she felt bigger droplets of hope leaching out her bottom, making her fingers wildly tap the edge of her seat to channel her unsteady soul.

Saeed perceived her anxiety. "Don't worry, we'll get there," he said genially before cutting the car on the right as soon as a gap opened.

The unsuspecting car they had just cut flashed its headlights and blasted its maddening horn. Inside, a man waved his hands and mouthed words.

Saeed continued cutting cars on the remaining two lanes, provoking ear-splitting horns to blare and blinding electric lights to flash. None of the drivers were giving at all. The other cars would stick their bumpers to the ones ahead just to not be cut off, even if the Lexus had been signaling with blinkers and its passengers had been using hand gestures. All the other drivers cared about was their own time. They didn't think that maybe not all who cut are assholes, and not all who flash their lights on the fast lane are jerks. Every now and then, some people do need to get by with imperative urgency to attend to some crisis that others won't comprehend.

After an excruciatingly slow ten-minute crawl, the Lexus got onto the right shoulder and illegally drove past the traffic. At the end of the lane, at the intersection where a slipway bends to the right, they passed a police car parked on the sidewalk. Its blue and red lights flashed, and its siren horn briefly wailed at the instant the Lexus appeared within view.

"Sharmouta!" Saeed yelled as he pulled over on the sidewalk. He turned to Luma and said, "Forgive me. Pardon my language."

The pair watched in silent torture as the traffic police officer glacially got out of his patrol car, put on his raincoat, and strolled towards them without any sense of urgency at all. Step. Step. Step. Step. Luma wanted to shout, *"hurry up!"* Step. Step.

At last, only two more steps. Step. Step.

Saeed rolled down his window.

Upon seeing Saeed's face, the officer jerked his chin, gesturing for the former to explain. It's a widely known gesture for authorities in the Middle East if they're asking for explanations—no words, just a jerk of the chin.

Saeed spoke, "Salaam-Alaykum! We're in a hurry. She needs to get to the hospital quick." He pointed to Luma.

The officer glanced at her. Her hair was wet, her clothes were soaked, her eyes were red, and she was shivering.

"What's wrong with her?" the officer asked, jerking his chin again.

"We don't know! That's why we need to get to the hospital in a hurry!"

The officer frowned in thought, then like a gentle sloth, he languidly lifted his chin, gesturing them to leave.

"Shukran jazilan! Thank you! Please tell your other friends we'll be speeding through," Saeed said.

"Yalla, go!" gallingly shouted the officer, and waived them off.

Saeed stepped on the gas and the SUV roared thickly over the sound of the winter rain. They went zipping through traffic lights, barely missing the reds. They only slowed down for the speed cameras, and when they were clear, they thundered once more.

A final right turn led them to the flooded streets of Al Mamriya. The water outside submerged their car halfway up its 20-inch wheels.

To a man, the depth was shallow, even so, it created a strong resistance against the powerful V8 engine. For a minute, the passengers of the off-roader thought that the torrent would disable their vehicle, but it soldiered easily on, as it was meant to.

"Over there!" Saeed pointed to the four-building apartment compound at the end of the road. "Xavi's apartment is in Building 4!"

A new sound echoed through the streets. It was the sound of a snarling engine as it powered through the sea of rainwater. The pair inside were so focused on the approaching building that they failed to realize the water was already up to the grill of their vehicle, breaching the engine bay.

The vehicle started slowing down, so Saeed stomped on the pedal. The car grumbled and growled, like a camel being forced to walk. But the steed still won't speed. Again, he pushed the pedal to the floor and the Lexus snarled loudly for the final time before oscillating and puttering to its death.

"Ya khara!" Saeed yelled, and banged the steering wheel; thoughts of a botched rescue mission readily pricked his mind.

The press of the push-button ignition did nothing to restart the unmoving engine. Saeed tried it again. Still, the vehicle won't respond. One more try, third time lucky, yet nothing. All the car's electrics stopped functioning the moment the engine drowned.

Saeed banged the steering wheel once more, loudly and brashly, this time with the force of defeat. With a leaden grunt, Saeed looked out to his side and studied the shimmering waters. "I think the flood is already waist-deep. Look at all the stranded cars," he said.

The vehicles outside bobbed with the flood's tender wave. The boot of the cars, which was more buoyant, floated above the water, while the bonnet, where the engine lay, stayed anchored to the ground. That scene seldom happens in the Middle East. But due to underprepared drainage infrastructure and climate change, it has become a common sight.

Luma, now with gripping panic towering inside, scanned the surroundings. There were about ten to fifteen marooned cars. Most of them were deserted in the middle of the road with the doors left open—a sign of abandonment. They were cars whose drivers encountered the same predicament as them, and the only way to escape was through the rising flood.

"Dammit, we have to walk the rest of the way," Saeed said. "I should have taken the other road. There's another way on the other street, but it's a long detour. We would have to go make a U-turn all the way from the next exit. I thought the car could handle the flood, but clearly, it's not—"

A sound of rushing water, like the rapids of the Amazon, cut off Saeed's sentence. To his surprise, he saw Luma wincing and forcing her door open against the dense wall of water outside. He wanted to protest, but he missed his chance. Before another word could leave his mouth, cloudy brown water had already submerged the car's bespoke leather and fabric interior.

"Sorry…" Luma simply said before jumping out.

Saeed was wrong, the water was not waist-deep, it was almost chest-deep.

Luma's figure glinted amidst the glimmering waters that dwarfed her. Walrus grunts and groans sieved through the raindrops as she journeyed the final one hundred meters with one functioning leg. She held her prosthetic leg in place, gripping the lip of its cup so it won't be inadvertently detached by the massive flood.

It's been five and a half hours since the last message of Xavi. That was all that had rung in her head as she pushed through the chest-deep water. She knew every minute and every second counts.

No time could be wasted, yet every second spent wading through the deluge was lost time. And then she stopped in the flooded street, which was now a lake in the middle of the city. She stopped for a moment to think. She then glanced down to her prosthetic leg under the muddy brown water…

Saeed observed Luma from afar. Beneath the torrential rain, she stooped down and submerged her head under the water. A breath later, she sprung up, dived, and swam across the deluge using her prosthesis as a kickboard. It took Saeed a while to comprehend that. When he did, he yelled, "Wait for me! Wait for me!" before he too dived and swam the chest-deep rainwater.

# Chapter 37:
# Enlightenment of the Rhino

Xavi raced ahead of the beast at his top speed. He hopped, jumped, and ducked obstacles, impeding low branches, fallen vines, and big rocks. Sharp palm leaves sliced his face, oozing warm blood that mixed with his cold sweat. Within fifteen minutes of hot-footing it, the speed started to take its toll. His lungs screamed for air, and no amount of wheezing and gasping can slake its thirst. Even in a lucid dream, the human limit makes its presence known.

The beast of despair kept on Xavi's trail. There was no hope of stopping it. Its ivory horn gorged and tossed anything obstructing its path, including tall trees, which plummeted with a shuddering thunder. The beast wasn't even running, it wasn't speeding, it was only trotting leisurely along the jungle floor. One step from it equaled ten paces for the man it was pursuing.

Xavi's breath escaped him faster than he could breathe. The thin, damp jungle air had constricted his chest to the point of an imploding pain. Only the fear of spending eternity with the giant rhino kept him going.

After a few more meters, he stopped behind a tree. The distant sound of snapping twigs and falling trees echoed behind him. They say the spirit is willing, but the body is weak; for Xavi, both were unwilling, both were weak. Both the spirit and the body had been broken by the relentless chase of the monstrous beast. He couldn't run any longer. Fear and exhaustion paralyzed his trembling limbs.

"Well, this is the end," he said to himself, as his heart excruciatingly pounded the walls of his chest. "Why don't you just take me now? Why are you still torturing me?" he yelled, bellowing to the trees, to the plants, and to the black clouds of the night ceiling. The reality of fear and distress sabotaged the expectation of a smooth and peaceful exit.

The thumping got closer and closer. Soon, after a few more gasps of air, Xavi knew the monster will impale him with its horn or toss him up like a matador hurled by a bull.

Then his ears flinched imperceptibly when he heard a faint voice call out to him. It wasn't Nicola whom he heard, she was long gone, buried under a thick layer of time. But this voice, this faint distant voice came from the living.

A level of peace descended upon him when he heard the voice. He momentarily forgot about the beast and only thought of the voice's face. That made him smile, and that made him more desperate to escape the jungle. However, no matter how desperate he got, he knew he had already signed his death contract with the fifty pills.

The faint voice echoed again. It was infinitely soft, but he still heard it.

"Wait, is that voice from the other side?" he asked himself softly. "I can still get out?"

He scanned the dark jungle. Only tall trees loomed beyond the tall grass. How can he get out? How can he get out of this purgatory of hell?

Then it clicked.

"If I can hear her voice, then I'm not completely dead yet. And if I'm not completely dead yet…"

His pupils expanded at the snap of an idea.

With a renewed vim, he jammed his hand into his mouth, and with his finger, he reached for his uvula, then pricked it. His throat gagged at once. It contracted and opened with a force so immense that bitter and hot liquid worked up the gullet, spilled to his mouth, and projected onto the moonlit forest floor, burning his throat from the hot stomach acid.

But nothing happened; he remained in the jungle. The beast continued closing in, and the vibrations on the ground kept getting stronger and stronger.

Xavi did it again. He pricked his uvula once more. Again, nothing happened. Still hopeful, he—

A sickening snap cracked in the air. The rhino's massive horns uprooted a tree, exposing the cowering man who took refuge from it.

Xavi whispered, "Dammit, Mia," like it was his last words.

The beast's white eyes glared down on Xavi. It snorted and exhaled lengthily, letting Xavi taste its breath's insidious warmth. The beast bowed its head, steadied its foot, and its neck muscles tightened as it prepared to swing its horn towards the measly man.

Xavi can now see the end. He's done. With his finger still on his mouth, he yanked his uvula for the last time, just for the sake of it. Then the last thing he saw before everything glowed white in pain was the tip of the beast's horn.

*** 

Two people tore through the stillness of a corridor in Xavi's apartment building. Their footsteps squished and sloshed as their wet shoes squeezed the water out of their soles. The walls around there boomed back their loud voices to their ears, heightening their already elevated senses.

"There!" Saeed shouted, pointing to the approaching door. "Number 24!" Out of habit, he tried to fix his ghutra. When he reached for it, his aged hands only touched his wrinkled scalp. Somewhere over the flooded streets below, his ghutra floated peacefully, oblivious to their plight to reach Xavi.

Luma rushed towards the doorbell with an extended hand. Her index pressed it with such conviction that her finger bent backward. It hurts, but she elided the pain.

In the instant the doorbell button dipped, her mind flickered images of what Xavi might be doing. She hoped for the best scenario, but prepared herself for the worst. Yet she knew that as long as the door never opens, Xavi is both there and not there; he is both doing well and doing badly; he is both breathing and not breathing.

DING-DONG! The first ring of the bell echoed faintly behind the closed door. The pair keenly waited for an answer, their ears almost touching the wooden door. Five seconds passed, no one had answered. Saeed looked at Luma worriedly. DING-DONG! She pressed it again. Again, they listened. Again, there had been no perceptible movement on the other side.

"Xavi!" Luma yelled at the door. "Xavi! It's Luma and…" She glanced to the man beside her.

"Saeed!" he yelled.

They waited for an answer.

After five, ten, fifteen seconds of vivid silence, Luma rang the bell once more and then hammered her fist on the door. "Xavi! Are you there?"

Silence. All they heard was the wind screaming, the rain crashing, and the electric humming of the corridor's fluorescent lights that added tension to their buzzing minds.

Saeed gently pushed Luma aside before stepping back himself. Across the hall, he got into a running stance and, with a speed so swift, he rammed his shoulder to the door.

THUD! Nothing happened. It left no mark on the door.

THUD! Again, nothing happened. The door did not even shift an inch. But this time, his shoulder left a mark. Not on the door, though. The mark was left on Saeed's face by the form of a blinding grimace. He remembered the days of his youth when he wrestled with friends under the desert heat; when he stood victoriously among those he tackled to the ground. That was more than forty years ago. In this instant, he was fifty years old.

THUD! He stooped down, bent to his waist, clenched his right shoulder, and scowled in pain. He did not say how much it hurt, but his scrunched face and twisted lips said it all.

Now, it was Luma's turn to push him aside. She stepped in front of the door, put her right foot backward, and got into a stance for a strong kick. She took a deep breath. Her muscles tightened and— she changed her mind.

"Hold my shoulders," she told Saeed before bending down and unclipping her prosthetic leg.

Though confused, Saeed stepped behind Luma and gingerly held her shoulder.

"Tighter. Don't let me fall," she said.

He nodded and tightened his grip, and his fingers pressed down on her bones.

Luma swallowed. She took a deep breath once more to brace herself. Then, clasping it by the pylon, she lifted her prosthetic leg above her head and aimed it at the doorknob. With one fell swoop, she swung hard. "Wa-argh!" Luma grunted like a tennis player. Her foot, or rather her prosthetic foot, hit the doorknob with immense crackling force. Today, she found many uses for her prosthetic leg: one, a crutch; two, a kickboard; and now, a sledgehammer.

With each driving pound of her prosthesis, her mind started raising questions.

BANG! *"What if you just did not want to reply?"*
BANG! The doorknob bent.
BANG! *"What if you just forgot your phone?"*
BANG! The rubber sole on the shoe peeled away.
BANG! *"What if you have some other reason?"*
BANG! The wooden panel cracked.
BANG! *"It doesn't matter, I'm here now! I'm here for you!"*
BANG! The door swung open viciously and its creaking sound reverberated down the halls to the tune of a mouse's thin cry. A pitch-black apartment welcomed the visitors, and a putrid odor, the stench of death, hugged them.

Lit only by the corridor's light slitting through the doorway, the pair found Xavi lying by the couch, motionless, lifeless. Vomit and bile percolated from his mouth down to the side of his face, to the fabric of the sofa, and to the floor where an empty pill bottle laid.

\*\*\*

Luma didn't bother reattaching her leg; it was all mangled into an irreparable twisted metal anyway. She dropped her prosthesis and lunged forward, hopping thrice before she stumbled down on the bitter bile. One second, she was now covered in sticky, pungent, and warm puke. Normally, she would have squirmed in disgust, but now, she felt nothing about it. She didn't even notice it. It didn't matter; she didn't care; Xavi was the primary concern.

She crawled up to his lifeless body, caressed his face, pulled him up, and shook him, making his limbs dangle flaccidly like a ragdoll's. He showed no signs of life. So, fearing the worst, she tried looking for a pulse around his neck. Under the hushed uncertainty of the dark, she pressed her fingers down below his jawline and... her breathing stopped.

Xavi was already cold.

Luma dropped to her knees and placed her hands over her face. She wanted to dissolve right there, as all hope completely leaches out of her body. She was too late. This was her fault. She shouldn't have erupted that morning. She should have been more understanding, more forgiving, more—

"No, wait! What am I thinking?" She distanced her palms from her face and stared at it. They were trembling and cold, which might have contaminated her senses. "Crap! Fudge!" Driven by fear and denial, she searched for a pulse once more.

There! A faint one. She tried counting the beats. In a breath, the beat faded.

She searched for another pulse again, but like the previous time, a faint pulse throbbed and then died. Luma kept going, pursuing that elusive pulse. After a few tries, she never found it.

Unsure of where exactly a pulse should be, she tried looking for her own pulse under her jaw. The same thing happened: it throbbed and died. Only for the sake of it, she pressed her fingers over her arm. A pulse throbbed and died. That made her realize that she had been feeling her own wild heartbeat through the tips of her fingers. She waited for a moment then, controlled her breathing, and tried again.

As she blew a thin stream of nervous air, there, below Xavi's jawline, she sensed a tiny thump.

A sudden jolt of hope lurched Luma forward. "Xavi! Xavi! Open your eyes! Open your eyes!" She jerked his body wildly, "Wake up!"

Saeed opened the lights and spotted the pill bottle lying on the floor. He picked it up and inspected it. "Ya Allah!" He started pacing around with his phone pressed against his ear. Luma looked at him, and without question, she knew that he was waiting for emergency services to pick up.

Back to Xavi. He's still not waking up. Luma yelled, "Wake up, you asshole!" and slapped him good.

The slap resounded loudly across the room, even making Saeed, who was already talking to the emergency services, turn in attention.

Both Luma and Saeed fell silent as they waited for a distant response from the unconscious man lying on the couch. In a tense heartbeat, the groan of a man waking up from a year-long slumber escaped Xavi's lips.

"He's alive! He's moving! Please come quick!" Saeed told the man on the other side of the phone, and he proceeded to describe the pill bottle in his hand.

Xavi awoke lethargically, quaveringly, halfway through. Gradually, the blinding whiteness from his vision faintly faded into a blurred image of a woman with red hair, whom he recognized without a moment's hesitation.

Without Xavi's knowledge, Luma was already eternalized in his mind. Even in an ocean of red and crimson hair, he could tell her distinct curls apart with one look and without thought. If you cut up a portrait of Luma into unrecognizable pieces and mix it into a million others, he can handpick each fragment and piece the puzzle together with ease. And even in a room full of perfumed woman, his nose could trace her unscented fragrance effortlessly like a bloodhound.

As soon as Luma's hazy image registered to Xavi's waking mind, his lips gradually curved a faint but rich smile.

Seeing him move, Luma wrapped her arms around his stretched-out body and embosomed him tightly.

"What have you done?" she asked, whispering to his fragile ears.

Still lying on his side, devoid of vigor, he answered frailly with a measure of serenity in his voice. "I... I was wrong..." he intermittently whispered, beholding Luma with his drained and weary eyes. "I... you... with you... I'm scared... I thought she still was... but... you... it's you... I'm okay..."

At Xavi's moment of weakness, he experienced the strongest emotion. An emotion that he preserved for over ten years. A feeling that he thought he'd never feel again. A passion that terrified him when it returned anew. A sentiment that is now mature enough to let go of the past and start over for a different tomorrow — Love.

"I don't know what I'm feeling right now," the words labored out of his straining breath, "I'm confused, but I want you by my side, and I by yours."

She heard his words and wanted to send a meaningful response, but her mind stuttered into nothingness. So, Luma held his cold and delicate hands close to her heart. It was the only answer she could think of without expressing any words, and it was still enough to send waves of ecstatic electricity throughout her shivering body.

Saeed stooped beside them with contagious merriment. "Xavi! You're alright! You're gonna be alright! They said that modern sleeping pills are designed to," he paused momentarily to think of the best words, "to, you know, not let you sleep forever. Die. Because they realized that some people use them to exit early. That's also aside from the fact that you bought the least strong sleeping pills. Ha! You're alright! They're gonna be here any minute now! We'll get you sorted out!" He then rushed to the kitchen and got some towels to clean the bile-soaked man.

Xavi gave Luma a sweet, delicate smile once more, and then his stare shifted to the poster on the wall. His breathing changed sharply but imperceptibly, like a minor note lost in a music of majors. Even so, Luma still caught his sudden change in demeanor, prompting her to turn curiously to the direction of his gaze.

There, alone on the bare wall, hung a digital art titled *The Beast of Despair*. The black and white digital illustration featured a lone man in a jungle, lit by the moonlight, facing a giant rhinoceros with glowing eyes. Standing taller than a coconut palm, you could almost hear the beast's fear-provoking snort and its thunderous footsteps if it walked.

The artwork is among a series of illustrations depicting the artist's depression, but *The Beast of Despair* was what resonated with Xavi. He had to have it. It reminded him of what had been haunting him for years. To him, the artwork represented his pain; it was his penance for Nicola's death. He feared it, yet he had to have it. It did not make sense, but to a mind battling despair, what does?

Xavi whispered, "Luma." He whispered again, even softer now that only their hearts can hear, "Luma."

Mentioning her name delivered a million smiles into the inner depths of his spirit. And now without reservations and remorse, he accepted his emotions for her as it is: maybe friendship, or maybe more.

Luma felt Xavi grip her hand a little tighter. From the poster, she switched her gaze back to him and read his languidly closing eyes. A smile lurked behind his placid face, and a bond flowed through their clenched hands.

What surged from their palms was a gentle exchange of energy and ardor; a force of yearning and vigor for each other's presence; an unspoken fidelity that was sealed by their converging souls. In that instant, Luma felt the same emotion as Xavi did: maybe friendship, or maybe more.

# PORTRAITS OF THE WIND

***

Under the faint glow of the lingering moonlight, Xavi once more stood in front of the giant rhino in the jungle. The creature loomed over him, dwarfing him. Its glowing eyes pinned him, and he shook with its staggering stomps.

Out of the shadows and from the tall brush, a woman appeared, carrying a burning torch to light her way. The beast cocked its giant head and took a step back in startled fear. The woman with the torch moved closer to Xavi, revealing her shimmering crimson hair. She looked at him with confidence. Suddenly, a dense peace overpowered Xavi amidst the terror of the night.

Luma extended her slender arms and offered her soft hands to hold, which Xavi clasped tightly so.

Together without trepidation, the pair confronted the giant rhino, the beast of fear and despair, and of guilt and shame as well. It snorted, tramped its feet, and bellowed a low growl.

The leaves of the surrounding trees started rustling as the heavens thundered a colossal squall. The creature growled another time and started stampeding towards them, charging at full speed. Despite the earth shaking beneath their feet, the pair held their ground like a lighthouse on a stormy night. They stared at the monster's glowing eyes as it grew bigger and brighter with the closing distance in between. With only a handful of meters left, the beast unexpectedly locked its feet and skidded forward, plowing the jungle floor, and wafting soil and dirt up the windy night sky. Still, the pair remained tranquil within the stormy dust that reduced the nearby visibility to nil. Then, a gentle snort.

The pair pierced through the cloud of dirt. Beneath, it revealed the giant rhino's head that gently bowed simultaneously with the settling dust. Its mouth touched the ground. Its glowing eyes squinted thinly like a friendly kitten waiting to be touched.

Luma released Xavi's hand and took a step forward towards the docile beast. She grabbed its front horn, pulled herself up the head, and balanced her way to its back. Her hand extended to Xavi, pulled him up too, until both were seated comfortably on the creature's spine. She tapped the rhino's head. In a jerking motion, it stood up and towered high above the trees where a gentle breeze blew.

The wind whispered songs to their ears as they rocked gently, side to side, to the swaying walk of their tamed beast. Together, they disappeared deep into the moonlit forest towards a new dawning day.

# Chapter 38:
# Friendship or Maybe More

A sunny blue sky beyond the vast landscape of beige buildings and black tarmac was the first thing Xavi regarded outside the window of his hospital room. As he slipped on the shoes that Luma brought with her, he considered what seems to be different about the panorama that appeared beyond his gander. Nothing. Nothing was different. He had seen the same view a hundred times, but somehow the blue, the beige, the black, and the white that he saw now seemed more vibrant and saturated.

Sounds of singing birds that were louder than the hospital machines and mumbled human chatter also entered Xavi's ears. He knew that this experience is only the beginning of exuberant days yet to come. As he admired the sparse clouds moving across the magnificent canvas of cobalt skies, he wondered how much life he missed or not missed during his fortnight stay at the hospital. For fourteen moons and fourteen suns, he remained under the watchful care of doctors and psychiatrists, who carefully assessed and evaluated his mental health while his physical body recovered from the futile attempt at an early exit in life.

He remembered the tedious daily sessions with psychiatrists, whom he spent more than two hours per day. He recalled the bland hospital food and the nauseating cleaning chemicals that he had to endure multiple times within his stay. He's not going to miss any of that, he thought.

He stood up, zipped up his jacket with the vim of a new tomorrow, put on his backpack, and faced towards the door. And then… he stopped breathing (figuratively).

There at the door was Luma looking out to the hallway, glancing left and right as if waiting for someone to come. Xavi watched her for a minute, oddly admiring her back. Even though he couldn't see her eyes, once more he felt that peculiar warmth brewing within him, only this time it was pure; there was neither guilt nor shame.

For two weeks that he stayed in the hospital, Luma never missed an hour of visit. She stayed beside him, for as long as the hospital allowed. She brought all kinds of food (take-aways, foods that her ma cooked, and meals that she prepared, including more of that cookie balls that Xavi loved) as a respite from the hospital menu.

They talked all day, talking about anything. And when anything ran out, sometimes they played board games. If they got fed up, they tried other things. One time, Luma even brought her painting materials just to not let them go to waste. But no, they really didn't like to paint.

Sometimes, she brought movies that they watched together on her laptop. And when they were apart, they would stream films simultaneously, through their phones, while texting each other, with the same phones, their reactions to certain beats and plots. When the movie would finish, they would discuss it over a phone call, simulating togetherness regardless of the many kilometers between them.

Despite all the time Luma and Xavi spent together, no one ever mentioned what happened, nor did anyone bring it up. A visceral understanding existed between them. They understood that there is no need to talk about their miseries and despairs. It is what it is. It was what it was. It happened, and it belonged to the past. Xavi kept silent about his attempt, and Luma kept quiet about her missing leg. It is what it is. It was what it was. Maybe down the road, in their relationship of friendship or maybe more, they would talk about it, or probably not. It didn't matter. They were content. What mattered now was that their presence is enough to quell each other's malaise.

Luma once thought of cracking a joke about it, that she had the bigger right to commit suicide, but she knew better. Depression should not be compared. Each person deals with it differently. One may seem depressed over something ridiculously small, like failing grades, but to that person, at that moment, it may feel like the end of the world. Depression should never be compared. It is unique to everyone. If a person is depressed over something trivial, it must not be laughed about. You have no right.

"Should we go now?" Xavi finally asked with an animated face.

"Hold on a minute. Your psychiatrist says he'll sign off some paperwork before you leave," Luma said without looking at him. She kept peeking out the door, expecting someone.

In a second, a balding Indian man with round glasses and a tweed jacket arrived from the opposite direction Luma's gaze was at.

When Luma saw the man, she recognized him in an instant. In the same instant, a chunk of embarrassment fell on her head, and the vinyl floor suddenly captured her attention. She knew the man was who she was expecting, but she wasn't expecting it was going to be that man. Within the period that she looked down and looked up again, the balding Indian man was already in front of her. Intuitively, she stepped aside from the doorway to let the man pass.

"Good morning." He nodded at Luma before going to Xavi to shake the latter's hand. "Hi, I'm Dr. Raju Khan. I'll be your consulting psychiatrist for your OP for the next... well, as long as you need to." Then he turned to Luma, studied her for a beat, and said, "You look familiar. Have we met?"

Luma shook her head rapidly with an exaggerated frown before falling silent to avoid any more attention drawn to her.

Raju turned back to Xavi. "Excellent. As you know, seeing that you are already dressed and ready to go, the hospital psychiatrist has already cleared you for outpatient treatment. But, as your OP Psych, I have a few questions before you go and before I do sign your paperwork." Raju turned to Luma. "Could you give us a minute, please?"

Luma nodded readily like saying, *"thank heavens!"* and then left.

Xavi sat on the creaking hospital bed and waited for Dr. Raju, who pulled out a visitor's chair and sat across from him.

Without glancing upwards, the doctor opened one of the folders in his hand and read through the papers. "According to the file that was handed to me, you were suffering from a closeted emotional trauma for the past ten, or almost ten years. Is that right?" he asked.

Xavi nodded.

Raju continued, "And then now, you acted on it because, you said, you were guilt-ridden and shamefaced that maybe you were falling for someone else and was replacing someone who was no longer with us."

Xavi nodded again.

Raju promptly shut the folder out of reflex, leaned forward, and asked, "Have you heard of complicated grief?"

"Complicated grief? No." Xavi shook his head and frowned overtly to show that this piqued his interest.

"Complicated grief, well, is the worst form of grief. In clinical terms, it's called Persistent Complex Bereavement Disorder. In the U.S., it occurs to roughly seven percent of those bereaved. When losing someone, by death usually, people experience grief. That's normal. They go through a period of sorrow, guilt, and even anger. Over time, these feelings diminish, and people move on. But for the seven percent, loss is life-changing, debilitating, incapacitating, and people don't move on, even as time passes. They have difficulty returning to their normal life. For some, it may last for months, for others, a year; worse, even a lifetime. Does that sound familiar?"

Xavi nodded with intrigue.

"Now, I believe, what you have, or what you currently experience is CG and MDD, major depressive disorder, combined. Worse, it also gave birth to an anxiety disorder. That's not uncommon, too, for sufferers of CG. And I've seen how terrible and how hampering it is to have one of those disorders in a person's life. Now, imagine having three."

"But my previous psychiatrist only diagnosed me with depression," said Xavi.

"Oh," Raju reacted with hints of fascination, "when was that?" He leaned back and reopened the folder in his hand.

"Weeks, months, after um… she died."

"And how long ago was that?"

"Almost ten years ago." Xavi tittered.

"There's your answer…" Raju smirked, "complicated grief is not easy to diagnose because it's like normal grief. It's only when it's compounded by time and your inability to move on… then it will be reclassified as CG. And how long did you see your psychiatrist for?"

Xavi sheepishly answered, "Three sessions."

The doctor abruptly chuckled. "There you go. How could have she diagnosed your CG if you only had three sessions with her?" He waited for a quick rebuttal. He could see in his patient's muted reaction that the patient had a sense of enlightenment, a new understanding, about the patient's own depression.

Xavi did not talk. He did not move. He only willingly absorbed the informed assessment that Raju conveyed.

"But how are you feeling now?" continued Raju.

Xavi sighed heavily. "Well, I think I have finally accepted her death after my own near-death experience. It's not how I imagined my life would be, but I think ten years of mourning should be enough. I think she would like me to move on now."

Raju repeated Xavi's words, "You think?"

"Yes. I mean, knowing her…" Nicola twinkled in his mind, who gave him a sidelong glance with a tight-lipped ear-to-ear smile. "…knowing Cola, she wouldn't want me to suffer longer."

"Who's telling you that? Is that your heart or your mind?"

Xavi answered carefully, "Honestly, I am still scared. There is still an amount of contrition swimming in my heart. But, at the same time, I don't want to let go of another chance for happiness. And happiness is waiting for me beyond that door." He glanced briefly at the closed door where he imagined Luma to be standing behind.

Xavi continued, "You know? I mean, I'm not exactly sure of what I feel about her, but I want her by my side. Friends or more. She's happiness. I'm tired of living in the dark as I had for a decade. I've experienced what's it like to be smiling and laughing, and simply happy again. I want that. I don't want any more brooding in misery and despair."

"Do you think you'll ever have another attempt with your life?"

"I don't think so. I hope not. I'm quite sure I won't." Xavi held up his palms in a conceding manner. "I know that's not the answer that you wanna hear."

Raju answered quickly, "The only answer I want to hear is the honest answer." He then showed a faint smile of approval and continued, "You know, I always tell the people who seek my help that depression can be cured, but it can only be cured if you are willing to be cured. Some people choose to remain depressed for reasons that only they understand. Like you, you chose to spend ten years ominously, when you could have gotten help sooner. So, the question is, are you... now willing to be cured?"

Xavi's lips curved to his ears. "Well, like I said, I am happy. I found happiness in the brink of death. Death... Death is easy; you won't feel anything when you die. Not any kind of gaiety, nor pain, nor regret, nor love, nothing. But right now, I don't want nothingness. I don't think I'll ever do, now that I'm experiencing a level of delight with Luma, who brings me a million fluttering smiles."

"Let me also just point out that there's a saying that when you decide to take your own life, you may have escaped your pain, but you're just giving it away to those who love you," Raju said.

"That's a grey area, I think. It depends on the reason why."

"Not really." Raju chuckled and continued, "We'll talk more about this in your session, alright?" He started writing notes on the document in his hand.

Xavi looked out the window once more. He was eager to be outside. Eager to be with Luma.

"Great," said Raju after signing the paperwork. He stood up and shook Xavi's hand. "I'll have my clinic contact you in the next hours to arrange your schedule. I'll see you within the week!" He waved his hand and left.

Luma quickly entered as soon as the psychiatrist left. The door didn't even close yet. As she entered, she glanced at the departing doctor. "You know, I heard he's good," she said.

"You know him?"

"Yeah! Remember back in that Filipino restaurant, I told you I went to a shrink?"

"Oh yeah!" Xavi remembered. "The expensive one! Oh my god! Is he a rip-off?"

Luma shook her head. "Don't worry! People do swear that he's good. He's just expensive. If I did have insurance like you, I probably would have continued with him."

"Would you like to? I mean, I can help you pay for it."

Luma waved her hands dismissively. "Nah! Thanks, but I'm okay now. It took a while, and yeah, maybe sessions would've helped me cope with my new life quicker, but here I am now. For some reason, I'm happy! Happy and content! Come to think of it, I think Raju's tips did work for me. I guess we really must work for our own joys. Depression is just the absence of happiness."

Xavi momentarily stared at the closed door, imagining the people on the other side of it. "See, what I don't understand is, people hate being depressed. I don't like it; nobody likes it. The only people who likes it are posers, people who seek attention. Yet, when it comes to art, we celebrate it. You know, Van Gogh, Munch, Beethoven. No wonder a lot of artists are depressed. Critics mistake sadness as a precursor for masterpieces. Why don't we celebrate monuments of happiness instead?"

"Yeah, well, what about you? Are you still going to use depression to capture timeless photos?" she asked.

"I don't use depression for my photos. I use nostalgia. There's a fine line between them. Nostalgia can dig up good and bad emotions. And I guess overuse of nostalgia will do crossover to depression.

"But timeless photos? That's the keyword, isn't it? Timeless. Sadness is timeless. Happiness is not forever. Your loved one dies, you lose a leg, you create something you're proud of, and then people start bashing it to bits. On the contrary, sadness will always be around like darkness. As you said, depression is the absence of happiness. When everything in the world is gone, all that will remain is darkness. Sadness, despair, and desolation are inevitable. They're the normal state of the universe. Darkness before light. I mean, even Adam was sad, that's why God created Eve. Sadness before Happiness.

"Happiness... now that's the prophylaxis that protects us from the misery of the world. Well, I guess it's up to the person, isn't it? If seeking depression makes them happy or not? So, for a photo to be timeless, there's always a touch of, I wouldn't say depression, but an inherent mix of happiness and sadness. That's nostalgia for me."

Luma approached Xavi and touched his forehead with the back of her hand. "Did they do something crazy to you that I'm not aware of?" she asked. "They zapped your brain? Fed you a hermit's blood? What happened? You achieved nirvana or something? Wooly the enlightened? Talking in uber long paragraphs?"

He laughed at himself. "Whaddayaknow, near-death experiences really do change you. Speaking of change, I think I might change jobs."

"What's wrong with your current job?"

"Nothing's really wrong with it. I just want a job where I'm free creatively, you know? Looking back at my childhood and what my young self had aspired to be, I feel like a disappointment right now."

Luma scoffed readily. "Really? Really? Seriously? What about me? Look at me!" She pointed all her fingers to her right leg. "I miss— oh my god! My dream, it's a fairytale to me now, without a happy ending. It's so far away I can't even grasp how intangible it is. Like seriously, it's in another quadrant of the universe." She shook her head as if trying to shake a stubborn fly off her hair, except that the fly was her bygone dream.

"I'm sorry. I didn't mean to upset you," Xavi said.

"No, don't be. It's something that I have to live with, and I will be okay with it, eventually." She shrugged. "Anyway, ready to go?" she asked.

Xavi stood up and dropped his backpack to the bed. "Actually, you know what? You go first," he said slyly.

"What are you up to now?"

"Meet me in the park in an hour, okay? Same place, under our tree."

"What, and now we have our own tree?" She inspected Xavi's temples. "How much voltage did they give you in the zapper, seriously?"

"Just go! You know what I mean!" Xavi yelled aloud, pointing to the door genially.

Luma giggled and then headed to the door.

"Luma…" Xavi whispered loudly.

Luma spun around with curious alacrity.

"Nothing," Xavi quickly said, but a vibrant look lingered on his face.

Luma chuckled, shook her head, and left.

# Chapter 39:
# Something New

Luma lay quietly on the grass, under the dancing shadow of the olive tree—their tree. With her eyes closed, she listened to the soothing music of the rustling leaves, and of the plovers that sung perched over the swaying twigs. She breathed in the gentle breeze that bristled her hair and tickled her lips. From the center of her chest bloomed an arousing yet aching, tingling yet relaxing, a kind of positive chill that ebbed to the ends of her person.

Her ears heard the whispers of the wind, good and bad, but she only listened to the good. It whispered memories of two wheels to which the hair in her arms stood in attention, and at the same time, it sculpted a smile in her tranquil face. She fondly looked back on the glorious memories of the road, of the bike, of the pain and of the pleasure, and of the aches and triumphs.

Slowly her forehead wrinkled at the heat of the filtering sun. Although it wasn't the heat that furrowed her brows; it was the crash that replayed in her mind. The memory became inevitable. Even if she tried to forget it, it would always pop up sometime, somewhere. She squirmed at the recollection of the pain, but no anger brewed within her. Perhaps, there was just the least bit of ire, but not enough to stir her mad. It was only a placid remembrance of the fateful past.

Now she wondered, pondered, and marveled how over the course of two lunar cycles, her anger gradually evanesced into the cobalt sky, leaving fragments of joy that she began reassembling into a steeple of bliss.

It's amazing how life works out to bring hope and happiness through the tiniest and unforeseen, sometimes bewildering circumstances, then letting it all coalesce together to form a bond centered in a sanguine existence.

In the blackness of her closed eyes, Luma saw the brightness of a life shared with love, even as simple as "friendship or maybe more."

Then she asked herself, was it only the novel friendship that made her forget about the pain of the past? She knew the answer was no. Sure, Xavi turned out to be instrumental in her healing. She longed for him; she yearned to see his face, to hear his breath, and to feel the touch of his lingering gaze. He is happiness in the shape of a man. Yet somehow, she knew Xavi was not responsible for everything. She knew there had to be another integral brick to her reconstruction, a keystone.

She rewound her life again starting from the accident, searching for that something, that one small brick in her tower of bliss. She flashed on the chapters of her life: the crash, the hospital, the school, the shrink, the train, Xavi— Then she knew. That was it! It was the thing that broke her in the first place.

She let out a restrained chuckle upon the realization of what refilled her waning tank of joy. It was bicycles. Bicycles. Somehow, she understood, that she became further appeased with her present being while teaching Xavi how to ride a bike. First love, she thought, first love; it's always lingering, waiting to be rekindled.

In a breath, she jerked her eyes open, breaking the train of wonder and nostalgia. She reached into her pocket and pulled out her phone, later scrolling through her contacts to find a name that was almost forgotten.

Energized, she sat up and leaned against the tree's fat trunk while pressing the phone over her ear. Finally, she knew she was on her way to the last stage of grief which is acceptance.

When she heard the line picked up after a few rings, she greeted with earnest fervor, saying, "Mrs. Wellbrock! Hello!"

Over the line, the noise of a million children playing and screaming in the background drowned Wellbrock's voice. "Hi Luma, how are you doing?" the principal asked, a little surprised but with hints of hope in her tone.

"I'm o… okay," Luma answered casually.

"Actually, let me rephrase that. How are you feeling?"

Luma laughed briefly. "And I'll answer the same, I'm okay."

"What can I do for you?"

Luma thought for a long while before answering. She wanted to be certain that the thing she was about to ask is indeed what she wanted to do.

"Luma?" the principal inquired after three breaths of silence.

"Do I still have a job waiting for me?" Luma asked.

Wellbrock livened. "Yeah, yeah! Of course!" She said it with such volume that Luma distanced the phone from her ear. "Are you ready to come back? We're all eager to have you back!"

"Not exactly, but I really want to."

"Oh," Wellbrock's voice fell a few decibels down.

"Instead of math, can I coach a cycling team?"

"What?" the astonished principal asked. Immediately, she lowered her voice to a softer and friendlier level. "What do you mean?"

"We could be the first school in Doha to have a cycling program," Luma explained, "and we can compete in various races around the country. I can train the students to be at their peak, and they could get handpicked by the national team."

The electrical hiss that followed overcame the cackle of children on the line. Luma tried to judge if Wellbrock was going to respond positively or negatively, but she can only hear a hiss; nothing can be extrapolated to deliver a verdict.

"Uh-huh," Wellbrock began.

Luma clutched the phone tighter.

"I'll run it by the board," the principal continued. "But you're not a certified coach. How do you plan to address that?"

"I will get certified, that's not a problem. I already have enough knowledge on training; it will be like taking a grade one exam!"

"May I ask why, though?"

"It's... I'm not sure ma'am. But I have a feeling this will completely free my spirit."

"Will you also be riding a bike?"

"Oh, no. C'mon. With one leg? No, I won't. Just the students."

"Okay. What about mathematics? Will you still teach that?"

"If you want me to, I don't mind."

Wellbrock let out a breath that sounded like either a scoff or a chuckle over the phone, but in Luma's imagination, she could already see her school principal grinning with approval.

"Alright! Let's see what the board says." Wellbrock lingered for a while, mauling over Luma's request. She let out another exhale with traces of approval. "I'm glad that you're feeling better now," the principal said before hanging up.

Luma froze momentarily in disbelief. "Am I really doing this?" she asked herself.

Taking a gander across the fields of green in front of her, she remembered the line from George Bernard Shaw's "Man and Superman": *"Those who can, do; those who can't, teach."*

## PORTRAITS OF THE WIND

She remembered Wally's words too: *"Some are born to succeed, while others are born to watch others succeed."*

Fear, frustration, and anger crept back and stirred inside her, prompting her to let out loud and forceful exhales. "Hoh!" And again, "Hoh!" And again, "Hoh!"

With each exhale, she felt the tightness in her chest ease. She continued dispelling air until the tremor in her soul dissipated to a tender pulse. She also reminded herself that life is inherently unfair, and all will wallow in misery if we dwell too much on the disparity of failure and success.

What is success anyway? she thought. Fame? Money? Achievement?

Success is when you're happy and content with where you are. Success is the ability to say no to fame and to more money if it means you'll live in misery. Success is personal; it is as subjective as it is objective. Some can see you as a failure, but only you can say that you are one.

"I can teach," she told herself. "I'll share to them the thrill of cycling, the pleasure of the pain, and the ecstasy of the wind. Why not? Just because I can't doesn't mean others shouldn't. Yeah, I can do it, yeah." She nodded to herself, earnestly convinced that she had made the right decision.

She lay back down on the grass underneath the dancing olive tree, closed her eyes, and absorbed the breath of the wind. In silence, she enjoyed the one word that the wind whispered: Content.

\*\*\*

"You okay?" asked Xavi as he looked down at Luma, who's lying down on the grass.

Luma stood up, patting her clothes. "Why not?"

Xavi rolled his mountain bike beside him. "Ready?"

"What? Again?" She abruptly laughed, surprised and pleased that Xavi hasn't given up on the bicycle lessons.

"Yeah, look!" Xavi animatedly pointed to the rear wheel. The training wheels were gone. "I'm ready to keep falling until I can move upright," he said.

Luma showed an impressed face. "Glorious! Hop on then!"

Xavi, empowered with the prospect of a fresh start, hopped on to the bike.

"Remember what I told you?" she asked. "Turn the wheel the other way if you're leaning too much to the side."

"Yup." Xavi nodded rapidly.

"Great! Another thing, now that you don't have training wheels on, don't be afraid to crash. Now chop-chop, move along!"

Without trepidation, Xavi pushed the right pedal down, and the bike lurched forward. His left foot involuntarily extended outwards as he tried to find the delicate balance between falling and not falling. The front-wheel shook violently. In a few meters, he saw the horizon tipping to its side, and then he knew that he was falling. With a loud thud and a whispery grunt, his body plummeted to the green grass.

Luma giggled from afar and asked, "Are you okay?"

Xavi groaned, stood up clumsily, saw a stripe of red dribble from his elbow to his hand, and wiped it with the bottom of his shirt.

Luma exclaimed, "That's nothing! Look at me!" She spiritedly pointed to her prosthetic leg.

Xavi chortled.

"Now, try going faster this time," Luma continued. "It's easier to keep the bike upright when you're moving fast."

"Alright," Xavi said as he remounted the bike.

"Also, you will crash harder when you're faster," added Luma.

"Well, that does nothing to boost my confidence."

"Just go fast, plebe!"

He held the handlebar tighter. The crash did not damage his will in any way. If anything, the crash made him tougher. Without hesitation, Xavi pushed the right pedal and then instantly drove down the left until his feet churned circles at a hundred revolutions a minute.

As the wind slammed to his face, his mind forgot about crashing, and his body ignored the pain of the previous fall. To his surprise, he stayed upright and sustained forward momentum. He pedaled so fast that the grass beneath him began streaking a solid green. To his side, trees whizzed by left and right. He continued pedaling until he realized—

"How do I turn?!"

"Turn the handlebar, dimwit!" yelled Luma from afar.

Xavi turned the bar, but too far to the right. The bike banked precariously, and he crashed once more. It didn't keep him down, though. Immediately, he stood up, punched the air, and he started screaming in celebration for his new accomplishment, like a toddler learning to walk for the first time.

When his ecstasy settled, he mounted and drove his scraped bike towards Luma's direction. With only a few meters left en route to Luma, he squeezed the brakes hard, and his front wheel locked up. Next, what he saw were the ground and the sky, tumbling over, as he went over the handlebars. And before he realized it, he was already staring at Luma's feet as he plunged to the ground... again.

"You know, I said crashing is a part of learning. But you don't need to be obsessed with crashing," said Luma.

Xavi stood up enthusiastically, brushed the dirt off his shirt with the back of his hand, and then looked at Luma with the demeanor of an eager child. "Wait here!" he said before running off into the parking lot.

Five minutes later, Luma watched Xavi jog back to her with another bike rolling on his side. The bike had a striking yellow paint and a sloping top tube. It had a straight handlebar, and its tires were fat and knobby—a mountain bike. "You bought another bike?" she asked as Xavi approached her.

Xavi grinned with such intensity that his neck veins showed, exclaiming: "Now that I know how to ride a bike, I'm gonna teach you how to ride a bike!"

"What?!" Luma grumbled. The absurdity of the idea prompted her to ask again with incredulous uncertainty, "What?!"

"Wally gave me a good discount when I told him it's for you. Also, look!" Xavi pointed to the clip-on pedals. "So your other leg won't slip. Now get on!"

"No!"

"And why not?"

"I don't want to!"

"Hey, come on, what's the use of me learning to ride a bike when you won't ride with me? Just try it out. Please? All you have to do is turn the wheel the other way if you find yourself leaning to one side."

Luma scoffed, shook her head, and took a step back. "Nuh-uh."

Xavi continued, "And the technique is to go fast so you don't fall." He giggled at his purported wittiness, but it quickly waned when Luma's brows and lips remained a straight line. She still didn't dare to touch the bike.

Xavi scratched his forehead. "Look. I'm not the best at giving encouragements, so I'm not going to encourage you. I just want to ask you to give it a try. See what emotions it brings you. Just ride. If you think you really hate it, then hate it. But what if there is still something there, some semblance of your love for bikes. Would you not want…"

Luma remained impassive given that she had not been listening to Xavi at all. The Luma in her head had its own set of words to embolden her: *Come on you legless biatch! You can do it! You want to become a coach, right? You need to show your students how to ride a bike! What is one leg? You'll get a lot of likes and hearts when you post that on social media! Oh, you don't care about likes and hearts? What about your own likes and your own heart? You won't listen to them?*

"Shut up!" Luma screamed.

Xavi stopped speaking, stumped.

Luma got wide-eyed. "Oh, sorry. I wasn't aiming at you. It's my… never mind. Give me the bike." She grabbed the mountain bike, swung her left foot over the frame, positioned her hands on the grips, and she didn't know what to do next. The right pedal was where her stare lingered, though, the side that will hold her prosthetic leg.

"I'll clip it!" Xavi said, and bent down to lift Luma's prosthetic foot onto the pedal. He strapped it in, and the clip locked with an audible click. "Good to go!" he exclaimed.

Luma faced Xavi with a terrified look. She didn't frown; she had no wrinkled muscles; she just had a face exuding uncertainty. She didn't want to move.

"Can you at least give it a try? Try pushing the pedals," Xavi said.

Luma lifted her right foot and tried pedaling backward. The clip-on pedals worked to keep the platform under her shoe. Satisfied, she looked forward and rubbed her hands on her pants to get rid of the anxious sweat before gripping the bars tightly. With her prosthetic leg, she began pushing the right pedal down, then the bike accelerated forward.

The bike stopped short in fewer than two meters later. Luma's hands were quick to the brakes when images of the accident exploded in her mind. The crash replayed over and over, sending phantom pains over her missing leg. She remembered the three nails, the harrowing ride back home, the blist—

"Break a leg!" Xavi cheerfully roared.

The words released a hearty guffaw from Luma. Just like that, her mind returned to the challenge at hand.

"Too soon?" Xavi asked.

"Wooly bastard!" replied Luma.

Unable to give up, she inhaled deeply to take a full breath of courage. Once more, Luma gripped the bars, positioned her prosthesis, pushed down on the pedals, and propelled herself forward. The bicycle wobbled side to side as her muscles recalled the memory of riding a bike. Then, after five, six, seven, eight pedal strokes, she caught her balance, and she began piercing the wind as she did many moons ago.

It only took a blink of an eye before all the zealous pleasure of slicing the headwind carved a smile. She had forgotten the sensation of freedom on two wheels, and here it returned anew, pouring a bucket of bliss over the dried-up river of joy. She felt weightless.

Xavi caught up to her with his own bicycle. He wooed and screamed at the euphoria of the moment. And then, the neophyte that Xavi is, he collided with Luma, sending them both hurling out of their bikes and onto the bermudagrass. They moaned and groaned over their painful scrapes, but the bright beam on their faces remained.

Xavi stood. And then…

"Oh my God!" he yelled in horror.

A gush of fear forced Luma to sit up. "What? What's wrong?"

"Your leg!" He pointed to her stump animatedly. "Where's your leg!" he said, in a more farfetched tone.

Luma spewed a tight laugh and laid back down to the grass.

"I'm getting good at jokes, huh?" Xavi said.

Luma shook her head genially.

"Then what's funny? Why are you laughing?" he asked.

"Us," Luma said. "We are like a math problem."

"Huh?"

"What do you get when you combine two negative integers?"

Xavi thought for a while.

"Come on you nitwit! It's simple math!"

"I'm not good at math!" he protested.

"Guess!"

"A positive?" he said questioningly.

"Yep! I always thought two depressed people combined will be like a nuclear explosion or something. But here we are." She sighed pleasurably.

Xavi laid down beside her. Together, they stared at the clear blue sky in a moment of fervent peace.

"So, what now?" she softly asked.

"I think if we stick together, we'll be okay," he said as his voice trailed off to tranquility.

Luma slapped Xavi's chest and stood up with one foot. "No, dimwit! I mean now-now!" She hopped towards her bike to reattach her leg. "What do you want to do now?"

Xavi stood up, embarrassed. "Oh!" He paused for a time. "Have you tried Ethiopian food? There's a nice African restaurant at the other end of the park."

Luma drove her bike forward under the wistful afternoon sun, and said, "Come on then. Let's do it! Something new!"

\*\*\*

# Acknowledgements

If you have reached this point in the book, I am deeply honored that you have endured my first novel. It's far from perfect, especially with English syntax, but you have persevered anyway. So, to you, reader, I thank you first. You're the one responsible for the circulation of this book.

Of course, none of these will be entirely possible without the support of my wife, Ronalie, who despite not ever reading anything I write, still indulged me and let me roost in front of my computer. She has this belief in what I do, but secretly detests what I do. I understand where she's coming from. And to my daughter, Alisha, who is only three years old as of writing, I am truly grateful to her for literally riding my back while I write. It's a distraction, yes, but I love it. I love it when she just crawls up to me and smothers me with her chubby little body.

My sincere and heartfelt thanks also to Marcel Villanueva and Charmaine Cordero for helping me edit this work, especially with the grammar. They had read my first draft and returned it to me bleeding red with revisions. For the second and third drafts, they're still bleeding red. Now, if you have spotted anything grammatically strange, don't fault them; I may have been stubborn sometimes. Like this. They hate this. Fragments.

To Ayessa Villanueva, Marcel's wife, my college classmate and former co-worker, thanks for marrying that guy. Otherwise, I wouldn't have someone check my work. Oh, and thanks to you, too, for being a real friend and for listening to some of my dark secrets. But still, thanks for marrying that guy. Because of him, you now have Haya. Now you will have to experience the sleepless nights.

Any acknowledgement won't be complete without thanking the family. So, to my parents, Philip and Janet, you didn't know that I was writing this book until yesterday. I wanted to keep it as a secret because I wasn't sure if it will ever get published. But it looks like it did get published, so thank you for, you know, everything. To my sister, Janzel, and husband, Herbert, thanks for the pizzas. To their daughters, Sam and Alex, thanks for keeping Alisha busy.

Finally, I would like to thank the cast and crew of Footprints on the Moon, my half-realized film. I'm not sure if it will ever be completed. Maybe someday it will, maybe not. But I would like to thank you guys too for helping me out, for enduring those turbulent times with me, and for not ever letting go until the very end. What do you have to do with this book? Well, the events of producing that film have compelled me to continue with my passion for storytelling through other mediums, like this one.

To Xavi and Luma, the fictional characters of my book, I'm sorry for making your life miserable, but you were inspired by my own life, so hang tight.

Now, if you've read everything until here, again, Thank You dear reader. I sincerely do thank you. I think there's just the "About the Author" page left, and that's it. You don't have to read that. You've done enough. Thanks!

# The Author

*Photo ©Billy Gene Gonzales*

Janix Pacle is a filmmaker from the Philippines but he grew up in Qatar, where he has been confined at home every day, except for school. Imagination became his friend, thus his aptitude for storytelling developed. Upon graduating Mass Communications at Saint Louis University in Baguio City, Philippines, he has written and directed a few award-winning films in the indie circuit. In his hard drive, he has a few unproduced screenplays that were written as a hobby, some of which became the inspiration for his first novel "Portraits of the Wind." An avid cyclist too, he has won only one race in his entire life before being bestowed the greatest award of all – a baby girl.

Made in the USA
Columbia, SC
31 May 2021